DEAR READER

On behalf of Geoff Davis and the team at Wattlebird Books, we'd like to thank you for supporting THE BLACK MIST. As a token of our appreciation, we'd like to invite you to join the Geoff Davis reader's group. To join the free group, head to:

www.wattlebirdbooks.com/geoffdavis

Members of the reader's group will receive exclusive content, behind-the-scenes glimpses, and updates on upcoming releases.

Thanks again for your support.

Warmest regards,
Wattlebird Books

THE BLACK MIST

GEOFF DAVIS

For Helen

1

FRIDAY, JANUARY 1, 2010

Riverina Hotel Car Park, Tenambra, New South Wales, Australia.

Gary Rogers didn't want to die.

He walked out of the Riverina Hotel at 3 a.m. on Jan 1, 2010, into an empty car park. The Riverina was the main pub in the town of Tenambra, population 4,000. Gary was slightly drunk. He had stuck with the lemon squash for most of the night, but there had been several raucous celebrations of his recent election victory. It would have been churlish to say no to the offered glasses of champagne. So, graciously, he had accepted and sipped as little as possible at the end of each set of "Hooray for Gary".

It had been a great party to welcome a year that, Gary hoped, would be significant. He was the newly nominated Liberal candidate for the seat of Riverina. There would be a federal election this year, and Gary was certain he could win.

Would win.

At the party, he had been the centre of attention and the focus of all the many toasts during the evening, plus those that followed in the early morning. He had spoken and smiled till his face ached. He had no doubt it would be an intense year, but right now, Gary was headed for bed. The long battle for justice could begin in the morning.

Most of the guests were his friends from before politics. Many of them shared his concern about the resurgence of the drug business in the area, just as many were simply his mates who loved him and supported him because he was their friend.

Most people in the Riverina were scared to speak up against the drug growers, but together they could fight and win.

But not right now.

Right now, Gary had to negotiate the journey home.

How many sips of champagne put a would-be politician over the legal limit? Jesus, how many had he had? Twenty? That would do it, especially for a two-pot screamer like Gary. He took out his phone and called his wife, Jennifer. She had gone home earlier, sober, and told him firmly to call at any time, to relax and have fun, and she would pick him up whenever. Don't drive drunk were her last words before she kissed him goodbye.

Gary opened the door of his car and pushed his bag of gifts and cards into the passenger seat. With the door half open and himself halfway into the vehicle, he took out his mobile phone and called his wife. His first attempt rang three times, then went to the answering service. She was, no doubt, asleep already, and he immediately felt guilty about waking her.

He lowered the phone, intending to redial. He heard a voice.

"G'day Gary." The jogger had appeared from nowhere.

"G'day mate," Gary responded, not recognising the voice or the jogger. He did recognise a pistol in the jogger's hand, rising toward him. With his right hand, Gary pushed the half-open door hard into the pistol. The jogger was quick and almost managed to pull the gun away. The pistol fired. Gary's first thought was that he had not been hit. With his right hand, he let go of the door and backhanded the jogger in the face.

Gary was ex-army, and he could fight, or he could have once. He hadn't had a real fight in a few years, not since Afghanistan. He had struck the jogger hard in the face. If he could get past the gun, he might be OK.

The jogger staggered back but did not fall. He also managed to hang onto the gun.

Gary wanted to move fast, to get close, get inside the arc of his attacker's weapon hand, do damage, and hurt the bastard. But he couldn't seem to get his legs working, couldn't seem to get around the car door. He looked at his left shoulder. He'd been shot. The wound was ugly, spurting blood through the small hole in his shirt. The pain and shock were swarming over his senses. He looked at his hand; it was cut and bleeding, and there were two teeth embedded there as though they were eating him. He looked back to the jogger, who was raising the gun slowly towards Gary's head.

"Not like this," he thought, "you won't beat me like this."

The gun fired, and Gary fell dead. His body lay on the ground between the car and the open car door. His phone had fallen into the car when Gary was struck by the first bullet. The jogger's two front teeth were stuck fast in Gary's dead hand.

The jogger stopped for a moment.

He had been angered by Gary's punch; it fucking hurt. He stood over the prone body and swore profusely. He aimed the pistol as if to shoot again but then, after a pause, thought better of it. Step one was done. The target was dead.

Calm the fuck down, he thought, make no more noise than necessary.

Be smart.

At the sound of the second gunshot, a white panel van had rolled quietly into the space beside Gary's car. A second figure emerged; the driver of the van. He had a bright blue tarpaulin in his hand, which he quickly spread on the ground behind Gary's car and then together, with the jogger, they lifted Gary's body into the centre of the tarpaulin.

"Hang on," said the jogger, speaking through busted teeth.

He went to the side of Gary's car, looking for the phone he had seen in his victim's hand. It wasn't under the car. He looked inside and couldn't see it.

"Fuck," he whispered.

He had to find the phone. Every second that passed was a second he could be discovered. Ruin a perfect job. He opened the back door of the car to see under the front seats.

"Shit."

Did he just drop blood, from his mouth, onto the floor of the car?

"You got a torch?" He asked the driver in an angry whisper.

"Yeah, one sec."

The torch made it easier. He saw the blood and wiped it up with his handkerchief. Do it properly, he thought. If some other cunt came now, he would have to shoot them too.

He handed the hanky to the driver. "Soak this in petrol; there is a jerry in the boot."

When the driver returned with the petrol-sodden handkerchief, the jogger cleaned what was left of his own blood from the floor of the dead bloke's car.

The torch was good; he used it to check there were no other spills.

Where was the fucking phone?

There it was, under the driver's seat.

Thank Christ.

He grabbed the phone, stood outside the car and listened. Shit, the dead bloke had been calling someone.

Fuck. Fuck. Had someone heard? He hung up. Always some shit goes wrong. Always.

He threw the phone into the centre of the tarpaulin, along with the body of Gary Rogers. He removed the plastic gloves he had been wearing and threw them in as well.

"Can they track those things?" The driver asked.

"Dunno."

The jogger stood up and stamped on the phone several times until it was crushed.

"Doubt they will track that."

They wrapped the smashed phone and Gary's murdered body in

4

the tarpaulin and then lifted the whole package into the back of their van. The jogger took the jerry can from the back of the van. It was full of petrol which he used to wash the area beside Gary's car. By the time he finished, Gary's blood, like his dreams, had been washed away.

The jogger returned the jerry can to the van, and then, back at Gary's car door, he shut the door, locking it. He then wiped the door handle clean.

"Job well done, mate," said the driver.

"Not done yet." The jogger stood still and listened.

"C'mon, let's get out of here." The driver was keen to go. Nervous. The sort that hurried and made mistakes. Would he be a problem?

"Shut up; listen for a minute."

They stood beside their van. The driver was too afraid to make another noise. He knew the reputation of the jogger, and now he had seen the man in action. If he wanted quiet, then he could have it. They listened to the sounds of the town.

The rattle of a fridge somewhere in the pub. The hum of a machine from somewhere in the distance. No cars, no trucks, and no traffic noise at all.

"Not a peep out of anyone," said the jogger, smiling. For the first time, the driver noticed the jogger's broken, bloody teeth. The jogger moved to the passenger side of the van. "You can drive; no rush."

And so, they drove their stolen van with Gary Roger's ruined dreams wrapped inside. It was their intention that Gary's body, his ambitions and the van itself should disappear forever.

2

TUESDAY, FEBRUARY 16, 2016

Six Years Later

Channel 10 Sydney Live Television Broadcast

"Good morning Australia. I am Tony Newton, and this is Channel Ten Morning news. An amazing twist overnight in the six-year-old mystery surrounding the disappearance of New South Wales anti-drug campaigner and political candidate Gary Rogers. We cross now, live, to Ten's crime reporter Angela Adams, on the scene in Rye, Victoria. Angela, firstly where is Rye?"

"Thank you, Tony. Rye is a holiday resort eighty kilometres southeast of Melbourne. It is close to the end of the southeast peninsula that forms Port Phillip Bay. We are standing here in the Rye Ocean Beach car park, about 30 meters from the surf. You can probably hear the surf as I speak."

"So, Angela, what is happening there?"

"Well, Tony, I can tell you, in a spot about 50 meters west of where I am standing now, police have discovered a hidden grave, and that grave contains a body, apparently male.

The body was discovered after Victorian police received an

6

anonymous tip. At this stage, police have offered no official confirmation or suggestion of who that male may be. However, according to my own police sources, I believe they have discovered the body of well-known anti-drug campaigner Mister Gary Rogers who disappeared without a trace, at least until now, on New Year's Day 2010."

3

TUESDAY, FEBRUARY 22, 2016

Media release from the New South Wales Police Force.

Melbourne Detectives have identified the body discovered in Victorian bushland last week as belonging to former Tenambra, *New South Wales resident Mr Gary Rogers. The body of Mr Rogers was found after a search of the area around the Rye Ocean Beach Car Park in Southern Victoria. The search was initiated after information was received from a member of the public.*

An autopsy indicated that Mr Rogers had been shot twice at close range, and death would have resulted from those wounds.

The identity of Mr Rogers was confirmed by a DNA sample taken from the deceased, which was matched to a sample taken from Mr Rogers' son John.

Mr Rogers was a well-known identity in the Riverina region and disappeared on the night he was selected to represent the Liberal Party in the Federal Election of 2010. Before his disappearance, Mr Rogers had been an outspoken critic of several Riverina identities who he accused of being involved in the growing, manufacturing and distribution of illegal drugs.

In 2009 Mr Rogers notified Sydney drug squad detectives regarding the location of a large marijuana plantation in the Tenambra *area. Informa-*

tion provided by Mr Rogers resulted in the arrests and conviction of four men who were subsequently convicted of various drug-related activities.

A press conference will be held at New South Wales Police Headquarters Parramatta at 2.00 pm today.

4

SATURDAY, MARCH 10, 2018

Two Years Later.

The Town Road, Jarrajarra, Victoria, Australia.

It was late Saturday night, and I was late to the scene. Being late to an emergency is hard to avoid when you're the only cop in a town of nine hundred people. It is a rule of thumb; at any single moment, nobody needs a cop, or everyone does.

I am that local policeman. Leading Senior Constable Chris Taylor, ex-army, now the local cop, the only cop. The sole police officer in the tiny town of Jarrajarra. Nine hundred people in an area of twenty thousand square kilometres. I had been here for three years.

The only real advice I received when I arrived as the new cop at the Jarrajarra station was from the retiring Senior Constable. He handed me a large pack of keys and said, "You can be friendly but don't be friends."

"With who?" I asked.

"All of them. They'll form a queue and take turns to bite you on the arse. Keep 'em at arm's length, mate," he said. "Arm's length."

He had been sitting on the front porch of the station when I arrived, already in his civvies. After he handed me the keys to the office, he jumped into his private car and backed out of the station car park. Before he drove away, he remembered some further procedural knowledge. He opened his car door and stood beside the driver's seat to talk to me over the roof.

The open car door and the running engine all indicated, to me, he was in a hurry, and this was some sort of added bonus information. I had best pay attention.

"That's your truck over there," he said, pointing at a Holden Colorado, a four-door, four-wheel drive utility truck. It had a canopied rear utility section; a narrow back seat, and it was filthy. "If it needs fixing, go to the Farrell brothers over the road there." He waved his hand in the general direction of the highway from which I'd just arrived.

"Could probably do with a wash. Oh and," he was thinking aloud, "oh yeah, you have a civilian assistant, Barney Trail; he's a bit of a girl but good enough at his job." He thought about that for a moment. "That's a bit harsh, to be honest; he's pretty useful."

He re-entered his vehicle and moved forward as if to leave, but no, he stopped again. More advice. This batch was delivered through the open passenger side window.

"There's a gun cupboard under the bench in the kitchen, the password is the postcode, and you're out of coffee." And then, finally, he drove off.

The news on the coffee situation made me hate him forever.

I was glad he had gone. He was supposed to stay for my first month and ease me in and himself out. He was taking the risk that I would not report his early departure and sabotage some part of his pension. It was a fair risk; very few cops would have phoned it in. But, there he was, gone. It suited me. I would rather make my own way than start out under the residue of his time on the job.

Over the next few weeks, I came to value his lack of instruction. I would hate to be a cop in his image. His share of the station was a pig sty. On the other hand, Barney Trail's domain, the front office and the reception area were immaculate.

When Barney saw that I was serious about keeping the back section of the station to his own high standard, he was keen to help. Soon the station shone, and for all our different backgrounds, Barney and I became close friends.

Here I was now, three years later, almost a kilometre or so north of town.

Ahead, I could see the flashing lights of an ambulance and a State Emergency truck as I approached. I had taken a call from Barney. The message was long in detail, not so rich in certainty. There was a badly injured male, possibly an assault victim, on the Town Road, 800 meters north of the Jarrajarra shopping strip or maybe more, say 900 meters. The victim was on the side of the road, maybe even dead already, maybe not. And there was a lot of blood.

I had followed Barney's directions to the area, and the flashing lights of the assembled vehicles guided me the last few hundred yards.

Barney was right about the blood. There was a lot. The two paramedics were loading their patient into the back of the ambulance as I pulled up beside them.

That was a good sign. If the victim had been dead, they would have waited for me. It was male, another point to Barney. The body was way too big for a female. He was also unconscious.

The ambulance driver, Jack Farrell, gave me a side glance. "Sorry, Chris, can't wait. Need to get him to Wodonga Hospital soon as." Jack was a 'Load-and-Go' paramedic; it was rare for him to attempt an on-site solution.

"No worries. Do you think he will be talking anytime soon?"

"If we don't hurry, I'm not sure he will be talking again, ever."

From the little I could see, the victim looked as though he had been badly beaten. A bloody mess.

I stepped back while Jack and his partner loaded their patient. Jack's new paramedical partner was a young girl in her 20s, new to the area. Jody Taggart.

I was watching as she followed the stretcher into the back of the truck while Jack hurried to the driver's seat.

I looked down at the battered body of the bloke on the stretcher when I noticed he was stark naked from the waist down.

"Oh!" I must have said as he was rolled into the ambulance.

"Oh indeed," said Jody with a cheeky smile. "Buck's night party gone wrong, maybe?"

"Maybe," I said, wondering where to look while talking to a young girl over the battered cock and balls of our roadside victim.

"This was how you found him? No trousers?"

"Yep, just like that."

Jack was in the driver's seat, the engine running. Jody reached over the stretcher to the rear of the ambulance, pulling the back door shut. "Go," she called, and, in a flash of lights and sirens, they were away.

I'd noticed before they'd shut the ambulance door the man's feet were bare and dripping with blood. The toes that I saw looked broken.

Greg Farrell, Jack's brother, stood beside me. Greg was head of the local emergency service team, Captain of the regional C.F.A. and unofficial Mayor of our town, Jarrajarra.

"Shit, he's a big guy, six-five, I'd reckon, huge," said Greg, referring to the body. "It looks like he has been worked over big time. Then maybe dumped here or walked here till he collapsed in that grass there, beside the road." Greg pointed, and I looked.

"Maybe you should be the local policeman," I said.

"Maybe, maybe not. Can't stand violence myself, but I'd be good at the investigative stuff."

We were standing in the light of our two trucks, both of us looking at the long grass beside the road where the body had been. The grass ran about ten feet off the gravel into a thick bunch of low scrubby bushes.

Beyond that, an old white horse walked up to the barbed wire fence between us and his paddock.

"Holy shit," said Greg, surprised, "look at that, it's a portend of death."

"A portend?" I said. "You mean portent?"

"Yeah, yeah, like the Clint Eastwood movie."

"Pale Rider?"

"That one, yeah, the horse is the portend."

"Mate, I think Clint was the portent. He had the gun. The horse was just the horse."

"Whatever, so why was he here? On foot, half-naked, where would he be heading, do you reckon?" Greg asked, back to the mystery of our wounded man.

"With any luck, I will get to ask him," I said.

"Nah, don't think so, mate. He will be done and dusted by morning."

"What constitutes morning?" I asked.

"I will give him till three A.M., to be fair."

I checked my watch, it was after midnight already, so our victim needs to survive three hours.

Greg sensed a lack of enthusiasm on my part.

"Alright, I will give you till four A.M. and ten dollars."

"No, I don't bet for money, plus this one seems,"

"Inappropriate?"

"Yeah."

"I get that," said Greg.

I took a couple of torches from my police truck and handed one to Greg. "Want to help me find where he came from?"

Greg examined the torch in his hand. He flicked it on and off a couple of times, looking at its beam with obvious scorn. "I'll help you mate, but not with these toys." He went to his own truck and returned with two headlamps and two larger hand torches. We put on our headlamps, and when they were turned on, the area in front of us lit up like daytime.

"Like morning already," I said.

"Not quite," said Greg. "Oh, and while you're checking your watch, don't forget to move it forward an hour. Daylight saving ends today."

He moved off, scanning the ground with his lamp and torch, eyes down as he walked slowly north, away from the town of Jarrajarra and me.

"Shit, you knew you had an extra hour when you tried to make a bet."

"What bet? Oh, that one, yeah."

I pointed my torch at the ground and headed back along the road toward the town. Looking for some evidence of where or how my unidentified victim had emerged.

Avoiding friendship with the locals would never work for me, especially with the Farrell brothers and their extensive clan. There were three of them – Greg, Jack, and Rob. Rob was the local mechanic, panel beater, bricklayer, handyman and whatever. Like his brothers, it appeared there was nothing he could not do or would not do if you asked nicely. Plus, Rob was ex-army, ex-Afghanistan, so we had some loose mutual history.

Now here I was, with the older Farrell Greg, searching in the darkness for our bashing victim's starting point.

Greg was heading north, away from town. I was searching south, toward the town. Ahead of me, in the distance, I could see the short row of streetlights that served the main drag of Jarrajarra. They were dim and shrouded in faint mist. After a minute, we were still only thirty meters apart.

"Why did you choose to go that way?" I shouted at Greg.

"Well, there is only one road through town, so I am thinking, from where we found him, there are only two options. After he was bashed, he either came from the south, heading away from town, or came from the north, heading toward town. From north seems to me the least likely of our two options."

"So, if anyone is going to stumble into the person who did this, you'd prefer it was me?"

"Exactly; I told you I hate violence."

As I spoke, my torch flashed across a footprint of blood. Under the full headlamp, I could see a long trail of bloodied footprints coming from the town toward me.

I called out to Greg. "I think we can rule out north."

We followed the trail of blood back to town, down a side street, and then left along the lane that ran behind the main shopping strip. The blood led us through the Jarrajarra Supermarket parking area, past the rear of the chemist, past some empty shops and finally up to the back door of the Jarrajarra Pizza house.

The back door of the pizza house was open, and our victim had obviously come from within. There was a lot of blood at this section of the journey. It was hard to imagine one person shedding this much blood and living to discuss his current situation. Had I taken Greg's bet, my money would have been heading to his wallet by now.

Greg had pulled up short of the blood and gore at the back door of the pizza shop; he clearly had no intention of going in.

"Well, what a surprise," said Greg.

"Yes indeed."

The pizza shop had a reputation. Joey Golino, the owner, was the local marijuana dealer. He sold grass. Coffee, grass and pizza. Nothing heavier. There had been a few punch-ups at his back door over the years and at other people's back doors when Joey had visited looking for money. I didn't see Joey as a major "crim". He was more of a bespoke retailer who kept one part of the town supplied with their particular preference.

Joey's weed enterprise did not involve any real dirty work. There were no heavies or weapons, just the occasional punch-up. Disputes were usually settled by the time I arrived, if I was called at all.

It had never seemed to me that Joey's side hustle needed crushing under the full weight of the law. He made great pizzas and perfect coffee, and most of it was free, for me at least. I quite liked him, though there was a section of the community that didn't.

Joey also had a beautiful wife and three beautiful children, and they had always seemed to me a very happy family. I was suddenly worried about my mate Joey.

"I know Joey is a big guy, but I don't see him handling that monster," said Greg.

"No." This scenario seemed a lot more serious than Joey's usual transgressions.

"Are you going in?" asked Greg.

There were no lights on inside the pizza shop, and the bloodied door was hardly an invitation. Before I went in with guns out and shooting at shadows, I tried a softer option. I took out my phone and called Joey's mobile; it rang out. I tried a second time and got the same result, no answer and no mobile phone sound from beyond the door.

I tried the pizza shop number, painted in red and splashed with a handprint of blood at the back door. I could hear it ringing on my phone, and I could also hear it ringing from somewhere toward the front of the shop. I dropped the phone from my ear as Greg and I listened to it ring out from within. There was no one taking orders.

"Maybe he's at home?" I said to Greg. I selected another number from my mobile and called it.

Greg looked at me, clearly noticing I had the home number of the local drug dealer on speed dial.

"Yes, and I have Kate Chalmers on my phone list as well, doesn't mean I go there." Kate was the lone prostitute operating in the area.

"I didn't say a word," said Greg.

The phone kept ringing.

"Your predecessor often knocked on Kate Chalmers' door," said Greg, "he always got in for free, I'm told."

Someone picked up the phone at Joey's house.

"Hello, who is this?" It was Georgie Golino speaking, Joey's wife.

"Hi, Georgie, Chris Taylor here. Sorry if I woke you. Can I speak to Joey, please? It's urgent."

"He hasn't come home yet, Chris. He should be at the shop." She paused, "What's wrong?"

"Could be nothing." I was lying to her already. "Do you have another number for him, maybe a business number?"

"Why would he need another number?"

Why indeed? Surely she knew her husband dealt drugs; I knew he did; he knew I knew, but I wondered, did Georgie know any of it? Unknown unknowns.

She waited a while, not speaking, then said, "Hang on a minute." She was gone, and then she returned with a mobile number I did not have on my list. I organised my phone, so I could type in the number as she dictated.

So, Georgie knew about the drugs. Interesting.

I ended the call with Georgie politely. Then I hit dial on the number she had given me. It crackled, as usual, then connected.

I held my mobile to my chest while I listened.

A mobile tone sounded from within the shop. It was a very tinny version of Puccini's Nessun Dorma. Joey's 'drug-business' phone was now singing to me from the darkness beyond the bloodied back door.

Eventually, the Nessun Dorma number quit. I dialled it again, then handed my phone to Greg.

"Keep going. If it rings out, then redial. OK?" He nodded, "And maybe step back away, down the lane a bit."

I took off the headlamp I was still wearing and handed that to Greg as well. I took my service weapon from my holster, flicked off the safety and aligned the weapon with my torch.

I nodded at Greg, quite the stoic hero, part of me wondered if I was overreacting, maybe looking like a goose. Better safe than sorry, I pointed my gun and torch into the centre of the doorway and stepped toward the darkness.

Inside the pizza shop, I moved slowly. Years of army training, followed by police training, had made me good at this, but practice makes perfect, and I had not practised armed entry for a while.

"Use it or lose it," My Nan always said.

I listened for anything other than the sound of the phone. There was nothing. I checked the shadows and doorways with the torch before I stepped near them.

The first door on my left was locked. I kicked it open and stood back. It was a pantry. No one in there. I moved past it, checking toilets and other side rooms. All dark except for the light of my torch, all empty. The floor was sticky with blood from the back of the building until the last side room, before the main customer area. The other phone was ringing louder here, and then it stopped. I stopped moving and listened. Nothing but my own breathing.

Greg obviously dialled again, as I had asked, and Joey's phone with the Puccini ringtone resumed. I stepped into the last side room. It was a kitchen, more for washing up than cooking. There was no one there and no phone, but there was blood all over the floor. I guessed it was here my victim had been beaten. Tortured, I thought. I knew where he was now, hopefully still alive in Wodonga hospital, but where was Joey Golino?

I left the side room, moving toward the front of the building and closer to the sound of the phone.

I stepped into the dining area. The customer tables were all bare, with no tablecloths and no obvious hiding places. The chairs were all stacked on the tables, the floors and tabletops were polished. Everything was set to start fresh the next day. There was nothing to see in the customer area. It was ready and efficient, like the owner.

My next move of the torch was toward the sound of the phone, and there it was, sitting on the counter, singing Nessun Dorma face down, flashing most of its light into the countertop.

Now that I was in the room, I could also hear the faint burr of the phone's vibration on the laminated top.

And there, on the floor, behind the shop counter, was my mate Joey.

Joey Golino was as dead as he could be.

He lay there face up, one eye open and the other battered beyond recognition. He was naked from the waist down. Strangely, he was still wearing his shoes and socks. It looked as though he had been hit one horrible blow to the left front of his head by something thin and heavy. Maybe a tire lever or perhaps the blunt side of an axe, perhaps a baseball bat. Not so much blood here. Joey's heart must have stopped pumping soon after he was struck.

I had always hated police procedure, and being a one-man show in a small country town suited me. Steady income and very little hierarchy to answer to was my preference. I very rarely called for outside police help, but this was beyond my pay grade and experience.

I backed out of the shop the way I came, touching nothing more than what I had already touched or kicked. The rules required I inform my higher-ups immediately.

Once outside, I retrieved my phone from Greg and put a call to Barney, letting him do the call-around to the people who would demand a part of this. He wasn't really a policeman, but he loved impersonating me, and he did a better me than I did. He loved pretending to be a copper. He could sit on the phones and find us the appropriate Criminal Investigator, or maybe two of them and the nearest available forensics team, sooner than I ever could. There were several such teams between here and Melbourne, all of them at least a couple of hours away.

Any useful information the investigation teams found would be weeks away from my desk. If the murderer's DNA was discovered and identified, I would probably find out after the accused. I was already sure I was looking for someone right-handed, around six foot tall and strong.

With Barney busy on the phone and Greg heading back down the road to retrieve his truck and then again to retrieve mine, I had some time to sit in the darkened lane and think.

This level of impact violence? Whoever did this was strong and knew how to swing their weapon. I thought perhaps the blunt side of an axe. The massive dint in Joey's head was thin and brutal but not cutting. Plus, I thought the perpetrator would be right-handed. The weapon had hit the left side of Joey's poor head and was heading down and inward when it landed.

The strike looked accurate, a deliberate killing blow. You don't fire a warning shot with an axe to the head, and you don't want to swing and miss.

Joey was a big man, tall, strong, and could be aggressive and belligerent. I was looking for someone at least as tall as him. Someone right-handed and big enough, and brave enough, to take on Joey and my other victim.

And what was the thing with no trousers? Both victims naked from the waist down? Was that a sex thing? Did they take their own pants off, or did the killer strip them? Hard to imagine Joey taking his trousers off and then putting his shoes and sock back on.

My murderer was either a psychopath or, maybe, just an extremely angry person.

Or both.

I waited in the dark till Greg had retrieved both trucks. We were sitting together in his truck, guarding the back door to the pizza shop, when my phone rang. It was Barney with a report.

"OK, we have a Criminal Investigation team coming from Melbourne, but they won't be here till very late."

"OK."

"I found a forensics team, coming from Seymour, that's over three hundred kilometres away, two ladies I know very well, Carole and Glenda, they're sisters and keen as mustard."

"Great job," I said. "How did you find them?"

"I cheated. They're my cousins."

I had Barney on speaker so Greg could hear both sides of the discussion.

"They are finishing a job now and will be on their way as soon as they can, so we need to hold the fort till then. They told me all the usual stuff, don't touch anything, keep everyone out, including ourselves, etcetera."

"The usual? Has this happened here before?" I asked. This was news.

Barney had to think a moment.

"Well, not a murder, no, but you know, the usual, like on television. Wear plastic gloves. Put up police tape to keep the press back from the scene."

"What press?"

"It's a double murder, Chris; the national media may well decide to visit. I don't know what motivates them. They always seem fascinated by murders and such."

"Do we have any police tape?" I was forced to ask.

"We've got some at the fire station," interjected Greg. "Norma uses it for the entry queue at the farmers market." Norma was Greg's wife, the power behind the throne.

"Well, we can use that," said Barney. "If Greg could go get it, I will explain to Norma tomorrow."

Greg and Barney had it all arranged perfectly. Saved me a dozen phone calls.

Barney was chuffed. Had he not been fifty-five years old, living with his Mum, and terrified of physical violence, he would have made a wonderful policeman. I was glad to have him.

Greg had a further thought. "Barney, if you could get some sandwiches and bring them over here, I can go get the tape and also make a thermos flask of coffee. We could have a picnic while we wait."

"Good idea, see you soon," said Barney as he ended the call.

"Greg, I can't believe you said picnic."

He was perplexed. "Why? I'm hungry, you live on coffee, and I don't think it makes any difference to Joey Golino what we do now. He wouldn't want us to starve."

"I suppose he did own a pizza shop."

"True," said Greg."

Before I indulged in a post-murder picnic, I needed to get over to Joey's home and speak to Georgie Golino, Jarrajarra's newest widow.

I was glad Barney was coming to join us. I would need him to sit with Greg, who also didn't like violence and, I guessed, would not be keen on babysitting Joey's corpse alone.

Hopefully, together, they could manage Joey while I gave his widow the bad news.

The Golino Home, Jarrajarra, Victoria, Australia.

"Chris, come in."

Georgie Golino looked worried, but a flicker of hope flashed across her face.

This was going to be sad and awful. My very first next-of-kin death notice.

"I'm sorry, Georgie," I said, standing on her doorstep. I just blurted it out before I did anything. I hadn't even moved inside the house. Mister Tact.

I was thinking the right words, 'I regret to inform you' and all that, but what came out was lame, "sorry Georgie, Joey is dead."

I chose not to mention that her husband had been beaten to death.

Georgie started to cry, one hand at her mouth, the other still holding the door to let me in. Her knees almost buckled, but the hand on the door kept her upright.

What happened next? I barely remember.

I did the best I could.

"How did he die?" She asked.

"It appears he was murdered."

I actually said that. I can't believe it, bloody hell. There has to be a lesson somewhere on how to do this.

After that, a lot of, how? Who? Why?

I don't recall her questions exactly, but they were plenty and tearful. I had very few meaningful answers and did my best to avoid the few details I had witnessed.

I told her to expect a visit from the Crime Investigation team. I didn't mention that she would be the first suspect on their list.

I wanted to tell her she should not admit to knowing about Joey's drug dealing. Definitely not.

If Joey was a known drug dealer, someone would ask why he hadn't been prosecuted and why he was allowed to operate unimpeded by law enforcement. Good coffee and free pizzas wouldn't really cut it with the police integrity unit. It even sounded shifty to me, but telling her not to tell was potentially worse.

I was thinking selfishly, my natural state.

My Nan always said, "it doesn't matter what you think or say; it only matters what you do." I phoned Georgie's sister Sue.

That was something I could do.

Sue promised to be there within the hour.

Once she arrived, I left as politely and quickly as I could without appearing to run away. I didn't do grief particularly well, and I was clueless about the art of grief support.

My only previous experience with this kind of unexpected death notice, I was the recipient of the bad news. My mother died when I was six years old, killed by my father; I learnt much later. My Nan had delivered the news, and I was still too young to appreciate the finality.

"Sorry, Chris, your Mum has died," I remember Nan's words as clear as day, but when and where they were said, I have completely forgotten. "You'll be coming to live with me for a while. OK?"

My Nan seemed sad and serious, so I mimicked her actions; I was good at that. I had spent my early years keeping my drunken father amused, anything to avoid his volcanic tantrums.

Nan was glum, so I played glum, but secretly, I was happy. The news meant I would be living with my beloved grandmother for a while. No doubt I would be back with my poor sad broken mother once she recovered from her latest calamity, this death thing.

My Nan took me on when she was seventy-four years old; I lived with her for the next eleven years till I reached seventeen and joined the army. I was too young to appreciate the enormity of what she was doing for me. I also failed to notice there was no one else who would have me.

5

SUNDAY, MARCH 11, 2018

Pizza Lane, Jarrajarra, Victoria, Australia.

The sun was coming up by the time I made it back to Greg's truck. We ate our picnic and watched the beautiful bush sunrise.

"He was no saint," said Greg, referring to Joey Golino.

"He had a beautiful family," added Barney.

"He didn't deserve to die like that" was my contribution to the spontaneous eulogy.

"Who do you reckon the other bloke was?" Asked Greg.

"Mister X," said Barney, naming him forever into local folklore.

Barney was getting tired, but he volunteered to go back to the station to make Greg and me another thermos of coffee before he headed home.

He did that, leaving Greg and me sipping coffee inside the warm cabin of Jarrajarra's State Emergency truck

"Who found the body of Mister X?" I asked.

"Ricky Chalmers, he was out on a training run."

"Jesus Christ, running at midnight? Is he ever not training?"

"I think he had a day off once when he broke his leg, playing for the juniors. I think he missed training, not sure."

Ricky was the captain of the Jarrajarra Football Club. What he lacked in football skills, he compensated with ferocity and fitness. Extreme, ridiculous fitness.

"He's a lunatic," said Greg. "But don't tell him I said that."

I took another sip of my coffee.

"Coffee's not as good as Joey's," said Greg, mind reading again.

"No, definitely not, but good."

We enjoyed a few moments of quiet contemplation.

"Oh," said Greg. "I should have mentioned. Jack rang while you were at Georgie's. The other bloke died in the ambulance before they made it to Wodonga. Jack's bringing him back here. He'll be waiting in the cold room at the Nursing Centre, with Joey, for your forensics people to do whatever it is they do."

"Great," I said.

I sometimes wondered if I was the head of a well-oiled machine or just window dressing for a town that needed no police assistance at all.

My first double murder, and the local fire chief and the head paramedic had it all under control.

Greg gave up and went home at about noon. The forensics hadn't arrived, and being a Sunday morning, the back lane of the shopping strip had seen no traffic. No one had come by. I had nothing to do but sit and wait for my betters and think some more about 'Who?' And 'Why?'

Why had Joey been killed with one whack while my other victim had been tortured?

Was my unknown victim the real target and Joey just collateral damage?

And where did the mystery body, Mister X, come from? Did he arrive at the pizza place with Joey? Were they mates?

If they were together, where was Joey's car? If Mister X was on his own, then where was his car?

. . .

I kept my eyes on the bloodied back door of the pizza house and waited. I was certain I would be dreaming about that dark empty door for a while, along with similar doors I had entered in my army years, gun in hand and scared shit-less.

Pizza Shop, Toowong District, Victoria, Australia.

By 5.00 P.M., the Forensic team from Seymour and the two Homicide Detectives from Melbourne had arrived.

On arrival, the two ladies from forensics gave me a bright, cheery hello, handshakes, and thanks for the directions and then practically romped into their crime scene inside the shop.

The two Homicide cops just walked straight past me.

I kept myself busy outside the murder scene holding back the non-existent Sunday horde of press and concerned citizens. I was alone with not a lot to do, so I did a quick canvas of the few houses between the pizza shop and the edge of the town. People were home, but no one had seen or heard anything.

It was 11 P.M. when the two Homicide Detectives emerged from the shop and walked toward me. The boss of the two was a bull of a man, six foot tall, muscular, thick, crew cut. Well-groomed and extremely well-dressed for a police officer.

His partner was a much larger clone of his boss. The number two was big but soft, fat, not muscle. He was big enough with his police badge to think he was tough. I wasn't so impressed.

"So, Senior Constable?"

"Chris Taylor, Detective Sergeant." I filled in the blank.

"Yes, Chris Taylor, right. That was you I spoke to on the phone?"

"Yes, it was." It was Barney he spoke to, pretending to be me, but no need to go into the finer detail.

"First names OK with you?"

"Yes, Sergeant, whatever suits you."

"I am Detective Sergeant Peter Jordan, and this is Detective Constable Leo Snow. Pete and Leo."

They both extended their beefy mitts, and we shook hands all-round. New friends, it was almost heart-warming.

Almost.

Jordan's voice belied his appearance, softer, gentle. I couldn't pick Snow's voice as he had still barely grunted.

"Great directions you gave us, Chris, got us here in no time. I can't for the life of me work those fucking voice directions on the mobile."

"Part of the service Pete."

"Maybe you could give Leo here a lesson. He's worse than me."

"Anytime."

I had a pair of technophobes to work the crime. The crooks were looking safer by the second.

"And that picture of the map you sent on my phone; you'll have to show me how you do that?"

Jesus Christ, Barney was making me look too good. If he got me promoted to another station, how would I cope without him?

"So, anyway." Pete was back to business. "What are your thoughts here?"

Oh hell, he wanted my thoughts. How about this - Joey was a low-level drug dealer operating with impunity in the same street as the police station. All in exchange for free Cappuccinos and the occasional large Vegetarian. And there, just down the road, someone killed him for money or drugs or both, and while that was happening, some other bloke got beaten and tortured to death.

How to say all that and leave me in a good light?

"Well, it appeared to me, Pete," I was still a bit cautious on my use of his name rather than his rank, "the weapon could be an axe, blunt-side, or something else thin and heavy, but not sharp. The murderer would be tallish, strong, very accurate with their axe and brave enough or angry enough to take on Joey and his massive mate."

By the time I finished, Pete was looking at me strangely. Did he think I was showing off? Or was he underwhelmed and waiting for more? Had I called him 'Pete' one too many times?

"But why do you reckon the pizza bloke?" Pete asked some good questions.

Why indeed?

"Well," I said, "the pizza bloke, Joey Golino, was probably dealing in small-scale marijuana, but nothing I could ever prove. But yeah, maybe a big, tall, right-handed axe expert had killed him for his stash. That's one possibility, or maybe he just got in the way of the real fight between the murderer and the big victim."

At last, Leo's lips moved. "Regular fucking Sherlock Holmes, we got here, Detective Sergeant. We can head home now, I reckon. Leave Doctor Watson here to wrap it up, and just send us the name of the killer."

Detective Constable Snow actually spoke. There's a surprise. I wanted to ask him how I could be both Holmes and Watson in the same simile, but I was interrupted.

"Ah Leo, come on," said Pete, "I asked his opinion."

Bloody Hell, the good cop-bad cop routine. Weren't we all on the same side? I ignored Leo Snow, the fat gutted clown and focused on my new friend Pete.

"Yes. You did ask my opinion Pete, and now you have it."

They were a pair, these two.

Detective Leo grunted. Nothing more to add.

Pete had a think and then asked me another question. "Chris, tell me where I can find the widow."

I called up a map to Georgie Golino's and shared it with Pete's phone.

I took Pete's phone from his hand, signed him into Maps and set his directions to 'Speak'. He now had all the Map's bells and whistles. All Pete had to do was point the car and listen to the phone.

"Thanks," said Pete. "Very impressive."

I might yet win a job on Pete's scientific task force.

The two of them went to their vehicle and made to leave. Pete opened his window and spoke to me.

"Just realised you must have been going a while."

"Since 5.00 A.M. yesterday. It is a one-cop town."

"Bloody hell, mate, go home, get some sleep. I think the forensics will be safe behind the yellow tape till morning."

They drove off, and I followed orders. I went home and slept.

6

MONDAY, MARCH 12, 2018

Jarrajarra, Victoria, Australia.

The next morning, I was up at 5.00 A.M. and took a 30-minute jog out to the river. I ran along the banks for a bit, then back home. I did another 30 minutes on the heavy bag under the old veranda, out back of my house. Knees, elbows, fists. I didn't kick much anymore, just enough to stay flexible.

I was too slow for kicks, and they rarely worked for me in a real fight. I could defend against punches and kicks well enough, but these days, while fighting, I kept my feet on the ground.

I inevitably beat the bag to a pulp; it couldn't punch back, leaving my martial fantasies to run wild.

I showered, togged up in my blues and then crossed the road to the police station. I was in hot pursuit of some coffee. I was trying to make a fluffy cappuccino just like Joey's, which wasn't working when my new best mate Detective Sergeant Pete caught me in the kitchen.

"So, Chris, where can I find this bloke who found the other body?"

"Ricky Chalmers, local footy captain, fitness fanatic, out for a run when he stumbled on Mister X."

"Yep, that's the one."

I dialled Ricky's address and sent it to his phone.

"There ya go."

"Thanks, mate. You couldn't do that phone talking thing with the directions, could you?"

I took his phone and set his maps to speak. Hard to imagine Pete getting lost when all he had to do after he left the station was turn right at the highway, but I set his maps anyway. I slipped in a question while my hands were busy with his phone.

"How did you go with the widow?"

Pete was watching his phone in my hands. "Nothing, mate," he said. "I think her grief is real. She didn't admit to much about the husband's business side, nothing about the drug thing. Maybe it's the traditional Italian housewife. Didn't know her husband was a crook or maybe didn't want to know."

I handed Pete his phone. "Not that we are racially profiling the victim's spouse."

"Heaven forbids," he smiled. Maybe the good cop thing wasn't an act.

I watched through the window as Detective Pete and Detective Leo Snow left the building. They were off to speak to Ricky Chalmers, I presumed.

By lunchtime, the forensic team were done at the pizza shop and returned to the station. Detectives Pete Jordan and Leo Snow were back from Ricky's place, and they had taken over my office for a conference with the two forensics women.

I was not invited to the meeting, so I wandered down to the Ambulance station next door to the Bush Nursing home. I wanted a chat with Jarrajarra's paramedic Jack Farrell.

"Sorry mate, not a lot I can tell you. Your victim never said a word, never opened an eye. Nothing."

Jack was sitting in a canvas chair, leaning against the side of his immaculate ambulance. We were in the 'ambo' garage beside the Jarrajarra Bush Nursing Centre. The Centre handled everything that didn't need a doctor immediately. If your illness could be handled by an experienced nurse, you ended up here.

For serious emergencies, you had to get yourself to the Wodonga Base Hospital ninety minutes away, which usually involved Jack and his ambulance.

Everything shone in Jack's garage, plus the coffee was perfect, damn near Joey-esque. I was on my second cup.

"He croaked about 30 minutes short of Wodonga." Said Jack. "He'd lost so much blood, nothing we could do. Greg rang and told me about Joey. We figured this might end up a bit of an investigation, so I turned back and stashed him in the Nursing Centre along with Joey."

"What does Wendy think about that?" Wendy Acheson was the head nurse at the Jarrajarra Bush Nursing Centre, a legend of the region and probably a saint in training. She was also my girlfriend.

"Wendy will be right with that. I put Joey and Mister X on a side table out of the way. Got clean sheets over both of them. Plus, I told her it was a police matter, and she practically glowed. Anything for her golden boy." Jack watched me for a reaction, but I gave him nothing.

"Could you see anything on him or about him that might help me?"

He thought about it. "Jody said he had a stab wound on the top of his inside thigh, just below hip level."

"A stab wound?"

"Yeah, she was looking for the blood source. Shit, it was everywhere. Head-wise, he was bleeding from the nose and ears and even from his eyes. But it was all down his legs as well. Did a closer search, and there it was, a stab wound, like a kitchen knife maybe, and deep."

"What about the other damage, the broken bones? I was thinking of an axe, maybe. Not the blade but the blunt side?"

"Maybe. Whoever did it was very brave or completely psycho. He was one seriously big, seriously ugly unit. I wouldn't have taken him on if you paid me."

Coming from a Farrell brother that said something.

"He might have copped an axe handle round the legs. His left ankle looked broken, and his feet were really busted up." He thought a bit. "Might have been an axe handle or a tire lever."

"The dent in Joey's head was pretty specific. I don't think the killer was using a lever."

"Yeah, maybe." He thought some more. "Anyway, what's the difference, unless there's like a bullet you could trace, what's it matter what hit him? Shit, there are literally thousands of axe handles, tire levers, cricket bats and whatever within a one-mile radius of here. Could be anyone."

"Yes, well, if you don't know all of the crime, maybe I can work out all of the little bits until I do. Really, everything matters until it doesn't."

"Yeah, OK."

Jack thought some more.

"What do you make of Detective Boofhead?" Asked Jack. "Struck me as a fat goose."

"Detective Boofhead," I tried it out loud. Jack Farrell nodded in approval.

Detective Leo Snow had been re-christened.

We sipped our coffee, looking through the open garage doors out to the mid-morning quiet of the main drag.

"I really liked Joey," said Jack.

"Me too."

"I like Georgie too. Even went on a date with her back in school. God, she was a beautiful girl. Still is, I suppose."

"You were keen on Georgie Golino?"

"Me and every other bloke in town, mate. She was way too good for the likes of us. I consider myself one of the lucky few that managed a date."

I sipped in silence.

Jack continued. "Georgina Mellish. The last person I would ever see owning a pizza shop right here in her hometown. We all had her classified as 'meant for better' or 'headed for elsewhere', you know the type. Then Joey, the rock star, came along, and she fell for him.

Then there are babies and marriage and pizzas in no particular order. Such is life."

"Joey wasn't local?"

"No."

"Where was he from?"

"Dunno, mate. Dunno. Never asked, and he never told me."

"Wait. Did you say, Georgina Mellish? No, she's not?"

"She most definitely is."

"Not a sister to the Mellish brothers?"

"No mate, first cousin. Her dad is Wally's older brother."

"Hard to see Georgie sharing the gene pool with Wally and his boys."

"Watch yourself with that clan. They're a local version of the Hatfields and the McCoys. The Mellishes and the Mellishes. Wally and his brother didn't speak for twenty years, then the brother died, and they didn't even kiss and make up at the funeral. Poor form, I say."

"Hang on, the Mellish brothers are, were, Joey's weed suppliers. How did Georgie feel about that?"

Jack looked at me like I was an idiot.

"Joey and the Mellish boys were a love affair made in cash heaven. Knowing Georgie, I would reckon she approved wholeheartedly."

I was back at the station by 2.00 P.M.

Carole and Glenda, the forensic team, were packed and leaving as I arrived.

They were thanking Barney profusely for the services he'd provided. Sandwiches, coffee, stationery, the works. Barney was glowing, soaking it up.

Barney had nothing for me, no calls, no cries for help, no cats up a tree. The town was extremely well-behaved, apart from the odd double murder.

As the forensics were leaving, Carole turned at the door and said, "We'll be communicating our results to Detective Sergeant Jordan. I'm sure he will fill you in on anything you need to know." As she spoke, she gave Barney a theatrical wink. I assumed that meant Barney would be getting his own unofficial copy of the report.

"Thank you," Barney said, and he winked right back at them.

They turned and left.

I looked in on the two Detectives, who were now settled comfortably in my office.

"All good here, Pete?"

"Yes, thanks, Chris. Are we right to park in here for the duration?"

"Absolutely, treat it as your own. Shout if you need anything."

"We will, mate, we will," said Pete.

"Couldn't get us some coffee, could you, Constable," asked Boofhead.

"Kitchens out the back," I said, "I am sure Barney would love to show you how the kettle works if you need it."

Fuck you.

And that was that. I had just lost my office for the term of their visit. Pete was all smiles, and no news. Detective Boofhead was no news and no manners. He hadn't even looked up when he asked me to play waiter. I would have to remind myself occasionally that his name was Leo Snow. Must remember that; I had settled too comfortably on Boofhead.

I'd lost my office, but I still had my truck.

I did a further canvas of the houses around the pizza shop and confirmed my first finding. Nobody had heard anything from within the pizza shop. No one had seen our Mister X on his slow and painful walk from the shop to his collapse beside the river road.

The famous forty-eight-hour window was approaching, and Detectives Pete and Boofhead had nothing to show. If they had been racehorses, you would suspect they were running dead. I wondered if the forty-eight-hour window was a real thing or just something I read in a book or seen in a film. I should ask Barney.

Two things bothered me, where was Joey's phone, and how did

Mister X get to the pizza shop? I had intended to drive to the caravan park, just north of town, to start looking for an abandoned car that might belong to Mister X. As I drove down the main street, I saw the front door of the pizza shop was open. I stopped, parked and went in.

From the front door, I could see through the building to the back door. There in the passage was Georgie Golino with a bucket and mop, washing the blood from the hallway floor. She heard me and looked up.

"Chris Taylor. What can I do for you?"

"Saw the open door."

"Thought you would come and rescue the grieving widow? Help her clean up?"

"I'm so sorry for your loss, Georgie."

"Well, if you're truly sorry, you can grab a mop. There's another one in the back room with a spare bucket. Start in there if you're brave enough."

She pointed to the side room, the room where Mister X had died two nights ago.

"Mop, bucket, clean, that would be very helpful, thanks."

"OK."

I found the mop and bucket and got stuck into it, helping her clean the bloody residue of the murders.

"So, where are the kids?" I shouted from the side room.

"One's at school. The little ones are at home with my sister Sue." I could hear her working the floor, hard and focused, on a mission of cleanliness. "Thanks for calling her. I couldn't think the other night, could hardly breathe when I heard."

"You know I could probably get a team together and get this clean for you," I said. "You don't have to do this yourself. People love to help." As a cleaner, I was a great team leader.

"No, I want to do it. Needed to get out of the house, do something physical."

I was mopping the side room; Georgie was now mopping the hallway. We were talking through the open door of the side room.

"Who was he?"

"Who was who?"

"The guy whose blood I'm cleaning. Was he a mate?"

She didn't answer for a while, so I let the question just hang there.

"I told those other two I didn't know anything about Joey's business or his business friends."

"Georgie, I think you knew about Joey's business."

I let that hang there for a while as well. I stepped to the doorway and looked at her.

After a moment, she stopped mopping and looked at me. She really was beautiful; I could see why all the lads at Jarrajarra Tech would have lusted after her.

"I'll tell you what I know, Chris. I know that mop won't work itself, and all this blood will lie here till someone cleans it away. Are you here to help me clean up, or maybe you think you can do a better job of interrogating me than the pig twins."

She put her head down and resumed mopping hard and fast.

I noticed she was crying. This was going splendidly.

"Georgie, I didn't mean to make you cry; sorry."

She stopped mopping and looked at me.

"Good old Constable Chris, you've been in town five minutes, and you think the grieving widow will spill her guilty guts for you, just you and no one else. Why would I tell you and not those other two fuckwits? Are you special, Chris? If you are so fucking special, why are you playing policeman in an up-country backwoods hole like Jarrajarra?"

"Georgie, look, I am sorry."

"You're not fucking sorry. I am fucking sorry. I lost my husband, and you haven't lost anything. You are just scared I will tell your mates about all your fucking freebies."

She had a point there.

"Fucking junkies everywhere, and Constable Clueless doesn't seem to care, as long as he gets his two extra-large, extra hot skinny lattes every day."

Junkies everywhere? That was a bit harsh, and she was just getting started.

"That's ten dollars a day, Chris, 245 working days a year. How

37

many years have you been here? Two? Three? Plus, all the pizzas, that is at least seven thousand dollars by my reckoning."

Seven grand? Bloody hell, I'd always thought of it as a friendship, not a fringe benefit. She'd have the tax man after me next.

She resumed mopping with increased vigour. Whoever said words couldn't hurt you had not taken a spray from Georgie Golino.

"Georgie, I apologise. I didn't mean to come here and interrogate you. I was trying to help."

Georgie looked at me for a moment, then reached out and took the mop from my hand.

"Just fuck off, you cop pig cunt."

That went well, I thought and left without another word.

I went back to my police truck to consider what further crime-solving magic I could work on today. I had obtained some sort of admission from the widow. She did know her husband's business, right down to the coffee money. She clearly knew Joey was dealing marijuana.

She had mentioned junkies.

Would the potheads Joey serviced really qualify as junkies? Did she mean heroin or amphetamines? Where were these people? We hardly ever had a burglary, and the few punch-ups that centred around Joey's pizza shop were as close as we came to serious crime. Whatever, or whoever, she was talking about, I was now certain that Georgie Golino knew her husband's business.

Barney called.

There had been a phone-in regarding a domestic disturbance at an address outside of town. The caller was a male and had been, or maybe still was, the target of a vicious assault, which maybe on-going. According to Barney, the caller was in fear for his life, and there were sounds of significant contact occurring in the background.

Who, or what, was conducting the assault, Barney could not determine. Nevertheless, the male was still conscious enough to contact the police, and my urgent assistance was required at the scene.

I recognised the address and wondered at Barney's description of 'domestic'. The farmhouse at the given address was a couple of kilometres out of town, along the River Highway. It belonged to Kate Chalmers.

Kate operated a one-woman brothel from her farm. Kate's farm was adjacent to her brother's farm, Ricky Chalmers. They had inherited the land from their parents and split it down the middle. Kate now owned the bit nearer the highway, and Ricky owned the section closer to the river. Neither of them was what you would call a farmer.

Ricky made his money from playing and coaching football and from working as the town gardener. He had quite deliberately turned his inheritance back into its beautiful native state. It was an organised bush oasis of birds, animals, native grasses and trees. Ricky had managed it as skilfully as he had managed the town's greenery. It was beautiful.

Kate's share of the farm was not so pristine, mostly unkempt bush. Kate's interests were more location, location. Her position along the highway was perfect for her true profession.

I arrived at Kate's to find her front gate locked. There was also a Toyota Hilux Utility truck stuck fast in the solid metal frame of the secured gate.

The Hilux was on the inside of Kate's gate, trying to get out, not trying to get in. My guess was that the driver of the ute had attempted to crash through the locked gate but failed, given that the gate was supported by two heavy corner posts and could only be opened inward.

Kate might let you in, but you could not leave without her permission. Knowing Kate, I doubted that was by accident.

So, the driver could not exit because of the gate. At the same time, he could not retreat because the rear end of his utility had been partially caved in by Kate's own pink Bedford tray truck, a vehicle that was significantly larger and heavier than the Toyota. The Bedford was rusty, to begin with, and had a truly massive front grill. It showed no obvious damage from its collision with the utility.

The smaller Toyota was a different story.

From my view, it looked as though the utility had suffered more than just the collision with the Bedford. The sides and windows had been systematically beaten to near structural death by Kate, using a cricket bat by the look of it.

I guessed this because Kate was now sitting in her underwear on the roof of the Toyota. Her bum was on the roof, and her feet were planted well apart on the damaged bonnet.

Her head was hanging down, and in her hands, she held a cricket bat. Her grip was textbook perfect. The working end of the bat rested on the hugely damaged bonnet, somewhat forward of her feet.

In addition to the doors of the utility, all of the windows had been smashed as well.

Fortunately for the occupant, the laminated glass had held together sufficiently for him to remain semi-safe within. The windscreen and side windows were splintered and fractured but mostly whole. There were several spots where the bat had penetrated the occupant's side of the glass. There was a fist size hole through which he was now shouting at me.

"It's about bloody time you showed up," screamed the guy in the ute. "This crazy bitch was trying to kill me." It appeared that Kate had tried exactly that, but right now, she was sitting exhausted on the roof above her victim. She looked spent

"Kate?" I asked, "Are you OK?"

She looked up at me.

"Chris, mate." That was all she managed before she dropped her head, heaved once and then vomited all over the bonnet of the Toyota. She dropped the bat and began a slow-motion collapse onto the bonnet and the vomit, and from there, she slid, gradually, toward its edge as though she were slowly melting over the bonnet of the car.

I had time to jump the gate, get to the side of the ute and catch her before she fell to the ground.

I then carried her to the nearest tree, where I sat her down in the shade, leaning against the tree and facing the conjoined vehicles.

At that point, the driver, presumably the 'victim' who had called Barney, exited his vehicle shouting things like "fucking bitch", "whore", and other insults.

Just screaming at her, really. Vile shit.

He seemed intent on running past me towards Kate, presumably to offer her further injury and verbal abuse.

Kicking her while she was down seemed to be his plan.

I let him reach my side, at which point I hit him with a left rip into his liver. He went down, retching before he could bother Kate. I dragged him all the way to the other side of the Bedford and cuffed him to the grill. I left him there, out of sight, heaving and moaning, cooking in the sun while I attended to Kate.

I might have been relatively new to Jarrajarra myself, but I would be dammed if I was going to take the side of some drive-through, ill-mannered, out-of-towner against a much loved, well-respected local merchant.

Kate's eyes were fluttering, and her breathing was ragged, so I called Barney. He called an ambulance for Kate and the tow truck for the Toyota.

I jumped the fence again to retrieve my first aid kit and some water from my police truck. I returned to Kate to see if I could revive her. I gave her a drink of water and wiped her face and chin with a damp cloth. She soon came around. I had some time before Jack arrived in his ambulance.

"What is this all about, Kate?" I asked.

"Bastard paid me up front, had his fun and then stole his money back, greedy turd."

"Well, he called Barney from inside his car. Sounded to Barney like a pretty serious assault was in progress. Looks to me like you were the attacker here."

"Nah, love, not me. Just wanted me money back."

"How much was it?"

"Five hundred. I put it in an envelope and wrote his registration number on the outside. I put it in me drawer. After we were done, I went to the loo, and when I came back, he was in his car and leaving, and me money was gone."

"Yeah, that's what he did." Confirming her own story.

"You fuck!" She shouted that last bit to her victim, cuffed and moaning on the other side of the Bedford.

"Kate, the ambulance is on its way. Are you taking anything they should know about?"

"Just need me medicine. My head is killing me. Just need me medicine. Ricky was supposed to bring me some yesterday, the shithead."

Ricky was Kate's younger brother. Ricky Chalmers, our missing football captain, the man who discovered our Mister X beside the road. Everyone knows everyone in a small country town, often as not, they are related as well.

Kate had always been a fit and attractive woman; I would have thought a twenty-minute assault on a Toyota Hilux well within the range of her stamina. Right now, she looked on the verge of a physical and mental collapse.

She groaned and turned her head to the side, and vomited again.

"Oh Jesus," she moaned. She closed her eyes and leaned her head back against the tree. She stayed there until the dynamic duo of Jack and Jody arrived in their ambulance.

"G'day mate," from Jack.

"Hi, Chris," and a smile from Jody.

The two of them were so adept and so efficient. Without words, they had Kate on their stretcher and in the back of their ambulance in barely a minute. They negotiated the firmly locked gate, the barbed-wire fence and the busted vehicle as though they weren't even there.

"What about this bloke?" Jack nodded toward the driver of the ute, still cuffed to the grill of the Bedford.

"No, he's alright, just a tummy ache. I'll look after him."

With that, the ambulance left, and I noticed this time, Jody was driving and Jack was in the back with the patient. What a team.

I called Barney, and he told me the tow truck was still about twenty minutes out. Rob Farrell was out of town, and his son Scott was running the garage single-handed. That gave me more time with my mate from the Toyota.

42

I un-cuffed him and stood back to let him stand up and regain some dignity.

"There was no need to bash me." He sounded as though most of the vinegar had drained from his attitude.

"Well, mate, for a moment, I wasn't certain if you were about to assault me."

"And I didn't take her money," he said, "I was just running late, and I had to leave. She was in the fucking toilet forever. What's the go? We had done the business. What's she reckon? I had to kiss her goodbye or something."

I felt unqualified to discuss the social requirements of post-coital departure from a serving prostitute. What were the rules, if any?

"Yes, well, have you got your driver's license there, Sir?" Falling back on a more comfortable procedure, I put my hand out. He found his wallet and handed it over. I took note of his details and also noted the wallet was empty of cash.

"I swear to God, Officer, I did not take that woman's money. I paid her in cash, like always. I don't normally carry cash. I had to get it on my way through Wodonga."

"Where are you heading?"

"Home. I live east of here, Towonga."

His driver's license confirmed his address.

"You married?" I asked.

"Yes." There was a touch of guilt there that I might polish into a compromise.

"Right. Well, how would you like to handle this then?" I waved my arm in the general direction of everything.

"Handle it? She wrecked my truck!"

'Truck' was a bit of a stretch; it was a utility. "That's my work vehicle. It's fucked." He had a good point there. "She has put me out of work, the mad woman. I can't afford a new truck. I can't even afford the time off to get it fixed."

I couldn't help thinking he had the time and money for Kate's services, but suddenly he was cash and time-poor. But then, who was I to question another man's priorities?

"It's your work vehicle? You're insured, right?"

"Of course, I am insured."

"Comprehensive?"

"Yes."

"Does that include a replacement vehicle while yours is being fixed or written off?"

"Yes."

"Hmmmmmmmm." I hummed and nodded at the same time.

"What?" He asked.

I spoke carefully, "Well, I look at all of this - this carnage! - And I see a man who ran off the road, trying to avoid a kangaroo, no, no, - Trying to avoid a family of ducks. He lost control and went through, no, he crashed through - a farm fence, luckily avoiding the family of ducks, coming to rest against a gate – Yes, there has been damage, but thankfully the family of ducks survived."

His eyes suggested he knew where I was going but was not quite there himself.

"Oh great, and I am still up for the excess on my insurance, which is four hundred bucks, plus the five hundred I spent on that mad cow, plus the pain and suffering you inflicted on me."

"Pain and suffering? That was resisting arrest."

"And yeah, well, what the fuck was I being arrested for exactly."

"Well, um," He actually had a good point there.

"And resisting?" Damn it, he was winning the argument. "I tell you what I was resisting. I was resisting getting my head bashed in with a bloody cricket bat."

I had to admit there had been a plague of head bashings going around Jarrajarra. He was wise to be careful.

I tried to get him back on track. "Four hundred dollars excess, you reckon?"

"Yes, and I don't reckon. I know, it's a fact."

I thought about that. "Hang on a minute," I said. "Wait here. Don't move."

I went inside Kate's house and went to the tallboy cupboards in her kitchen. I poked around a bit and eventually found a cleverly hidden wad of half a dozen envelopes wrapped in an elastic band. Each envelope had five hundred dollars inside in cash. Each of them had a registration number written on the outside of the envelope. I thought the rego number was clever, but keeping this much cash in your tallboy was not so smart.

I went to the door and shouted at my new partner in crime.

"What's your number plate?"

He told me, and I checked that number against the batch of envelopes. His rego number wasn't there.

I put Kate's money back where I had found it.

I looked around a bit more and noticed a small bunch of household bills and invoices pinned to a pegboard above the kitchen bench.

I checked another cupboard, under the kitchen bench, directly under the pegboard. The top drawer contained pens, elastic bands and writing paper. It also contained an open box of new envelopes. There, at the back of the box of newbies, was another envelope, not new, but used and opened, with cash inside. It also had the correct registration number written on the outside. Kate must have mistakenly put it back where she had taken it.

I went back outside, extracted the five hundred dollars from the envelope and showed it to my new mate.

"OK, four hundred dollars for your insurance excess, one hundred dollars as a co-operation bonus, nothing for your pain and suffering, no refund for your fun with Kate." The fun with Kate was the only thing he hadn't complained about.

"In addition, Kate needs to be compensated for the damage to her fence and her Bedford. That can come from your insurance."

Also, I threw in the obvious. "Once the tow driver gets here, you can have a free lift back to town to Farrell motors, where I am sure they can arrange a replacement vehicle." That last bit was a guess.

"What do you think? Do this the easy way, keep it out of court?"

He took the proffered cash. We had a deal.

I called Barney.

"Mate," I said to Barney. "I have an accident victim heading your way. Could you scoot over to Jack's garage and help this poor bloke with his insurance claim?"

It was a given that Barney would write it up in my name and forge my signature wherever required.

Scotty Farrell arrived not long after. He was huge and muscular like all the Farrells. With brute force and some finesse, he eventually separated the vehicles from the gate and each other, and soon after that, he had the Toyota, and its owner, on their way.

After they left, I went back inside to see if I could find evidence of this medicine Kate had been talking about.

I checked the bathroom cabinet, and there was not much there, just a half-used packet of Neurofen.

There was a wastepaper basket beside the bathroom sink. I opened it. It was stuffed full of empty packets. I took one out to check the label.

It was an empty box-of-12 Oxy-Contin, prescribed by a doctor whose signature I could not read, to a patient I had never heard of.

Oxy-Contin? Bloody hell.

I went to my truck and called Jack Farrell. Jack was in his ambulance, on another call already.

"Jack, I have found about 20 used packs of oxy in Kate's bathroom. Looks like she has run out."

"Damn, I knew she was coming down off something. I was guessing ice or oxy or both. Yeah, oxy makes sense."

"So, where did you take her?"

"We dropped her at the Nursing Centre, too much hassle at Wodonga, left her with Wendy."

"OK." If Kate was in withdrawal from Oxy-Contin, she would be there for at least a week. I knew Wendy would provide Kate with the care that was needed for as long as it took, but if Kate couldn't get off her addiction, then what? Jack read my thoughts.

"Look, mate, it's the best place. Kate's no addict. I guess this is something that just got out of control really quickly. You can't handle these things alone, Chris. You know Wendy, she will either kill her or cure her."

"Yep. OK. Talk later." I ended the call. I didn't tell Jack what Kate had said about her brother Ricky providing the drugs. It didn't seem to fit at all. He was a fitness fanatic, not a drug pusher. I would have said his sex-working sister was not far behind in fitness.

I was tired and thought the mysteries surrounding Kate's sudden addiction could wait until tomorrow. As always, Jack had made the right decision. Right now, Kate was in her best possible place, given her current condition. She was under the care of Wendy Acheson.

Wendy and I had a history.

There were three people I knew in my current sphere who had served in Afghanistan. Rob Farrell, the local mechanic; Senior Sergeant Bruce Palmer of Wodonga Police Station, my immediate boss; and then there was Nurse Wendy Acheson.

On my last tour of duty to Afghanistan, I had been badly wounded during an engagement with the enemy. This had occurred near the village of Khas Orusgan. I played a minor part in a very major battle. The battle had been famous for a while, but that fame was fading. I had struck out early in the event. Thankfully, when my wounds occurred, I quickly lost consciousness, so I missed the nasty parts that followed. When I woke up a week later, I was in the Medical Mission in Kabul, under the care and attention of Australian Navy nurse Lieutenant Wendy Acheson, Officer-In-Charge of the Holding Facility at the Mission.

Wendy had been the officer in charge of just about everything she had involved herself with since. She had been the boss of the world since she was a girl. In Kabul, ten years ago, I was her patient. I hadn't died, but I had gone to heaven.

In 2015, when Wendy was back home, working as a civilian in Jarrajarra, she heard that the job at the local Police Station would be available later that year. She got together with Barney and filled out my application. She had also called Sergeant Bruce Palmer of Wodonga Police, a fellow veteran.

According to Sarge, she had instructed him that if he hoped to receive medical care east of Wodonga anytime during the rest of his life, then I should get the job.

I got the job, and Wendy called to let me know of my success after it was all settled.

So, there I was, at the time, the youngest, lowest-ranking officer in charge of a police station. That was no great honour, Jarrajarra being the smallest one-cop station in all of Victoria. I found out later, when my excitement had eased that after my word-perfect application and all the glowing references from the region's finest, the deciding factor with the appointments board had been that I was the only applicant for the position.

So, now, I was happily ensconced in my new hometown Jarra-jarra, courtesy of Wendy Atcheson. She had decided, she told me after I arrived, it was way past time that she cut me from the herd.

7

TUESDAY, MARCH 13, 2018

Jarrajarra, Toowong District, Victoria, Australia.

I was up at 5.00 am and took off on a long run into the hills west of town. Jarrajarra existed on a five-mile-wide river flat where the Murray River cut through the Eastern Highlands. The Highlands run for over three thousand kilometres along the east coast of Australia, separating the temperate east coast from the dry desert inland. If you were looking for a hard run out of, and then back to, Jarrajarra, you only had to run east or west of town into the hills. That's where I went.

In the day ahead, I wanted to check in on Kate Chalmers and see how she was doing. I also wanted to see her brother Ricky and ask him what he knew about the bucket of used Oxy-Contin.

I also needed to get out to the Caravan Park to see if I could find Mister X's means of transport.

I ran for about an hour, returning to town. Just a few hundred yards from my home, I passed the Bush Nursing Centre, where I could see Wendy's push bike leaning against the wall outside her office. I cut my run short and headed inside. Wendy was at her desk, writing some notes.

"Howdy, nurse."

"G'day soldier." She looked up at me, "Oh yuck, you need a shower. Room 1B across the hall is free. There's a shower in there."

"I haven't got any clean clothes. I only need a minute."

She took a towel from a drawer behind her and threw it at me.

"I know," she said, "But if you want to talk to me, then go take a shower. Go. Now." She continued writing, and I headed for Room 1B.

Five minutes into my shower, I heard the door to 1B open and then close and then I heard it lock.

A few moments later, Wendy stepped, naked, into the shower.

"Make some room here, Corporal." Wendy was referring to my army rank. She had outranked me significantly and always called me Corporal when she was in a bossy mood, which was most times. She pushed her way into the shower, backed me against the wall and gave me that beautiful smile. We had a standing cuddle and a lovely, soft kiss.

"Hold that thought," she said and stepped out of the shower. Within ten seconds, she had returned with a white plastic chair, the sort that old people might use to take a shower. "There ya go. Sit down," she said. I sat, and she straddled, sitting in my lap, facing me. She reached across and adjusted the hot water, making it harder and hotter. "Oh, that's so nice."

"What about some foreplay?" I asked politely. "I might need a moment here to prepare myself."

"Foreplay? You?" She thought about that and then reached behind me. She grabbed a cake of soap from the tray and handed it to me. "Here, wash my back. I'll give you foreplay."

So, I soaped her back, and we made love, just like that, till the hot water ran out, and her back was shining.

I got out of the shower, leaving Wendy to wash under the cold water. She spoke about Kate without being asked. "I'm keeping Kate here for at least a week, her heart is strong, so I am taking her cold turkey. She is in lockdown and drug-free as of right now."

"Did you ask her about that?"

"Look, mate, her head is on another planet, and I never ask a junkie for permission, not even a new one."

I found the towel Wendy had given me earlier on a chair beside her folded uniform. I went to grab the towel.

"Oiy!" She called from the shower. "Leave that; it's for me."

"Oh."

"You haven't finished your run yet. What's the point?"

By the time I had shaken off as much water as I could and redressed into my sweaty running gear, Wendy was out of the shower and drying herself. I was ready to go. We were always discreet, so it was a given that I would leave the room now, and she would exit later. Not that there was anyone here in the small bush hospital at 6.30 A.M. other than the two of us and the comatose Kate.

"Come here," she said, smiling broadly. She gave me a kiss and then let me out of Room 1B, locking the door behind me. The halls of the small hospital were empty.

I ran home and got ready for work.

I made it to the station after just 8 am, arriving to find Detective Senior Constable Boofhead standing in front of the reception desk, speaking at Barney.

"Fuck me. Have any of you yokels in this shithole even heard of a fucking camera?"

"Firstly, Detective Senior Constable, I don't like being referred to as a yokel." Barney Trail may not be a modern Rambo, but he was not to be bullied by anyone. "Secondly, yes, we have heard of cameras. We have also heard of Closed-Circuit Televisions, which I doubt very much you are aware, are actually not cameras, or even 'fucking' cameras as you describe."

Barney even made the finger quotes in the air.

"They are actually, as their name suggests, television broadcasting systems which include both camera, broadcast and viewing components."

Boofhead's mouth was open, ready to talk back, but nothing was coming out.

"Sorry, Detective Senior Constable Snow, I can see I am confusing you with big words. So, yes, we have three privately owned CCTVs in town, one at the pub, another at the garage, and the third belongs to Mrs Copeland on Dunlop Drive. That one is at the other end of town, and she only ever uses it to keep an eye on her roses. None of these systems is in range of the Pizza Parlour, and all of them are focused on the owner's premises.

"And furthermore, if you'd read the notes Constable Taylor left on your desk, sorry his desk that he so kindly loaned to you, you would know that he had already spoken to the owners of all three CCTV systems. And he had viewed the footage from those systems and found nothing of interest in the immediate hours before or after the Pizza Parlour closed on Saturday night."

I did all that. A viewing? A report? On Boofhead's desk? I had impressed myself. I had no doubt Barney had done it all on my behalf. I could take credit for the delegation.

Eventually, Barney stopped talking. It was Boofhead's turn.

"Alright, OK. Fuck me. Shit, mate, I hear ya. No need to get your panties in a twist."

With that, Boofhead disappeared into my office, slamming the door as he went.

"Barn mate," I started. I was going to suggest, very politely, that going out to interview the CCTV owners was over the mark. What if Mrs Copeland on Dunlop Drive was the murderer?

"Yes, Chris," he said before I could elaborate, "I know I over-stepped the line. I can see you would be worried about me stumbling over the actual murderer and ending up ravaged and destroyed. A carcass by the roadside, God forbid. I get it. Sorry. "

Bloody hell, was the community of Jarrajarra some lost tribe of mind readers, or was I so transparent I didn't need to speak.

"But to be fair to me," he continued. "I was only speaking to Gloria at the pub, Wilma Copeland with her roses, and young Scotty Farrell at the garage, and I very much doubt any of them are our murderers."

"No, I suppose not. You spoke with Scotty, so Rob wasn't at the garage?"

"No, he wasn't. He was off in Melbourne, I believe. Look, I won't do it again, I promise."

"Good."

"Now, Wendy called just before you got here. Kate is as well as can be expected. So, I guess you will be heading out to speak to Ricky Chalmers about his sister. You also mentioned the other day about checking out the caravan park, which I noticed, you didn't get around to. So, I guess you will be off to do that as well. I suppose you'd rather be on the road all day doing meaningful work rather than hanging around here at the beck and call of those morons." He nodded in the direction of my office.

"Yes, I guess you're right."

"I am sure I can handle those two if something comes up."

I had to laugh at that. "I am sure you can, Barn. I am sure you can." I saluted Barney and headed off.

I went looking for Ricky Chalmers. The Jarrajarra Football Club Captain, fitness fanatic, football enforcer and younger brother of Kate Chalmers, the freshly minted Oxy-Contin addict. I had always found Ricky easy to deal with. His fearsome reputation was something he reserved for the football field. I had seen him play, and the reputation was well deserved. He was a genuinely tough guy and a brave competitor. Off the field, he was a good man, solitary, with no wife and no kids, but a solid and reliable person.

Ricky's apparent turn to drug pushing was as surprising to me as Kate's addiction to pills.

You couldn't make a living playing Australian Rules football unless you were very good. You needed to be good enough to play in the national league over an extended period. Ricky had managed two seasons playing for the Sydney Swans in his early career. That was a worthy effort in such a competitive sport, but he was never good enough to make it last. Talented but too slow in a game that loved speed was the final verdict.

After he was dropped from the Sydney list, he returned home and settled for local stardom. He was paid to play locally, and while it paid reasonable money for a weekend hobby, it was never enough to live on. He made his daily bread as the Jarrajarra groundsman. He was employed by the Towong Shire to manage the various grounds around town. All the locations under Ricky's care were, like himself, maintained impeccably. Damn, near perfect, in fact.

Between 10 am and noon, I looked in all his various workplaces. I looked in his shed behind the Football Ground where the Shire-supplied tools of his trade were kept, the tractors, the mowers, the trimmers and chainsaws. I drove out to his farm; nobody was there.

His front door was unlocked, so I took a quick peek inside. Even the milk in his fridge smelled old, 'on the turn,' my Nan would say.

In all the places I searched, there was nothing to suggest he had visited in the last few days.

I knew Ricky had reported the dying body of Mister X to Greg Farrell late Saturday night. But where was he now?

I decided to start the afternoon by searching for someone I was certain I could find. I grabbed a sandwich from the local milk bar and headed to the Jarrajarra Caravan park.

Wally Mellish was the day-to-day manager of the Jarrajarra Caravan park.

The caravan park was a couple of kilometres north of the town. You drove to where the town road hit the Murray River Road. You crossed that road and followed a dirt track another half a kilometre till you hit the Murray River itself. Here at the head of the river, it was wide and full and beautiful. The caravan park sat right on the river and ran for several hundred meters along the river's banks. The park attracted fishing enthusiasts, grey nomads and boaters. It also attracted seasonal workers, drifters and people who couldn't afford permanent housing. The camp sites were cheap if you had your own van, plus the permanent cabins were almost as cheap and reasonably clean if you didn't. It was a lovely place for a holiday or even a place to live if you didn't have much money, but it would never be mistaken for luxury accommodation.

It was conceivable to me that my unidentified victim had come through here. It was close to town and reasonably discreet. If you had some secret business, then this might be a good place to meet. There was also the question of how Mister X had been transporting himself. Where was his car or motorbike?

I drove into the park and stopped at the reception. Wally Mellish was a slightly shabby little bloke, more the cleaner than the concierge. I had never stayed at the park, but he struck me as a bloke who would remain seated while tossing you the keys. The type of bloke to point you at your cabin rather than walk you to your door. As long as I had known him, Wally had that musty smell of cigarettes and beer.

On a typical day, Wally parked himself on a bar stool behind the counter inside the reception cabin to the park. And there he stayed until his outdoor responsibilities screamed at him to move. I stood at the door to the reception area. Wally was behind the desk, a cigarette in his mouth, a full ashtray and a racing guide aligned in front of him. He was watching the horse races on a small black and white portable TV with twin overhead rabbit-ear aerials. The TV was at arm's length, and Wally was holding one arm of the antennae and wobbling it gently. The aerial was not cooperating. The sound of the race preliminaries droned along, but the picture was mostly hissing fuzz.

"Wally, mate, how are you?"

"Terrible Chris, terrible, fucking television."

"Maybe the fates don't want you to see what comes next."

"It's me third leg of the quaddie, Chris. I am two for two. I can't miss this, and I can't leave me seat. Don't want to break the spell."

"Right, so who are we cheering for."

"We got two going, Mantel Piece or Trailer Trash. Either will do, but Mantel Piece is the better odds. This will pay huge, mate, huge."

Wally was still fiddling with the aerial as the race was ready to start."

"Fucking TV. Works better if two people hold an arm each mate."
He waved me forward to grab one end of the aerial contraption. I did
that.

"Move back," I followed his instructions, moving back away from
the screen. "Further . . . A bit more." I moved accordingly. "Perfect
mate, right there, don't move, don't move."

"OK," I said. I was now staring at the back of the TV.

"And they're racing." That was the race caller on the TV. Wally's
eyes widened.

"Come on, Mantel Piece. Come on, Trailer Trash run my little
darlings."

Wally took a massive drag on his cigarette and, with his free hand,
stubbed it out in the ashtray. He would need his full lung capacity to
cheer his horses home. His free hand was now fake whipping the air
behind the chair as if the barstool was a saddle, and there, beneath
him, was his horse.

"Go! Go! Go, babies, go." Wally was shouting. I held firmly to my
end of the aerial.

The sound of the TV went scratchy. It was obvious Wally, waving
his imaginary horsewhip at his imaginary horse, was wobbling his
end of the aerial. Where was the teamwork?

"Wally, your bouncing the reception, mate."

"Shit, sorry, Chris."

He froze in a semi-horse-whip position, still watching the TV.

The race progressed, and as the horses approached the final
straight, Mantel Piece and Trailer Trash had taken the lead and were
both well clear of the rest of the field. It was now a race in two. Wally
had to make a choice.

"Fuck off, Trailer Trash, you slut, fuck off, you bitch."

"100 meters to go," came the sound of the race caller via the back
of the TV. "It's Mantel Piece stepping clear, half a length to Trailer
Trash."

"Come on, Mantel Piece, go baby." Was that me or Wally
cheering?

"Mantel Piece crosses the line one length to Trailer Trash," said
the TV.

"Aaaargh!" Wally punched the air in celebration. His eyes closed, facing the ceiling above him, fists clenched at his chest. "Shit, shit, shit! Oh God, oh Jesus."

He sat back in his chair and grabbed his cigarette pack, and lit up another. He breathed it in as though recovering from a heart attack.

"Oh, Chris mate, oh shit. Mate, what have you got planned for the rest of the day?"

"Well, actually, I came here to ask you a question or two. I am pretty busy."

"No worries, mate, ask anything, but you have to stay here, OK? You can't leave, mate. We have to stay exactly where we are for the next race."

"Jeez Wally," my late grandfather had the same affliction, gambler's superstition. Better to nip this in the bud. "I don't think I can."

"Please, Chris, please, just one hour till the next race is done and dusted."

"Wally, tell me what I want, and I will try and get back here in an hour, OK?" An hour was hopeful.

"Anything, mate, anything."

"Has there been anyone through here in the last two or three days? Anyone new at all, and are they still here?"

"Yeah, mate, the bikies. They come here once a month. They sleep in cabins 141 and 142 and party in 143, down the far end. They usually stay for a night or three and then shoot through real early on checkout day. When they leave, it is like still-night-time-early, like pre-sun-up. Usually, they go together, but yeah, today, one of them is still here, or his bike is, so yeah, can you stay till the next race?"

"These bikers, there were four of them?"

"Shit, Chris, what is this, a fucking test? Four, I think, maybe three, I forget. Yer staying for the next race, right?"

"So, if they are awake, they'll be in 143 down the far end?" I asked.

"Yeah, mate, last cabin before the bush trail starts."

"Thanks, Wal."

"No worries mate, I'd come with you, but I can't leave me seat.

Remember, you gotta be back here in," he checked his watch. "Fifty-five minutes. Fifty minutes to be safe." He sounded desperate.

"I'll try." I headed back to my truck to make my way down to the end of the park.

With his bum still fixed to his seat, Wally lent to the side so he could see me through the door. He shouted to me.

"Chris, I think if you stay within the boundaries of the park, we will be alright. Don't leave the park, OK? Don't break the spell!"

"OK, Wal, I will do my best." Was I being detained by the caravan park manager? Did Wally have that authority? Surely not.

Apart from Wally, the park was truly beautiful. The vans and cabins were all well-spaced, and the gravel road wound its way through magnificent old river gums. The beauty of the bush and the river overcame Wally's shortcomings as a groundsman. The vans and cabins were mostly immaculate. By the time I reached cabin 143, I was fully reminded of the park's appeal.

There was a Harley Davidson V-Rod Special parked outside number 143. Black, sleek and beautiful. I guessed it was the 2015 model, the Night Rod Special. I couldn't help thinking it was the perfect ride if you were moving drugs or money across the border. I walked past the bike and knocked on the cabin door. There was a sound from within the cabin, but it wasn't human; it was the steady buzz of blowflies. A lot of them.

I took out my gun for the second time in two days. The cabin door was locked, so I kicked it in. It was flimsy and caved in easily. The blowflies went crazy for a moment, then settled on their meal. There at my feet, just inside the door, under the carpet of blowflies, was the owner of the Harley. He was face down on the linoleum. His head had obviously exploded in a bloody mess across the cabin floor. Another big scary bugger, almost as big and just as dead as Mister X.

I stepped over the body into the cabin and did a quick check inside. There was nothing and nobody. No food, no spare clothing, no cupboard to store clothes. It was empty and grim.

I stepped back over the body very carefully and out of the cabin. I checked the other two bikie cabins, 141 and 42. They were both empty.

I went to my truck and called Barney.

Within minutes, Barney had loaded up Detective Pete's phone with appropriate directions to guide Pete and Boofhead down the straight line from the police station to the caravan park.

Within forty minutes, the two detectives had finished their first inspection and were now stationed outside cabin 143, waiting for the forensics team. The team from Seymour were very keen to be involved, and they were, at that point, according to Barney, halfway to Jarrajarra.

Barney had police under his direction, running all over the district. He must have been in heaven.

With the police tape in place, I excused myself from the two detectives. I told them I needed to alert the park's caretaker, Wally, to what was happening in his park. They didn't seem to listen or care, so off I went.

Exactly fifty-two minutes after leaving Wally guarding the television, I was back in the park's reception room. I was just in time to grab my end of the twin aerial and stand with my arms extended behind the little black and white TV.

"Jesus, mate, you are cutting it fine." Wally was annoyed. I could tell.

"So, Chris, mate, what's with the other cop car?" Wally clearly maintained some interest in his responsibilities and had noticed the arrival of the detectives.

"Wal, you have some serious problems down at number 143."

"Problems? Problems? Chris, mate, stop right there. We don't have time for negativity, mate. After the race, mate."

I held my tongue. Who wants negativity?

"Wally, you realise I can't see the screen from here."

"Chris, life is not always just the way we want it to be. You have to take the magic where you find it. You are present at what may be a special moment. Don't move. Don't think. Just be."

"It would be nice to actually see the magic."

"Shut your eyes and watch with your ears. For fuck's sake.

I closed my eyes and accepted my lot.

"And they're racing," said the back of the TV again.

"Who are we on, Wal?" It didn't seem too negative a question.

"Barbecued-Banana and Kiss-Me-Hardy. The banana is a red hot favourite, and Kiss Me Hardy is my 100 to 1 long shot. The banana is a certainty. I can't lose, not now you're here. If you can shut your grizzling for two minutes, we might be rich."

And so it went, and as the race transpired, there was no real need to cheer for either horse. The un-favoured Kiss-Me-Hardy led from start to finish, winning by ten lengths, and the red-hot banana finished dead last. Wally sat transfixed on the screen, stunned to silence. The race was done, and he had selected four winners in four races. Wide-eyed and speechless, he was trying to calculate his quadrella winnings with pencil and paper, but neither the pencil nor his hands were functioning.

He gave up his calculations, sat silently for a moment, and then, at last, he spoke.

"Chris, mate, I think this is big, very big."

I was still holding my end of the aerial five minutes later when the race caller announced, over the television, that the quadrella had paid twelve thousand, one hundred and thirty-three dollars per unit. Per unit? Surely that couldn't be right, but the TV said it again. It was right.

"Oh," said Wally.

The race caller also announced that there were only twenty-five successful units in all of Australia, hence the large payout.

"Oh," whispered Wally again. "Fuck me, hooray!" His voice was almost inaudible.

"Jesus, Wally," I asked. "How many units did you have?"

He stubbed his last cigarette, his hands shaking; he lit another, inhaled half of it, held on for the calming effect, and then exhaled slowly at the roof.

"Just the twenty, Chris," his voice was soft and shaking. "Just the twenty."

"Twenty?" Wally was now, cash-wise, probably the richest person in Jarrajarra. Certainly, the richest instantaneous self-made man I had ever met.

"Wally, I better take a picture of that ticket. If you lost it, you'd need the ticket number for a claim."

"Good thinking Chrissy, police evidence, yes, good thinking." He laid the ticket flat on the reception counter and smoothed it with his hands. I took a clear photo of the ticket getting it to fit and focusing on the number. Once I was done, he went to shove the ticket back in his pants pocket.

"Wal, could you do me a favour and put that in your wallet." I could see him losing the proof of his fortune the next time he took out his cigarettes.

"Oh mate, you are on fire. These are good suggestions, really good suggestions." He put the ticket in his wallet. While he did that, I emailed the photo of the ticket to Barney as a third leg to Wally's insurance. Was that enough to secure his quarter-of-a-million-dollar victory? Bloody hell, a wealthy Wally Mellish, could Jarrajarra cope?

It was time I returned to duty.

"Sorry mate, I have to go. This is sensational news, but I really have to get back to work."

"Chris mate, no, no!" He was genuinely shocked. "Celebrations, Chris, celebrations. You're a big part of this, buddy."

I didn't have the heart to tell him I would not be celebrating with him tonight.

"Can't Wal, sorry, work," and off I went.

As I got to my truck, Wally came running out of the reception cabin, now unglued from his stool and the TV, running toward me, his arms raised to heaven. He charged into my chest and embraced me, tears streaming down his face. He had me in a bear hug, sobbing like a child.

"Oh mate, mate, mate. You are the best thing that ever happened to this town. I love you, mate."

"Thanks, Wal," what else could I say? After Georgie Golino and Kate Chalmers, Wally was the third person I had made cry in two days.

He looked up, still hugging me. "So yeah, what's the go in 143?"

"You've got a murder victim in there."

"Oh." He finally stopped the cuddle. His hands dropped to his hips. Was this all too much excitement for a single Wally afternoon?

"Murder victim? Fuck me." He looked in the direction of 143, then looked at me. "Bloody hell. Big day all-round, hey?"

"Yes, Wal. Big day."

"Good for some, hey."

"Yeah," I said.

"Not so good for others."

I left, feeling sure that Wally would cope with the loss of his customer from 143.

By 5.30 P.M., I was back at my third murder scene in three days. In Jarrajarra, that was unbelievable.

I was standing guard with the two Melbourne Detectives. They sat in their car chatting to themselves while I stood protecting the police tape that surrounded both the cabin and the last fifty meters of track that led to the cabin.

We were all waiting for the forensics.

Jarrajarra football training was probably starting now, and I was missing another chance to track down Ricky Chalmers.

At 6.00 pm, Greg Farrell arrived in the Jarrajarra fire truck, accompanied by his wife Norma and two of their teenage children, Narelle and Brett. The four Farrells were all seated in the large front cabin of the truck, all wearing full C.F.A. uniform, including the heavy, bright yellow, hi-vis overcoats to protect them from the evening chill.

Greg parked the big red truck two inches from the police tape that surrounded 143. He had glided the massive truck off to the side of the police tape without causing so much as a flutter from the tape. He could park on a sixpence, and I had seen him do it many times.

Greg, Norma and the kids emerged from the truck and proceeded to set up a gas barbecue and picnic table at the front of the truck, creating a natural barrier against public intrusion upon our crime scene but leaving enough access room for the two police investigators.

Within five minutes, Greg had fired up the BBQ while Norma and the kids laid out the folding table with plastic forks and paper plates beside a hand-painted sign saying, 'two dollars a snag and five dollars a drink'. As I wondered what flavour the drinks might be, the younger Farrell boy, Brett, dumped an ice chest full of beer cans, stubbies and a single bottle of pink lemonade beside the table.

"Half price for members of the police force," he winked.

The residents of the caravan park all dutifully arrived, as if summoned by the sound of sausages cooking on a plate, and quickly formed a queue at the front of the table.

Narelle, the older Farrell teenager, had carried a large stack of folding chairs from the back of the fire truck. She aligned them outside the perimeter of the police tape, facing cabin 143 but off to the side so as not to impede the catering or the police.

Norma, who was already selling drinks and taking cash, promised me faithfully that she would ensure that no member of the public would cross the line.

At one stage, Detective Boofhead stepped out of his vehicle, which was behind the tape, and shouted, "Oiy! Everyone. This is a crime scene. You, people, can't stay here. You have to move on."

To which young Narelle Farrell turned and, smiling beautifully at the detective, said, "We will, officer. Soon." Then smiled again and then turned back to serving sausages.

Jarrajarra had not had a murder before, and now we had three in as many days. The fire brigade was determined to do it in style. The barbecue, the booze and the spectators would remain. Detective Boofhead would just have to cope with the public scrutiny.

Cabin 143, with its battered corpse inside, sat silently behind us all.

Over the next hour or so, Norma had, as she had vowed, made it very clear that no one was to venture beyond the tape for any reason whatsoever, and they obeyed. I found the people of Jarrajarra were mostly cooperative when they saw the sense of it.

Soon, the word was out, and it seemed half the town had joined the audience. There were over one hundred people who had self-organised in an orderly fashion outside the tape, eating sausages, drinking beer and heading back to the table for a refill whenever they felt the need. Many had brought their own canvas chairs for that extra bit of comfort. There was even a small queue outside the ladies' toilet further back inside the park.

Eventually, the forensic team of Carole and Glenda Johnston arrived. They were in their smallish Volkswagen van with 'Victoria Police Crime Services' printed along the side. What they lacked in numbers, they made up in energy. They almost burst from their van into action. Greg Farrell had guided them to their parking spot, and both greeted him like old buddies. I did see a small glimmer of surprise as they first noticed their seated audience, but after a quick word from Greg, they were down to business.

When the ladies from forensics had unpacked their gear and were making their way toward the cabin and the crime, two taller members of the crowd stepped forward and gallantly held the police tape aloft. As the two-cop crime services team stepped under the tape, the two Melbourne detectives stepped out of their vehicle to greet them. With that, a spontaneous round of applause burst from the assembled audience.

One of the uniformed C.F.A. guys shouted from the back, "Three cheers for the police who have come to solve our murders. Hip, Hip!" and the crowd responded with the "Hoorays."

The two Melbourne detectives looked stern and unimpressed. The two forensics seemed quite impressed. Carole turned to smile at the crowd and punch the air.

The four cops all made their way toward the entrance to Cabin 143.

The show was about to begin.

As the two tall locals lowered the tape, I stepped into the gap to ensure that no one from the audience lost total control of themselves and burst forward in pursuit of an autograph. It didn't happen. Everyone was remarkably well-behaved once the Crime Services went to work.

When they finally set up their spotlights, focused them on the cabin and then opened the door, you could clearly see the naked soles of the dead man's feet facing out towards the crowd. Did he have his shoes on when I found him? No, I was sure he didn't. Had he been in bed when his killer arrived? Perhaps he didn't need his shoes to let his visitor in?

The naked feet looked cold and dead.

Murder had come to Jarrajarra, and the town was reacting in its purest form, disrespectful, extremely curious and not missing the opportunity for some important community fundraising.

Greg stepped up beside me. "Nice little earner, this."

"The BBQ and folding chairs?" I asked, "It's a bit 'Welcome to Woop-Woop', don't you reckon?" Greg's favourite movie was the closest analogy I could find.

"Nah, we're just taking the piss. Boofhead there came over to the Fire Station early on. Just started looking around without so much as a hello."

When Greg said Boofhead, he was pointing at Detective Snow. Jack Farrell's nickname was spreading through the town already. How long would it take till he heard it?

"Anyway, Norma goes to speak to him, and he says he's looking for the CCTV."

"And you don't have one?"

"No, mate. Who'd fuck with the fire truck, for fuck's sake?"

I could imagine in another world, or even another town, the fire captain might be concerned about the safety of the truck, but not in Jarrajarra.

"Financial priorities." Greg was mind-reading again. "What's a camera system cost compared to a locked door? It is a lot more expensive, I can tell you, and we don't have a whole lot of cash to play with. So anyway, Norma sets him straight on the lack of a CCTV to solve his crime, and off he goes. No 'by-your-leave', nothing, just some smart-arse comment about small country towns. While he is walking, he is not even looking at her. Mate, your colleague is a rude prick, so we thought we'd fuck with him a bit. Hence the BBQ. If I'd known we'd get a hundred or more, I'd have organised a raffle and sold the prick a losing ticket."

"He certainly has a way about him."

"Chris, he was rude to Norma. He's lucky the boys just took the piss. They could just as easily take him out the back of the shed. Now that really would have fucked up your investigation."

"I get the feeling the two Detectives think I'm too backwoods to be any value," I nodded towards Cabin 143.

"The Detectives? Who gives a fuck what they think? The forensics? Mate, I know them, country girls. You're with me. You'll be right."

I had seen it many times since arriving at Jarrajarra. When two people argue in a small town, the rest of the town will take a side, even before they know what they are arguing about. It is 'Who' that matters, not 'What'.

"Greg, mate, could I ask you a favour?"

"Anything Chris."

"Could you hold the fort here for ten minutes? I just want to scoot over to footy training and see if I can have a word with Ricky Chalmers."

"Save yourself the bother. He called me earlier. He had to go to Melbourne for something important, he said. Be back for Thursday night's session. He promised."

I stared at Greg, thinking Ricky Chalmers had missed training. That seemed impossible.

"I know," said Greg. "First time for everything, hey."

"Who is taking . . ."

"Jack's taking the training tonight, he's doing the ball work, and then he's getting Jody to finish them off with a running session." He laughed to himself. "Those poor bastards won't know what hit 'em."

What the hell was going on with Ricky Chalmers?

I would have to wait till Thursday to find out.

"Listen, Chris," Greg had more to say. "If someone from out of town did this, then it is not your concern. No one will be looking at you to assist. If someone from within the town did this, well, it will be you, and only you, who will find them, trust me. You are a good cop. Have some faith in yourself. You are the best thing that ever happened to this town."

That was what Wally said earlier today, cuddling me as he wept. I thought about that for a moment.

66

"Fucking Wally, hey?" said Greg. "How about that? All that money." Greg had read my mind yet again.

By 9.00 P.M., footy training had finished, and a few of the players had wandered from the footy ground to the caravan park to join the crowd. By 1.00 A.M., curiosity was satisfied, and everyone had gone home. The Firefighting Farrells had cleaned up and left.

The show was over, but the activity inside Cabin 143 continued.

Outside the cabin, there was only me and the town's two paramedics, Jack Farrell and his co-driver Jody. We were leaning against the ambulance, waiting for forensics to clear the body. Another one for the cold storage room at the Bush Nursing Centre. The pathologist still another 48 hours away.

At 1.30 A.M. Detective Pete emerged from the Cabin.

"We are mostly done here on the inside," he said to Jack. "You guys can grab the body now if you want."

Jack and Jody went off to do that. The forensics team stepped out of the cabin, getting some air and moving out of the way of the paramedics.

Glenda from the forensics shouted to me. "Wouldn't have any of those snags left, would you, Chris?"

"There's a plate full of them on the front of my truck, wrapped in plastic. Hope you like sauce." Norma had thought of everything.

The two women raced to be first to a pile of sausages and cold drinks that would feed ten.

Detective Pete stood beside me, watching them.

"What's the story, Pete?" I asked. He still didn't object to first names.

"Mate, right now, I know exactly what you probably knew five seconds after you opened that door. He's opened up to someone. He's turned his back on them to lead them in, maybe, then he gets a bang on the head from behind, and he drops to the floor, face first, dead. After that, the killer vanishes into thin air. Was he expecting them? Was it someone he knew? Who knows? It is a fucking cluster fuck. That's what it is."

"How much longer will the forensics be at it?" I asked.

"Ha! All night I reckon, they want to finish inside the cabin, then outside and up that trail behind there." He was pointing to the bush trail that ran from behind the cabin, out of the park and into the hills beyond. "Probably do that in the morning."

We both thought on that one for a moment.

"A sausage sizzle at a murder site," Pete continued, "it is a strange little town you have here, Chris. Very strange."

"Takes a while to settle into it, I guess," I answered.

He tapped me on the shoulder, it was friendly, "and I suppose you were up at 5.00 A.M. again for your morning run, hey?"

"I was. Seems a while ago now."

"Go home to bed, mate. Leo and I will look after this."

"Thanks, Pete." I meant it.

"What is it you lot call him when he's not listening?" Oh shit, he'd heard. "Detective Boofhead?"

I swore to myself that I had never said that out loud. Had it slipped?

"I might have heard it, maybe."

He laughed. "Go on, piss off home."

8

WEDNESDAY, MARCH 14, 2018

Supreme Court, New South Wales, Australia.

TRANSCRIPT OF PROCEEDINGS.

THE HONOURABLE J. CAIN AC QC, Commissioner

In the matter of the alleged Murder of Gary John Rogers by Johnathon 'Jack' Hayes and others.

Thursday, 15 March 2018. Continued from Wednesday, 14 March 2018. DAY 9

Ms J. Berlic QC appearing with Mr D. Hume and Ms. P. Blake as Counsel Assisting.

Mr R. Dickson SC appears with Mr J. McKenna for Mr Alexander 'Tiny' Sheahan.

9.45 AM: Mr Alexander 'Tiny' Sheahan.
ON OATH, Cross examination resumes.

Commissioner: Please continue, Ms. Berlic.

Ms. Berlic: Thank you, Commissioner. So, Mr Sheahan, yesterday we were discussing your remuneration for your involvement in various activities leading up to the murder of Mr Gary Rogers on the first of January 2010. Quite a significant amount I recall.

Mr Sheahan: If you say so Miss.

Ms. Berlic: What I want to talk about today is those people that paid you those monies which we have discussed and why you were paid those sums.

Mr Sheahan: OK

Ms. Berlic: Those people I refer to being Mr Azzolino Pisano and Mr Michelle Folliero.

Mr Sheahan: Azzy and Mick, yeah.

Ms. Berlic: As you explain in your statement to police, you were not a full-time employee of either Mr Pisano or Folliero.

Mr Sheahan: Nah, no way. I had my own things going with my club in the town. I was my own man.

Ms. Berlic: The town being Griffith?

Mr Sheahan: Yeah, like I say, I had my own thing going, never liked having a boss or anything. But, you know, money is always tight in the entertainment industry and so I would do favours for Azzy every now and then. He paid really well, which was good.

Ms. Berlic: It was always your understanding that 'Azzy', Mr Pisano was an employee of Mr Folliero, and that these occasional jobs you did for Mr Pisano were at the request of Mr Folliero?

Mr Sheahan: Yeah. Azzy was my man, but Mick was the boss.

Ms. Berlic: And when you were paid for your effort, you were always paid in person, in cash, by Mr Folliero.

Mr Sheahan: Oh yeah, absolutely. Mick was pretty tight with the cash, he made sure you got exactly the correct weight and that, once you took it, you had better not stuff up.

Ms. Berlic: By 'correct weight' you mean the exact amount of cash negotiated.

Mr Sheahan: Yep.

Ms. Berlic: And by 'better not stuff up' you mean that Mr Folliero emphasised to you that you should not fail in the performance of his request.

Mr Sheahan: Exactly. Failure was not the option, like they say.

Ms. Berlic: So, Mr Sheahan back to these favours you did for Pisano and Folliero. The nature of those favours was usually driving someone to a location, assisting your passenger in their endeavours, as required, and then returning your passenger to a location of their choice?

Mr Sheahan: Yeah

Ms. Berlic: And these endeavours, for which you were the driver, on one occasion, involved murder?

Mr Sheahan: Yeah.

Ms. Berlic: So, on one of these drives, January 1st, 2010, to be exact, you drove a man that you have identified as Mr Johnathon 'Jack' Hayes to the Riverina Hotel car park in Tenambra, New South Wales?

Mr Sheahan: Yeah, I drove Jack to the Riverina, and that is all I did. I didn't sign up for murdering anyone. I'm a driver not a fucking hit man, sorry, excuse my French.

Ms. Berlic: Yes Mr Sheahan, we shall come to the question of your responsibilities later, right now I want to focus your attention on Mr Hayes.

Mr Sheahan: OK, but just so you know, like I told the police, I didn't know he was going to shoot the bloke.

. . . Cross examination of Mr Sheahan continued until 12.30 pm at which time proceedings postponed for lunch.

3.15 PM: Constable Lucille Jans.
ON OATH, Cross examination continues.

Ms. Berlic: So, Constable please state your current position with the New South Wales Police Force

Constable Jans: Yes, I am an investigator with Forensic Evidence & Technical Services Command, which is a division of the New

South Wales Police Force. It is my job to provide technical services to assist investigations,

Ms. Berlic: So, Constable, once a body is found, your job involves the identification of that person through biometric means, finger-prints, DNA and even voice prints, in order to assist in various investi-gations and Commission Inquiries such as this.

Constable Jans: Yes, that is correct.

Ms. Berlic: And in the identification of Mr Rogers' body via means of his DNA, you also discovered other DNA material belonging to other individuals.

Constable Jans: Yes.

Ms. Berlic: Commissioner, I am now referring to Constable Jans' report to New South Wales Police, Special Task Force, dated June 18, 2017. That document is now Commission exhibit 7.23.01.

Commissioner: Noted.

Ms. Berlic: So, Constable, in your report to the Special Task Force, you mention that you found tooth fragments embedded in Mr Rogers' right hand.

Constable Jans: Yes, that is correct.

Ms. Berlic: These were not Mr Rogers' own teeth.

Constable Jans: No, they were not.

Ms. Berlic: Constable, to summarise your report to the Special Task Force, it is your opinion that the tooth fragments embedded in Mr Rogers' hand, his dead hand I should mention Commissioner, that the DNA of those teeth match the DNA found on another victim, a sexual assault victim from a totally separate incident. That victim is identified in your report, who we shall refer to here as Jane Doe.

Constable Jans: Yes, the DNA of the teeth found in Mr Rogers' hand match the DNA of the fluid matter found on the person of Jane Doe.

Ms. Berlic: The fluid matter being semen?

Constable Jans: Yes, the semen which was discovered on Jane Doe after a sexual assault on her person, in July of 2015.

Ms. Berlic: Which means what? In plain English.

Constable Jans: It means the perpetrator of the assault on Ms.

Doe in 2015 was the same person whose teeth were embedded in Mr Rogers' hand in 2010.

Ms. Berlic: Is there any possibility that the man charged with assault on Jane Doe is not the original owner of the teeth.

Constable Jans: No, none whatsoever.

Ms. Berlic: And do we have a name for the perpetrator of these two separate crimes.

Constable Jans: Yes, the man's name is Johnathon Elvis Hayes, also known as Jack Hayes.

Ms. Berlic: Thank you Constable, and to the best of your knowledge, where is Mr Hayes at this present time?

Constable Jans: Mr Hayes is currently resident at Her Majesty's Prison Barwon, in Victoria.

Ms. Berlic: Thank you constable. Now Constable I would like to focus on some other evidence that you were asked to investigate in this matter, in particular the telephone that was discovered with Mr Rogers body. Can you describe that please?

Constable Jans: Yes, we found the remnants of a mobile phone that had been buried with Mr Rogers' body. The phone has since been identified as that belonging to Mr Rogers at the time of his disappearance.

Ms. Berlic: What is the significance of that phone.

Constable Jans: Well, since the time of Mr Rogers' disappearance we have had possession of a recording, taken from the answering service of Mrs. Jennifer Rogers, the wife of the deceased. In the moments prior to his murder, Mr Rogers was attempting to call his wife.

Ms. Berlic: And we are talking about a recording of that call?

Constable Jans: Yes. On the recording you can hear clearly, Mr Rogers responding to a greeting from another party who, at the time, we were unable to identify.

Ms. Berlic: So, you didn't know who Mr Rogers was speaking to, other than his wife?

Constable Jans: No, not then. Mrs Rogers did not pick up and presumably Mr Rogers was intending to leave a message.

Ms. Berlic: How did you eventually identify this other person on the recording.

Constable Jans: Firstly, Mr Hayes left a fingerprint on Mr Roger's phone. We established a 15-point match to Mr Hayes' right forefinger on the screen of the phone.

Ms. Berlic: You say firstly?

Constable Jans: Yes, in addition to the fingerprint, we had also established Mr Hayes as the owner of the broken teeth.

Ms. Berlic: Anything else?

Constable Jans: Yes, in addition to the teeth and the phone, we were able to use a sample of Mr Hayes' voice and match that sample to the voice of the other person on the recording. Using what we call a wave file match on chosen words, we matched the voice on the recording to the voice sample taken from Mr Hayes.

Ms. Berlic: Is that even possible.

Constable Jans: Yes it is most definitely possible.

Ms. Berlic: And is a voice match considered as accurate as a DNA match.

Constable Jans: No, and I am not suggesting that the voice matching would be sufficient to convict a person of a crime where that was the only evidence. In this instance it was used to confirm Mr Hayes actions in relation to Mr Rogers. The teeth and the fingerprints put Mr Hayes at the scene but don't necessarily prove his role in the events.

Ms. Berlic: Well exactly, how do you know Mr Hayes was in fact the same person that attacked Mr Rogers, he may well have been a bystander or someone wandering by.

Constable Jans: Well, Mr Rogers and the other party greet each other, then there is a gunshot. Then it sounds like a very brief struggle occurs. Then, after the first gunshot and after the struggle, there is another gunshot and the struggle ends.

Ms. Berlic: So, presumably at this point Mr Rogers has been shot and is dying, if not already dead, and he does not speak again?

Commissioner: Was that a question or a statement Ms. Berlic.

Ms. Berlic: That was a question Commissioner.

Commissioner: So, Constable, did Mr Rogers speak after the second shot.

Constable Jans: No. Mr Rogers does not speak again.

Ms. Berlic: So, after the second shot, what happened?

Constable Jans: Well, after the second shot Mr Hayes speaks, quite emphatically, in such a way that indicates he fired the gunshots that killed Mr Rogers.

Ms. Berlic: What did Mr Hayes say that established him as the shooter?

Constable Jans: He said, "Hit me will you fuck head?". Then there is a brief pause, you can't hear much at all, and then Mr Hayes says, "Well cop that you cunt."

Ms. Berlic: Commissioner, can I suggest that now might be an appropriate time to listen to the actual recording.

Commissioner: Yes, I think that would be wise.

. . . The tape is played for the Commission after which proceedings are postponed to the following day.

9

THURSDAY, MARCH 15, 2018

Jarrajarra, Toowong District, Victoria, Australia.

I was out of bed by 5 A.M. Today was weight day, so I went to the shed and huffed and puffed through thirty minutes of lethargic lifts and grunts. I wasn't much interested in lifting weights, but you can't run for hours every day, and they say weights help you maintain your strength and libido into old age, not that I am old.

After the weights, I managed thirty minutes of slow jogging to the river and back and then thirty minutes on the heavy bag. I had rechristened the bag 'Boofhead'. That name would probably last for the length of Detective Constable Leo Snow's visit to our town. I gave the bag a father of a hiding, and not once did it attempt to hit back. I had it totally intimidated, as usual.

I arrived at the station by 7 A.M. to find a television broadcast van parked near the main entrance. The two-person television team consisted of a young bloke holding a camera. He was also wearing headphones over a baseball cap on backwards, dressed in a dirty white T-Shirt and some nasty floral board shorts that had slipped so far down his muffin belly he was in danger of being arrested for offending public decency, not that I was offended.

In front of the camera, holding the microphone, was a woman, approximately 35 to 40 years of age, whose personal presentation, hair, make-up, clothes, you name it, was as opposite to her cameraman as was humanly possible. I recognised her as the well-known TV journalist Angela Adams, who had a mixed bag of specialities but had made her name as a crime reporter. Standing in the light of the camera, Angela was possibly the most glamorous human I had ever seen.

She almost sparkled.

I had seen her the previous day on the Morning Show, standing outside the Supreme Court of New South Wales. She had been reporting on the Commission Inquiry into the death of Riverina Politician Gary Rogers. Rogers had vanished nearly a decade ago. When his body was found just two years ago, it was apparent he had been murdered. He had not run off with other people's money, as had been alleged at the time of his disappearance. There were now confident allegations of mafia involvement and political corruption. There were also allegations that certain police had not tried very hard to find Rogers when he first went missing.

Late last year, Rogers' wife Jennifer had successfully sued her husband's former political foe, the current Riverina parliamentary incumbent, Mister Thomas Field MP. Mrs Rogers also sued the former New South Wales Premier, Mister Leon West. Both men, West and Field, had suggested that Rogers had shot through with funds embezzled from a charity he ran, which was not true. The charity money, even if it had been stolen, would hardly have paid for a bus ticket out of town. The discovery of Rogers' body had exposed Field and West as liars. The Rogers family had claimed they were lying in exchange for drug money from the pocket of Michelle 'Mick' Folliero.

The Rogers Inquest, being held in the Supreme Court of New South Wales, was the biggest show in the country. There was talk that Thomas Field would soon be resigning from Parliament. The former premier West was safe. He had died three months ago of natural causes. His reputation was barely intact when he passed away, but his former good name was not looking too flash right now.

In addition to the crooked politicians, there was a whole bunch of formerly respectable New South Wales farmers who looked certain to go down for conspiracy to murder.

I had to wonder what was a famous reporter such as Angela Adams doing here in Jarrajarra. Our three murder victims, a small-town pizza cook and two other complete unknowns, paled in comparison to her reporting from the Supreme Court.

Standing beside her, apparently waiting for a question, was Detective Pete. Behind him was the Boof, just being his own best self, not doing anything much other than standing and breathing and looking like a horrible pig. Between the camera guy's bum crack at one end of the line and Detective Boofhead at the other, it was hard to know where to look.

Angela was talking to someone off in the cloud, probably the host of the Morning Show somewhere beyond the horizon. The two cops were dutifully waiting their turn to talk. I quickly drove into the station yards and parked around the back, just in case Angela had the notion of pointing her microphone at me.

I came in the back door of the station, into the kitchen, to find Barney using his mobile phone as a TV. He was watching the Adams' press conference from just outside our front door, Live on Channel 7. Sitting next to Barney, squeezed in to watch with him, was my fearless leader, Sergeant Bruce Palmer of Wodonga station.

"Sarge, Barney," I greeted them as I grabbed a chair. "Let me in."

"Shoosh!" they both whispered loudly.

I had to hand it to the camera guy. What he lacked in the sartorial, he overcompensated in the professional. He had Angela and the police station and the blue hills in the distant background, all looking magnificent on Barney's phone. There wasn't much he could do with the two Melbourne detectives, but at least they were standing in the correct positions.

While I was in transit from the front gate to the kitchen, I missed the middle bit of the interview. Angela was now interrogating Detective Pete.

"So Detective, are Victoria Police prepared to confirm that one of the three victims murdered here in Jarrajarra, Mister Edward "Joey" Golino, was, in fact, the nephew of Mister Michelle Folliero? The same Michelle Folliero who at this moment is the main suspect in the conspiracy to murder former political candidate Mister Gary Rogers."

"Yes, Miss Adams, I can confirm the family relationship. Joey Golino was a nephew of Mister Folliero. Mister Golino was the child of Victoria Golino, nee Folliero, the sister of Michelle Folliero."

"Holy fuck!" Sarge and Barney were in harmony. I had never even heard Barney swear before, and the Sarge swore almost never. No wonder Angela had come to Jarrajarra.

"So, Sergeant," the TV reporter continued to Sergeant Pete. "Can you confirm or deny that the three murders that occurred here on Saturday are linked to the very recent disappearance of Mister Folliero and his alleged accomplice Mister Azzolino Pisano?"

"No, I can't confirm or deny anything in that regard. This is an ongoing investigation, and it is too early to determine if these murders are related to the activities you describe."

"Are you aware, Sergeant, that both Michelle Folliero and Azzolino Pisano are, as of today, in breach of their bail conditions, and their whereabouts are currently unknown to New South Wales Police?"

"I can't discuss that subject today. The current location of those gentlemen is not the concern of Victoria Police."

"He hasn't got a clue," the Sarge saw through the Detective double speak.

"Do you concede, Detective," Adams continued, "that those gentlemen are now missing, possibly absconded."

"I won't comment on that suggestion. No."

And so it went.

· · ·

The phone at the front desk rang, and Barney left the kitchen to attend to it. He took his phone with him, the selfish bugger, leaving the Sarge and me alone in the back room.

"Coffee, boss?"

"Absolutely, son."

"So, Sarge, to what do I owe the pleasure?"

"Well, I was thinking with three dead bodies and two Melbourne detectives, you might need some managerial assistance. After that interview, I am certain of it. Holy hell, a Folliero nephew? Your pizza guy? In Jarrajarra? "

"I wonder how many nephews he had. It might have been a big family. Could be like a second nephew or a third nephew."

"You only number cousins Chris. A nephew is just a nephew. Like a brother or sister, you can't have second brothers on your mother's side. You're a nephew, or you're not."

"You can have a half-brother." I wasn't prepared to concede.

"That's a step-brother Constable." The use of my rank, Constable, indicated the Boss was getting serious.

"I suppose." I handed him his coffee and sat down beside him.

"Can't say that I am impressed by these two?" He nodded towards the front of the station, clearly meaning the two Melbourne Detectives. "The older one is affable enough, but the other one, my goodness, what a troglodyte."

"They'll never be accused of collaboration."

"No."

We both took a sip of our coffee. I was learning to live without Joey Golino's special skill,

"Tell me, son, what have you worked out on your own."

I told him the little I knew.

I mentioned that the three men had all been bashed to death with an unknown weapon. That the various bashings went from short, sharp and brutal for both Joey and the man from Cabin 143 to a long and tortuous assault on our Mister X. I told him that Mister X and Mister 143 were bikies that stayed in the Jarrajarra Caravan Park once a month. Sometimes, according to Wally Mellish, there was a third member of the party, sometimes a fourth. They always stayed in the cabins around number 143, at the bush end of the park. I had no idea what that might mean. I mentioned that the crime services report was not yet available, but according to Jack Farrell, our ever-reliable ambo, our Mister X, had also been stabbed in the thigh. Probably by a large kitchen knife, maybe, but certainly something long and sharp.

Also, Mister X was probably bashed and stabbed at the Pizza Shop and survived all of that, only to bleed out on his ill-fated journey back to the caravan park, where I suspect he was heading.

"Anything else?" Sarge asked.

"Well," I said, "I canvased most of the town, and so far, no one has told me anything of note. I've checked with the owners of the three CCTVs in Jarrajarra, and "we" viewed all the relevant footage, of all the relevant times, and nothing showed up."

I almost forgot the bit about the CCTV because I hadn't really done that myself; Barney had. I used the royal "we" to cover that fact. I was embarrassed by exactly how much I was relying on Barney for real cop work, but that wasn't why I lied to the Sarge. I lied because if the higher-ups knew how much police work Barney did, especially the stuff when he impersonated me, we would probably both lose our jobs. Barney would hate that.

"Oh, and one other thing, according to both Jack and Barney, the pathologist would be here for the autopsies tomorrow."

I was reaching the end of my update, running out of things to say, when Barney entered the kitchen carrying a wad of sticky notes.

"Sorry, Sergeant Palmer," Barney handed the notes to the Sarge. "They are all for you. Except for this one."

He handed the last note in the pile to me. It was from the desk Sergeant at Warrangatha Police. It said words to the effect 'Mellish Brothers have allegedly destroyed Warrangatha hotel. Please detain for further questioning.' I groaned out loud. I also toned my language for Sarge's sake.

"Jason and Justin Mellish, shit! They have been so well-behaved lately." I felt like crying, not the Mellish boys. Please, God, anything but that.

The Sarge stood up, "I will leave you to it, Constable. I am going to claim back your office for the region, shift those two clowns over to the - um - somewhere." With that, the Sarge, and any hope I had for backup, was gone.

"I'm so sorry, Chris." Barney sounded appropriately sympathetic. "I'd love to help, but you know my thoughts on conflict."

"No worries Barney, if I am not back in three hours, no two hours, get all the Farrells, especially Rob and Greg, but also Scotty, and maybe Norma. Definitely Norma." Amongst her other civic duties, Norma was the principal of the local primary school and had allegedly established some semblance of control over the younger Mellish brothers. Whether that control still held fifteen years after they gave up their pursuit of education, I didn't know.

So, it was back to being the local policeman.

I called the desk Sergeant at the Warrangatha police station to ask how I became the lucky duck assigned to managing the Mellish brothers. Warrangatha wasn't my town, not even my district.

"Constable, they are from your town. I want them arrested."

I didn't like the bit about 'arrested'.

"Well, Sergeant, that is not strictly true. Technically, they are from twenty kilometres outside of my town." I was not above begging.

"Whatever, in-town, out-of-town, they belong to you."

I was trying to think of an excuse not to visit them.

"Constable," he interrupted, "I could send a ten-man SOG team from Melbourne, and if we were extremely lucky, those two idiots would be the only ones killed. Or I can ask you nicely, bearing in mind your past success in this area; I could ask you to do your duty and follow my instructions. Go and sort this out."

"Sort it out? Your note said detain them?"

"Sort out, detain, sneak up close and shoot the bastards. I don't care what you do; just get it sorted. I have had calls from the president of the Warrangatha Chamber of Commerce. The publican has called me; his place is wrecked, and his staff are in tears. I went over there myself, and I almost shed a tear."

"Did the pub have bouncers?"

"This is Warrangatha Constable, population zero-fuck-all. They can't afford bouncers. Who would they bounce? They don't have fist-fights, and if you hired twenty of the locals, how the fuck would they bounce the Mellish brothers. Just get it sorted, Constable."

He hung up the phone. I had my orders. Get it sorted. Not detained. Not arrested.

Huge win for me.

I called the Warrangatha hotel. The phone was picked up by a staff member, a local woman named Shirley.

"So," said Shirley, "they've come in the pub with their dad, Wally, around 9 P.M. Already drunk but, give 'em credit, everybody was happy, no trouble. The dads had a win on the horses, apparently."

"Anyways, all's sweet till closing time, right? At which point they get a bit testy, nothing threatening or anything, but don't want to leave, right? So, I give them another hour's grace and, give 'em credit, one of the boys gives me a large tip. A very large tip, the largest I've ever had to be honest with you. Anyways I let them keep drinking while I did me standard close-up and clean-up."

Shirley seemed to be enjoying the retelling of the tale.

"Like it's now an hour or more past closing, OK? Probably shouldn't be telling you this, what with the licensing and all that, but anyways they're still drinking like fishes, right? I'm falling asleep behind the bar. By this time, their dad's out like a light, sound asleep, drunk, on the floor. The two boys are so drunk they were beyond driving themselves anywhere, let alone the forty kilometres or what-ever home to Jarrajarra."

"They don't live in Jarrajarra." I corrected.

"Yeah, yeah, whatever. Anyways at this stage, It's like 2 A.M. So, don't ask me how but I manoeuvre the both of them, one at a time, onto the cushioned benches we've got along the wall of the public bar there, hoping they would sleep it off there. I didn't think it was right to just chuck them into the street or let them drive. Anyways it was the best I could do."

"Sounds like you were very generous with your time Shirley, more than they deserved," I said. Both Mellish boys were over 6'4" and more than 240 lbs of steroid-boosted muscle. It was amazing she could move them at all. In fact, it was very kind of her to do anything. None of the Mellish clan are attractive drunks.

"Anyhow," she continued, "I get them to sleep, locked up the grog cupboards, and turned off the beer taps. I locked the front door and went home."

"Then what happened."

"Um, I think the boss wants to talk to you about that bit, yeah."

They shuffled the phone between themselves, and a very angry man came on the line.

"I'll tell you what happened here, Constable. This morning, I arrived to find my public bar totally destroyed, my main windows all smashed, and the main doors of the pub busted open from the inside. From the inside," he shouted.

"It looks like we have an open and shut and re-open case," I said.

He either didn't get my joke or didn't think it was funny.

"Not funny, Constable," he said, clearing up his position on my attempt at humour. "In addition to all of that, the wine and spirits cabinet and all the expensive drinks therein have been totally destroyed. Demolished."

He fiddled with the phone for a moment, then shouted, "I am sending you photos off my mobile phone. See for yourself." Then he hung up without a further word.

The photos arrived in moments, and I inspected them. The brothers had outdone themselves. The Warrangatha pub was a complete and utter wreck.

The Mellish boys were a pair of massive, muscular, chemical-fuelled meatheads. They lived on heavy weights, protein powders, steroids, testosterone and weed. Whatever they were taking would be illegal in professional sports. But they didn't play sport. They just liked being bigger and stronger than everyone else.

They lived twenty minutes east of town, in the hills, on a 500-acre bush block. It should have been paradise, but the whole place looked like a junkyard.

They could fight a bit, untrained, thankfully, but their size made them formidable. My one advantage was they were all fists, no knees, no kicks, no headbutts, no elbows and not much defence.

They'd learnt their boxing at the local gym until the trainer there, Brad Henderson, had ended their membership for beating up the smaller kids.

The Mellish brothers grew marijuana, and lots of it, in underground crop rooms in the area around their farm. Undetectable by air and almost impossible to find by foot.

I knew about their crop, and I knew they supplied Joey Golino, but I didn't care so long as it was only weed, and it only went to adults. I had drawn my own line in the sand upon the never-ending drug wars. Smoke as much grass as you want, but for the people in Jarrajarra, there would be none of the hard stuff.

I parked near their house and followed the noise. I could hear the sound of a loud revving engine coming from one of their sheds. Inside the shed, they had pushed back the rubbish pile and brought forward a massive deck of tools and equipment that they were applying to a 1976 Valiant Charger.

I stood there watching as Justin tinkered under the hood and Jason sat in the driver's seat, pushing the accelerator pedal to the floor.

'Revving the shit out of it' was a term that came to mind.

Eventually, they saw me and turned off the Charger engine.

"Wow, guys, I'm impressed."

They both looked back at the car. "Yeah, she's pretty fucking good, one of only 200 SLEs ever made in Australia," said Justin, the older of the two.

"I wasn't talking about the car, Justin. I am impressed by you blokes. Look at you both. Up and about playing with your Charger after being pissed to the point of oblivion a few hours ago."

"Bullshit, no way we were pissed," said Jason. "Who says we were fucking pissed?"

"Well, mate, the Warrangatha Police say you were."

"That is fucking crap. Give me a name. I will fix this."

"Jase, you don't get a name, but I can show you lots of photos."

"Bullshit." They harmonised in their denial.

I took out my phone and showed them the photos I had received from the publican at Warrangatha.

"Fuck me," said Justin.

"I'll be buggered," added his brother.

The photos were supposed to be damning. The boys were on the verge of chuckling with pride.

"Fucking good morning's work, hey," said Justin.

"Fucking hey," said his brother.

Neither of the brothers, in my experience, had ever shown a hint of wear and tear after a hard night on the grog. I had let them sleep the night off in the police station cell a couple of times over the years. Better than having them risk the community's life and limb by letting them drive home paralytic.

"So, all that damage," I said. "What happened?"

"None of your fucking business what happened," said Jason.

"Well, the Warrangatha cops want you incarcerated, and they want me to do it, so I guess that is my business. The Sergeant over there says you need to be held in custody for a trial by jury," the bit about the jury was a fib.

"No fucking way, I am not going down for this. We were no trouble; we even gave the barmaid a fucking tip. A fucking huge tip."

"Jase, will you shut the fuck up?" said Justin. I could see Justin was trying to curtail Jason before he admitted to the whole crime.

"Who the fuck do you think you are talking to," Jason said to Justin. "Don't fucking tell me to shut the fuck up."

"You just admitted we were there fuck-wit."

"Course I was there. How do you think I knew about the tip we gave Shirley? You're the fuckwit, you fuck-wit."

"Next, you will be admitting to wrecking the joint."

"That wasn't me. That was you, you fucking idiot. I only broke the window to get out of the joint, remember fuck-head, they locked us in!"

Justin rolled his eyes.

Jason's rage suggested he was on something more than grog.

86

"Why the fuck did you go and smash the other window?" Jason asked a valid question.

"Because I wasn't going sloppy seconds to you, is why. If I need a fucking window broken, I will break it myself, and I will break it properly."

"How do you break a window properly?" Asked Jason. Mellish mentality right there.

Justin closed his eyes and then rubbed the bridge of his nose, a picture of despair. Which only served to enrage Jason more.

"Don't go the poor sooky big brother on me. You were the one bought the ute in through the door to load up Dad. That was your fucking stupid idea, not mine."

"Oh, fuck-me-hooray, did you expect me to carry him back to Jarrajarra, for chrissakes. I was pissed, you idiot."

"Not as pissed as me. I woulda carried him!"

"Who smashed up the drinks cabinet?" I asked.

"What?" they asked in harmony.

"The drinks cabinet. With all the spirits."

"Mate," said Jason, "we smashed it all right. We drank the fuck out of it is how we smashed it."

I showed them the photos again. This time I highlighted the much-demolished drinks cabinet.

"That is fucking bullshit. We never did that."

"Jesus, Jase can you stop screaming half a second?" asked Justin, maybe showing just a trace of a hangover.

"I am not fucking screaming," screamed Jason.

"You're screaming in my ear, dumb arse. I can't think."

I had to take Justin's side; his younger brother was screaming. Spitting as well.

"But it's bullshit. I smashed one window. You smashed one window. You smashed the front door when you drove the truck in, and I smashed it a bit more when I drove it out."

"Jason, we are talking to a cop. How many times have I got to tell you it's not a pissing contest when the pigs are listening, sorry Chris, no offence. I always tell you, tell 'em fucking nothing, tell 'em fuck all. You always fucking spill your guts and tell 'em fuck-everything."

"I never give 'em anything," said Jason

"Fuck me," replied Justin.

I knew from experience they could argue like this all day.

"So," I thought to ask, "Where's Wally?"

They looked at each other, was that worry on their faces?

"Shit," said Jason.

"Where the fuck is the old bastard?" said Justin.

They walked past me, out of the shed that contained the Charger, to another shed containing a Ford F150 truck. I followed at a safe distance. Justin jumped into the rear of the F150 and pulled back a tarpaulin that had been covering the tray floor.

There was Wally, sound asleep. With the coverall removed, the sun was now shining on his face. He let out a long deathly moan. "Oh, Jesus in heaven above, what have I done to meself." He sat up, checked us all out, and then lay back down with his back to the sun.

"Good to see you, Chrissy," groaned Wally from the bed of the F150 tray. "Would someone Get some coffee?"

"Get your own fucking coffee," said Justin.

"I'll pay you a thousand dollars."

"I'll get it," said Jason, and off he went to earn his money.

"I'll fetch the milk and sugar," said Justin, angling for his share.

I leant over the side of the F150 to talk to Wally. "So, what were you drinking, Wal?"

"Oh Jesus, what didn't we drink? The boys set themselves to drink the wall of grog behind the bar. Oh, God."

His voice was coming from a long dark tunnel of self-inflicted pain. He grabbed the edge of the tarpaulin and pulled it over his head. I was now talking to a human cocoon.

"You mean all of the stuff in the spirits cabinet?"

"Yeah, mate, and they were about half-way through by the time I passed out."

That was interesting. The smashed bottles in the photographs were all empty.

"Oh shit," moaned Wally. He started dry heaving. He held on till he had dragged himself out of the F150 and found himself a water pump with a hose attached beside one of the other dilapidated sheds.

With the water running, Wally vomited profusely, relieving himself from the intestinal wreckage of his previous night. When he was done, he sat on the ground and turned the hose, so the water ran over his head. And there he sat, tilting his head back and drinking from the hose, then dropping his head again and showering himself. He just continued in that soggy, thirsty loop until the boys returned with coffee and biscuits for all.

The biscuits were on a separate tray from the coffee. Justin's tray carried a supermarket selection of sweet biscuits. The other tray was carried by a very attractive woman in her mid-thirties, wearing a light sleeveless dress and thongs on her feet. She also had an intricate Maori tattoo, looping from a circle on her shoulder down to her wrist. I had fought in Afghanistan alongside a few Kiwi soldiers, and the tattoo looked, to me, like a Ta Moko, which only a Maori can wear, as opposed to a Kirituhi, which anyone can wear. Ta Moko was a statement of identity.

"Chris, this is Jenny." Justin looked a bit sheepish if that was possible. True love?

"Kia ora Jenny, lovely to meet you." I used one of the many Kiwi versions of hello, even pronounced it correctly.

"Kia ora Chris," she replied.

Justin lowered the back of the F150, and we set up the morning tea right there. Jenny set down the tray, and we all helped ourselves to coffee and food.

Wally had semi-recovered and was now dunking his biscuit in his coffee and taking in the scenery around him. He finally looked at me with a puzzled look on his face.

"Hang on a minute. How the fuck did we all end up here? Last I remember, I was in the Warrangatha pub."

I showed Wally the photos from the previous night and brought him up to speed with the events that had occurred during his drunken coma. Then we all stood and contemplated our coffee.

Eventually, Wally pushed the food and coffee back, and he made a seat for himself on the lowered tailgate of the F150. We had finished the first round of coffee, so Jason went off for more.

Justin went off to find some canvas chairs.

With the chairs and a second round of coffee, it was a picnic already, and the Warrangatha cops had thought about a SOG team. This was going well.

Halfway through the second pot of coffee, Wally spoke. "Chris, mate, I think you should do one of your negotiations."

"My what?"

"You know, you do your thingy where every Tom, Dick and Harry has their say, and says what they want on the day, and you have a think, and then you come up with the something in the middle, the win-win. You're good at that, mate. It's ya gift."

"My gift?"

"Yep, that's what it is, a negotiating gift."

"And what am I using my negotiating gift for Wal?"

"Law and order, mate, peace in the valley, goodwill to all men. Especially the man from this pub we're talking about."

"Talk to him about not busting up hotels and going to jail for it?" I asked.

"Yeah, mate, that's it, exactly."

Anything would be better than trying to arrest the Mellish boys, especially after such a nice picnic. I was on my third Tim-Tam, and there was still half a pack of Scotch Fingers.

"OK," I said, "Won't hurt to try."

I called the Warrangatha publican.

"Are those animals in jail yet?" he asked.

"Not as yet, Sir, no." I had the phone on personal, not speaker, and I had stepped a few yards away from the Mellish clan. I wanted them to hear just what I needed them to hear and nothing more.

"They're not?"

"No, Sir, that is correct. They are not incarcerated at this moment."

"Why the fuck not? You've seen what they did to my pub."

"Well, Sir, Wodonga police may need time to organise a SOG team. You have seen how dangerous these men can be." I raised my eyebrows at Jason, sharing the joke. He seemed quite chuffed at the idea it would need a team from the Special Operations Group to take him down.

"There are a few other issues as well, I'm afraid, that we may need to discuss before this can be resolved," I continued.

"Issues? Resolved? I'll resolve your issues, officer. I've got an insurance assessor here right now; he's put the damage at thirty thousand dollars, and I've got a fucking five-thousand-dollar excess on that. That is five grand out of my pocket to fix the damage those two fucking animals did," he stopped for a short breath. "And my premiums will probably go up, and the public bar is out of action for fuck knows how long."

He took half a second for a breath and kept shouting.

"I am fucked, Constable, fucked. Totally and utterly and completely fucked, and you reckon there are other issues. What other issues could there possibly fucking be? You tell me."

"Well, Sir, the suggestion has been made that not all of the damage was done by the Mellish brothers."

Silence on the other end of the line.

"They are claiming that the liquor bottles behind the bar were only half empty when they left and that they did not damage the cabinet or any items behind the bar." I was guessing a bit.

Still nothing from the outraged publican.

"They claim they have a few trophy photos of the liquor area after they half-drained it."

The Mellish brothers were looking at each other, puzzled. Whispering "Photos? What photos?"

"I also have a corroborative witness who heard them boasting about how much they drunk. Hence the photos as evidence."

Corroborative was a good police word. I was warming to the task. Maybe I did have a gift.

"I know it is hard to imagine, sir, but they were quite proud of their drinking effort. Shameful, really." I gave the Mellish clan a corroborative shrug of the shoulders. "Should I send the photo to the insurance assessor?"

The publican spoke, "No, don't do that. We will, we will, Aaaaaah?"

"Seek compensation?" I filled in the gap.

"Compensation?" He asked, surprised.

"Yes sir, some form of direct compensation, paid by the perpetrators, might be in order?" One moment while I discuss this with my colleagues." I put my hand over the phone and spoke to Wally.

"Wal, he's going to need twenty-five thousand to solve his problems. Otherwise, he wants to go to court."

"Fucking bullshit, give the cunt nothing," from Jason. He was definitely sniffing every time he spoke; cocaine, probably.

"Oiy! Language." From Justin, nodding toward Jenny, who was sitting quietly, taking it all in.

"Sorry, Jen," said Jason, all contrite.

"Jesus, bloody costly night out," said Wally.

"Can you pay it, Wal?" I asked.

"Dad's not payin' it. We'll pay it," added Justin, suddenly quite serious with Jenny present.

"It's a shit hole anyway, whole place not worth twenty-five," added Jason.

Justin looked at me. "Offer him ten."

I offered the ten.

"Don't fucking insult me, Constable."

"No, Sir, of course not. It wasn't meant as an insult. I understand it is still very sensitive. Let's just leave the money side to the insurance assessor, and we will take the property damage through the courts. Might take a while sorting out how the liquor section got damaged, but justice will be done, I promise you."

"Twenty," That was the publican.

I mouthed the word Twenty toward Justin. He shook his head, a firm no.

"No Sir, I think at best the alleged perpetrators could go to twelve, with no admission of guilt."

"Fifteen," he replied.

I lip-synced a fifteen at my team, and they all nodded.

"I think they can manage that, Sir."

"In cash today," he added.

"Yes, I can have that to you today. I will bring a letter for you to sign absolving the Mellish brothers of any further action by you in this matter. That will need your signature, of course, and they will give you the cash in your hand."

I sounded more like the Mellish family lawyer than the local cop.

"Jesus fucking Christ," the poor old Warrangatha publican sounded defeated. I tried to close the deal.

"Would that be alright, Sir?"

"Alright? About as alright as a hole in my fucking head." He paused and had a think. "OK, OK, let's just do it," he said.

The matter was settled, but he was not happy.

"And you can tell the lot of them for me, the two gorillas and their useless old man; they are banned for life from any pub I ever own. Life! Two lives!"

"I will, Sir. Have a nice day." And we both hung up.

"There you go," said Wally, "Chris does his thing, and it's a win-win."

"Except it's not," said Jenny, "it's not a win, really, is it, Constable?" She had read me like a book.

"No," I said.

"How come?" asked Wally.

"Well, Wal, firstly, the boys are now down fifteen grand and for what?"

"We can afford it," said Justin.

"Yeah, but the pub in Warrangatha is now out of bounds."

"It's a shit hole anyway," from Jason.

"Yeah, you said that already Jason. Nevertheless, they let you in, treated you right, and you put them out of business for a few days with your standard Mellish brother's death and destruction tour."

"Death and destruction?" Jason still thought it was a joke. "Just a bit of fun, mate."

"No way it was death and destruction," said Justin.

"A kerfuffle at best," added Wally.

"Wal mate, you were in a drunken coma. How would you know what it was?"

"My boys wouldn't hurt a fly, not in a deathly fashion. They're just straight up and down, old fashioned,"

"Marijuana growers," I said, "which, you shouldn't need reminding, is against the law."

"What's your point, Officer?" Jenny was joining in.

"My point is this," I said. "We have just had three murders in town. Turns out one of them is the nephew of the biggest drug pusher in the country. Your business partner, no less."

"No one is going to miss that cunt, Golino," said Justin.

That surprised me. The Mellish brothers and Joey Golino had been in business for years.

"Well, Justin, whatever you think of Joey, you already have two Homicide Detectives in town looking into these murders. Plus, I have had the Warrangatha cops on my back, wanting to lock you three up, and why? Because you lot went out and splashed a whole heap of cash two days after Joey Golino had his head bashed in. The same Joey Golino you have been supplying weed for years. And what do you three come up with, just to put the cream on the cake, just in case anyone within a hundred miles should forget that the Mellish boys have a capacity for violence? You fucking wreck the fucking Warrangatha hotel all on your own-some."

"Fair go, Chris," said Wally. "I think we already established that was only a kerfuffle."

"What are you saying, Officer," Jenny took a step forward. "You want some money, maybe? Help make this go away?"

"I beg your pardon, Miss?"

"Whoa, whoa," said Wally, "Hang on, hang on there. Chris is not like that. We don't do that here. Fuck me, girly. Chris is not saying anything like that at all."

Jenny eyed me off. She wasn't convinced. What had happened to our lovely picnic?

"What are you saying, Chris?" asked Justin.

"You boys need to show some contrition beyond just throwing money at the pub you wrecked. You need to show all the cops in town that these are separate matters."

"They are separate fucking matters. What fucking idiot says they aren't?" Jason had chimed in with his usual added value.

"Public perception." I was getting angry with these idiots, fuck

94

their picnic. "Everyone in town will know by tonight what you've done, and so will all the visiting cops. You need to do some visible time."

"No fucking way!" They sang in harmony. They both did a side-step so that they stood side by side facing me, prepping for action. I stepped into a shooting-ready position and put my hand on my gun.

"Stop, stop, stop," said Wally as he stepped between us. "No one's going to jail. What do you mean by 'visible time, Chris?"

I was not really listening to Wally. I was watching the brothers. Particularly Jason, who would lose it first. It was worse than herding cats with these two. They were about 9 feet away. If they came at me and I stood still, I wouldn't have time to get the gun out and fire, but I would get it out. Jason was on my right and would be running. If I moved fractionally right as he ran at me, and if I threw a left hook, then I would have time to shoot. That would leave a wounded Jason between Justin and me. There would be no turning back at that point. I would shoot Justin too.

Fuck them.

The black mist was descending on me.

I was getting angry. I hate bullies. I had kidded these two long enough. I had been beaten up by experts in my past. These two did not frighten me in the slightest. Whatever they thought of their chances, I had done more of this than they could ever guess. After such a good start, this was ending badly.

"Chris?" prompted Wally. "What do you mean visible time?"

"Well," I said, "I think you boys need to do some community service. Something to show the town that you are remorseful for your actions."

"Community service? What fucking community service?" said Jason.

"Well, Ricky Chalmers is away for a while, and the town is short its one and only gardener." Where did I think of this stuff? Maybe Wally was right. It was a gift. "You boys should come into town this arvo, and get on the mowers, let everyone see you. I am sure Barney could spread the word that you are doing community service right now. Showing remorse."

"Mowing?" asked Justin.

"Yes, mowing. Some say it is therapeutic."

Justin smiled. "Can we use the new ride-ons?"

"Use whatever you like, just be seen, and smile and wave at people, maybe."

"I want that new Husqvarna I saw," Jason had apparently chosen an afternoon mowing in place of getting shot in the guts. I wonder if he realised.

"Sounds good to me," said Wally.

"We'll be there by two," said Justin.

"You should do a week," I said.

"Yeah, yeah, till next Friday, no worries."

"There ya go, like I said, win-win," said Wally.

"You coming too, Wal?" I had to ask.

"Me, no way I have me park duties, busy as all hell at this time of year."

"And I want you boys to put yourselves on probation. No more kerfuffles for at least a year, please."

"Yeah, alright, one year."

It was settled.

Jenny spoke, "I will type up that letter for this publican bloke to sign, and I will take him the cash."

"Great," I said

Jenny turned and headed back to the house without any further comment. She was angry, probably at being called girly by Wally, or maybe just angry at me for being a cop. She might be a problem, I thought.

At this stage of the relationship, I definitely would not have shot her, even if the boys and I had got to fighting.

"Settled?" I asked Justin.

"Yeah, mate, settled. See you after lunch," he said.

With all that done and dusted, I left.

. . .

I checked my watch as I got back into my truck. I had warned Barney I might need backup. I was cutting it fine. I called Barney. He answered before it rang.

"Oh, Chris, thank goodness, I was getting worried. I had Greg, and Scott Farrell set to go; Norma wouldn't be coming since she cannot condone fighting."

"That's why I wanted her to come."

"Yes, well anyway, Jack and Jody were going to follow in the ambulance. That was only as medical support. Jack said he couldn't be involved physically because of his hypocrite's oath.

"You mean Hippocratic?"

"I know the word, Chris. I think he was being ironic."

"OK, got it, like it was a joke, yeah?"

"Anyway, I am glad you are safe again from another Mellish encounter. I will call off the battalion. Meanwhile, you better get back here now. Things are happening in the best possible way."

"What?"

"We have our station back. Come and see."

I made it back to town by noon. Barney was the only person at the Station.

"Hi Chris," Barney was smiling. His empire was restored. "Sergeant Palmer has moved the investigators over to the back rooms of the Community Centre. We have our police station back."

"Nice." I meant it.

"Here, I made you this." Barney handed me a coffee from behind his desk. It had a lid. "Thought you'd need it."

"Oh, Barney."

"I timed it from when you told me you were heading back. Should be perfect."

I sipped the coffee, "Oh, mate. It is perfectly perfect." I had some more. "Do you think I should check in over there at battalion headquarters?"

"No, I've done that. I took Sergeant Palmer some sandwiches and coffee."

"Just Sarge?"

"Yes, just Sarge."

"Not even a dry biscuit for Sergeant Pete?"

"Nope, not a one. I made sure they noticed too."

We both had a smile at that. The Melbourne cops had broken the golden thread of Barney's courtesy and henceforth would be catering for themselves.

"I guess I will go back to being the local plod."

"I am sure if our elite force from Melbourne needs our lowly services, they know where to find us."

Three murders in my town, and all anyone wanted from me was to man the yellow tape.

"I might head down to the Nursing Centre and investigate Kate Chalmers."

"First the Mellishes, now you double up with a visit to Kate Chalmers. You are a brave man Chris."

That made me stop and think. "You know Barn visiting those two is a raffle. One day sooner or later, it won't go so well. How did I ever get the job as the Mellish whisperer?"

"Chris, they are bullies. You are the first person in this town who ever made them take a step back. If push ever comes to shove with those two, I am sure you will do the right thing."

"The right thing?"

"Yes, as in you shoot them before they shoot you."

"Jesus Barn, for someone who doesn't like physical confrontation, you sure talk a good shoot out."

"Well, I don't like to participate, but I'd pay to watch, and I'd bet on you."

"Thanks, I think."

I left to visit Kate Chalmers.

I was passing the Pizza Shop on my way to the Nursing Centre, and there, out front, was Georgie Golino's Car. I was still irritated by her words the other day but equally sorry for her plight. I did a U-turn and went to the bank. I withdrew some cash and had the teller place it in an envelope. I borrowed the teller's pen, and on the outside of the envelope, I wrote the dollar value contained inside. It was a lot of money, but I could afford it. I had saved almost all of my police wages since I started in Jarrajarra, and I had hardly touched my army benefits.

I had a house and a car, and my uniform courtesy of the Victoria Police. All I paid for was food and running gear. Money didn't really mean that much as long as you had enough, and I had plenty for my simple tastes. I went back to Joey's Pizza with my envelope of cash.

I braced myself for another bout with Georgie.

She was standing on a table, painting the ceiling. She had already done the walls, and the shop now had the clean smell of fresh paint. Her sister Sue was with her, equally as beautiful, just a few years younger. Playing happily on a blanket on the floor was Georgie's youngest baby. I liked the numbers; Georgie was less likely to give me another serve in front of her sister and baby.

"Hello," I said as cheerily as I could, given the circumstances of my last visit.

"Hi, Chris," said Sue.

"Hi Sue, thanks for coming when I called the other night."

Sue gave a sad nod to that.

Georgie put down her brush and jumped from the table to the floor. Still athletic, still capable and still clearly sad and angry. She stepped toward me.

"More questions?" She hadn't softened from my last visit.

"No, Georgie just dropped by to settle my tab." I handed her the envelope.

She looked at the envelope and saw the number printed on the outside.

"Seven grand?" She nodded and put the envelope in her back pocket. "Good, I need that." She looked at me, "Better late than never, I guess."

Ouch.

"I might get a receipt from you when it is convenient."

"I'll do it now."

She went to a drawer behind the serving counter and pulled out a pre-printed receipt book. She wrote in it while I stood there awkwardly. She finished writing, tore the page out of the book and handed it to me. It said 'Coffee and pizzas, $7,000. Paid in full. Georgie Golino.'

"There you go," she said.

"Thanks." I folded the receipt, tucked it in my shirt pocket and turned to leave.

"Bye, Chris," said Sue.

"Yes, bye Sue, see you later," and I was gone.

I don't know what I expected. It didn't have to be a brass band, a bugle would have been nice, or a thank you. But in her mind, what would she be thanking me for? Paying for my coffee, finally?

I pushed on toward the Nursing Centre, certain I would receive a warmer reception.

Nurse Practitioner Wendy Acheson was in her office.

"Howdy, Nurse."

"Howdy, Soldier." Her beautiful smile wiped away the misery of the morning.

"I guess you are not really here to see me."

"I only ever come here to see you."

"Yeah, bullshit baffles brains but not mine, Soldier boy."

"Well, OK, after gazing at you lovingly for a bit, I was hoping to talk to Kate."

"Right, well, it's a bit early for that, mate."

"How is she?"

She thought for a moment. "Come around here."

She tapped a few words into her computer keyboard. I came around the desk and stood beside Wendy to check her screen. She was searching for 'Oxy-Contin withdrawal'. The search finished, and she clicked on an article she had obviously read before.

"OK, this is the official word for getting a patient off Oxy." She highlighted a paragraph, and I leaned forward to read it.

The highlighted section contained the following words: 'The Department of Health has received reports of serious harm in patients dependent on opioid medicines where these medicines are suddenly discontinued. Serious withdrawal symptoms include uncontrolled pain, psychological distress, extreme irritability, loss of appetite, anxiety, paranoia and suicidal thoughts.'

"You got all that?"

"Wow."

Wendy selected another paragraph further down the page and highlighted it.

"Now read that bit."

I did, and it said, 'About 48 to 72 hours after cessation, symptoms are typically at their worst. During this time, early symptoms can become more severe. New symptoms may occur, such as chills, stomach pain, nausea, vomiting and diarrhoea.'

"Sound like our girl?" Wendy asked.

"Well, I reckon if you replace the suicidal thoughts with homicidal, that just about sums her up when I brought her in on Monday."

"Exactly. From the few coherent words I heard, when you brought her in, she was somewhere between 48 to 72 hours cold turkey. She said she ran out of her so-called medicine sometime Friday or Saturday. She can't remember."

"So where is she at now?"

"Right now, I put her at five to six days into total withdrawal. Doctor Google says that around a week, 7 or 8 days, she will be fit enough to make her own decisions. Till then, I figure we classify her as under arrest and locked up in the hospital. Can we do that?"

"A week under arrest without any charges? Not really. Might ask Barney if he can work something out."

"OK. Till I hear from you, I will keep her locked up here. If she complains afterwards, I will deal with that stuff then."

She turned the screen to herself and started typing again.

"Here, read this." She turned the screen back to me.

It read, 'Sex your place, 10 pm tonight. Yes/No?' As I was leaning forward to read, she grabbed my bum and gave it a healthy squeeze. I looked up, and there was no one in the foyer beyond her office window. I kept reading.

"This font is so small it is hard to read."

"Lean closer, Corporal." I did, and she squeezed harder.

I read out loud, very loud, 'Sox, my place. Ten pair. Really?'

She laughed. I laughed. "Sounds good. Sox it is."

I left Wendy and drove to Rob Farrell's garage. Rob wasn't there, still, but his son Scotty was busy working under a car raised on one of their two hoists.

"Scotty, your dad still away?"

"Yeah, mate, still in Melbourne, might not be back for another week. Can I help you?"

"I want to get into the rifle range, get some practice."

I had drawn my gun twice this week already, and this morning, I was mentally prepping to shoot the Mellish brothers. It was time I had a practice run.

"Dad left the keys with Uncle Greg. Do you want me to call him?"

"I'll do it. Thanks, mate."

I called Greg to ask for a loan of the keys to the rifle club. He said he had a better idea; he would meet me at the range and waste some ammunition along with me.

Fifteen minutes later, we were on the range. The beauty of living in a small town; everywhere is close.

I had laid some human silhouettes over one of the standard bullseye targets and was planning on some pistol shooting from five yards to start, then moving back five yards at a time, all the way back to thirty. With my pistol, anything over thirty yards was probably a waste of time, but it wouldn't hurt to go the extra.

Practice makes perfect, my Nan in my head again.

Pistols on a 500-yard range meant for rifles. But, it was Thursday afternoon. We were the only ones there, and the safety flags were up. It was cool.

I was using my standard police issue .40 calibre Smith and Wesson military and police semi-automatic pistol. This had a magazine capacity of fifteen cartridges. One magazine cost over thirty dollars, but Victoria Police were paying me to be competent, so I bought ten mags and, hang the expense, the government were paying.

Greg had his own pistol, all shiny and clean. We set ourselves in position and got stuck in.

I was good.

Lack of recent practice and nearly eight years in the police force hadn't totally ruined my army training, which had been as good as anything in the world.

Of course, in the modern Australian Army, the targets are often real people, and the people were plenty. Aussie soldiers had live targets to shoot at almost every single day of the twenty-first century. The new wars just never ended, and if you keep going back to war, it will eventually get you, it got me on my last tour, and it was almost fatal.

Greg and I were on our last magazines each.

"Chris, I don't think you missed at all."

"Use it or lose it, my Nan always said." I wasn't sure my Nan meant that for killing practice. It was more of a directive to get off my bum and go soak up the great outdoors.

Greg was looking at me carefully. "What's the matter, mate? You look a bit glum."

"Just thinking. Haven't really seen a dead body since the army. Couple of car crashes I suppose. But three different heads smashed to pieces in a week. All done deliberately. It's like being back in a war zone. Just feels wrong."

"It's like Wally winning the quadrella," said Greg. "Wally, with money, it goes against the laws of nature."

"It does."

"Come on, let's do the last magazine from fifty yards," said Greg. "If you get over half your fifteen, I will make you two cappuccinos back at the fire station. Norma's bought the boys a new machine."

Joey's death was affecting the caffeine habits of the whole town. "You're on."

Thirty minutes later, we were back at the fire station. I was leaning against the front of the fire truck looking out on the main street, and Greg was in the kitchen making me the first of my two cappuccinos. Damn, I was good at killing those silhouettes. I hope Greg was half as good at making the Cappas on his new machine.

Greg bought out two large steaming cups of brand-new machine coffee. It looked delicious.

"Tell me, Chris, how did you end up in the army?" Greg was curious, which was fair enough. We were becoming solid friends. Usually, I never discussed my personal history; I preferred to listen rather than talk.

"After my mum died, I lived with my grandmother. When I was seventeen, she was eighty-six, poor old Nan was running out of ways to feed a growing teenager, and my Muay Thai teacher suggested the Australian Government might share the load. So, after my birthday, I joined, and he was right. There was more food than I had ever seen in my life."

"Muay Thai? How long did you do that?"

"Started when I was about six or seven, done it ever since."

"Shit, hey, Jarrajarra's own lethal weapon."

"Hardly," I laughed. "One thing I learnt from martial arts; is there's always someone better, and usually, they have at least six mates."

"Must have done you some good when it came to your SASR training."

"Greg, nothing on this earth can prepare you for that training." That was a different question from Greg. I never discussed my army life with anyone much. "How did you know I was in the SASR?"

He had to think about that.

"It was part of the town gossip; I picked up on it when we found out we were getting a new cop. A war hero, SASR, a good mate of Wendy Atcheson, and I use the word mate liberally. Didn't realise just how matey you two were at that early stage. I heard lots of good stuff, didn't hear about this Muay Thai stuff though."

"That was something my Nan got me into. I needed discipline, apparently. She found me a great coach, and I stuck with it; loved it."

We were sitting on the front bumper of the main fire truck, gazing through the open doors of the fire station. I was happily contemplating my little part of the world when I heard machinery approaching. Eventually, a ride-on mower, driven by Justin Mellish, turned into the driveway of the fire station and headed toward me. By the time he reached us, he was inside the station, and the noise of the mower was echoing loudly from the steel roof above. Justin turned off the motor and stepped off the mower. He was wearing a set of industrial-strength ear protectors, so the noise would not have bothered him at all.

My head was still ringing.

"Chris."

"Justin."

"Jase is doing the footy ground, and I was going to re-do the flower beds in the main drag."

"Great." You couldn't go past a veteran drug grower for getting your gardens done.

"You wouldn't know where Ricky Chalmers has left that front-end loader he's always running around in, would you? That Chinese tractor?"

"Not in the council shed?"

"No mate, not in the shed."

Ricky kept a shed full of heavy-duty gardening gear in the council-owned shed. It was next door to the fire station, right behind the football ground. The shed and the gear were usually kept in immaculate condition, like Ricky himself. He was very much a 'place-for-everything' and 'every-thing-in-place' kind of guy.

If Greg was surprised to see a Mellish brother in his fire station, he didn't show it.

"Sorry Greg, I have to go. Justin is helping out on the gardening while Ricky is away."

"Right. Good to know." Greg was pretty much the town mayor. We had no official mayor because we were just a small town in a much larger shire. Greg's correct title was Liaison Officer to the Shire. The title was irrelevant. Greg was the fire chief which made him the top dog in town. I probably should have warned him about my latest win-win deal with the Mellish brothers, but it wasn't in Greg's nature to be fazed by incidentals.

"OK. Hang on a sec." Greg kept the coffee and returned to the kitchen. He was back in less than a minute with the two coffees transferred from proper cups to the cardboard takeaway kind.

"There you go. You boys can share." He gave one coffee to me and the other to Justin.

Oh, the irony, Justin was now drinking a coffee I had won in a practice bet while getting my skills up to the mark, just in case I had to shoot him or his brother. Should I explain that to him or not? Mostly not.

"Thanks, Greg. OK, Justin. See you back at the shed."

I took to my truck, with my hard-earned winnings now halved. Justin put his ear protection on, picked up his coffee and took to his ride-on mower. With the elaborately nursed coffee held clear in one hand, he followed me on the mower back to the council equipment shed.

And there it was. Gone.

Among all the beautifully maintained, shiny-new, council-owned equipment, the front-end digger thing was, most definitely, not there. Not there at all.

"Maybe it's at his place," I said.

"Maybe."

Justin parked the mower, and we headed out to Ricky's place in the police truck. Justin was now drinking one of the coffees I'd won from Greg. I still might shoot him before the day was over. After a long, loud slurp, he let out a soft pleasurable moan.

"Bloody good stuff this. I might have to join the C.F.A."

"I can't see you taking orders, Juz."

"Nah fuck that."

My mobile rang. I answered.

"What the fuck sort of extortion racket are you running in that wild west town, Sheriff?"

It was the Warrangatha publican shouting at me yet again.

"Sorry, Sir, I am a Constable, not a Sheriff."

"Could have fooled me, bunch of fucking cowboys."

I pulled off the road and turned off my engine. We were about fifty yards from Ricky Chalmers' place.

"Could you explain the problem, Sir?"

"The problem? The fucking problem is that bitch you sent to finish our totally-fucking-dead-in-the-water transaction. That woman, that's my problem."

"I take it she is not with you now, Sir."

"No, she is in the bar your mongrels wrecked. Waiting for me to find a pen to sign."

"Can you tell me what she has done, please?"

"What's she fucking done? She told me to pay her fifteen fucking thousand. That's what she's done. Me pay her Constable. ME PAY HER!" He was shouting again, in duplicates now.

"Are you hearing me, Sherrif? Oh, and if I didn't pay her, she would be back with more of her friends. Not two but twenty, and all of them crazier than the pair who have already been here. So yeah, that's what she has done. Just a little touch of blackmail and not a word about me RECEIVING fifteen grand in compensation."

What the fuck. I couldn't even think what to say. "OK."

"No! No! Not OK. Very much not OK. She told me last night was just a taste. Just a fucking entree to the main fucking course. And I can tell you this, Constable, as soon as I hang up on this call, I am calling Wodonga police, and I am putting in a report on you and this whole fucking scheme."

"Whoa, whoa. Sir, did you say the woman is still in the bar there right now?"

"Yes."

"Can you hand her the phone, please?"

He had to think about that for a moment.

"Alright. One second."

Shit, shit, shit! What happened to win-win? I offered my phone to Justin.

"Jennifer will be on in a second. Can you ask her, for me, exactly what is going on?"

Justin looked perplexed. He took the phone and waited.

"Hey babe, what's going on?" He listened and then looked at me.

"Hang on, Chris." He got out of the car and stepped away, presumably for a private word with his beloved. I couldn't hear much. I heard mumbled words like "We made a deal" and "will you just do what we agreed." That amped up to "Just do what was fucking agreed." Then after some listening time from Justin, I heard him say, "Give him the money, get the fucking receipt and get the fuck out of there. Will you please?"

I said to Justin, "I want to speak to the publican after it's done."

He kept listening but managed to look at me and give me a thumbs up.

After a few more minutes, he returned to the truck and handed me the phone. I put it on speaker so Justin would hear the next bit.

"Hello."

"Hello, Officer." I wasn't the Sherrif anymore. That sounded positive.

"Sir, do you have the compensation we agreed upon?"

"Yes." My God, he was angry. Angry but frightened.

"Did you sign a receipt for the money?"

"Yes."

"Did you sign the receipt willingly?"

"Yes."

"Has the young lady left?"

"There was no lady here, Constable, but yeah, that woman has gone, and I don't ever want to hear from her or those animals again. Not ever! Understood?"

He'd hung up the phone before I could make a promise of forever.

I looked at Justin, but he was looking straight ahead.

I started the truck and pulled back onto the road, resuming the short journey to Ricky Chalmers' place.

After a few awkward minutes, Justin broke the silence.

"Women, hey. Fuck me." He let out a sad deep sigh.

"Mate, that was simple, straightforward extortion. You do ten years inside for that." I didn't really have a clue what the punishment for extortion was, but ten sounded good.

Ricky sighed; I pushed a bit harder.

"Juz, I don't give a shit about the weed you grow and sell. It's a victimless crime in my book. Fly as hard as you like under that radar, but there is stuff I can't ignore. Your new girlfriend is way over the line, and your brother has stepped up to sniffing coke. My boss in Wodonga won't let me ignore it, and I won't."

Justin looked doggedly ahead. No reaction. I went up another notch and made it as clear as I could.

"If either of them steps over again, I will arrest them and let the system sort them out."

He said nothing.

"Are you hearing me, Juz?"

He looked across. "I hear ya." And that was the end of the conversation.

We pulled into Ricky's drive and went straight to his shed.

And there it was, the front-end digger thingy. Keys in the ignition and, uncharacteristically for Ricky, it was covered in mud from its very top to the tip of its sharp forked teeth. Bloody hell, even the roof of the roll cage was thick with mud.

"Not like Ricky to leave it like that."

"No." Justin agreed.

We stood there contemplating the totally mud-coated machine.

"What say I drive it back to town, get those garden beds done and give it a clean for you." Justin sounded extremely conciliatory.

"That would be good. I would appreciate it. Thanks, mage."

He went to the side of the machine and half-turned the ignition.

He wiped the mud from the dashboard with his hand and checked the gauges.

"Diesel's good. Oil's good."

He jumped into the driver's seat and turned over the engine. It kicked into life, and he gave me a thumbs up.

I left him to it and headed back to Jarrajarra.

Twenty minutes later, I walked into the station to find Barney positively glowing.

"You've had a victory?" I asked.

"Oh yes," said Barney. "The forensics ladies faxed their report through on our machine. I sealed it in an envelope and carried it over to Detective Pete."

"And?"

"Well, he asked me if I had read it, and I said, of course not, which was true. At that point in time."

"He believed you."

"I think so. I had the ring of truth. My heart was pure. I glowed sincerity, Chris. God, I even believed myself. I assured him it was the only printout, and no one had seen it. That was true as well."

"At that point in time," I added.

He pulled out a data stick and held it aloft.

"I don't think Detective Pete is familiar with the history option of the modern fax machine."

Barney was positively gloating; he had put one over the cops from Melbourne, and they didn't suspect a thing.

We went to my office, and he plugged his data stick into my computer, and we settled in to read the fax-fresh forensics report.

Mostly, it was as boring as old soap. A lot of dull technical detail, but it had some serious highlights in the summary section. Firstly, they could not identify the murder weapon. They were convinced by the shape of the wounds that all three men were killed by a single weapon. That weapon was heavy, blunt and deadly. But whatever it was, it remained unknown. All three men had their skulls fractured.

For Joey Golino and the mystery guy in the caravan, the fractures had proved fatal.

Mister X, we found by the road, also had a fractured skull. In addition, he had a fractured ankle and numerous other bruises and abrasions. Despite his massive list of broken parts, he had actually died from loss of blood. The bleeding was caused by the stab wound to his inner thigh.

I wondered what he had done to deserve all that punishment. Whatever it was, he was one seriously tough bloke. To get halfway from the pizza place to the caravan park with all those injuries was incredible.

Who the hell was tough enough to take him down?

Finally, according to Barney's copy of the report, and most importantly, the previously unidentified victims now had names.

The first of those names was the guy by the road, Mister X. His real name was Allan Jarrad Davies. He was from New Zealand. Another Kiwi, the second one I had encountered today in my duties, though this one was dead.

The second name belonged to the corpse in the caravan. This one was a blockbuster, Azzolino "Azzy" Pisano. The very same Azzy mentioned in the Royal Commission into the conspiracy to murder Riverina politician Gary Rodgers. Pisano had been mentioned extensively in the Royal Commission only yesterday. The press had declared him missing only this very morning on a TV broadcast from right outside our station.

"Holy fuck," said Barney as he read.

"Barney mate, you have sworn twice today. Standards, please."

Azzy Pisano was the right-hand man, and bodyguard, of Michelle Folliero. These were the men who had paid for the murder of Rogers, the anti-drug campaigner. The infamous murder set to bring down a host of corrupt politicians and police in New South Wales.

Folliero was an old-time drug baron, allegedly worth a billion. A man, according to the Royal Commission, willing to murder anyone who stood in his way. A man with enough money and connections to make anyone his minion. To get away with anything until one of those minions, Alexander 'Tiny' Sheahan, started pointing his finger and naming names. Sheahan had turned informer to keep his own evil arse out of jail.

Folliero was also the uncle of my freshly deceased coffee wizard, Joey Golino. Another thing we found out from Angela Adams today. Maybe she should be the Melbourne detective.

"So, Barney, if we have Azzy Pisano dead in the caravan park, then where is Michelle Folliero?" I was thinking out loud to my favourite Admin Assistant.

"Wrong question Chris. The one they will be asking tomorrow is, 'Where is Folliero's money?'"

"Holy Fuck," I said.

"Chris, please, language."

I'd had a weird day, but it turned into a wonderful night. Wendy arrived at my place at the appointed hour of ten pm. I loved the sound her push-bike made as she parked it against my back wall. We had dinner, we made love, and then we lay in bed together, chatting as we always did when we had the chance.

"So, how's it going with Sherlock Holmes and Boofhead?" Even Wendy had encountered the intrepid Melbourne detectives and was curious about their methods.

"Buggered if I know. They sit in the back rooms of the Community Centre and mumble at each other real low, so the Sarge can't hear them. Then they get in their car and drive somewhere and come back and sit down and mumble some more. And that appears to be it."

"Every second time I pass the Community Centre, Boofhead is out the back talking on his mobile."

"Why out the back?" Wendy asked.

"Probably saying things he doesn't want his buddy Pete to hear," I said.

"Weird man,' she said, dismissing the topic. "More important, the Greg-Norma-Jack grapevine tells me that you and Greg went pistol shooting today."

"Yep, going again tomorrow as well."

"The grapevine told me you were very bloody good."

"You really need the Farrell family to tell you that?"

"No, but when my Corporal starts practising with his service pistol, I know he's not thinking about getting good at target practice."

"No, that's true."

"Do we need to re-read your famous psych report?" She asked, with a cheeky smile an inch from my own.

Back in our army days, when Wendy was nursing me back to health from what should have been my Afghanistan graveyard, she managed to lay her hands on a psychological profile that had been done on me after one of my early infractions as a fledgeling soldier.

On my first weekend break after basic training, I found myself drunk on the street. I had been in some sort of blind-drunk argument with someone inside a pub when I found myself in the grip of half-a-dozen bouncers who deposited me in the gutter outside. I was lucky that was all they did. I probably deserved worse.

I wasn't the only one in that position, drunk and in the gutter, but I was the only one in an army uniform.

Whoops.

Next, I ended up in a fight with a group of Military Police who had come with the intention of arresting me. Naturally, I came off second-best. I swung a few punches, missing most, till the weight of numbers wore me down, or that was my view of it, an honourable loss. I think it all lasted thirty loud, abusive seconds. Twelve years of Muay Thai training does not amount to much when you are too drunk to stand up.

Anyway, amongst my punishments, I had landed on the couch, not really a couch, more a chair, in the office of an army psychiatrist, who wondered if this stupid seventeen-year-old might have a death wish. It didn't help that my father had similar violations recorded against him during his stint in the army; twenty years previous.

"Child of a violent alcoholic," said the report. "Private Taylor appears passive and disinterested until he is not. When provoked, he is capable of sudden anger and extreme violence. Corporal Taylor tends to hyper awareness, and constantly evaluating threats to his safety, real or imagined."

What the psych got wrong was the 'sudden anger'. There was nothing sudden about it. It was always there. As a kid I had masked it to avoid provoking my terrifying father. On my first night out with the army, I got drunk and let the mask slip. Hence the glorious but unsuccessful fistfight.

Never fight drunk. You are not as good as you think you are, was the real lesson.

Somehow I was allowed to remain in the army, and I quietly swore off grog forever.

The key findings had become a joke between Wendy and me. She could recite phrases verbatim when it suited her.

"Capable of extreme violence," she said. "Sudden anger, I recall."

"That was done before eight years of army training sorted me out, completely irrelevant to the man before you, under you, whatever," I said. "In my own mind, I am a great bloke. Soft as custard. Wouldn't hurt a fly."

"Yes, you are, just a big jelly custard, but here you are, brushing up on your gun skills. What's going on?"

"Someone's killing people in our town Wendy. One of them was a local."

"And two outsiders."

"Yeah, well, Joey was murdered. The other two victims, well, that was just plain rudeness. Anti-tourist. People can't help being born out of town. I was one myself, once."

"Can't you just leave the whole thing to the two detectives? You just roll along as required and roll out the yellow tape when they need it."

"I don't know about those two. They are not like any homicide cops I've seen on TV. Harry Bosch says you have to solve it in the first forty-eight hours. The old bloke on Midsummer Murders just mucks about for fifty-two minutes, then, in the last three minutes, he points the finger at the last man standing, or woman, whoever is the most famous actor. These two from Melbourne have been here for four days. All they know is what the forensics have told them."

"And what's that?"

"I shouldn't say, but I bet you will be seeing it tomorrow on TV. One of the bodies is a big-name criminal. I reckon Angela Adams will be back to interview Detective Pete and Boofhead."

"So, we are all settled on Boofhead?"

"Yeah, Jack Farrell christened him Boofhead, and I don't think you have the civic authority to override Jack's nicknames."

"Boofhead. OK. Boofhead it is. Just for the record, what's his real name?"

I thought for a bit.

"Fuck me, I've forgotten."

"OK. I will,"

"Will what?"

"Fuck you," she said. "See if it helps you remember."

So, we made love again, and then she fell asleep. She was the most beautiful person I had ever known, inside and out. It was her birthday soon and, come the day, I would ask her to marry me again.

Most likely, she would answer as she always did. Yes, but not yet.

10

FRIDAY, MARCH 16, 2018

Jarrajarra, Toowong District, Victoria, Australia.

I woke up at 4.30 am. Wendy had already showered and was ready for work. We shared a cup of tea before she left, and then I took off for a long run. I headed to the caravan park. I ran through the park, along the river, to the very last cabin, the now infamous Cabin 143. The police tape I put up two nights ago was still in place. I had defended it bravely against the cluster of locals who came to have a barbecue while they watched the forensic team. Eventually, we had all gone home, and since then, the tape survived remarkably well without me to defend it. Plastic is forever.

I followed the bush path out of the caravan park and along the banks of the Murray River. It was certainly the most beautiful running track I had ever taken. I didn't do this trail very often in the hotter months as the path beside the river tended to be populated with snakes. I had the usual fear of snakes, and I didn't fancy being bitten by a tiger snake while out jogging in the early morning alone.

This morning I had a plan, and I was prepared to take the risk. I also had my pistol in a back holster concealed under my loose T-Shirt. The weapon wasn't to defend against snakes. It was protection. I was going snooping.

No one had seen Ricky Chalmers since he reported the body beside the road on Saturday night. The body, my Mister X, had since been identified as Allan Jarrad Davies. I was still none the wiser as to who that person was. More importantly, I had not seen Ricky Chalmers since the murders. That was beyond strange as Ricky was the captain-coach of the local Jarrajarra football team, and pre-season training was on in earnest. Ricky was also the town gardener. This was a time of year I would normally see Ricky several times a day, every day. Where was he?

Yesterday, when I drove Justin Mellish out to Ricky's place looking for the town's digging machine, it had occurred to me that, with a shortcut through the bush on his property, Ricky could have easily put himself on the trail that led to cabin 143. That, and his strange disappearance since the night of the murders, had me wondering. Could Ricky be the person that visited cabin 143 and murdered its occupant, Azzolino Pisano. I couldn't picture Ricky, the town's beloved football coach, as a murderer, but why the disappearance?

Azzy Pisano was the right-hand man to the richest drug dealer in the country. He was a professional bodyguard, and he was huge. It didn't matter how big or tough Pisano may have been, Ricky was a guy with the strength and physical courage to take on anyone. He was one local I could picture taking out both Allan Jarrad Davies and Azzy Pisano on the same night. I wasn't a homicide investigator, but I was curious about Ricky's alibi. As the local cop, I was allowed to be curious. In fact, it was my duty to be curious even if I was only officially the custodian of police tape.

It was my morning jog, and I could plod where I pleased, so I did. It was a beautiful run, and it took me to the place where Ricky might have joined the trail if, indeed, he had wanted to visit cabin 143 without being seen from the highway. I turned off the path and cut through the thin bush at the rear of Ricky's property. I headed towards his house. He lived on a long stretch of about 40 acres of mostly bush. His land had a thin highway entrance at the front and a wide stretch of land, along the river, at the back.

I walked quietly from the river and was about one hundred yards from the rear of his house when I saw Ricky's motorbike, semi-hidden in the bush. Why would he park so far from the house if he wasn't in hiding? I felt the engine and it was warm. It had been ridden very recently.

I walked towards the house, as I got closer, I could hear someone in the shower.

If Ricky was a murderer, I could be destroying the case against him right here. How did my curiosity stand up legally? I wasn't looking to search his house; I wasn't looking to arrest him. I was a friend jogging by. I saw the bike, heard the shower and wondered if my good friend, the footy coach, was back from his trip.

Shit.

I could only imagine what a hotshot city lawyer would make of me just dropping in on a murder suspect. I needed Barney to fill me in on the appropriate procedures.

Fuck it.

I crept in through the back door of the house to take a look. The sound from the shower told me someone was in there. A quick check of the house revealed there was no one else inside apart from myself and, presumably, Ricky. I took a chair at the kitchen table, facing all the entry points, sat down, took out my pistol and rested it on my knee, under the table and out of sight. I waited. Ricky finished his shower, then took a while fiddling about in the bathroom. I sat quietly, wondering if I should risk a 'Hey Ricky', but I let that thought pass.

I could hear him go to his room, getting dressed, then finally, his footsteps told me he was heading my way.

And then, there he was, in the much-battered flesh. Ricky had entered the kitchen wearing shorts, a t-shirt and runners. His arms and face were a mass of bruises. His eyes were both blackened. His right eye was swollen to the point it had closed, and his football-damaged nose looked freshly broken.

"G'day Ricky."

He looked at me out of his one good eye. The unbattered section of his face revealed no surprise, and his demeanour betrayed no fear at my sudden appearance. He didn't speak, just stood there looking at me. I thought he might be preparing to run, and I would struggle to match him in a foot race, so I very casually lifted my hand, the one with the gun in it, onto the table.

"So, where have you been?"

Nothing. He was just looking at the gun now. I persisted.

"And don't tell me you've been away in Melbourne on business."

"No, I have been camping further upriver."

"Hiding all those bruises on your face."

"Yeah, I guess." He was still looking at the gun. "Why the fuck are you in my kitchen pointing a gun at me."

"Well, Rick, I am not pointing a gun at you. It is sort of pointing at the fridge, really."

The gun was a mistake, legally, morally, every which way. In the army, you have your weapon at hand and ready for action at all times. No exceptions. If you don't, you are as likely to get killed by your sergeant as the enemy.

Police are different, pistol training takes forever, and much of it is about when not to use it, how to avoid using it, and how to keep it away and out of sight as though it is not even there. The civilians around you are not the enemy. You are there to protect them.

But here I was, weapon out, army training imprinted on my brain forever, and the civilian I was not exactly pointing at was not impressed. Not impressed at all.

"You are always such a smart-arse, Chris. What do you want?"

"I want to know where you have been. You report a murder and then disappear in the middle of the pre-season. Not like you at all. I was half worried about you as a mate and half curious to see what you had to say about the dead body you found. The one who had been in some sort of fight, all bashed up. You remember him?"

He thought long and hard about those issues.

"You're worried as a mate, alright." He semi-sneered at that. "Cop first, mate second."

"Well, there's that, plus there are all those bruises that tell me you have been in a serious punch-up. And don't tell me they are from last week's practice game; I was watching."

Long pause while he thought about it.

"I was in a fight."

"Who with?"

"I don't want to say."

"Let me guess. You were in a fight with the bloke beside the road for whatever reason. Looks like you won, given he is now dead. Then maybe you panicked and ended up in a blue with Joey Golino, and he ends up dead as well."

"Stop, Chris, for fuck's sake. You are embarrassing yourself."

"Well, it was only a first draft."

"I got in a fight, and yeah, I reckon I won since the other bloke was unconscious when I left. But he wasn't dead or even dying. I didn't kill anyone. Not accidentally, not deliberately. No one."

"OK. You didn't kill anyone."

"No."

"Three dead bodies, and you know nothing whatsoever about it."

He seemed to twitch at that statement. He definitely knew something.

"I didn't kill anyone, Chris. I am not a murderer."

Unfortunately, as always, I believed him. This was my fatal flaw as an investigator. I tended to believe everyone, whatever they said. My Nan had always said it doesn't matter what people say. It is what they do that counts. I thought about that. I would give Rick something to do and see how he behaved.

"You got any coffee? Instant will do." It was all I could think of.

He made some coffee while I guarded the fridge with my pistol. He made one for both of us, then sat down opposite me. Actually, he was sitting between me and the fridge, so I shifted my aim to the chest of drawers that was standing against the wall. The drawers looked dangerous.

"So, why did you come back home?"

"It was a hit-and-run visit. I just wanted a hot shower, grab some more food and gear. After that, I was heading straight back to my campsite."

"Did you know your sister is in hospital?"

"Kate? What happened?" He was genuinely concerned and surprised.

"Well, that's a long story, but the main part is she is in detox. Locked in a ward. Coming down off Oxy-Contin."

"Oh, shit." That shook him.

"Oxy-Contin, which, according to Kate, you supplied her."

For a moment, he looked ready to run again. Then he settled.

"She wanted it, she nagged me, so I rode up to Sydney and spoke to some people I knew there." He had no qualms confessing that. "Yeah, I bought it for her. Her money, once only, one-off. That was months ago. I told her I was not doing it again. I didn't do it for anyone else, just my sister. I am not a drug pusher, Chris."

"Who were these people you knew that sold you Oxy?"

"Some bikies I met when I was playing up there in Sydney. When you play in the big league, you meet all sorts."

"So, you just went up there and spoke to your bikie mates and bought drugs for Kate?"

"Yep. Not something I enjoyed. It is one thing to meet them in the footy rooms, totally different world back at their place."

"And that was the only time you ever did it?"

"Yes, and only because she nagged the shit out of me. You know my sister. Try telling her no; see how far you get."

He definitely had a point there.

"OK, let's put that aside for now. There are two Melbourne homicide detectives in town, and they want to talk to you about the dead body."

"I know. They left a note under the door. I was gonna pass on that for a few more days till the face healed up."

"So, you reported a body, you knew your current state of appearance would make you look guilty, so you disappeared."

"Yeah."

"Mate, you are talking yourself directly to jail."

"So, is this an interrogation? Don't you have to read me my Miranda rights or something?"

"For fuck's sake, Ricky, everyone's a fucking procedural expert. Miranda is American, bloody hell."

Maybe I should just shoot him, claim he confessed, then attacked me. Self-defence. The annoying bastard. I was trying to help him, for heaven's sake.

The black mist was hovering but had not descended.

Shooting Ricky Chalmers would not work. No one would believe me. Jesus, only last year, barely six months ago, he'd coached the Jarrajarra footy team to its first premiership in over forty years. He was a local God. I'd be run out of town.

"Ricky, mate, I am not here to interrogate you, but you should talk to these Detectives sooner rather than later. They are after a murderer. They see your face and that busted nose, and you don't explain yourself, they are going to assume bad things. The sooner you get the truth out, the better for you."

"The truth? I would be better giving them the truth after my face heals." He laughed at that, then looked at me. "So, are you going to take me in?"

"Take you in? Like on television." I hadn't really thought of it. I just had the gun out to discourage any fight-or-flight intentions. I wouldn't like my chances in either option.

"Mate, I am not going to take you in. Way above my pay grade, plus I thought we were friends. I would like to help you if I can."

He looked at me, thinking all that through. He knew I was not big on arresting people if a more peaceful solution could be found. For my part, I was certain he was not a murderer or did I just hope he wasn't?

"Hang on," I said. "I need to make a phone call."

"What? Get yourself a SWAT team to handle me?"

Jesus Christ. Suspicious prick.

"Ricky, have you ever seen someone who has been shot?"

"No."

"Well, mate, I have. I've seen way too many, and it is really simple, I have a gun, and you don't. I don't need a SWAT team to get you to behave."

He didn't answer that.

"I am going outside to make a phone call. Please don't run away. I will come back with some advice, and you can either take it or leave it. Either way, I will get out of your hair while you make your choice."

"Who are you calling?"

"A higher power."

"Who?"

"Barney, of course, you suspicious prick."

He nodded; Barney was clearly acceptable. Barney and Ricky were as far apart on the scale of conventional masculinity as could be. But they were locals and had known each other since birth. They trusted their knowledge of each other. They probably even liked each other. Most importantly, Ricky knew Barney would do the right thing for all of us.

I put my gun away and took out my mobile phone. I finished the coffee, and then I called Barney. I gave him the details of my morning's activity.

Barney wasn't too impressed by my not-so-legal entry into Rick's home. He could not see any possibility that anything I had discovered during my uninvited visit would be admissible in a murder trial. I had virtually guaranteed a not guilty for anything Rick may have done since childhood.

That was harsh but cool. I really hadn't discovered anything beyond Ricky being home and very bruised.

Barney also wasn't keen on my other idea of shooting Ricky and claiming self-defence. In Barney's words, that would be a lie. It would also severely affect the football team.

As for what to do next, Barney explained in simple sentences. I listened while he nailed it, and then I went inside to convey my Barney-fresh ideas to Ricky.

Ricky was still at his kitchen table drinking his coffee.

"OK, Ricky, here is my advice to you," and I told him what Barney told me. "Go into town, find yourself a solicitor. I suggest Eddie Doolan in Main Street."

There were only two solicitors in town, and one was on maternity leave. Not Eddie, the other one.

"Then, with Eddie beside you, go and report to the two detectives. Just tell them you are responding to the note they left under your door. Don't be interviewed alone. Insist on having your solicitor present. Don't say anything without first asking his permission to speak. If he says no, then don't speak. Whatever you do, don't lie. Don't speak if you don't want to, but don't lie. And, if they ask why you thought you needed a solicitor, let Eddie answer. Definitely don't speak on that one. You have every right to representation."

"That's it?"

"Yep. That's it. If they reckon you're a murderer, then they have to prove it. You don't have to help them."

"You don't reckon they will ask about this?" He pointed at his battered head.

"I am sure they will, but you say you didn't murder anyone, so just follow your lawyer's advice, answer their questions if he lets you. Otherwise, keep your mouth shut. You will be free and clear in time for footy training.

Famous last words.

I left Ricky to mull over Barney's brilliant advice and jogged home to have a shower.

I made it to the station by 8 A.M.

The media was back, which meant the forensic report had obviously leaked. The media had grown from a two-pack to a throng. It had also shifted location. They were now gathered at the rear of the Community Centre, the new home of our intrepid homicide investigators.

The most startling thing was that standing there, in the spotlight, beside Detective Pete and Detective Boofhead, was my own beloved leader, Sergeant Bruce Palmer, our very own Sarge. They were facing a row of microphones, and all cameras were on them. The Sarge was in full uniform, with all his medals pinned to his chest and his hat on. I actually felt quite proud of him. He looked fantastic.

I raced inside the station to find Barney at the front desk watching his mobile phone TV. I grabbed a chair and joined him.

The Sarge was in the middle of answering a question from one of the reporters.

"Yes, we can confirm that the deceased person found in the Jarra-jarra Caravan Park has been identified as Mr Azzolino Pisano. This is the same Azzolino Pisano under investigation by the Current Royal Commission into the death of Gary Rogers. Mr Pisano was on bail and had failed to report to Police on Saturday morning. He was, as of noon Saturday, in breach of his bail conditions, and a warrant had been issued for his arrest."

There was another question that I could not hear, but the Sarge had it under control.

"No, Police were not aware that Mr Pisano was in Jarrajarra. As I stated previously, there was a warrant for his arrest and, up until last night's identification, we considered him missing."

Another question.

"No, we are not aware of any large amounts of money found at or near the location of Mr Pisano's murder."

Another question.

"No, I repeat, there was no money, nothing."

Another question on a different tack.

"No, we are not aware of the whereabouts of Mr Folliero. He is also in breach of his bail conditions, and yes, there is a warrant out for Folliero. That warrant is current."

Another barely audible question. I noticed Detective Boofhead was looking a bit agitated. No limelight.

The Sarge continued.

"No. At this stage, we have no information as to whether Mr Folliero is alive or dead, and I am not prepared to speculate on that." The Sarge was on a roll. "As I said, the warrant for his arrest is current. As for Mr Pisano, I think we can all assume that particular warrant is now closed." Police humour, bloody hell. There was even a small chuckle from the throng. "As of now, in regard to Mister Pisano, we are handing that matter over to homicide. Detectives?"

The Sarge looked over toward Detective Pete and the Boof, then gracefully stepped back as the two Homicide coppers stepped up to the microphones. I swear they nearly bumped shoulders as the Boof jostled for the lead position in front of the camera. Seniority won out, and Detective Pete took control. He unrolled several pages of notes, leaned into the microphone, and away he went.

After Sarge's effort, it was all just waffle. The two Melbourne Detectives went on and on without anything beyond what the Sarge had said so perfectly. Barney and I lost interest.

"Wafflers," said Barney, reading my mind again. Did I mumble when I thought, or was the whole town telepathic?

"Barney," I said, "holy hell, how good was the Boss?"

"He was absolutely incredible. Who knew?"

"What a trooper."

"Honestly, that man is born for television."

And on and on, we prattled in that mode for another ten minutes while I made some truly crap fluffy coffee, and Barney tried to work out how he could get a replay of the Sarge's speech.

When the coffee was made, I passed Barney his cup. He took a sip and rolled his eyes in despair at the taste of my effort.

"Don't be so theatrical."

Barney doubled down, took another disgusted sip and went more theatrical.

Eventually, we found another TV station re-broadcasting what we had just watched. Barney started recording.

Then Sarge walked in alone, thank goodness. Barney and I just stood and gave him a round of applause. A standing ovation. He blushed, as he would, and then we all sat down while I fluffed up some coffee. Sarge was practically sparkling.

"What did you boys think?"

"Oh, Sergeant Palmer. You were honestly magnificent, truly magnificent, really. I actually mean it, and I am not lying to make you feel good," said Barney, who would always lie if it made you feel good.

"Thank you, Barney. Are you sure you aren't saying that just to make me feel better?"

"No Boss, no, no, no." That was from me. "You were bloody sensational. You were fucking brilliant."

"Language, Chris, please. Brilliant, really?" He was positively flushed red with delight.

"Absolutely," from both Barney and me. "Absolutely."

"So, you both reckon I did OK."

"Yes! Yes!"

"I have never spoken on TV before. To the whole nation, no less. National television, my word."

"Boss, you were great, really."

"Don't know about great." He was blushing again. "Vilma always says I say 'um-and-ah' too much when I speak in public."

"No way," I said, "you didn't say one 'um' or one 'ah'. You were perfect."

"And so natural and eloquent," said Barney. "Like you were reading a script. Honestly, Tony Bonner could not have done better." Tony Bonner was the Boss's favourite actor.

"Tony Bonner?" He chuckled, "My goodness me."

"Tony could play you in the movie Boss," I said, thinking further ahead.

"I was glad that Angela Adams woman wasn't there. She would have made me nervous."

"She is probably off chasing the money, Sarge," I added.

"Did you like my little joke about the Pisano warrant expiring? That wasn't a bit off, was it? Vilma says I shouldn't try humour when I speak."

"Oh, for heaven's sake, Sergeant Palmer, you are looking for faults." Barney was getting annoyed with all the humility. "Give me your phone."

Barney put out his hand, and Sarge took out his mobile phone and handed it over.

Barney typed in the passcode, which he knew because he had set it up, then dialled. We waited.

"Hi Vilma, it's me."

We listened to Barney's end of the conversation..

"I know, I know, yes, yes, I know. Yes. Absolutely. Oh my God, wasn't he though? And didn't he look so handsome? Oh yes. And those other two, oh good heavens, the fat one? Yes, I know, oh, you should meet him in the flesh. Actually, no, you shouldn't."

At that point, Vilma must have said something about the Boof-head, and Barney burst out laughing. He laughed so hard he had tears in his eyes. His voice went up an octave through the laughing. "Yes! Yes!" He let out a huge post-laugh sigh and wiped his eyes. "OK, I will put him on. You just tell him what you told me. He doesn't believe anything we tell him. OK, OK, kiss-kiss bye. Here he is."

"Kiss, kiss?" I whispered to Barney. He gave a defiant shrug of his shoulders and then handed over the phone to the boss. Barney and I then sat there, sipping our shit coffee and watching, smiling, as Missus Sarge gave the Sarge a fine dose of praise. He deserved it, and he loved it. By the time she had finished, he was positively glowing.

I never served with him in the army. The little I had found on the record suggested he was a very good officer. But here and now, back in the world, I just couldn't imagine a better person to work for.

Eventually, after we had all praised him to the skies, the Sarge went back to the Community Centre, and I left the station, walking down the road to the Nursing Centre. Wendy told me Kate Chalmers was doing really well, surprisingly well, in fact. I was allowed to see her.

The door to the holding ward was unlocked, and in I went. Kate was lying on the bed, looking totally spent but calm. She was also unhooked from all the monitors and drips. As bad as she looked, she was clearly better.

"Hi Kate, how are you?" She looked as though she had been in a war. She was a tall, striking woman, but she was showing every part of her recent ordeal.

"Chris, mate, I am feeling really fucking terrible. How are you?" Her voice was barely a whisper. A very croaky whisper.

"Better than you at the moment." She smiled at that. "Do you remember the other day?"

"Oh fuck, do I have to?"

"Just wondered how much of it you recall."

She actually laughed at that one.

"Oh God, mate, I remember every horrible bit of it. Please don't tell me you found that bloke's five hundred bucks inside the house."

"I did. It was in the receipt book. Not that far from the leftover boxes of Oxy."

"Oh Jesus, oh shit, I suppose that he wants me strung up now."

"No, he's OK. All settled. We treated it as an insurance thing. He ran off the road and hit your fence and your truck. Turns out he swerved, trying not to hit a family of ducks."

"Ducks?"

"Yeah, a family, daddy, mummy, baby ducks. Plus, you are going to get a payout for repairs."

She looked at me, bewildered.

"Bullshit. I don't believe you."

"It's true. Catch up with Scotty Farrell when you get out. He will give you the insurance details. It's all done and dusted."

She started a laugh which turned into a long fit of coughing. Eventually, she recovered,

"Just how in the hell did you manage that?"

"Well." I said, "a bit of argy-bargy, a bit of looking at the possible reverberations, his wife maybe finding out he visited you, the family scandal and so forth. Then we looked for a win-win, and there you go. Insurance is a wonderful thing, it turns out he had some handy."

"Wow, incredible. You are a step up on our previous copper."

"Is that a compliment?"

"Not much of one. He was a pig."

She started coughing again and then looked at me.

"Jeez, Chris, I would kill for a cigarette."

"Hang on a sec." I went to the door, which had been unlocked, in order for me to enter. "Promise not to run away on me."

She looked at me, a picture of physical misery. "You are joking, right?"

I went to find a wheelchair and a cigarette. I found a wheelchair in the hall and borrowed a cigarette and lighter from one of the cleaners. I went back to Kate's room, helped her into the chair, and we went out the back of the hospital to find some sunshine. We found a lovely spot against the back wall facing the car park and the bush beyond.

She lit up and took a very long drag.

"So, did these ducks of ours survive?" She asked.

"They're fine. Our driver did a big curve, and thankfully, the ducks were saved. You're the one we need to fix now."

"Fucking ducks, hey," she said. "I always loved ducks."

"Me too," I said.

She smoked her cigarette for a bit, basking in the sun. It really was a beautiful place, Jarrajarra. There were so many nooks and crannies where you could grab a moment of peace. Even in a hospital car park, there were huge ghost gums and the beautiful sounds of the bush just there, beyond the concrete.

"I am not a junkie, Chris. I won't be going back on any of that shit. I promise you."

"Don't need to make any promises to me, Kate."

"Are you going to charge me with anything?"

"Like what?"

"I dunno."

"I could do you for loitering on the roof of his car. Not sure it is actually a crime. Car was a wreck anyway. You could argue that you were trying to help him out of the vehicle before it exploded."

She smiled at that one, sitting there in the wheelchair, contemplating. I was leaning against the wall. The sun was beautiful.

"You get on that shit, and it is all you think about," she said. "You miss the little things like this, sunshine, silence. Everything gets so complicated. Your brain just stops working. Shit, I was getting so fucking angry."

"There are other addictions, you know, Kate. Good addictions. When I first came here, I often saw you out running."

"Yeah, I loved it. I had a bit of trouble a while ago, got in a fight, hurt my back and my neck, stopped running, everything got worse, got on the pills."

"And you couldn't get off them?"

"Not on my own. Would never have got off them without your girlfriend, Nurse fucking Evil. She is one hard bitch. Sorry mate."

"I will pass Wendy your compliments," I said.

"Don't bother. Our relationship is past saving. One good thing is my back and neck aren't hurting anymore."

"Who was this fight with?"

She looked at me with a smirk. "I think I will claim professional silence on that one. Just say it got sorted. Eventually."

"Being a hooker isn't like being a lawyer, Kate, or a priest. You don't get any professional privileges. There's no right to silence."

She looked at me to determine if I was serious. I wasn't. She burst out laughing. Throaty and loud.

"Fuck off, copper," she said in the friendliest possible manner.

She closed her eyes and took another long drag of the cigarette.

"Maybe you should start running again." I offered.

"Maybe."

I was not sure if that was a maybe-yes or a maybe-no.

"Whatever bothers me, I just run it out," I said. "Alternatively, I punch the shit out of the heavy bag."

"Maybe. Might get myself one of those."

I let a bit more sun soak into the conversation.

"Tell me about Ricky and the Oxy."

She rolled her eyes at that.

"Oh, Jesus. Bloody hell, poor kid. His big sister nagging him to death, wanting painkillers. Don't blame Ricky. Jesus. It is all on me. I hounded the poor bastard. I think I am the only person on earth he is frightened of, and look what I made him do. Jesus Christ. I would be ashamed if I were able. Don't take it out on him. He's a good kid. Thinks with his dick like most men, but hey."

That was pretty much the same story that Ricky had told me, apart from the bit about his dick. Confirmation. Fair enough. I wasn't on the drug squad.

"What do you mean thinks with his dick?"

She looked at me. Her natural cynicism shone through the recent wear and tear. She practically snorted in derision.

"Jesus, Chris, you are such a goody two shoes. My little brother has slept with almost as many wives in this town as I have with husbands. For free, too, the idiot."

That gave me pause. I was too embarrassed to ask who. I didn't really want to know.

She looked at me. "No, I am not talking about your girlfriend, for Christ's sake. No one is wedging between you two lovebirds." Was I that transparent? Really?

We contemplated the sunshine a bit more. I had a thought.

"You know Kate, the C.F.A. organise a five-kilometre park run every Saturday, starts 8 am. You can walk if you want, don't have to run. Why don't you come? Cost is five bucks. Nice run in the fresh mountain air. Better than Oxy."

"Oh, Jesus. Spoken like someone who hasn't tried both." She liked her little joke, even if it was wrong.

I had done the whole painkiller addiction thing myself during my long and hard goodbye from the military. The only thing that worked for me was a change of addiction, from drugs to exercise, with a big help from my beloved Wendy. Kate was right. Nurse Wendy could be a hard bitch.

Kate looked at me. "Anyway, how will that go down, me running with the C.F.A. blokes? What would the wives and girlfriends think of that?"

"It will be fine. Maybe give some of those firefighters a chance to get some money back, even if it is only five bucks every Saturday."

She gave a smoky laugh to that.

"I will swing by one Saturday morning after you get out of here. See if you need a lift."

She looked at me. It seemed to me she was suspicious of someone trying to be kind.

"I will think about it."

"Do that. Let's get you back inside. I need to get back to work."

I wheeled her back to her room. On the way, she asked me a question.

"When do you reckon that girlfriend of yours will let me out of here."

"She will probably say it is up to you. It's a hospital, not a prison."

"OK."

I didn't really need to get back to work. I was heading to the rifle range for more practice. When I got to the range, I was happily surprised to see my friend Rob Farrell waiting for me. Rob had been away, and now he was back.

Rob was ex-army like me, had served in Afghanistan like me and, just like me, he enjoyed maintaining those skills he acquired during his service. He was the best person I knew for partnering up at the practice range.

"Hey, stranger." I was smiling just to see him there.

"G'day corporal." He loved reminding me that he had outranked me in the army. It wasn't much of a boast. Most people in uniform had a higher rank than me.

"Set up already?"

"Yep, since we are here alone, I thought we might work some situations."

"You put up the steelies, nice."

Rob had arrived early and set up some steel targets. Steel targets were fun. You could hear the ding when the bullet struck, so you knew from your position if you had scored. With the paper targets, you weren't sure you had struck till you checked the target after you had finished shooting.

He had also put down five numbered markers at various points on the range. They were placed from fifty metres down to about ten. The markers were in random positions, but each one was closer to the row of steelies.

"I thought I might get on up the roof of the flag house and cover you while you worked your way in close with your pistol."

"OK. You got your Scout?" Rob had a Steyr Scout lightweight rifle. He had traded it with a US marine he knew in Iraq. It was chambered for .308 Winchester ammunition. The Steyr was designed to be accurate to at least three hundred to four hundred meters. Rob could manage that distance easily, but the club's flag house was only about two hundred meters from our targets and a bit off to the side. At that range, he was deadly.

"Do you really need to cover me that close? You could just shoot them all, mate."

"I like to see your fat lazy arse working."

"OK." We were smiling, I wasn't fat, and I wasn't lazy, but Rob would never admit either to me. It was good to see him.

I changed out of my uniform into a pair of overalls, didn't want to dirty the uniform, and away we went. I would start at the fifty, and while Rob shot, I ran from one marker to the next. Then I would hide behind the marker and take some shots myself. The markers didn't offer any protection, but the targets weren't shooting back, so I could pretend.

Rob would shoot in bursts of three shots, then four shots, then three, then five. After the last bracket, he would need to reload. Theoretically, I would be safe to run in the open while he was shooting. I just need to remember which bracket he was up to. I could fire from the cover of the marker or on the run. I just didn't want to be in the open while he wasn't shooting.

And so, it went till I worked into the ten-meter mark. Then I would start back at the fifty. I did a lot of running and sliding while Rob lay there on the roof, hitting the steel targets with monotonous regularity. Any misses were greeted with utmost scorn from the non-shooter. After an hour, I was exhausted, and the miss-to-scorn ratio was about even between us.

We called it quits. I showered and changed in the rifle clubhouse while Rob boiled the kettle and made us some cups of tea. We sat in the shade of the clubhouse porch, sipped our tea and chatted.

"Where have you been?"

"Melbourne."

"And?"

"And I've been sorting out some family stuff."

"Family stuff?"

He looked at me. I sensed he was debating whether to confide in me or not. I wasn't good at confidentiality. When a friend had a problem, I always wanted to solve it.

"OK, this is my problem. You don't need to solve it, alright?" Another mind reader. Was I really that transparent?

"Absolutely, your problem. Not mine."

"So, Joanne, the oldest. Started university this year. Went down, end of January. At the start, she keeps in touch daily. Then it tapers off, it gets to last week, and we haven't heard from her for two weeks. Nothing. Not a word. So I went down to check her out, see what was going on."

"OK."

He took a long sip of his tea before he continued.

"I tell you, mate, I am not too convinced about this university stuff. Cost a fucking fortune, and the kid was way off the rails. Been there barely six weeks and has gone totally fucking native. Told her if she

134

wanted to continue, she could come home and earn her way back. She wants to go to university; she can pay for it herself."

"Wow." That seemed harsh from a guy devoted to his family.

"Fuck it. I get down there. She hasn't attended a single lecture. Hasn't written a single study note. The money she had to buy books is spent and not a book in sight. Night times she is playing tambourine in a fucking rock band."

"Tambourine?"

"I know, who plays fucking tambourine in a rock band, for fuck's sake. What bloody life skills are required, or can be gained, banging away on a fucking tambourine? Bachelor of bloody Koombayah! Jeez-us."

"She is a very beautiful young girl Rob. She would be an ornament to any band, even with a tambourine."

"I did not raise my daughter to be an ornament to anything or anyone. Especially anyone on the male side of the equation. She is not an ornament, OK?"

"Sorry mate, bad choice of words. Maybe she was just sowing her oats."

"Fucking oats? Bugger me. I get to her house down there in Melbourne, if that's what you would call it, more like a pig sty. Anyway, there is drug shit everywhere. She says it is not hers, just her boyfriend's. Jesus Christ. It's all good, Dad, she says, like it's only this week's boyfriend is the junkie. Not me. Holy Jesus."

He took a long sip of his tea. I don't know if it is possible to sip angry, but he was trying.

"Anyway, she is not twenty-one yet, so I tell her she can get her butt home and get a job."

"Maybe learn electric guitar," I added, trying to cheer him up. "I mean, you can't condone tambourine."

He looked at me, totally unamused.

"OK, sorry, not funny. I apologise."

"Accepted."

"A job?"

"Yes, a job."

I finished my tea. We sat and contemplated the state of the world while Rob calmed himself down.

"That was nice shooting today, Rob."

"Yeah, you too, hot shot. I'd hate to have you on my tail."

"I'd hate to have you as a dad." It was meant as a joke, but it made me think about my own father. "Actually, I take that back. I would have loved to have you as a dad."

"Is your old man still alive, Chris?"

"Fucked if I know, mate."

Back at the station, I asked Barney if we could find a job for Joanne Farrell. I gave him the reason. He had to think about that. Joanne was a super girl, but our biggest problem was we had no money and no budget. Mere detail, I was sure Barney would sort it out.

The yellow post-it notes on the corkboard told me that Barney had taken a few phone calls and there were a couple of real police type errands for me to run. Not your murders, just some graffiti to check out at the War memorial, and Mrs Gillespie in Royal Avenue had made too much chocolate cake for her granddaughter's birthday, and she wondered if Constable Chris would like to take home the extra to share with that lovely nurse he is seeing.

I gave Barney a look.

"Chris, I am just reporting the words as they were spoken," said Barney as I rolled my eyes. "You know Mrs Gillespie really likes you, and she is very old and very lonely."

"How many birthdays has her granddaughter had this year?"

"Seven." Barney handed me the post-it notes. "You go and do the post-its, and I will write them up in the book," he said. And off I went.

The first post-it I addressed was the graffiti. I knew this would be an easier issue to solve than Mrs Gillespie's loneliness. Plus, it would be good to do some real work before feasting on chocolate cake.

The problem with being the only graffiti artist in a very clean town of 900 souls is you quickly get a reputation. The good news for me was that Jarrajarra's one-and-only street artist was very easy to find. I didn't bother inspecting the crime. I went straight to the criminal. Saxon Tyson-Howard was, as he always was on a weekday afternoon, ensconced in the granny flat in the backyard of his grandmother's house. He was sprawled on a rotting hard-rubbish couch with two of his mates, playing on his computer gaming thing. I walked in and unplugged the big screen that had them all hypnotised. This was greeted by a chorus of "Shit, fuck, shits" and groans with all eyes glued to the now dead screen. Eventually the three teenagers looked sideways and registered my presence.

"Saxon," I said, "you promised me no more tagging."

"It wasn't me," he said. "It wasn't even my tag."

There was a solid defence if ever I'd heard one. Plus, there was the fine mist of Saxon's favoured yellow spray splashed across his dirty black track pants. Saxon was the guiltiest perpetrator I had ever seen, yet again.

"Mate, you can change your tag, but you can't change your handwriting. It is as culpable as your DNA or your fingerprints." I was sure I had just misused the word culpable, but it was only Saxon.

"That's not what culpable means," said Saxon, the little smart-arse.

"Whatever. I sent a photo of your latest effort to forensics, and they confirmed the handwriting match." I nodded toward the other two gamers. "You two can take off. I am here to get Saxon's DNA."

I pulled out my pair of rubber gloves and inflated them ostentatiously, maybe insinuating a rectal probe.

"Police headquarters needs DNA and handwriting before we go to the judge."

Saxon's buddies were open-mouthed in shock. The judge? Rubber gloves?

"Sorry, Saxo, but someone is doing hard time for this one. What were you thinking mate? The war memorial?"

The two gamer buddies stared at Saxon, then looked back at me, then they sprang from the couch and scrambled for the door. They fought over each other to get out quickly.

"I tried the soft approach with you, and look where it got me." I am sure the two youngsters heard me and took it as a life lesson.

Saxon burst into tears.

"Please, Chris, Constable, I am sorry. I was depressed because I lost my job." Saxon had a job; news to me.

"What job?"

"Pizza deliveries. Mister Golino told me not to come in anymore, said it wasn't worth it, people could come and collect their own pizzas if they were hungry."

"When did he say that?"

"Last week."

"How long have you been doing pizza deliveries?"

"Last three months or so."

Bloody hell, so that was why there had been a lull in weekend vandalism. Our man Saxon had been gainfully employed. The notion that Saxon had killed Joey in revenge for losing his delivery job and then went on a graffiti rampage lasted about one second in some part of my brain, then melted away.

"I'm sorry, Chris," he blurted out, almost crying. "I really am. I don't know why I do it. I don't even enjoy it anymore. I even started buying that washable stuff, make it easier to get off."

He had actually anticipated both his capture and his eventual punishment. I looked at him, incredulous.

"I don't know, mate; I have given you so many chances." I looked to the ceiling for inspiration. "I suppose we could go and see how the victim feels about it."

I put away the rubber gloves and let the boy recover his composure then I drove him over to the Jarrajarra R.S.L.

Alf Longmuir was president of R.S.L. and head of the war memorial committee. Alf found us an appropriate bucket and filled it with water, suds and rags. We walked over to the memorial and set young Saxon to work cleaning the damage he had inflicted.

We watched him for a few minutes. He was actually doing a good job; he had the skills.

"You know Saxon, I am surprised Constable Taylor let you off so easy," said Alf. "He is a much-decorated war hero, you know, ex-SAS. Real killers. You desecrate his memorial, you might just disappear one day, no one would ever find you."

That annoyed me. I rarely discussed my army days or even my attitude to war memorials with anyone. As for killing locals, I would more likely shoot pompous fucking Alf than sad young Saxon. At least the kid still had time to grow out of his problems. I knew Alf was just trying to put the wind up our indentured painter, but it was my war service, which was my business, not his.

How did he find out about me anyway?

"I'm sorry, Constable Taylor. I promise it won't happen again," sniffed the still-delicate prisoner.

"You know Saxon, my Nan always said, it's not what you say. It is what you do that counts."

Saxon stopped for a think on that one. "But I was promising not to do it."

He had a point, the little smart arse. Nan hadn't covered that side of it.

"Yeah, well, sometimes not doing something negative is the same as doing something positive or thereabouts." I decided to leave before I shot the little shit for questioning my Nan.

"Just make sure you do a good job, Saxon. Tell Mr Longmuir here when you are done. Let him check it before you leave. If he is happy, I won't put you before the judge. Maybe we can keep your DNA out of the system, OK?"

"OK," he whispered, intent on his repairs.

I took the older bloke to the side to have a word away from Saxon.

"Mr Longmuir, if you really have to talk about my military career, and I don't think you do, the correct term is SASR, and we were soldiers, not killers, thank you very much." I gave the old goat the snake eyes and headed off to Royal Avenue to collect my chocolate cake from Mrs Gillespie.

. . .

Mrs Gillespie took over an hour. She was a lovely old lady. She was 95 years old and still lived alone and looked after herself. Always busy. Still fit and trim and sharp, but she had outlived her husband and most of her friends. I stayed for a chat and looked at photos of her granddaughter, who had to be at least fifty years old herself. The granddaughter was surprisingly thin for a woman who must be living on chocolate cake.

Mrs Gillespie had informally adopted me and my nutrition when I first moved to Jarrajarra. Her chocolate cake was very good, and her fruit cake, which she called health loaf, was positively addictive. It took me a year of cake and tea before I realised she was my boss's Mother-In-Law.

The Sarge's wife, Vilma, was Mrs Gillespie's daughter.

In a small town, everyone knew everyone, and a large portion were related. I learnt early in my Jarrajarra years to be careful about who you discussed. Chances are you would be talking to one person about another, only to find they were cousins. It was Doris Gillespie who told me that in Jarrajarra when two people argue, most people will take a side in the argument before they even know what it's about. It proved to be true.

I saw no harm in spending an hour with Mrs Gillespie. I was only two streets away from the police station and only a few doors down from Wendy at the Nursing Centre. Everyone that mattered was a stone's throw away, so I sat and chatted with the lovely old lady.

We usually talked about her late husband, who had served in World War 2 with the R.A.A.F. He'd had quite a war and a box full of medals to show for it. I was genuinely interested, and the time always passed quickly.

Eventually, I finished my third cup of tea and headed back to the station with a large box full of yummies and a belly full of cake.

I only had time to deposit the mountain of chocolate cake and biscuits on Barney's desk when the Sarge walked in looking for me.

"Got a minute, Chris?"

"Absolutely, Sarge."

"Let's take a walk to the cafe."

He was back to business. Focused, the glory of this morning's TV appearance a thing of the past.

We settled into a booth at the back of the "Jarrajarra Breakfast and Lunch". Sarge ordered coffee, and I had water, still recovering from tea and cake.

"The news, your local footy coach is being held on suspicion of murder."

"Oh."

"Yes, oh indeed."

I sat mute, struggled to think.

"Murder of who?"

"All of them, the trifecta."

"No way. He didn't do it."

"Based on?" Which was a bloody good question.

"Based on," I had to stop and think. "Well, I would say it is based on knowing him."

"Anything else you want to add? Like evidence to the contrary."

The Sarge had that one step ahead of you look on his face. Time to spill.

"OK. Just so you know, this morning, I was worried that I hadn't laid eyes on him since he reported finding Mister X, this Allan Jarrad Davies bloke. So, on my morning run, I went by his place, found he was home, so I had a chat."

"A chat?"

"Yes, I called in for a chat. When I got there, I could see he had been in a fight. I knew the two Melbourne Detectives wanted to speak to him. I advised him to lawyer up and get on in there to get his chat out of the way."

"You told him to lawyer up?"

"Yes."

"Were you in uniform?"

"No, I was out running, called in on him as a mate."

The Sarge had a long think about that while I sipped my coffee. "OK," he said, "that could possibly work."

"Why are you worried about making it work?"

"Well, they may be able to use his DNA to put him in the fight with Davies and Golino. This is going to court, son, and if Ricky Chalmers is guilty, I don't want your actions ruining the case."

"Oh." I hadn't realised there was more DNA. There had been no mention of it in the report Barney and I had secretly read. More DNA, possibly Ricky's, and I sent him off to have a friendly chat with Detectives Pete and Boofhead. Holy shit.

When I came back to earth from my revelation, the boss was looking at me very carefully.

"I didn't know about unidentified DNA," I said.

"I know you didn't." The Sarge said. "Those girls had hurried through their report as a favour to me. Turns out they missed something on their first pass. Carole just called me half hour ago. They found some DNA traces on Davies that may belong to his assailant."

"Taken from Davies' knuckles," said Sarge.

"Ouch."

"Exactly."

"So, I just sent my friend into the belly of the system, and they may have his DNA on the victim."

"Exactly."

"Shit."

"Chris, you are a police officer. If Chalmers did it, you've scored a goal. If he didn't, then you had better get around to proving who did."

"Hang on, Sarge, when did the two Melbourne cops find out about the DNA?"

"Twenty minutes ago. I told them just before I came to tell you."

"Where is Ricky now?" I asked.

"Right now? I am guessing he is still cuffed to a chair in the community centre. When I left, Detective Snow was watching him while Detective Rogers was getting his DNA swab into the system, probably marked urgent. They have called in a divvy van, and they are going to ship him over to Wodonga lockup. He will probably face the magistrate next week."

"Any chance he will get bail?"

"Not a prayer. He murders one of the Folliero henchmen right in the middle of the Rogers' inquest. They will be looking at him as part of some broad conspiracy. He will be front page everywhere. You think you have seen some press lately. Son, it hasn't even started."

"And the dynamic duo will be front and centre."

"Probably. My personal view is they are more interested in finding Folliero and his money than working out who is killing the drug minions and their sidekicks."

"OK."

We sat in silence. I was thinking about Ricky and Kate, brother and sister, same but different.

"Boss, you are a rugby man, right?"

"Yes, why?"

"I am guessing you never saw Ricky play football."

"No, never had the pleasure. Is that relevant?"

"Personally, I'd be concerned leaving Ricky cuffed to a chair in the care of Detective Boofhead, especially if Detective Pete was distracted. I don't think both of them, together, can handle Ricky if Ricky decides to leave. We should be getting Ricky into our holding cell till the divvy van arrives. The sooner, the better before someone gets hurt."

"Really?"

"Better safe than sorry, boss."

My pertinent observations were interrupted by the sound of a very loud motor. I looked out the cafe window to see a motorbike gunning down the main street. It was a quad bike with a Toowong Shire sticker on the side. The bike was being ridden hard and fast. It had come from the direction of the Community Centre, past the cafe where I sat with the Sarge, heading out of town toward the river.

Driving the bike was our newly arrested murder suspect, Ricky Chalmers. His face still battered, with no sign of any new bruises, but his T-Shirt torn half off his chest and now blowing in the wind of his escape.

The Sarge was watching too.

"Oh, my God. Was that who I thought it was?"

"One and the same."

"Oh, bugger," said the Sarge. Oh, bugger, indeed.

I sprinted from the cafe toward the police station. The Sarge could not keep up, after about twenty seconds of flat-out sprinting, he gave up.

"Go, just go!" He shouted after me as he lagged further behind.

I made it from the cafe to the station and was in my police truck in less than a minute. I followed the main road north out of town to the intersection with the river road. I was there in 90 seconds. I turned right towards Ricky's home at speed, my siren screaming.

I arrived at Ricky's place within ten minutes of his escape. The council quad bike was there, abandoned in front of Ricky's tool shed. Ricky's trail bike had gone. I did a quick check of the house. There was no one there. Back to the shed, and I found fresh tire marks from the shed into the bush. The same bush track I ran this morning.

My guess was Ricky was heading across the river, over the border into New South Wales. If he was smart, he would be going to the nearby Bogandyera ranges, thick scrubby mountain country. He would be near impossible to track and find.

Ricky Chalmers, the local football hero, someone I admired, someone the town loved, was now officially a wanted man. A suspected murderer. His escape seemed to me a statement of guilt.

Why would Ricky Chalmers kill Joey Golino? It made no sense at all.

I gave up the chase. I had missed what little chance I may have had. I had neither the tools nor the weapons to pursue a fugitive into the bush beyond Jarrajarra, especially one who knew the area better than me, someone who grew up there. Ricky wasn't even my prisoner. I would be the lowest man on the official police pursuit totem pole. I headed back to town and waited on my orders. I was sure they wouldn't find him, but once they gave up and went home. Once I had a chance to prepare, I knew that I would.

Only this morning, Ricky had come home for a hot shower after less than a week. One week? I could hunt and travel in rough country longer than that. A lot longer.

~

As I drove toward the Community Centre, I could see Jack Farrell's ambulance outside the main entrance. Parked behind the ambulance was a string of news vehicles with their satellite dishes pointing at the clouds. In front of the broadcast trucks stood the highly manicured talking heads and their not-so-glamorous camera teams. All the same but different.

I parked down the street, walked around the collection of cars and cameras, and into the Community Centre. Just a lowly constable, I was invisible.

Inside the Centre, it was post-escape mayhem.

Detective Pete was seated in a chair being, attended by Jack Farrell. His shirt was covered in blood, his eye and nose were swollen. He would end up with a major shiner by tomorrow, and his nose was probably broken,

Detective Boofhead was being attended to by Jack's off-sider Jody. Boof was flat on his back on a stretcher. She was attaching some fluids to him. What little I could see of his face was broken and bloody. He had obviously fought and lost badly.

There was blood on the floor. A table overturned, and a wooden chair smashed beyond repair. In the middle of the floor, one broken arm of the chair had one end of a handcuff attached to it. There was another broken chair arm, with a similarly released cuff that had fallen on the overturned table. They had cuffed Ricky's hands to the separate arms of a wooden chair. That was dumb.

Ricky had, most likely, demolished the chair and then wreaked havoc on the two detectives. Used their keys to un-cuff himself. They had totally underestimated him.

The Sarge had two Smith & Wesson police-issue pistols in his hands, both still in their holsters. I guessed Sarge had taken them from the two injured detectives to keep them safe. I was glad Ricky had not taken either cop's gun after he had incapacitated them. It would be just one more excuse for the search teams to shoot him.

I checked in with the Sarge. I brought him up to date on my failed pursuit of our fugitive, then asked him what I should do next, thinking I would be back on police tape guard duties very soon. It turned out a little different.

I was given the task of organising the local motel to allow for half a dozen police higher-ups who would be arriving soon. There would be some senior New South Wales police, some Federals and SOG teams from both Victoria and New South Wales. There would be no motel for the SOGs. They could camp in the park behind the football ground.

Ricky Chalmers, local hero, now fugitive, was at large, and the hunt was on. The machinery of three separate police forces was gearing up for action. There were so many hired guns. I just hoped they didn't kill him.

Over the next few hours, the ambos got the injured detectives off to the Bush hospital. More police cars and trucks and two extra police choppers arrived, and I was kept busy, ferrying people from the choppers to the motel and then to the Community Centre, which was serving as task force headquarters. It was feeling like my army days, except the army did it better. Plus, in the army, I was one of the guns, while here, I was just a traffic cop and chauffeur.

Later in the night, a Victorian Police Superintendent named Hughes stepped out of the Community Centre to meet the press. Why he had the honour, I had no idea. I had never seen him before.

Hughes had more ribbons on his chest than I had ever seen on a policeman. He looked very impressive. I found a quiet spot out back of the Community Centre where I watched the press conference live on my mobile phone. Hughes started off with an outright lie and kept at it from there.

"I can report that a suspect had been bought in for questioning earlier today." That was a lie. He came in under his own steam.

"During questioning, the suspect produced a blunt weapon with which he assaulted the two Victorian Detectives who were questioning him." Another porky. Ricky had already been arrested. Question time was over. And what was this about a magically appearing blunt weapon? From the little, I could see Ricky had done over both coppers with his fists.

"After severely injuring both officers, the suspect then left the building and escaped into the nearby bush." I guess that bit was true.

There was a barrage of questions after that. Hard to decipher what any of the reporters asked but since Superintendent Hughes had the microphone, his answers came through loud and clear.

"Yes, this is the man who was assisting police with our inquiry into the three murders."

Another question.

"The suspect's name is Richard Chalmers. He is local to Jarrajarra."

"DNA evidence places Chalmers at the scene of the murder and in some sort of altercation with two of the deceased, namely Davies and Golino." My dead Mister X now had a name, and people were using it.

"No, we are not previously aware of any relation between this suspect Chalmers and either Azzolino Pisano or Michelle Folliero. There is a suggestion that Chalmers and Davies were acquainted." Ricky knew Mister X? Really?

It was weird. The reporters would shout over the top of each other to the point their questions were unintelligible, and then Hughes would just say what he wanted as though answering a specific question.

"No, we do not believe we will find Michelle Folliero in this area. We believe Folliero has left the country, and yes, there is now a warrant issued for his arrest in relation to the murder of Gregory Rogers in 2010."

As I was watching Hughes, someone walked up behind me.

"Thought I'd find you outback, avoiding the brass," said Sarge. Something I could not deny. Together, we listened to Hughes waffling on.

"We do not know why Pisano was here in Jarrajarra," said Hughes, pretending to answer a question. "No, we do not believe he was travelling with Folliero. Intelligence made available from the Federal

Police indicates that Folliero left the country as early as Saturday and, at that point, was headed to Spain."

The few words I could hear from the reporters seemed to be pushing for answers on how two big burly homicide detectives allowed an alleged triple murderer to walk out of their custody without so much as a see you later.

"No, I believe Detectives Jordan and Snow have done an outstanding job identifying the alleged murderer as quickly as they did. Yes, they were unable to detain him, which indicates how dangerous this man is to the community."

"Yes, Chalmers is most definitely considered dangerous. We believe he is armed. Members of the community should be aware he may still be in the area, and under no circumstances should they approach him if they see him."

"Yes, the search for the fugitive will commence at first light tomor- row. I believe with the resources we have at hand Richard Chalmers will be in police custody very soon."

And so it went. Bullshit baffles brains. Waffle and more waffles.

The Sarge let out a long sad sigh. "Turn it off, Chris. I can't watch."

"Bloody hell," I said, "this sounds like a setup for a shoot-on-sight approach."

"I don't know, son. Surely they want him alive and talking. I get a sense the Feds and the New South Wales coppers think Joey Golino might have had some of the Folliero money. Maybe Chalmers was chasing that."

"Sarge, trust me on this. You can lose that notion. Wipe it from your brain cells. Ricky Chalmers is the only bloke I know who is less interested in money than I am. The only thing he is interested in is football. First, last and always, football. He doesn't give a shit about money."

The Sarge looked at me for a while. "Well, here is a notion for you. They aren't really after your boy, they are all after Folliero, and some of them are after his money. Chalmers is incidental, they want what he knows, and if he can't tell them where Folliero is or where all that drug money is, then the next time they get their hands on him, they will squash him like a bug."

"If they can find him," I added.

"This is my fault," said the Sarge, looking down. "I should have hustled Chalmers into your holding cell while I had the chance. Now all the sharks have smelt blood in the water and have come looking."

"And all the cracks had gathered to the fray."

The Sarge looked at me, surprised. "Didn't pick you for a Banjo Patterson man."

"Man from Snowy River, my Nan's favourite poem and her favourite movie."

"One of Tony Bonner's best roles."

"Absolutely."

The boss looked at his watch. It was close to midnight.

"Goodness, Chris, did you do your 4.30 run this morning?"

"Yeah."

"Of course you did, stupid question. Go home, and get some sleep. You'll need it."

Home I went.

I walked, staying on the backstreet away from the throng of officer types inside the Community Centre and the press mob in front of it. I thought about my Nan and how she loved that poem, 'The Man from Snowy River'. She always finished with the second last stanza. It reminded me of Ricky Chalmers.

"But the hardy mountain pony he could scarcely raise a trot. He was blood from hip to shoulder from the spur. But his pluck was still undaunted, and his courage fiery hot, for never yet was mountain horse a cur."

"Read the rest of it, Nan," I would demand.

"No, mate," she would say. "The last bit is just waffle; those two lines are the guts of it. That's all you need to know about that."

Mountain ponies and good people don't quit, ever, my Nan's philosophy on life in a poem.

Ricky was like those mountain ponies; I couldn't see any of this mob catching him.

. . .

I came through the back gate. My whole body smiled when I saw Wendy's bike against my back wall. Inside, she had left out some cold cuts of turkey and a bowl of freshly cut fruit salad on the kitchen table. I ate that lot way too quickly and headed to bed. Wendy was asleep. I tried to spoon in without disturbing her. She moved just right, and we snuggled in. She spoke in a sleepy mumble.

"Just so you know, both those Detectives, Pete and Boofhead, were released from the hospital. Detective Pete has a few cuts and a slight concussion. Boofhead has a broken nose and concussion. I wanted to keep him in overnight, but he wasn't too keen on that idea. Rude ungrateful pig."

She breathed heavily and went back to sleep. I kissed the back of her head and headed for sleep myself. I was just about there when she mumbled again.

"They won't catch him. Not a chance. That will be your job, my love."

11

SATURDAY, MARCH 17, 2018

Out and about, Jarrajarra, Victoria, Australia.

I woke at 4.30 am, two seconds before my alarm went off. I was still exhausted from yesterday's epic duty, and today was going to be just as bad. Wendy was up and awake and sitting on the bed.

"You going running, soldier?"

I let out a long lazy groan. I managed to half open one eye.

"You will be feeling the guilts all day if you don't."

I didn't respond.

"This hurts me more than it hurts you, Corporal," she said. With that, she stood and ripped the doona off the bed, leaving me stark naked and cold.

"Shit."

"You will thank me later," more laugh than sympathy in her voice.

I opened my eyes, and there she was in her own running gear.

"Come on," she said, "I'll go with you."

I struggled out of bed into my running gear, then stumbled out the door in her wake. We had been running together for twenty minutes before I truly woke up. She had the headlamp, and I had just been dragging along behind. We were running along the bush trail that went behind the town across the River Road and on, towards the river.

"Hang on." I was awake at last. "What are we doing?" I asked.

"Well, I thought we would have a run, finish at the footy ground, do some exercises and maybe check out the weekend warriors."

Her 'weekend warrior' comment was a typical military Officer's snipe at the Victorian Police's Special Operations Group. There was not a lot of mutual respect there.

"I am sure they are very capable and very dangerous to criminals," I said in defence of my colleagues.

"Let's go see."

I followed Wendy for forty minutes, finishing our run at the footy ground to check out the SOG teams and their preparatory actions.

There wasn't any preparatory action going on, not with the SOG teams. They were all still asleep.

We wandered through the campsite, past some police caravans, past about thirty tents.

It was nearly 5.30 A.M., and there was not a peep from any of them.

"That's impressive," said my beautiful girlfriend, clearly unimpressed.

We ran back home. As we passed Rob Farrell's garage, there was a light on inside. We went in.

"Hello," said Rob, "The love birds. Let me guess. You have been down to the War camp. How scary is that lot?"

Rob and Wendy, the ex-Army officers, had a good laugh at that. I maintained some police solidarity and merely chuckled.

Rob made some pretty good coffee, and we sat on the smoker's bench out back of his garage and watched the sun come up. Rob had quit smoking a while ago, but he wasn't going to give up his bench, which was his favourite escape, and mine.

Sitting there in the morning sun, I had to agree with Wendy. She was right again. If I hadn't run, I would have had the guilt trip all day. This way worked for me.

"Thanks for the Joanne thing, Chris."

"What thing?"

"The job."

"Oh yeah, the job. Yes." Barney had clearly found some money and a job that only a young girl could perform, especially one dragged home to Jarrajarra by her parents, worried about her drugged-up mates in Melbourne.

"She will be fantastic," said Wendy. "It's a great idea. The police and the hospital have always needed an extra hand in Community liaison. Isn't that so, Chris?"

"Absolutely," I added as if I had a clue.

"I hope she doesn't embarrass you both," added Rob.

We all sipped some more coffee and soaked up the last bit of the sunrise pink in the sky.

"Rifle range today?" Rob asked.

"If I can get away, yeah. Practice makes perfect." Nan's rules.

"Text me if you get the time, and I will meet you there."

Wendy was leaning back against the wall, coffee in both hands, her eyes closed, just soaking up the sun. I could have sat there, next to her, forever.

Police Station, Jarrajarra, Victoria, Australia.

I made it to work by 7.30 am.

The Sarge and some other leadership types had taken over my office. I could hear the racket as I came through the door. Barney was at the front desk, and I parked myself in the spare chair beside him. It would be a brave man who joined the argument inside my office.

"They have been going at it for twenty minutes," said Barney. "I must say Sergeant Palmer is giving a good account of himself."

The raised voices were coming through the walls loud and clear. I could recognise the voice of Inspector George Murray, the Sarge's regional boss, but I wasn't sure about the third voice.

"There is a Superintendent Hughes from Melbourne in there," said Barney. "The one on the television last night, he really thinks his team have done a wonderful job. Apparently, we are the ones who mucked up."

"He has to be taking the piss."

Barney shook his head. "No, sadly, I don't think he is."

Barney and I sat and listened. I could hear the Sarge loud and clear.

"With all due respect Super, it was my bloke who found the suspect and got him to present himself to your Detectives, and that was done peacefully, with no harm to anyone."

The 'my bloke' Sarge referred to was me.

"Your team have had nothing but cooperation from everyone in the district," added Inspector Murray.

"No! No!" shouted Hughes. "My two detectives had Chalmers wrapped in a ribbon with a bow on top. Guilty as sin with the DNA, ready on a platter for the courts. Apparently, no one in this bloody backwater could manage to keep him cuffed to a chair for five fucking minutes."

"He was in the custody of your team, for God's sake," shouted Sarge right back at Hughes. "He was only arrested after we delivered him. I really can't believe this. In fact, it is you. I can't believe you, Superintendent. In fact, I don't believe even you believe you! Is this some kind of setup?"

The Sarge could shout as well as anyone. The trouble was he was shouting at a guy light years above him in rank. "My Constable put him there with no fuss or bother. Your pair of idiots lost him. Spin it any way you like but don't throw my bloke under the bus."

"You need to be careful how you speak to me, Sergeant."

"You need to get your facts straight, Superintendent. Start speaking the truth. Shouting a lie doesn't make it so. It is what you do that matters." The Sarge was now quoting my Nan. He was also pushing the envelope of appropriate respect for his superior.

The door to my office opened. Hughes emerged and shouted back towards the Sarge and Inspector Murray.

"I will be heading back to Melbourne after we catch this bloody killer of yours, and when I get there, you pair and your fuck-wit constable will be going on report. Enjoy your last days in the police force, gentlemen, and from now on, stay out of my way. All of you."

He slammed my office door and headed for the exit. Then he saw me.

"And who are you?"

"Constable Chris Taylor, Sir."

"Right," he said, "of course you are." Then he walked out.

"What a pig," said Barney.

"They breed them rude in Melbourne Barn."

Barney handed me a bunch of yellow post-it notes.

"Here's your phone-ins Chris. Maybe you should get out of the station and get busy and avoid all this hostility. I will let Sergeant Palmer know where you are." Barney was smiling. He loved the verbal dramas, and he knew I hated it. He would cover for me if necessary.

I looked at the post-it notes in my hand.

"There is one there from Georgie Golino?" That one stood out from the rest of the day-to-day stuff.

"She called here?"

"Yes, she will only speak to you."

I looked at Barney.

"And who are you?" I asked in a poor imitation of Superintendent Hughes.

"Constable Chris Taylor, Sir." Said Barney, sounding more like me than I did myself.

"Right," I said, "of course you are." Then I walked out to attend to my jobs.

I was keen to see what Georgie Golino had to say. The last time we spoke, she had not been friendly at all. I had forgotten about the Melbourne Superintendent already. If he really did file a complaint against Sarge and me, he would lose. The Sarge had spent years fighting against the Taliban. I was confident when push came to shove; he could handle this bloke.

As I walked out of the station, our new employee, Joanne Farrell, was walking in. She had three large takeaway coffees on a cardboard tray in her hand.

"G'day Chris, here's yours." She handed me one of the coffees. I tasted it. It was perfect.

"Thanks, Jo." As her theoretical boss, I was trying to conjure some managerial instructions for her first day.

"I am going to order a new coffee machine," she said. "A proper one. I also started a community funding page for the Police Station and the Hospital facilities. That was Mum's idea. That will pay for the new machine, so don't stress. What's that you got?"

I tried to process all that, and I noticed the last statement was a question.

"Oh, these?" I held up my yellow notes from Barney. "Just my phone-ins. Barney usually puts them on post-it notes for me, he does the paperwork, and I do the police-y bits."

"Great idea. I can do that as well," she said. "I mean the post-its, not the police stuff."

"Terrific," I said. I took another sip of my coffee for lack of anything meaningful to say. It was still perfect.

"Sorry if it is a bit cold. I have been sitting at the back window listening to those three blokes abuse each other."

"Oh," I answered.

"Don't worry. It doesn't put me off the job, not at all. I love the conflict. So passionate."

"Well, it is not like that every day. We usually get on pretty well around here. And don't believe what you might have heard that bloke from Melbourne say. It wasn't like that at all."

"Doesn't matter what I think, Chris. It is a post-truth-fake news world, I reckon. He who shouts first and loudest gets the cherry pie. You should watch out for that one."

Bloody Hell, she hadn't even set foot in the door yet.

"Anyway, see you later, Chrissy, you action your post-its, and Barney and I will find you some more." She headed inside to face her first day with the cops.

She didn't seem to need me at all.

Pizza Shop, Jarrajarra, Victoria, Australia.

"Hi Chris, thank you for coming," said Georgie Golino, friendlier than last time but still dour.

Georgie was at the Pizza Parlour; it was now all fresh paint and clean floors. No signs of a double murder, none at all.

"Where is the rest of the Golino gang?" I asked.

"Well, Sue is at home with the kids, getting them off to school. Joey is at the funeral parlour, still dead, basically." She flashed a half smile. My gosh, black humour.

"OK."

"And I'm here," she continued. "Fixing this place up. For sale, as a matter of fact."

"You wanted to talk to me?"

"Yes, I wanted to ask you for a favour."

Interesting. A favour? Our last meeting had not been that cordial.

"OK, ask away."

"Tell my uncle, Wally Mellish, this place is for sale."

"Why can't you tell him yourself?"

"Family feud, haven't spoken for twenty years."

"I'm the local cop Georgie, not the estate agent. Why not get them to do it?"

"They will want a commission, plus Wally loves you. If you tell him, he might really think about it, and if he actually thinks about it for five minutes, he will do it."

"And, let me guess, you know he just came into some money, and you also know his sons need someone or somewhere to sell their weed."

"Yes. All of that."

Bloody hell, Georgie had it all worked out.

"Is there any reason on earth why I would get involved in your real estate plans?"

"Because I know some things you don't, and if you do just this little thing, then I will tell you what I know."

"Georgie, if you are withholding information, I could arrest you right now and hand you over to the two homicide cops from Melbourne."

"Yes," she said, "You could do that. But you hate arresting people, and even if you did, those two idiot cops from Melbourne won't get anything, and that won't help me sell my shop. This way is better."

Which, in Georgie-speak, meant better for her.

"What if Wally doesn't want to buy the place."

"He will. Eventually, but if he doesn't, I will still tell you what I know anyway. Just ask him."

"How do I know this information you have is worth having?"

"You don't. But it is."

She just stared at me. That was all I was going to get.

I thought about it for two seconds. Curiosity won the day, and I called Wally at the caravan park. I put the phone on speaker. After an epic wait, Wally answered.

"Jarrajarra Caravan Park, Wally speaking." He sounded fully alert and even respectable. The fake tone in his voice suggested I had just woken him up.

"Wally, mate."

"Chris," he croaked. His fine answering technique crumbled when he realised it was me. I would guess from his voice that, last night, he had still been in celebration mode.

"Wally, I am with Georgie Golino right now. I have you on speaker."

"Georgie Golino? My niece Georgie?"

"That's the one."

There was a long pause. A very long pause. I used my intense police interrogation training and did not fill the vacuum. I was starting to question the pause-vacuum technique when Wally finally spoke.

"OK. What's she want?"

This was clearly not going to be any kind of loving family reunion I was negotiating.

"She wants to know if you are interested in buying the Pizza shop."

"And you're with her right now?"

"Yes, Wal, I am."

"Call me back when you're on your own," he said, then he hung up.

I looked at Georgie. "There you go, I asked. Now your turn."

"Grab a chair," she said. "I will make you a coffee."

I took five dollars out of my wallet and put it on the counter.

"I was going to give you this one for free," she said.

"Thanks anyway. I'm happy to pay."

I left the money on the counter and seated myself at one of her tables. She made two coffees and brought them over, and sat opposite. She had pocketed the money, and I hadn't seen her do it. So, there we were.

"Ricky Chalmers and I were having an affair," she said.

Well, that was a surprise.

"For how long?"

"Since we were kids, really, teenagers."

"How often?"

"How often? Jesus, Chris, I don't know, once a week, twice, whenever we could find time, really. Not so often recently."

"Your husband knew about this?"

"Joey? No. He didn't know. No one knew."

"How did you manage that in a town like this?"

"We were very careful, I guess. Picked our time and place."

"Bloody hell. Twenty years and you think no one knew."

"I am certain no one knew."

"Why did you say, 'not so much recently'?"

"Why? I grew up, I guess. Joey worked hard, we had the kids together, I struggled with the whole motherhood thing, and he was such a good dad. Something I never had. The longer Joey and I were parents together. I suppose I appreciated him more. I actually started to like him a lot."

"So, you were trying to end this thing with Rick?"

"The thing?" She laughed. "Yes, I suppose I was trying to end the thing and not lose my family while I did it. Not get Ricky angry, not incite anything, not make anyone angry. So yeah, I was trying to end it."

"Why keep it going after you were married."

She looked at me like I was an idiot.

"Why have an affair?" She practically rolled her eyes. "For sex, Chris. I liked it. He had a fabulous body, and he was like a wind-up battery."

"You're talking about Ricky?"

The look of scorn on her face.

"Of course, I am talking about Ricky. Jesus Christ, he was beautiful, dumb as dog shit in the important things, but that body."

She was on a roll. I kept nodding, hoping she would keep talking. She did.

"I like sex, so does he and I could always turn him on and turn him off like a light switch whenever I pleased. Whenever I had the itch."

The itch? Shit. She stopped; my pause-vacuum had lost its magic.

"OK. So why marry Joey?" I asked.

The scorn factor on her face rose another notch. She had moved to full sneer in confronting my stupidity.

"Money, Chris, money, security, a chance to move up. Why do you think I got married? I wasn't going to be married to a football bum the rest of my life, stuck in this shit hole town."

"Stuck here? Ricky played two seasons for the Swans. You could have moved to Sydney." I felt offended on Ricky's behalf. On the run for murder, and here I was defending his footy career. Surely I had better things to ask. "He was no bum Georgie. He almost made it."

"Almost. Bloody hell." She shook her head. "Men and their games."

She took a sip of her coffee, put the cup down and started tapping the tabletop with one angry finger. Something I had seen somewhere before.

"He came to the caravan park on holiday."

"Joey?" I was struggling to keep up.

"Yes, Joey. We met up one summer. We were both swimming in the river. He was good-looking, not Ricky good-looking, but nice and smooth, and he had plenty of money, and like an idiot, I thought all that money he flashed about was his."

"The money?"

"Yes. The money. I thought he was rich. More fool me. Fucking asshole. He always carried a wad of cash that you could barely get your hand around. All hundreds. Turned out everything he owned belonged to his uncle, including the flash car. I thought I would be moving up into a more glamorous world. I could see myself in Sydney, first nights, red carpets and opera houses. I ended up married to the guy running the pizza parlour in downtown Jarrajarra."

"Sorry, Georgie, I just don't get it. How could you be sleeping with Rick as a teenager, all the way through to your thirties and then just go and marry someone else in the middle?"

She didn't like that. There it was again, flashed across her face, the angry woman she kept under tight control. The finger tapping increased.

"What? You're the morals police now?" She said. "I thought the cops collected the evidence, and the courts decided what to do with it. When did you become the judge?"

She was right. I was judging her. I really didn't like her. There was something uncontrollably self-indulgent about her responses. She didn't go from point A to point B like most people. She could be polite and courteous in one moment, but she had that instant anger that came from nowhere whenever her wants were questioned. She had the self-centred empathy of a two-year-old.

"Typical fucking male. No idea how hard it is for a woman. No money for a decent education, not one person pointing you in the right direction. Grew up with nothing. My so-called father was all over me like a bad rash from the time I had tits. All the men in your life after just one fucking thing."

So-called father? What did that mean? The angry finger tapping was getting angrier. She was looking at me as though I had murdered her husband. Then I saw it. The same face, the same rage, the ever-present willingness to explode.

"You're not Jason Mellish's cousin, are you? You're his sister."

"What's that got to do with anything?" She was bright red with barely controlled fury, just like Jason.

"I am right, aren't I?"

"Yes, as a matter of fact. I am his half-sister. My father is his father. My late auntie May, Wally's wife, was his mum."

"So, Wally knew about this?"

"Eventually, yes. I reckon he found out."

"Hence the family feud?"

"Yes. The family feud. I assume that was part of it all."

"So, your dad and Wally were brothers, and your dad has a baby with Wally's wife?"

"Yes. 'Had-a-baby-with' is a bit of a stretch. I am sure my auntie did most of the work. My Dad would have just involved himself with the early running. He might have even asked permission. He certainly never asked mine."

She clearly had no reason to love her father. Maybe we had something in common after all. Suddenly I wasn't so judgmental.

"So, Jason is about twenty years plus, and the two families haven't spoken for around about twenty years?"

"Yes. That's it in a nutshell. Dad fucks my auntie, and my uncle cracks the shits. Who would have thought?"

I drank the last of my coffee while I let it all sink in. It was all very interesting, a good bit of gossip. Barney would love it, though he probably knew already. But what did any of this have to do with the murders in town?

"So, Small country towns, full of big surprises," I said.

"Yes, a surprise, but that's not what I wanted to tell you."

"Good." There was more. I was glad. So far, it had hardly been worth the mobile call to Wally.

She took out her mobile phone, entered a passcode, then fiddled around a bit with the phone and then finally handed it to me.

"That's the history of my phone calls on the night Joey died. You can check what I tell you against the list of calls and the times they were made."

"OK." This was good.

"I know Ricky didn't do it, and those calls will prove it. Plus, I can tell you where he is most likely hiding right now."

"OK." This was promising.

"Ricky told me he was at the shop before Joey and that other guy were murdered. I know, for a fact, he did get into a fight there with the other bloke."

"Davies?" My Mister X.

"Yes, Davies. Apparently, Ricky beat him up. Pretty badly."

"How do you know this for a fact?" I asked.

"I know because both Ricky and Joey told me."

"Hang on a second. They both told you this. Both of them?"

"Yes, separately, but yes, they both told me the same story basically, just different points of view."

"OK, take me through that?"

"It was after midnight. The store would have been closed. I was expecting Joey home any minute when he called me. He said there had been trouble. According to Joey, this bloke Davies had been there to discuss business, Joey's uncle's type of business. Davies worked for sweet old uncle Michelle Folliero, gangster, murderer, rapist, pig number one."

"Rapist?"

"Yes, rapist. Didn't you know? They didn't mention that in the Royal Commission, did they?"

She stopped for a moment.

"Anyway, according to Joey," she continued, "he and Davies were talking in the front area of the shop. The place was locked, the shop was closed, all of that, then next minute Ricky bursts in and, according to Joey, Ricky and the other bloke just go at it."

"Did Joey tell you why they started fighting?"

"No, he didn't. I have no idea why they fought. Joey just said as soon as they laid eyes on each other, they were both straight into it."

"Did Joey ever tell you anything about Davies?"

"Nope. He was one of those blokes I am not supposed to know about, one of Uncle Mick's henchmen. They come down from time to time to see Joey, have a pizza, sit in the shop till it is closed, do business with Joey and then go."

"What sort of business?"

"I don't know. If they ever showed up while I was there, Joey hustled me out. To be honest, I was usually happy to go. They are all scumbags, and the little I knew of Davies, he was the scariest. Apart from good old uncle Mick of course, who is downright evil."

"Not nice men?"

"No."

"So," I asked, "tell me how you knew Ricky didn't murder your husband?"

"Well, a few minutes after I had spoken to Joey, Ricky came through my back door, all bloodied up and looking for help."

"Ricky came to your house after the fight with Davies?"

"Yes."

"I thought you and Ricky were careful about where you met."

"Yeah, well, this was different."

"OK." I wanted to get this straight. "So, Ricky turns up at your back door a few minutes after you speak to Joey. Exactly how many minutes?"

"Five max."

That was hardly an alibi.

"How do you know he hadn't used that five minutes and already murdered your husband."

"I know Ricky didn't do it, the murder, I mean because while I was talking to Ricky, Joey called me again. You can check the time of the calls on my phone." She pointed at the phone she had handed to me earlier. "You can see the two calls from Joey, and between them, you can see I missed a call from Ricky."

I checked her phone, and there were the calls, just as she said.

"Ricky had called me while I was speaking to Joey, probably looking for help, whatever. Anyway, he didn't get through to me, so he just showed up at my back door."

"All battered and bruised?"

"Yes, and scared. He said he had just been in a fight with a guy he knew from Sydney. The guy was a big-time crook."

"So why come to you? You and Ricky are having a secret affair, and he gets into a fight at your husband's place of business, and then he comes directly to your home. Why?"

She looked at me like I was an idiot. She tried again.

"OK, just forget the affair for a moment. Think of it from Ricky's point of view. He and I have been friends since we were kids. He was hurt. He was on foot. He asked me to drive him back to his farm. He wanted to get his dirt bike and disappear before anyone tracked him down. I assumed he knew something about Joey's uncle and his friends. Maybe he assumed they would be after him."

"Georgie, you realize that these calls could easily be interpreted as a sign that you and Ricky conspired in all this."

"In what?"

"In three murders. Ricky kills your husband and another person at the pizza shop, then heads out to the caravan park and knocks off another victim in cabin 143. In the middle of all this mayhem, he phones you and actually then visits you. Maybe he was just keeping you up to date on the body count."

I could see that last bit hurt.

"Ricky came here, alright? While he was here, Joey called me, and he was still alive and well. It doesn't matter if you believe me or not; a judge will."

She was probably right about the judge. She stood up and left the room. When she returned, she threw a T-shirt into my lap.

"That belongs to Ricky. I gave him a clean one of Joey's before he left."

The T-shirt was covered in blood and ripped past repair.

"OK, he came here," I conceded that much. Doesn't mean they weren't conspirators.

"You should probably put that in a plastic bag, Chris," she said, "it's what real policemen call evidence." She even handed me a plastic bag. I used it as she had suggested.

"So, tell me, Georgie, when the two Melbourne Homicide detectives came here for a friendly chat, you chose not to mention any of this."

"No, I couldn't trust those two cops from Melbourne. Jesus Christ, Joey's uncle owns half the cops in the country and those two are in the wrong half."

"Georgie, all this, the phone calls from the pizza shop to you, the missed call from Ricky to you, the hidden T-shirt, it all makes you look as guilty as hell."

She let out a long sigh of exasperation. But I pushed the point.

"Those Melbourne cops, the ones you don't trust, will paint their own interpretations all over this. They will see it as an obvious conspiracy between an unhappy wife and her lover."

"I didn't murder Joey Chris, and neither did Ricky. I just told you the truth."

Speaking those words almost brought her to tears. Georgie Golino was either telling the truth or was a very good actor.

"OK, tell me about the second call. Why did Joey call you back while Ricky was here?"

"He needed help. Davies was badly hurt. Joey needed to get him somewhere to see a doctor. He could barely move him; he was so big. Joey wanted me to get the Mellish brothers to come and help him."

"Why ask you? Why not call them?"

"It was late at night. I'm the family connection. I don't know why he called me. Maybe I was the easiest number to dial. Maybe I can get the boys to do naughty things they won't do for others."

I could believe that.

"So, what did you do?"

"I didn't do anything. He was in the middle of a sentence, and then he stopped for a moment. Then he told me someone had come to the shop door; he told me to wait while he got rid of them." She paused, back to the verge of tears. "And that was the last words he said to me." She stared at me, just holding herself together.

"So, someone else came through the door of the pizza parlour?"

"Yes."

"Not Ricky?"

"No, Ricky was here with me, swapping T-shirts and begging me to drive him to his farm."

"And Davies was still alive."

"Yes, Joey needed help getting him to a doctor."

"So, who was it at the pizza shop door?"

"I don't know; I don't have a clue."

"Did you hear anything? A voice? Violence? Anything?"

"Nothing, really. I heard Joey shout, 'go away, we're closed', or something like that. Then maybe the sound of someone being struck with something, I don't know." Now she was crying again. "Someone was hitting somebody, maybe, Joey most likely. Then after a few moments, someone hung up the phone at the other end."

"Then what?"

166

"You know what came next. Joey was dead, is what."

"What happened with Ricky?"

"Nothing. I wasn't driving him anywhere in the middle of the night. The kids were asleep, and he looked like someone from a horror movie. I had already told him no before the second phone call from Joey. By the time the second phone call ended, Ricky was heading out the back door."

"So, you just told him no, and then he left."

"I might have said worse, but it was the same message. Probably told him to fuck off out of my house and never come back."

She grabbed a tissue and wiped her nose, wiped her eyes. Composed herself.

"OK, you told me that you know where Ricky was right now."

"I am pretty sure I know where he is. I want you to go there, arrest him and bring him back safely."

While she was talking, she reached out and took back her phone. She fiddled with it for a moment, then handed it back to me. It showed a map with a red pin and GPS coordinates in the centre of the map.

I used her phone myself to send the coordinates to my own phone. Next, I played with the map to see where it was. How far from Jarrajarra? It was south, deep in the Wabba Wilderness Park, a thickly forested mountain range. South from here, and quite a climb.

I could get most of the way in my truck, but the last ten kilometres would be a solid uphill hike along a path called the Mitta Mitta trail. Tough, dense bushland. Uphill all the way.

I wasn't going to discuss with Georgie what I would be doing next.

"What does he have here?" I asked, nodding at the phone map in my hand.

"He has a cabin type of thing he built. We went there together once."

"What do you mean cabin type of thing?"

"It is a sort of underground dugout thing, pretty neat, really. You know how fussy Ricky is with the things he does."

"It sounds like one of the Mellish boys' marijuana-hot houses. Underground and neat?"

"Yeah."

There was a flicker there in her eye.

"Who did he build it for? The Mellish brothers."

Her head jerked in a spontaneous backward motion.

"No, no, God, no!"

"For Joey?"

Her eyes dropped to the floor, and she whispered.

"Yes, for Joey?"

"Why?"

"For his horrible bloody uncle."

She had her head down, looking at the floor. She was back, again, on the verge of tears.

This spot on the map was a ten-kilometre hike from the nearest road, a dugout, invisible from the air. Of course, it had to be for Folliero.

"How often did Joey go there?"

"He only went once with Ricky. They looked it over, unloaded some furniture."

"Was Joey happy with it?"

"Yes, at first. He was trying to impress his uncle with a secret hide-out, Joey the genius, but Uncle Mick told him it was dumb, stupid, too far away, and too hard to get to. After that, Joey lost interest. He told Ricky he could use it however he pleased. I am certain Joey never went back there."

"And you have been there once yourself? With Ricky?"

"Yes, he thought it would be perfect for our little meet-ups."

"But it wasn't."

"Fuck no, it was three hours there and back, in the middle of total fucking nowhere, worse than nowhere. There was no way in hell I could get there on my own. We had to go together on his dirt bike, for god's sake. A fucking dirt bike, Jesus."

"Not how you like to travel?"

"No, definitely not. Not me and not Uncle Fucking Mick."

"So, you couldn't get there under your own steam?"

"No way. Not a chance. Ricky was the only person who could find it. You had to follow a GPS location on a road barely fit for humans, and that's even before you get to the track."

"The track?"

"Yes, the track, the Mitta Mitta trail, it is just a hell ride. I can't begin to describe it. The whole thing was just too much effort. By the time we got there, who wanted to fuck? I needed a cup of tea and a rest. Ricky's freaking love nest, my god."

"Why tell me and not the Homicide cops? They questioned you, and you gave them nothing."

"Jesus, Chris, you are so naive. Those Melbourne cops you are working with are as crooked as hell, and if it suits them, they will kill Ricky and me, and even you, to get what they are after."

"If they are not really here to arrest Ricky, what are they looking for?"

"Michelle Folliero and his money, of course, that's all any of them want. Wake up, Chris. Even the government wants the money. God spare me. You are so fucking thick."

Fucking thick? I had been called worse, I suppose. I actually thought I was doing a pretty good interrogation, what with all the pertinent questions, but apparently not.

"You should be careful," she added, "these people won't hesitate to kill you. If you don't believe anything I say, at least believe that."

For someone who supposedly didn't know anything about her husband's associates, she had some strong opinions on what they might do.

"Georgie, just up and shooting people won't be so easy, now. There are more police around town than there are locals. You can't just go shooting suspects or fellow coppers for a bit of a payday."

"I am not talking about a payday. This is fuck-you money, this is disappear-forever, never-work-another-day-in-your-life kind of money, and Ricky is just a nice little package to wrap up my husband's murder and let them get back to what they really want. If you don't get up there and get him out of harm's way, he will be dead before the weekend is over."

She really was crying now, the tears streaming down her face.

"These homicide police you are talking about, which ones specifically?" Did she mean Detective Pete and Boofhead, or did she include Superintendent Hughes? "Do you mean the first two or this new bloke Hughes?"

"I mean the fat one and the one that just arrived from Melbourne, Hughes. They are both on the take and worse. Just trust me, Chris, Jesus."

"It is all good having me trust you, Georgie, but can you really prove they are corrupt?"

She looked directly at me.

"I don't think I can prove it. I know I can."

Quite the statement. No doubt or uncertainty at all.

"When I know that you have Ricky safe and sound, I will give you all the proof you need to put those two away for a long time."

OK, I could work with that. It would be a nice twist to send Superintendent Hughes off the long jump before he managed to drive the Sarge, and me, off the force. It would be better still to put Constable Boofhead behind bars just for being his natural self. I wasn't so sure either way about Detective Pete. He was a smarmy bastard, but he didn't seem corrupt.

But what if she was right?

"You are telling me that you have hard evidence that will put Snow and Hughes away? Both of them?

"Yes, I have. I guarantee it."

Police yards, Jarrajarra, Victoria, Australia.

"So why trust you with all this, and why now?"

The Sarge was leaning on my truck inspecting my supplies. Ticking off my small pack of food, my weapons, ammunition, cuffs, protective vest, knives, backpack and various weapons.

I had called Sarge and Barney as soon as I left Georgie Golino's place. It was just after 1.00 P.M. We met up at the police yards, out back of the station, where I was loading the police truck for my impending manhunt. I told them everything that Georgie Golino had told me.

I was going after Ricky right now, no delay; the sooner, the better.

I would follow Georgie's GPS coordinates, and if Ricky was where she said he was, I would bring him back safely before the assembled militia found him and started shooting.

I was assuming my target, Jarrajarra's much-loved footy coach, may not be too keen on returning to town to face his various consequences, so I was going prepared. Ricky was not a guy I would enjoy force-marching back to civilization, so I was making sure I had all the tools.

For the Sarge and I, ex-army, feet-on-the-ground soldiers, packing our kit was second nature, to both of us. He was double-checking everything I placed in the truck. His silence told me he approved of my choices.

"Why does she tell you, and why now?" he said.

"I don't know, Sarge." I had no idea why Georgie had burdened me with the rescue of her former lover. "Why not? Maybe she needs someone she trusts to keep her and the kids safe through all this. Maybe Ricky is her choice."

"He won't be much protection if he is in jail." The boss wasn't convinced.

"If the judge believes Georgie, then he won't be in jail for long."

"You could be right," said Barney. "I can't recall a time when Georgie didn't have some devoted male following her around like a puppy." Barney knew her better than any of us. "If the judge is a heterosexual male, Georgie and Ricky will be free as birds."

I did a final check of my phone to ensure the GPS markers were safely stored. They were. I was almost ready to go.

"What about these Melbourne cops?" The Sarge was as puzzled as I was. "Could that be true? They are here just chasing the Folliero money?"

"Maybe," I answered.

"Or else," interrupted Barney.

The Sarge and I both looked at him. Barney did not usually offer his policing opinions in the presence of most real coppers. He usually just presented them to me, knowing that most members of the force preferred civilian administrators to stay in their lanes. But the Sarge was not like most.

"Or what?" we both asked.

"Well," said Barney, "they say, historically, that sometimes the bigger crimes occur in the cover-up."

"A cover-up?" Both Sarge and I were puzzled.

"Yes, a cover-up," Barney continued. "Maybe what we are seeing now, the weird behaviour of these police from Melbourne, the urgency to blame Ricky Chalmers for everything, their desire to push the local police away from the investigation. Maybe they aren't really trying to solve our murders. Maybe they are trying to cover up their own crimes. Something that happened somewhere else. Maybe they were scared that Folliero might spill something to the Royal Commission about them. Maybe they are going around killing anyone who could send them to jail. Maybe they are our murderers. Maybe they are after this evidence that Georgie has."

"Jesus Christ." I could see from Sarge's face that Barney's idea had landed. "My goodness Barney," said the Sarge. "It could be anything. They may have been involved in Rogers' murder eight years ago or something trivial like taking money to kill a parking fine."

"Who knows what," added Barney, "I doubt they would be murdering people over a parking fine, but what does it matter? If there is evidence they did anything for Folliero, their careers are over."

"If it involves taking Folliero's money, they will end up in jail, Barney," said Sarge.

I looked at my two friends and colleagues. Barney was positively glowing with the exchange of 'crime-solving' ideas with a real cop other than me. The Sarge was equally impressed by Barney. They were think-tanking.

I felt almost jealous. I was Barney's favourite policeman, surely. Now I had to share. Three murders and my life had changed forever.

"OK," I joined in. I couldn't leave all the hypothesising to the boss and Barney. "So, three of Folliero's henchmen are dead in Jarrajarra, so where is Folliero?"

That stumped them.

"Well," I continued, "I don't trust any of them out there with guns chasing our footy coach."

"Yes, indeed, Chris." The Sarge was on my page. "Let's you and me get this boy Ricky Chalmers back safely, out of harm's way, and then we go see what Mrs Golino has to show on our fellow policemen."

I was not so keen on the 'you-and-me' bit.

"Boss, I don't need backup on this. In fact, I will be better without it. This is straight in and straight out there and back to the red dot. It's a total of twenty kilometres on foot. Not saying you couldn't do it, just thinking about the speed factor." This job was right in my lane. The Boss was somewhere around sixty years old. I didn't want to be rude, but he would slow me down.

"It's not your decision, Chris. I will drive with you till you leave the road and go bush. You can do all the footwork while I coordinate what we need from there. We need to make young Chalmers safe, and then, you and I and Barney can make war on these crooked cops."

Barney's chest nearly exploded with pride at being included.

All I heard was 'make war'. Sarge was back in the army, and that, it appeared, was that. The Sarge would drive me to the end of the road, and from there, I would go and collect Ricky Chalmers. That could work.

There was just one more thing I was waiting for.

As if on cue, Rob Farrell's truck drove into the yard. He pulled up parallel to my own truck. He was out of his truck in a moment, carrying his Steyr Scout. It may not have been the best rifle in the world, but it was unquestionably the best weapon in Jarrajarra on this day. He opened my truck door and set his precious rifle inside behind the driver's seat.

"Barney, Sarge," said Rob with a nod. "Show me your kit, mate," was all he said to me.

We went to the back of my truck and opened my kit.

"Too much food Chris," he said with authority as he ripped out over half of the calories I had packed. "You need five thousand calories there and back; five thousand max. Eat it on your way in the truck. If you need more in the bush, shoot a rabbit."

"Should I take a gas cooker?"

"Funny man, eat it raw."

He kept looking over my kit.

"Your water is good."

"Thank you."

Finally, he nodded in what might have been approval, then went back to the cabin of his truck. He returned with seven magazines for the Steyr.

"Right, there is none in the gun, and there are 20 rounds in each magazine. They are 308 Winchesters if anyone should ask you what you shot them with."

Rob wasn't taking prisoners, apparently.

"So, mate, load up the gun when you are ready." Rob continued. "I don't need to tell you to double-check everything I just told you."

Rob was back to being an army officer and loving every minute. I put one magazine in the truck next to the rifle. While I was at it, I also checked that the rifle was empty and safety on. I packed the other magazines in my kit. With the added rifle and the extra ammunition, my pack was now pushing 30 kilograms, which was heavy for a twenty-kilometre sprint. Rob looked at me, reading my mind.

"Fun times, hey. Would love to be coming with you."

Sarge did not like that idea.

"We appreciate the weapons, Rob, but I can't allow you to participate in a police matter."

"No, no, I understand, absolutely, coppers only." There was a glint in Rob's eye. His blood was pumping. He winked at me over the top of the Sarge's head. God help the rogue coppers if they were crazy enough to shoot at me with Rob Farrell at my back.

All was in order; departure time was at hand. I took the two body Armor vests from the back of my truck and handed one to the Sarge. We put them on, and we were set to go.

The Sarge chose to drive, so I took the passenger seat.

Sleep while you can, they always said. Was that something I heard in the army or something I read in a Jack Reacher book?

I wasn't sure, but at a time like this, old Jack was good enough for me.

With the Sarge's careful driving, I was asleep in five minutes.

Jarrajarra to Mitta Mitta Region, Victoria, Australia.

"You awake, Chris?"

"Yes."

"Did you hear that?"

"Yes."

We were thirty minutes into our drive to find Ricky Chalmers. My boss, the Sarge, had been letting me snooze while he drove. Apparently, he also adhered to the rule of sleep when you can. I had been woken by the sound of motorbikes coming up behind us. Big ones.

I woke quickly and re-arranged myself to check the side rear vision mirror. There was nothing visible, but the sound was getting louder as the bikes got closer.

This was not a major highway. It was barely a road. In one sense, it was a road to nowhere, two hours dead straight to some of the highest and thickest bush in the country. The road was mostly used by the few farmers that ran cattle in the region. It was not the place you would expect to encounter a Saturday afternoon motorbike run. No place for a joy ride.

I checked the road ahead. There were a few side tracks into the bush. I pointed toward the next on the left.

"Maybe sneak up there, Sarge, and we check them as they go by."

"Good idea, son."

The Sarge turned sharply onto the side track. He drove hard and fast along the rough ground till we reached a point that was invisible from the road. Over the last few meters, the bush had been snapping closed behind us as we pushed past. By the time we stopped, our side track had shrunk to little more than a meter wide path.

I grabbed the rifle, exited the car and headed back to the road. I found a spot under some bushes where I could see the road without being seen. The Sarge crept up beside me, and we waited together as the sound of the bikes got louder. Closer.

I positioned the rifle and focused on the road.

"It's like army days, Sarge."

"Not quite, Chris. Technically speaking, we don't have an enemy, and you can't just go shooting at people passing by."

"Not even if I perceive a threat."

"Not funny, son."

I focused on the road, and after a minute, the bikes appeared. They were flying.

We watched as they went by. Within a moment of their appearance, we both began counting guns and rifles. You couldn't miss them; the riders had made no attempt to hide their weapons. They looked like the team from hell in some apocalyptic bikie movie.

They passed quickly, disappearing around a bend further down the road.

"Holy fuck," I said.

"What did you see?" asked the Sarge.

"Five bikes, the middle three had AK-47s, either over their shoulders or sticking out of their side bags, the leader had some sort of machine pistol stuck in the ass crack of his trousers."

"What about the guy in the rear," said Sarge, "he had some weird thing with a hook."

"That hook," I said, "was a fold-over shoulder brace for a SPAS 12 shotgun."

"Oh, my goodness."

"No goodness involved, Sarge. That is one evil weapon. Costs a fortune unless you stole it. Never fired one myself, but if they are chasing Ricky Chalmers with that arsenal, well, I don't think they are planning to bring him home peacefully."

"They are going to kill him?"

"That would be my guess."

"Oh, dear."

"Sarge, the guy with the shotgun, did you notice his leather gear."

"I noticed none of them was wearing club patches. They were either hiding their patches or were not part of any gang we knew."

"Yes, but the front four clearly ride together, the bikes, the tattered leathers. My guess is they are a team. Shotgun-guy is an add-on. His whole gear is new, the helmet, the jacket, the lot."

"So?" The Sarge was not getting my point.

"His leathers, they all fit, which for a fat bastard means it is all his and all relatively new. So, I am guessing he isn't part of that crew."

"Oh," said Sarge. "So, he is extra?"

"Yes, extra, and not the man in charge either. Otherwise, he would be in the lead."

"Where do they get the nerve to be riding a public road so obviously armed to the teeth? Banned weapons clearly visible."

"I don't know, boss."

The Sarge was right. You never saw that in Australia, ever. Quite apart from being against the law, it was guaranteed to win you some serious police attention.

"I guess they either know that every cop in the area is heading in the other direction."

"Or else," added Sarge, "they know we are out here on the road, and they don't really care. Maybe they are looking for more than just Ricky. Maybe they are after us as well."

"How would they even know we are here?"

That made me stop and think, how, indeed?

"What if that guy at the rear was our fat Detective from Melbourne."

"Detective Snow?"

"Yes, Boofhead himself."

"He's the right shape."

At this point, my phone vibrated in my pocket. I answered.

"Hey, Barney."

"Oh, Chris, oh God." Barney stopped talking. He had broken down in tears.

"Barney mate, what is it?"

"Oh, Chris, Georgie Golino," Barney was sobbing. "Georgie is dead."

There was an old saying that my Nan loved - Everyone has a plan till they get punched in the face. I had just taken that punch. For a moment, I just stopped. I could barely think. I handed the phone to the Sarge.

"Barney, this is Sergeant Palmer. Can you repeat that, please?"

The Sarge tapped the phone to put it on speaker. We both

listened. Barney made an effort to regain his composure, then continued.

"Sir, Sergeant Palmer, Georgie Golino is dead. She was just found a short while ago by her sister Sue. Sue called the ambos, Jack Farrell and Jody Taggart. They got her to the hospital, but she died pretty much on arrival."

"What do you know?"

"I just spoke to Jack at the hospital," Barney was bravely speaking through tears, holding it together as best he could. "According to him, the cause could be heart failure or loss of blood. Mainly, he said, she had been beaten to death."

"Sweet Jesus."

"The task force has moved off North in pursuit of Ricky, but Detective Sergeant Jordan called to let you know that he was at the scene and taking charge of the investigation."

Detective Pete is at the scene. I had a thousand thoughts and not a good word to say.

"Thank you, Barney," said Sarge. He thought for a moment. "Stay off the air for a while. If we need you, we will call you."

I waved a hand at the Sarge, asking for the phone.

"One second, Barney, Chris wants a word."

"Barney."

"Yes, Chris?"

"Call Rob Farrell, tell him where we are headed and tell him we have a situation developing," I said quickly.

"OK."

I ended the call. I knew Barney and Rob would work out what to do. I also knew the Sarge was not impressed.

"Chris, listen, you can't be inviting civilians to participate."

He stopped talking. I was already on my way to the car. I took over the driver's seat without asking. The Sarge was still fastening his seat belt when I took off, fast. He may well have assumed I had stopped listening.

The Sarge grabbed the satellite phone, not the police radio and not his mobile. I was travelling fast on a mountain road; it would not be easy making calls. He was hanging onto the overhead strap with one hand and thumb dialling the sat-phone with the other. It looked difficult, and he grumbled a few times, not enough to make me slow down.

Somehow he managed. He found the person he wanted.

"Will!" he shouted over the sound of my truck. "We have a situation here, son." Will Walker, I guessed. Sarge's number one right-hand man from Wodonga Station. "I need you to get yourself and some of the lads to the Car Park at the southern tip of the Mitta Mitta trail. It is on the map. Ninety minutes south of Jarrajarra."

He listened while Will talked. It took a moment.

"Six officers in two cars and a van would be wonderful," he was still shouting."

He listened some more.

"Come armed. Do not alert any members of the Chalmers task force. I repeat, do not alert anyone involved in hunting Chalmers."

More talk from Will, more listening from Sarge.

"Yes, yes, come armed and ready. Need to know only and only our guys."

A brief pause.

"Yes, Will, get there as soon as you can, son, as soon as you possibly can."

I headed in the direction of Mitta Mitta and Ricky Chalmers.

There was nothing I could do for Georgie Golino, but if those bikies were involved and intended to do the same to Ricky, I was about to bring some serious opposition to their plans.

The Sarge stopped talking about Rob Farrell. He knew there were no police in Jarrajarra. Rob was our best close back up. The Wodonga cops were a further hour away.

"What speed are you doing?" Sarge asked.

"Around 130 kilometres an hour. That's as fast as this thing will go."

"Alright, alright," he tapped away on his phone, grabbing the strap whenever the truck bounced too hard. "OK, say they are doing around 130 on those bikes, I would say, so we are going to arrive around fifteen minutes behind them."

I didn't answer. I was going to get there as soon as I could and do what I had to do; the timing was irrelevant.

"We get to the car park at the start of the Mitta Mitta track," said Sarge. "Once you are on the trail, you have to cover another ten kilometres to get to Ricky. Now, if the track lets them use their bikes while you are on foot, then that gives them a further advantage."

"Sarge," I said, "you're overthinking it." His voice was distracting me. I was pushing the truck as hard as it would go on a road that was barely fit for traffic. "We are behind them. How far? How late? Doesn't matter. They are going down."

Enough talk.

"Sorry, son, I can't help myself," he sighed. He was worried. I knew there would be one more platitude. "It is what it is, I guess."

I didn't answer. He put his phone away and grabbed the hand strap above his head.

I was flying. As much as you can in a truck.

After a while, the Sarge spoke again, "Chris, is your body camera turned on?"

"No."

"Better turn it on. If that was a dirty cop with those bikers, this could get ugly."

I turned my body camera on, and the Sarge did the same.

"Bikers and crooked cops, what next?" The Sarge was mumbling now, angry.

In the next hour, we never saw or heard the bikes again. They were too fast. We had not anticipated that this would ever be a race. It had been my plan to find Ricky, catch him off guard and arrest him. Now it was a chase to save his life, a chase for which my police truck was hopelessly inadequate. But it was all we had.

I didn't need to think this through. I just needed to get there before they killed him. I had the weapons. I had the training, and I knew where they were going.

The black mist had descended upon me. If those bikers, or any crooked cops, stood between me, and Ricky, they would be standing in a world of pain.

The time passed in focused silence.

We were approaching our planned parking point. The start of the Mitta Mitta track.

The Sarge spoke. "If these bikies are involved, they would possibly leave a lookout."

"Probably." If I were them, I would definitely leave a lookout.

We had driven south from Jarrajarra for 90 minutes. Then, at the last section, we turned west toward our destination.

The car park was ahead of us. It wasn't so much a parking area as simply the end of the road. The bitumen road ended, then widened to about two-and-a-half car widths of gravel and weeds. It stretched like that for another 300 meters, then thinned out into what I presumed was the track into the wilderness.

I slowed down at the park entrance. As we crawled forward, I saw the back wheels of three motorbikes partially hidden in the bush, about one hundred meters ahead. They had been parked nose-in, facing the bracken that bordered parts of the car park, a lazy attempt at concealment, or maybe just sloppy parking.

I was thinking, the boss was thinking.

Too much thinking.

A single gunshot hit the truck, exploding the rear window and the windscreen.

The shattering glass told us the shot had come from behind.

There was a second shot, but it missed altogether.

I hit the accelerator hard and pointed the car to the far end of the small gravel-based car park.

"Go!" Shouted Sarge. It wasn't necessary. I was already going, charging forward as fast as I could. My foot pressed hard to the floor of the truck.

Another burst, this time semi-auto fire. Another hit on the truck. A third single shot.

There were two shooters in action. Lucky for me, neither of them in full auto.

"Jesus H Christ." The Sarge was blaspheming full volume. "Go! Go!"

I was, but it was hard to outrun a bullet in a clapped-out Holden

Colorado.

I'd recognised the clunky metal sound of an AK-47 at the sound of the automatic fire. Not a good memory. The barrel noise was like a solid metal hammer on a hollow steel pole. Add to that the dull, ugly thud of the strikes on my much-loved Colorado, which was now being shot to the shit.

Glass was smashing all around, burst by bullets and ricochets. The flying glass cut my face and hands.

Their first effort had been in single-shot mode. If the shooter was aiming at me, the driver, he had missed by a lot.

The second shooter was using semi-auto, firing in short bursts of three or four. I hadn't heard that evil unfriendly noise since Afghanistan. It wasn't a sound you forget.

We charged forward and away. I took the slight curve in the parking area. Trying to put some distance and trees between our truck and the shooters.

I caught a flash of the three mud-covered Harleys parked ahead, to the side, almost but not quite in the bushes to our right.

These must belong to our new friends. Fuck them and their precious choppers. Give them something to think about.

I hit the first bike, and the truck went airborne. Then my driver-side front wheel landed perfectly on the guts of the second bike. There was an ugly metallic screech as we dragged the first bike into the body of the second and over it into the third. Then my back wheel hit. It bounced and dragged over the pile of metal and wheels for a few more meters of metallic screaming.

The Sarge had dived under cover of the car's back wall, his head practically in my lap.

"I'm OK," he shouted. "Keep going"

His face was bleeding, but he wasn't complaining, still active. Probably glass cuts.

I was leaning over the Sarge, keeping low, with just enough vision to keep going forward and not hit a tree.

I was running out of driving space. The path ahead of us narrowed quickly. The thin bush path was lined, either side, with scrub, bracken and large thick grey-skinned ghost gums. Hitting one of them at speed would be like ramming a concrete wall, about as much fun as getting shot by the idiots chasing us.

Both shooters were now shooting in short bursts of semi-auto. More short, loud bursts slammed the back of the truck and the window behind me. The Sarge let out a scream of pain. Was he hit? I couldn't tell.

Three bikes. Two shooters?

Shit! Where was the other guy? Shit, shit, were they herding us like sheep into the firing line of the third biker? How could I be that stupid?

In my fractured side mirror, I caught a glimpse of the bikers behind us. They had broken cover and were chasing us on foot down the centre of the car park.

There were three of them. Fuck.

I wasn't so stupid after all. They were.

Three fucking machine guns. But totally exposed, I had seen two of them firing. The third was running but not firing, at least not when I looked.

I caught another glimpse.

They were in the centre of the car park. Running at us. They were either drugged out, suicidal or stupid. Or all three. I would settle for just stupid.

They were obliterating the back of my truck.

I was now lying across the seat on top of the Sarge. Thankfully, we were still moving forward, away and fast.

Driving.

Steering with one hand on the base of the steering wheel. My foot jammed hard on the accelerator. It was a weird angle, but it was working.

Driving blind and fast, buried in a wafer-thin cone of safety, below the window line of the truck.

Glass, bullets, deafening sound, everywhere.

Still, the clatter of the two guns. One shot, then semi-auto bursts, then singles.

I was trying to judge the centre of the track.

Tree branches, outside the shattered side windows, flying by.

Getting closer on both sides.

The track was rough as hell, like driving on a trampoline.

Sarge grunted in pain at every bump. He was bleeding every-where from his wounds.

With the bikers behind us, we had four layers of steel as protec-tion. The back of the truck, the back wall of the cabin, and then there was my tool cabinet screwed in tight in the tray against the outside of the cabin. Custom-fit to the width of the truck. Those four layers of steel, plus the tools within, would protect us unless these fuck-heads had a missile launcher. I worked on the assumption they didn't.

We had to keep down, keep moving.

While they were shooting from behind, we were safe. If we stayed in the truck and they got to our side, we would be dead.

I was still charging forward as hard as the truck would go, but we were running out of room.

The path ahead was not meant for motorcars, and it was getting very narrow.

The sound of tree branches bashing against the truck wall roared at us from both sides. The last thing I wanted was to be jammed between two of the giant gums lining the path.

We would be trapped in the truck and as good as dead.

I could see by the trees above us our track was disappearing fast.

Our hostiles were still chasing and still firing. The last few bursts had missed. Small mercies.

My forward options were gone. There was no more room for the truck.

We crashed hard and loud into the trunk of a thinner sapling. A wattle tree, thank Christ. The tree trunk snapped, and a large burst of steam exploded from the engine of my poor, battered truck.

The Sarge screamed in pain from the collision. His face and shirt were now drenched in blood. This was more than glass cuts.

Did the shooting just stop?

They may have emptied their magazine, or was I just miracle shopping?

Maybe they thought we were already dead.

It was no time for playing possum. They would be beside us in moments to finish the job.

We had to move.

I revved the accelerator, but the truck was stuck fast on the busted trunk of the wattle tree. The engine sputtered, sighed and stalled.

Steam and muck spewed from the engine, into the air above and over our cabin.

I kicked open my door.

I slid out of the driver's side of the truck and rolled to the safety of a nearby gum tree. It was a good four meters wide at the base.

Our opposition was about seventy meters away, still walking towards us, side by side, like actors in a cowboy western.

They hadn't fired at all as I had hustled to the safety of the giant gum. For a moment, they still didn't fire. I could hear them walking toward our position.

I could hear the crunch of their boots on the gravel.

I could hear the heavy struggled breathing of the Sarge in the wrecked cabin of the truck.

The Steyr was in the truck, under the Sarge.

They were too far for my pistol.

They walked, fully exposed, surrounded by miles of cover. A "face-me-like-a-man" type of walk. Movie star heroic; real-world stupid.

I stayed behind the tree.

They were not showing much respect for our skills.

"Keep walking," I prayed, and they did.

They were close enough that I could hear the crunch of their feet on the gravel Getting closer.

A small win for me. Very small.

Then they resumed firing. I guess they had been changing magazines simultaneously. If so, they really were stupid, terminally stupid.

They were also firing in full auto. In tandem. Destroying my truck and shredding the base of the tree. The leaden clack-clack of the AK-47s was loud and getting louder.

Terrifying if the noise was what scared you.

I wasn't scared of the noise; it was telling me they were getting closer.

Closer.

I was definitely scared of 'Closer'.

I could see the Sarge hunkered down, as small a target as he could be. He had his pistol in his hand, but he had few options amongst the flying glass and metal.

"Stay down, Sarge," I shouted. Probably didn't need to say that. Both the Sarge and I were as down as we could get.

I was practically buried in the dirt behind the tree.

Waiting.

The machine rifles continued screaming their approach.

Still waiting.

I would not be waiting long. I knew something our biker cowboys clearly didn't. The more they sprayed fully automatic mayhem across my poor truck and my big innocent gum tree, the more certain I became they didn't know what I knew.

On a twenty-cartridge AK-47 firing on full auto, you had about 4 seconds of fun. With a 40-capacity magazine, you could double that shooting time to eight seconds max. I figured our opponents were getting close to a full ten seconds' worth of violence. Firing in tandem. Exhausting their magazines together, in synch, like a boy band on a violent mission. Equipped but not so capable.

Then there was a pause. The shooting stopped. Either they were empty, or I had gone deaf in the sound of their attack.

I knew I wasn't deaf.

The Sarge looked at me from the floor of the truck.

I winked at him. Why the fuck not? They had used their turn and wasted it.

I came out from behind the tree, my pistol in my hand, my bog-standard, police issue .40 calibre Smith and Wesson semi-automatic pistol. The very same weapon I had been practising with daily for the last few days and for years before that.

I had a full magazine of fifteen cartridges.

My heart was pumping so fast I could hear it. Someone was screaming like a mad, raging bull. It could have been me.

I was not ready to die just yet. Especially not at the hands of these fucking morons.

My new friends from the bikie gang were now about 50 meters away and fumbling to remove the empty magazines from their guns.

I took a shot at the man in the middle. He was the fattest, the biggest target and, being in the middle, a near miss on either side might score a lucky hit. Who knew?

I knew I was too far away, but I was fully loaded and advancing and thought getting a taste of return fire might fuck up their concentration.

I had the right line, but I was way short.

I kept walking forward. Walking fast.

Middle-guy wrestled the magazine out of his gun and dropped it to the ground.

I kept walking forward.

He took another mag from a denim bag he had slung across his shoulder. With all his shooting, the bag had swung around and was hanging awkwardly over his fat gut near his knees.

I realised a moment before he did that he had grabbed the mag upside down.

The Right-hand guy had extracted his own used magazine and had dropped it on the ground, out of the way. He was now waiting for middle-guy to make the ammunition bag available.

I couldn't believe it.

The guy in the middle was carrying everybody else's ammo.

Three guns, one bag.

That ruled out drugged-up and arrogant as their excuse. These guys were just simply fucking stupid.

I took another shot. It was short again, A few feet short this time but in perfect line with middle-guy. He was still my number one.

My second shot unsettled him. He dropped his fresh mag in fright. Now they were all out of ammo.

I kept walking forward.

The middleman bent and picked up his dropped magazine. The shoulder bag hanging around his knees made it an ugly move, but now he had his bullets.

Mister Left and Mister Right were still waiting for Mister Middle to sort himself out.

I kept walking forward.

Middle-guy pushed his mag into his rifle.

I was now about 25 meters away.

Time was up, boys.

I fired again. I had the right line yet again, and this time, I had the perfect length. I hit Middleman in the stomach, dead centre. The impact sat him on his fat arse. He landed with a thud, dropping his rifle in the process.

I kept walking forward, watching him carefully. He was still sitting up. He was shocked, maybe processing his predicament. Maybe oblivious. I could see the blood oozing from the small hole in his stomach.

I could imagine a bigger hole in his back.

Middle-guy was reaching for his AK-47.

The guy on the right beat him to it; mister-right had dropped his own empty weapon and reached over his fallen friend to grab the loaded rifle. He lifted it towards his shoulder to aim.

I was fifteen meters. I fired again and hit him.

Stomach, dead centre. I was close enough to hear the wind burst out of him like a solid vicious punch to the gut. Only this punch went all the way through.

He dropped the rifle and then folded to his knees.

The guy on the left just stood there, his unfired weapon useless in his hands. Up close, he was just a kid. Physically he was the mirror of his mate on the right. Lefty had huge steroid-pumped shoulders but a puppy face. Probably nineteen, twenty at best. He was open mouth, stationary, speechless, useless in this fight. He just stared, helpless, at his guy on the right. They could have been brothers.

Right-guy was still functioning, deep in shock. He still hadn't registered that his perfect gym-toned body had been fatally penetrated by a nine-millimetre bullet.

He grabbed for the rifle again. One hand tried to cover the hole in his stomach. The other hand struggled to lift the rifle into his lap. He might have been trying to keep up the assault. He might have been ready to talk. He might have just wanted to use the rifle as a crutch, maybe, to get to his feet.

I'd never know.

At that moment, with the weapon now in his hand, his head exploded into a fine mist of brain and bone and blood. He fell back to the ground.

Dead.

His knees folded awkwardly. The AK-47 was laying across his lap.

Lights out. Permanent.

Did I hear the shot that killed him?

Yes. It was the Steyr. It had to be Sarge.

I focused on Mister Lefty.

"Drop your weapon!" I screamed. He dropped it.

"Face down on the ground!" Down he went.

"Hands behind your head," and that was what he did.

I was on a perfect roll of command and response.

Mister Left was much better at being arrested than he was at fighting. I guessed he had been arrested before. He knew the drill better than me.

I had never actually said "Drop your weapon" out loud to a real person, not since I left police training college.

In the army, if someone had a weapon and was not on my team, I would either shoot them or hide or do both. There wasn't much cross-team negotiation in Afghanistan when the war guns were out.

I cuffed Mister Left. Extra tight, hands behind him. I zip-tied his feet just to be extra careful and a little nasty. He was now out of the game and going nowhere.

Mister Right was as dead as he could be.

Mister Middle guy had now collapsed onto his back and was staring at the sky. He was struggling for breath. Blood was bubbling from the hole in his gut. A separate, larger puddle of blood was pooling on the ground beneath him.

He was also coughing up copious amounts of blood, not a good sign. He wasn't far behind his mate. I guessed he would be dead before I could arrange any meaningful help.

I grabbed the three rifles. With the first two, I took out the ammunition magazines and threw the rifles into the bush. I took the third rifle, the one that had started in the middle and been taken by Mister Right. I knew it worked. I had seen it trying to kill me.

I put the spare magazines into the mag bag that was looped over the shoulder of the fading Mister Middle. The bag itself was now saturated with his blood.

I cut the bag free and placed it beside me.

Better safe than sorry, I rolled the dying Mister Middle onto his side and zip-tied his hands and feet.

He hardly made a sound. Beyond pain already. "Circling the drain" was a thought that came to mind. Alive or dead, he was now secure.

I grabbed the bag of ammunition and the loaded AK-47. I left the three bikers and sprinted back to the Sarge.

He had lowered the Steyr rifle and slumped to the ground. Landing in a sitting position, leaning against the truck.

I checked him out. His face, neck, hands and shirt were totally covered in blood.

I couldn't see bullet wounds, just a ton of glass cuts and blood everywhere.

"Good work Chris, good work son. Bloody hell, that was amazing. Holy Jesus. What possessed you."

"Them or us, Sarge?"

"Better them, I think."

He sounded strong. By luck or good management, he was still wearing his unbroken spectacles. His eyes looked un-scarred. I helped him find a comfortable position against the truck. He winced in pain as I moved him. He pointed to his shoulder.

"There's something sticking under my shoulder."

I looked at where he was pointing.

I felt around the shoulder and under his arm. There was a piece of metal sticking out through the arm hole of his protective vest. Stuck fast.

I gently turned him, just a fraction, to check it out. Holy Jesus, it was ugly. The Sarge groaned with the pain.

Metal, like a badly made knife, jammed under his shoulder. It wasn't his armpit, thank God. A lot of blood flows through the armpit. Damn, I wished Wendy was here.

The metal looked to be a piece of the support strut from the back window of the vehicle. It had somehow been blasted to pieces by the shooters and embedded itself in the Sarge, in the far right of his shoulder muscle. It must have flown through the arm hole of his protective vest.

"Oh God," he groaned. "It hurts like buggery. Get it out."

I looked at the surviving metal strut. Amazingly, it was still in place in my otherwise-demolished rear window. I compared it to the broken strut sticking out of the Sarge. It was hard to tell how deep the broken piece was embedded. I guessed about three inches, hopefully less.

From his grunts of pain and the location of the wound, I guessed he had cut a tendon. They hurt like hell. I hoped that was all he had damaged.

Would he bleed to death if I pulled it out? I couldn't tell.

"Get it out, Chris. For God's sake, just get it out."

I wasn't a medic; I cared about his pain. Still, he was the boss, so that's what I did. Except, it wouldn't come out. It was wet, bloody and stuck tight.

Fuck. I suspected it was stuck in the bone.

I tried again and failed.

"Holy Jesus," He screamed in agony.

I dried my hands on my trousers and tried again, tighter grip this time. It came out after a second hard tug, and the Sarge let out a loud yelp of pain. That was followed by a long, deep sigh.

I removed his vest and cut off the underarm of his shirt sleeve. I was terrified I would find blood gushing from the wound. I watched and waited. It was bleeding, but there was no torrent. Thank God.

I quickly retrieved my first aid kit and smothered his wound in Betadine. That made him shout again.

"Holy mother of God. Bloody hell."

Then I bandaged him as best I could over the blood and ointment. I tied it all in place with a stretch bandage wrapped around his body and shoulder.

I watched the wound carefully. The bleeding was not too bad. He seemed to be in reasonable shape. It was a remarkable effort to make the shot on the biker with this wounded wing.

"Jesus, Sarge, you are one tough old bastard."

"Chris, please. Bad language and the Lord's name in one sentence. Do you mind?"

I think he was joking.

"Get me the Satellite phone," he said, back in boss mode. "I am going to make some calls. You need to load up and get going."

I dug out the sat phone from the wreckage of the truck. It was unscathed; I handed it over. I also found a tarpaulin and camping blanket in my tool bin in the back of the truck. I threw them both over the Sarge. We were in the mountains, it could get cold, and he wouldn't be moving till help arrived. He would need the warmth.

I took the Steyr rifle and checked its load. It was ready to go. I checked my pistol. It was ready. I stripped everything from my backpack except ammunition and water. I was packed.

I put the bikers' shoulder bag of magazines beside the Sarge. I intended to take the Steyr.

I held up the loaded AK-47 and showed it to him.

"Have you fired one of these before, boss?"

"While ago now, son."

"Do you remember how?"

"Yeah, yeah, give it here and get going."

I lay the dead bikie's rifle across the Sarge's lap. It occurred to me that the next person to visit the car park here might not be so friendly.

"Sarge, maybe we should move you into some sort of cover."

"Be buggered with that. I am not moving. You get going."

"Listen, Boss. You are too exposed sitting here. I might not be the next person who comes back along that track. It could be our bikie mates."

"Well, Christopher," he looked at me as he drew a pained breath, "you just better make sure that doesn't happen."

We held that moment of eye contact. I could see the stubborn old bugger was not going to be moved.

"Listen," he said, "just get my pistol out for me, thanks?"

I could see the pistol was a better option if the next person in the car park was hostile. With his bung arm, a quick draw with the rifle would be out of the question. I took the pistol from his holster, checked the safety was off and laid it in his lap.

"It's ready to go."

I stood back and checked him out. He was as comfortable as I could make him. For a wounded man, he was armed to the teeth. He had the sat phone out and was dialling.

"You're not going to lose consciousness? Not feeling faint?" I had to ask. His look of scorn told me he was good.

"I'll manage," he said. "You need to stop worrying about me and get after your mate." The old bugger was indestructible.

I strapped on my backpack, clipped my pistol into my holster, and clipped my hunting knife to my belt. I picked up the Steyr rifle in one hand and the small screen GPS strapped to my wrist.

I had my destination on the screen and the path in my head.

Locked and loaded.

I did a quick check of our trio of dead and captured bikies. They weren't moving. I jogged over to check Mister Lefty. He was belly down where I left him. He had turned his face to the side, away from the other two, who were now both dead.

"You shot my brother."

"I did, mate." Softly. "Sorry about that."

I checked my body cam was working. The light was on, all good. We were recording.

"Is he OK?" The biker asked, Still weeping.

"Your brother? He's stable, I guess. Should be an ambulance along soon," I said. "They will take a look at him." None of which was a lie. He couldn't be more stable, really.

"Listen, mate," I said, "you are in police custody now, so you need to remember you are not obliged to say anything unless you want to, but whatever you say may be used in evidence. Do you understand?"

"Yeah, yeah," he said. The young biker wanted to talk.

"You can wait till you speak to a lawyer before you say anything if you want."

"Fuck lawyers," he said. I had him on record. This arrest was going seamlessly, apart from the two mangled bodies lying beside him.

"They said this would be a piece of piss," he said through his tears. "Be some fun."

"Not my idea of fun, mate, shooting at people." It seemed like we were pals now after our little gunfight, just like sparring at the boxing gym. You punch on with some young bloke, and then, afterwards, you chat like old buddies.

"How come you didn't shoot while you could?" I asked.

"I tried to, but it wasn't working. I tried to tell them, but they weren't listening. Too busy shooting themselves."

"Had you fired one before?"

"No."

This was some top-line hit team we had taken out here.

"Where are the other two?" I changed the subject.

"They've gone to get that bloke, some footballer."

"I know the footballer. Who are your bikie mates?" I kept it conversational.

"Not my mates," he answered. "Gerry's buddies."

"Gerry's your brother?"

"Yeah."

"Who are they? The other two."

He was in shock; I don't think he realised I was questioning him. We were just two blokes chatting among a puddle of blood and a pile of bodies. Absolutely normal.

"One was Butch Davies; his brother got murdered up here last week."

Davies, that name, I was chasing the brother of my Mister X, Allan Jarred Davies. Oh, dear.

Welcome to my town, guys.

Mister Left was still talking.

"The other one is some fat pig cop cunt. Don't know his name."

Fat pig cop cunt, very good ad-hoc description of my very own Detective Constable Boofhead.

"Interesting," I said as I tightened the straps on my backpack. "Well mate, you just wait here, and some more officers and an ambulance should be along shortly. They will get you sorted."

I jogged over for a last check on the Sarge. He was as good as I would get him. I gave him a salute. He waved back, all OK. I turned toward the trail and started running.

Ready or not, here I come.

Mitta Mitta Trail, Victoria, Australia.

Running.

The Mitta Mitta trail was slick and wet, cut to ribbons by years of deer invasion and the chaotic wheel prints of two very recent motorbikes. At ground level, I could see muddy and broken shapes of bike trails fractured from one side of the track to the other.

The random profiles where the bike wheels had gripped and moved forward were joined by long, erratic smears of wet shining mud where the wheels had slid sideways and back. The bike riders had come to this part of their journey badly equipped. The road bikes were struggling, not meant for the slick bush trail.

The local deer weren't helping the bikies. They had destroyed this trail, and it was now a soft, squelching, deer-ravaged nightmare.

I was probably faster on foot than the men ahead of me were on their bikes.

From the little I had seen, none of them were runners.

From their choice of vehicle and their erratic tracks, I could see they were not much as trail riders either.

The insane rage I felt when Barney told me about Georgie's death had calmed for now. I was in action; I was moving, and I had seen enough to know these bikies were my enemy. An enemy, someone to target and destroy.

Running easily.

This particular enemy did not know it, but they were already three men down.

My blood rage had given way to process, I was in a battle, and I had been in plenty. I was adrenaline-fuelled, my backpack felt weightless, and my only concern was the ache in my gut that I would be too late to save my friend Ricky.

I blocked out the flash thought of Ricky Chalmers lying dead and alone in his weird mountain hideaway.

Visualise a victory. Visualise the fifth bikie in the store-bought leathers. Our very own Detective Constable Snow, Detective "Boofhead".

Payback would be good.

I kept running. It was uphill but not so steep.

The ground was wet and muddy but manageable. I was surely gaining on them.

I hadn't heard the sound of motorbikes since they left us behind on the Mitta Mitta Road. I hadn't seen a bike since I left the bush car park.

Nothing. No sounds of engines, no shooting, Just the bush and me.

Fifty minutes into my rescue run, I stopped to check my position and take a drink.

The wheel tracks told me they had got this far on their bikes. That was either a remarkable testament to their biking skills, or else they just refused to walk.

The GPS told me I should leave the trail and cut west.

The Sarge and I had driven nearly 150 kilometres south, then southwest, from Jarrajarra. Then, after the gun battle in the car park, I ran a further nine kilometres north.

The GPS points that Georgie Golino had given me were now due west of my position, but if I headed west now, there was no trail to speak of. Nothing but thick, dense, hard Aussie bush.

If Ricky had made himself a permanent hideout here in the rolling depths of the forest, he would surely have made himself some sort of track from the trail to his squat. If such a track existed, I hadn't seen any evidence of it.

I checked the elevations on the GPS.

I was currently on a ridge, and the track ahead of me stayed on that ridge, curving around in a northwest circle. The ground to my west was all gullies and rises filled with very forbidding bush and scrub. Anything other than the ridge I stood upon looked impassable.

My contour map suggested there was a fork in the ridge about a kilometre ahead of my current position. One part of the ridge broke south toward Ricky's hideout, and the other part broke west, away from Ricky.

If I followed the track another kilometre uphill, then I would be at the fork in the ridge and above the hideout. There would still be one kilometre of bush to negotiate to my target. If I was going to make a track for myself, then that is where I would start.

If I were Ricky, my track would be running downhill, where the bush and scrub would be thick enough to hide the track from above. Theoretically, I could bike to such a point the first time and then carve myself a secret path. After that, I could just bike in and out as I pleased.

Finding the secret path was the tricky bit. The fork in the ridge seemed the best option.

I still hadn't heard any shooting, nor had I seen any evidence of the bikers themselves.

Would it be too much to hope they had lost themselves in the bush and I could sneak Ricky out of their clutches without being discovered? Worry about them later.

I decided to go further along the track and try to find Ricky's secret track if it existed.

Less than two hundred meters into my search, I saw a glimpse of chrome through the bush ahead of me. I stopped, quickly checked my weapon status then double-checked my surroundings for signs of ambush.

Nothing.

I crept slowly forward, keeping to the outer edge of the path. I was ready for anything, sight or sound, anything.

Further metallic glimpses confirmed I had found the bikie parking point.

Two bikes.

I stopped and listened.

Nothing.

Crept closer. Still nothing.

Just the sound of the bush. Birds, crickets, wind.

I was alone. Still trailing. Still running last in the hunt for Ricky.

My two remaining opponents had pushed on ahead. There was no one waiting in ambush to shoot me. Not here, at least.

I took a breath and stretched for just a moment. A wave of fatigue swept over me, this had been a long day, and there was a long way to go if I was to get home safely.

I was looking at the two Harleys and thinking about the bikers.

Why park here? Why, suddenly, decide to go by foot from this point? Did they look at their map and decide this was the place to start cutting a path? Just go due west, straight through the bush.

There were gum trees every few meters.

Between the gums were tall skinny wattles.

Ground level was dense with thick shrubbery, a metre or so high.

Between the standing greenery, there was fallen bark, broken limbs, wombat holes and water erosion. This was not impassable terrain, but extremely difficult. There was no level ground. Try to run, and you could step in a hole and break a leg.

This was a dumb choice, almost as dumb as their choice of bikes.

But you don't have to be smart to shoot someone. Even getting wounded this far from home would, most likely, be a death sentence.

This was not a contest to lose.

If these two guys got past me, they would no doubt head back down the trail the way they came. Getting back downhill would be a lot easier than getting up. If they got back to the car park before help arrived, it would be bad news for the Sarge.

I took my knife and cut the fuel lines on both of the motorbikes. The petrol drained out of the tanks, over the engines and onto the ground.

Whatever happened next, these last two blokes would not be going home on their Harleys.

Another fifty meters on, and I found the freshly hacked path taken by Detective Boofhead and his mate.

I could see their footprints. Heading west. There were several deep gullies between them and Ricky. I couldn't guess how long it would take them to cover the last kilometre. I hoped it would take an hour.

I kept going north. If the ridge idea worked, I could still beat them there.

Within five minutes of hard running, I found the fork in the ridge. There was no obvious track South towards the GPS points I had been given. No path, nothing.

The bush along the southern ridge was overgrown with bracken. It was forbidding but not impassable.

I tried the ridge anyway. I walked south. The bracken was about a meter tall and thick enough that I couldn't see the ground. I tread very carefully.

I stumbled in a few holes. Nothing too dangerous at walking speed.

Fifty meters in, I found what I was looking for. A track had been carved into the bush. I'd headed south on the rounded crest of the ridge. Right there, before me, in the mud, I could see the recent tracks of a trail bike. This had to be Ricky.

The downhill run towards the GPS location was easy. I was going to be there soon.

I thought I was going to get there first. I was thinking about how to approach Ricky. Would he just see a cop and then start running? Would he see me as a friend there to help him?

Thinking how to get him to come back with me before Boofhead and his biker buddy arrived and started shooting?

I was thinking all of that while focusing on running, not tripping, not stepping in a hole, not breaking an ankle.

Then I heard it. That old familiar song.

Gunfire.

Due South.

I had lost the race to Ricky Chalmers.

I could hear the clack-clack of an AK-47 and the punching sound of the shotgun, maybe two hundred yards ahead.

The trouble with fighting in bush this thick was that being in sight of my opponents put me in range of both their weapons. I knew the shotgun was good for fifty meters, maybe even one hundred. Pistols were good for twenty if you knew what you were doing. How close would I need to be to see these shooters?

I would find out soon enough.

I kept low and hustled toward the gunfire. Toward the action. Not really heroic, just years of solid training backed with years of practical application in the army.

I crawled the last thirty meters through the thick bracken that surrounded the path.

Felt the whoosh of bullets passing overhead.

Surely they hadn't seen me. I stopped, lay flat, poked my head onto the path and took a very quick ground-level peek ahead.

There was a clearing ahead of me. I couldn't see any buildings or structures but through a gap in the scrub, I could see two shooters. They were firing back in my direction.

But they weren't firing at me, not specifically, just in my general direction.

Ricky's hideout must be underground. I guessed they were firing at his front door.

They were in the solid cover of some large gum trees. Hiding behind trees that were meters thick. Good old, very old, Aussie hardwood.

Here was me, in the approximate line of fire, hiding in the grass. A truly shit position. I'd need a cannon and a tree of my own.

I compromised and found a tree, a big one. I would have to make do without a cannon.

Please, God, Ricky had something solid to hide behind.

The two shooters were laying it down thick and fast.

I saw another gum tree on higher ground, away from the line of fire. I crawled over to it. It was better for me but not so good for my opposition. They still hadn't seen me.

Time to get involved.

I had the Steyr rifle, and I was above them. A good start.

Detective Boofhead was partially covered by his own personal gum tree. Firing single-round bursts from his shotgun.

The biker had an MK-47. He was firing towards my left, towards what? If there was a door to Ricky's hideout, I couldn't see it. Was it a door or just a hole in the ground? I couldn't tell.

Whatever it was, door, hole or cavern, it appeared to me that my opposition had concluded that Ricky was behind it.

All the shooting was in one direction. There was no response from Ricky. None that I could see. Maybe he did not have a gun.

Maybe he was already dead.

The biker must have felt immune and, like his friends in the car park, he had, quite suddenly, stepped out of cover, advancing in the direction he was firing.

Confident or careless?

These blokes all seemed to think the machine gun made them indestructible.

I did the ritual welcome. Pointing the Steyr rifle at the biker, in a moment between gun bursts, I shouted, "Police. Drop your weapon!"

He didn't drop the weapon. Of course, he didn't. I didn't expect him to. He turned and fired at me. He missed.

I shot him in the chest, and he went down.

Another man with a wrong plan.

The instant the biker fell, Detective Boofhead fired a shot in my direction and then withdrew.

His shot shattered bark and chunks of a tree beside me. Something hit my face. Nothing serious, but he'd used the moment to hide behind his personal tree and bury himself in the bracken that surrounded it. Invisible.

I waited. I could see the biker on the ground where he fell. He was still alive, barely.

Silence.

Like a good sniper, I waited to see what care and attention the rogue cop might offer his companion. Precious little, as it turned out.

I waited.

The biker had fallen on his side, facing me. Forty meters from me. He was sucking for air.

Some movement in the thick bracken that surrounded Boofhead's gum tree.

A single gunshot. Holy fuck.

The biker's head exploded.

From somewhere within his bracken-covered lair, Detective Boofhead had shot his partner in the head.

This was the second exploding head I had seen today.

Jesus Christ.

Movement in the bracken. Detective Boof was scurrying away. I could track him from the movement of the bushes that surrounded him. He was like an elephant crawling through long grass, dreaming he was invisible.

I fired several rounds into his general vicinity.

He could die as far as I was concerned. A dead Boofhead would make it easier to tend to Ricky if Ricky was still alive. I could make up a story later. I kept firing at a line just below Boofhead's trembling bracken ferns.

"Aaaargh," a scream from the long scrub. "Stop! Stop! Ceasefire! Oh god, oh god! Stop shooting, please."

After a week of treating me and my town like pieces of shit, he was appealing to my better nature.

"Please stop," he was crying. "I am a policeman. I am a policeman." Whimpering.

"Throw your weapon out!" I shouted.

"I can't. I can't. I've been shot. I can't do it."

"Try!"

I had crept closer, keeping in cover, I could hear him, but I couldn't see him. I had his general position. I was sure he couldn't see me.

I heard him fiddle about in his bush hide then I heard a loud pig-like grunt.

I saw a police-issue Glock fly out from the bracken into the clearing near the dead biker.

"And the shotgun."

"I haven't got it." I could hear the pain in his voice. "It's by the tree. It's empty."

"What else have you got?"

"Nothing, for fuck's sake, I'm unarmed. I need help. You shot me. Bloody hell, I am a policeman."

I crept toward the safe side of the gum tree he had been using as cover. My fellow policeman was still pitching.

"Just get me to a hospital. I will tell them you didn't know I was an officer. I know you didn't mean to shoot me."

I was pretty sure I did mean it but keep talking.

I made it to the relative safety of the huge gum tree.

Whatever this pair had been shooting at was now behind me. It would be a perfect irony if Ricky Chalmers was to now emerge from his hideout, guns blazing, and shoot me in the back. I really hoped Ricky did not have a weapon at this point.

I peeked around the tree base, and there was the shotgun. I grabbed it and checked it. It was indeed empty. Bloody hell.

This was not an elite hit team. They had surrendered a numerical advantage and a weapon advantage with hardly any resistance. I doubt this victory would end up on my CV.

I dismantled the shotgun just to take it out of the game.

I listened.

Detective Constable Leo Snow, "Boofhead" to his friends, was wheezing in the bushes about 20 meters away. He certainly sounded as if he was in pain. With the grunting and groaning, he couldn't be that good an actor.

"It's OK, mate. I am unarmed. You're safe."

I was his 'mate' now. These were the most polite words I had heard from his mouth all week.

To be safe, I circled around him, moving carefully and very quietly through the low scrub until I could see him.

I was behind him. I could see him through the thick hedge of bracken stalks.

He was on his back, head lifted from the ground, facing toward the tree I had just left.

Surprise.

He was holding a pistol in a two-handed grip, pointed at the bush, waiting for me to emerge. He had lied to me; he did have another weapon.

Who would have thought?

Unfortunately for him, I was emerging from the wrong direction.

I crept forward silently to within arm's length. He was either deaf or the pain had blocked his ears, or maybe I was just that fucking good.

I moved my Steyr rifle till the tip of the barrel touched the back of his head.

"Throw that gun to the side, very slowly, please," I whispered.

He did exactly that. Very slowly.

"Just put your hands on your head. Thank you."

He did that as well. Very compliant.

As he placed his hands on his head, I eased back, out of his reach, and then stood.

"Roll over on your face."

"I can't move. I've been shot," he whimpered.

I could see a puddle of blood beneath his fat bum. It looked to me like I had hit him in one butt cheek, and it exploded out the other, maybe smashing his hip bone on the way through. The exit wound was pumping blood onto the ground beneath him. It looked extremely painful.

"Roll over on your face," I said more firmly.

"I can't. Fuck it, you fucking shot me."

I stepped around beside him, still pointing the rifle at his head, over his leather biker gear. He was now wearing the same style of protective vest as me, the word "Police" emblazoned on his chest. What a disgrace.

We made eye contact for the first time since I had arrived.

"Fuck," he said. "You, the local plod. You are fucked for this, shooting a superior officer."

"Superior? Really?"

I kicked him hard in the ribs. He convulsed, his knees went up from the pain, and I used his movement to push him over onto his stomach. Hard.

He screamed one long agonised shout of pain.

"There you go," I added in casual insult. "Easy-peasy."

He was bleeding badly from the exit wound; he would be lucky to make it down the mountain.

I took two zip locks and, very roughly, cuffed his hands and feet. Tight. Skin cutting tight. Fuck him.

"Fuck you. You're dead. You're fucked. I'm a policeman, you fuck."

Whimpering, angry, face down and zip tied in the mud. Suddenly he was a tough guy again.

"Bit late for big talk, Detective."

I lifted my knee off his back and stood.

I was beyond exhausted. If these clowns had reinforcements on the way, I was about ready to surrender.

A sudden burst of fatigue just rolled over me.

I walked over to the gum tree Boofhead had been hiding behind just minutes ago. I sat down and just breathed slowly. Just a moment's calm.

I could see from my position a wooden door frame built into a low earthen mound. This was what they had been shooting at.

An entrance.

To what?

It was about thirty meters away. I checked my GPS one last time. I was bang on the spot Georgie Golino had given me. Ricky's hideaway.

What was beyond the doorway? A tunnel.

I could hear the crooked cop whining in pain behind me. Not a sound from the doorway before me.

I was so tired, but this was no time to sleep.

I stood, disarmed my rifle and lay it up against the tree. I took out my pistol and walked toward the mystery door.

Please, God, no more surprises. I was nearly dead on my feet.

Pistol in hand, ready for action.

"Ricky, are you in there?"

No response.

I sprinted to the edge of the doorway. I hid at the edge of the frame. I would be invisible to someone inside looking out.

"Ricky, it's me, Chris!"

Nothing.

I took my phone and turned on the flashlight app and the camera app. I set it to video and hit record. I held the edge of the phone around the frame of the door. A makeshift spy cam. Adequate.

I waved it around, up and down, side to side, trying to keep my hand and head outside the frame.

I withdrew the camera, hit stop, and then hit replay.

It was hardly cinema standard, but within my shaky, jerking video, I could make about a dozen steps down to a dirt floor. There at the bottom of the steps, was what looked like a human leg. It wasn't moving, and it was hard to tell if it was still attached.

Oh, dear. Oh, Ricky.

I went down the stairs quickly, using the phone flashlight. Found a light switch. As I flicked the switch, a generator kicked in, and the lights came on. It was an underground bunker, done in Ricky's typical fastidious fashion.

It looked amazing, unbelievable, really. There at the bottom of the steps, lay Ricky Chalmers himself. He was shot. It looked like shotgun pellet wounds to his face and sides.

He was unconscious.

He was still breathing, raspy, strained, but breathing.

Thank God for small mercies.

He had been hit down the right side. There was a range of wounds. I lifted his blood-wet sticky shirt. The pellet wounds looked deep enough to do some damage. Not good, bloody, but no significant bleeding. No gushing blood spurts that I could find.

I checked the other side of his shirt. No through wounds.

The wounds to his face were also pellet-like wounds, not deep, maybe a ricochet. His eyes looked intact, thank God.

His eyes fluttered and opened. He looked at me. "Chris, mate? What the fuck?"

"Ricky, mate, what happened here?" I asked as I checked his wounds.

"That fat pig cop shot me," he groaned.

"So it seems" there was nothing I could do for Ricky here.

"The prick," grunted Ricky.

"Forget him. He's done. We need to get you to a hospital."

"Chris, mate, I'm fucked."

"No, you're not. Just hang on. I'll get you down the hill."

"I don't think I can make it."

"Listen, the footy season starts in two weeks. It's too bloody late to find a new coach."

He was fading out. Eyes rolling back, I slapped his face, not too hard.

"Ricky, where is your trail bike? The trail bike?"

"He opened his eyes and looked at me, then turned his head and looked to the far corner of his underground bunker. There it was, a farm-built modified trail bike. Leaning against a chest of drawers. On the wall above was some religious artwork, hanging over that was a large crucifix on a chain. This place really was built for Joey Golino. I knew Ricky did not have a religious bone in his body, excluding Aussie rules football.

The bike was an old Honda but with a dozen, Ricky-style home improvements. They looked like they had been welded on to assist in carrying heavy material up the mountain. Most importantly, the bike had an extended driver seat. Room for two. Perfect.

His eyes shot open, half-conscious.

"Chris, don't leave me here."

"No mate, no man left behind, not today."

The thought of leaving him never occurred to me. I was more concerned about how I could achieve this.

I was already exhausted.

It was too far to carry him over my shoulder. Theoretically, I could take him down the hill on the dirt bike, but how the hell was I going to keep him on board while I drove?

How to turn the thought into action?

There was a large hiker-style backpack in the corner near the bike. Maybe I could hoist Ricky onto my back using the cut-down backpack.

I attacked the backpack with my knife and cut the shoulder straps free from the front of the pack, leaving just the straps, the back, and the base of the pack in one piece.

It looked like it could work.

The backpack now looked like a giant, crude baby carrier, but for a grown man weighing over one hundred kilograms.

I could keep him attached to me while I rode the bike using the cut-down backpack. Daunting but possible. Stupid but possible.

Barely possible, mostly stupid.

I would need a belt big enough for two men to hold us all

together. I could think of two belts, not being used, just outside the bunker.

First things first, I wheeled the trail bike up the stairs, out of the bunker, and parked it by the door.

I ran over to Boofhead, still where I had left him. Barely conscious. I rolled him on his side and undid his belt. He grunted in pain with every movement, but he was all out of trash talk. I put a foot on his ample belly and ripped his belt out of its loops.

I went over to the dead biker and did the same. The end result, two very long, thick leather belts.

I had my plan and my materials. Now it was just a matter of doing.

I took the belts and went back into the bunker to Ricky. With the stripped-down backpack and the two leather belts at hand, I knelt beside him.

I joined the two belts into a single long belt.

Next, I slid the backpack under Ricky as though he were wearing it himself, but with the shoulder straps very loose. I had the base of the pack around about his bum level.

"Ricky, mate, this next bit is going to hurt. I am going to get you to your feet, and then I need you to try and stay standing as long as you can."

He didn't answer. I hoped he heard me. His eyes fluttered open. That was something.

I grabbed him by the front of his shirt and hoisted him to his feet. He barely made a sound beyond a small moan.

Miraculously he stayed standing, pain all over his face.

I stepped into the shoulder straps. I now had the means to carry him on my back, but I had to make sure he stayed there.

I took my belt contraption and wrapped it around us both high on my chest, just under armpit level. I then tied it as tight as I could bear.

Once again, Ricky let out a low moan as I tightened the belt.

I stood as tall as I could manage and lent forward. Ricky stayed in place. It was like piggybacking a grown man, but with no help at all from the passenger. It might work, but, God-in-heaven, it would be hard going.

I walked us both up the stairs. Ricky's arms flopped down towards the ground; his head just lolled about like a drunk.

Step by heavy step, I made it up the steps and out of the bunker.

This was ridiculous.

I couldn't even stretch for a breath once I made it outside. If I stood up straight, I would fall over backward. So, I remained bent at the waist and waddled myself and Ricky, my human tortoiseshell, over to the dirt bike.

With great difficulty, I managed to get both of us straddled in place, and seated on the bike.

That was a lot easier for me, seated like this. I didn't have to carry him, I only had to balance him.

Ricky was still conscious. The pain was probably keeping him awake. His ragged breathing at my shoulder was the only audible hint he gave of the pain he was feeling.

The quicker I could get this done, the better it would be for both of us.

The bike started on the first kick. I expected nothing less from a machine owned by Ricky Chalmers.

Bit of throttle, and away we went. Slowly. So very slowly.

Away from the clearing, back the way I had come. The first kilometre would be uphill along Ricky's secret path. We slipped, we slid backwards, we stopped and started again, over and over. Mostly, we moved forward. It was slower than my entry on foot, but we were moving.

Small victories.

When we finally made it to the bush barrier between the secret track and the main Mitta Mitta track, I decided to just keep going, hoping I might just push through the bracken.

Bad decision.

The bracken ferns were so thick I couldn't see the ground.

Five meters in, we hit a wombat hole and over we went. Strapped together, we hit the ground hard.

Ricky cried out in pain; I cried out in anger.

I had no option but to unhook from Ricky. Put the bike upright and walk it through the fifty meters of ferns.

I went back to Ricky. We re-hitched using my ridiculous backpack and the long-joined leather belts.

Then I had to turtle walk Ricky, up the hill, through the bracken, back to the trail and the waiting bike.

Bloody hell, it was hard going.

I was travelling on fumes. Utterly exhausted. My inner demon suggested if Ricky were to do the right thing and die, I could lie down right there and have a sleep.

Inner demons are not your friend.

Strapped together, we trudged up the hill, through the ferns, to our modified Honda bush bike chariot.

I couldn't tell who was grunting loudest. Was it me or Ricky?

He breathed, grunted and spoke.

Not so much spoke as laughed and groaned.

"Chris Taylor, you are a serious fucking idiot."

"I have been told this before."

We made our way to the bike. We did the stupid straddle manoeuvre into the seat. Ready to go.

Like a loyal steed, the bike clicked into action with no complaint. We were off again, downhill this time. Surely this would be easier.

Of course, it wasn't. Who would have imagined?

Down we went, Ricky belted to me like a nearly-dead weight. The bike wanting to slip away down the hill. My arms aching from controlling the speed while keeping the two of us upright. Both of us wanting to drift away and just sleep. Sleep would be good for me, but maybe not so much for Ricky.

We kept at it. What else could we do?

Glorious notions of carrying him over my shoulder for the last nine kilometres never entered my head. I had carried men before over rough terrain, and it is near impossible to make it one hundred yards, let alone a single kilometre. It is why they invented stretchers. It is why medics usually work in pairs.

No medics here, no stretchers. No help from my passenger. We laboured on.

The time dragged by in the agony of total exhaustion. I didn't know the trail, so I had no idea how far we had come or how far we had to go.

"I have come too far to only get this far," my Nan used to say. We had no option but to keep going.

Then we crashed again. The worst crash of the lot.

I don't know what happened. I was concentrating on staying upright and moving forward. Not watching the right bit of ground, maybe looking right when I should look left. Maybe it was just fatigue-induced brain fog.

I hit something not sure what. A tree stump, another hole in the ground, who knew? The bike jerked as though it had been punched. Whatever it was, it was enough to throw us off. We landed harder this time, much harder. I hit the ground face first, copping the full weight of Ricky landing on top of me.

"Oh God," I groaned. Every muscle ached. I might have broken my nose, lucky I hadn't broken my neck. I unhooked the belt and removed the shoulder straps and stood up to take one selfish, lazy, indulgent breath. Just for me. Free of Ricky's awkward weight for just one second.

I looked at the trail ahead and wondered how in hell I was going to make one more yard, let alone make it the rest of the way back to the car park.

Should I go and get help and come back for Ricky? It didn't feel right. I was scared he might die if I left him. Plus, my mind was mushing under the strain of fatigue. I looked at my GPS and tried to calculate how much further I had to make it to the car park.

My brain refused to do the math, let alone work the buttons on the screen.

No man left behind, I had said. Easily said, not so easily done. Too late to change now.

I set the bike up on its wheels. I knelt beside Ricky and gently turned him over onto his back. Making sure my carrying contraption was still in place.

Then we did it all over again. The hoist, the belt, the bike straddle. I can't say our technique was improving. Start the engine, and off we go.

I had no idea how far we had left to go. No idea how much longer I could keep going.

Painful ages passed, and then I turned a corner in the trail.

A lengthy stretch of maybe one hundred meters of straight, gradual decline, and there I saw a miracle. My own personal miracle.

My own Wendy Acheson, here in this dark and desperate bush. Running hard up the hill toward me.

I stopped.

I wasn't sure if I believed what I saw.

It was getting dark. She was running with a headlamp switched on. I couldn't see her eyes through the light, but I knew that run.

I stared. I prayed she was real and not some mirage from my exhausted mind.

She was real, all right. Absolutely real. Running toward me, and there, beneath the light of the headlamp, her smile.

And there behind my very own army nurse, the dynamic duo, Jarrajarra's very own ambos Jack Farrell and Jody Taggart, back-packed, kitted out and carrying a stretcher.

Finally taking up the rear, struggling with the pace of the three trained runners, was Rob Farrell, ex-soldier, loyal friend and a man who had been in a firefight or two.

Further behind him a cop I didn't know, or did I? Yes, I did know him, one of the younger brigade from Wodonga, one of the Sarge's boys.

Thank God.

Help at last, thank God Almighty, help at last. More than that, the very best help that the universe could send.

I was done for, finished, spent, kaput, all-over red rover.

Ricky and I collapsed one last time, off the bike, onto the ground.

A controlled descent this time, landing nicely, side by side on a cushion of bracken ferns.

I slipped off the backpack harness and stood to greet our rescuers. Well, 'standing' was the plan. I half stood and then thought better of it and sat down next to Ricky. I checked him out. He was still breathing. That was a plus. He would be in better hands in a moment.

Then they were beside me. Wendy came to me, and Jack and Jody went to Ricky.

Rob Farrell and the Wodonga cop just stood there. There was no one to shoot at, so they were suddenly redundant.

Wendy greeted me as though I had been away for a month.

I didn't complain. We hugged and kissed. Then she set to checking me out.

"Any more bad guys we need to worry about?" Rob asked.

"No, mate. Bad guys all down."

"How is it down at the car park?" I asked.

Rob shook his head. "There is some serious carnage back there," he said, nodding toward the car park.

"Sarge?"

"He should be OK, I think," answered Jody.

"Some hospital time," said Wendy. "But let's look at you."

Wendy removed my vest and shirt and then started cleaning my back.

"Chris, you have cuts all over your shoulders and through your hair." She said.

"Glass, I would reckon."

I could hear them working on Ricky.

"How's Ricky?"

"Not sure," said Jack, almost a whisper. That was a worry.

"Don't think he will be coaching for a while yet," answered Jody.

I lay down on my front while Wendy tended my back.

"I love you, Soldier," she whispered.

That was the last thing I remembered for a while. Wendy and her team of medics did their thing quietly and efficiently while I drifted away into a limbo of half-sleep and total fatigue.

"Roll over, Corporal," Wendy whispered to me through the fog. She was in officer mode, giving orders. I loved it. I rolled over. I noticed my arms were back in my shirt sleeves. I was dressed and wearing my protective vest again. How did that happen? I drifted off again. Not sure how long.

. . .

"Come on, Chris," Wendy said. "Let's go." She was helping me to my feet. "You are a bit of a mess, my darling."

"Just tired," I said.

"No, you have glass cuts everywhere and maybe some shotgun pellets in the mix around here." She pointed to my chin.

I touched the spot and felt cuts and bruises.

"That must have come from Detective Boofhead," I said. "I thought he missed."

"Just as well," she said as she pushed me to walk.

The others had already gone.

"Where are the others?" Ricky Chalmers, Rob, Jack, Jody and the extra cop had vanished.

"We stabilised Ricky while you slept, we put him on the stretcher, and I sent then down the hill. I let you sleep a bit more. You need rest more than anything."

"How far are we from the car park?"

"About a kilometre and a bit."

"Bloody hell, we made it nearly nine kilometres."

"You did," she laughed. "Stubborn bugger."

She handed me a pack of soft sugar lollies, snakes and gummy bears, pure sugar. Some water. I practically inhaled the food and drink. So hungry.

Down the hill we walked, hand in hand. It was, for the fifteen minutes we took, like a Sunday stroll in the bush with my beautiful girlfriend. Not a care in the world.

I think we were both so happy and relieved I had survived two shootouts in one day that we just forgot everything else for a few moments.

Then we arrived at the car park, and that was one hell of a scene.

Like Rob Farrell had said.

Carnage.

Mitta Mitta Car Park, Victoria, Australia.

"I better get back to work," said Wendy. She left my side and hurried over to a pair of ambulances.

First thing I noticed on my return to the car park was some serious support.

Three police cars, a police van, a fire truck and two ambulances. The police, medicos and emergency services were all in attendance.

I recognised the cops; they were from Wodonga station. That was good. Like the young cop on the trail, these were the Sarge's team. People I knew and trusted. More importantly, the Sarge trusted them. Good news after a week of dealing with dirty cops.

Whichever way you looked at it, I had a bit to answer for. There were two dead bikers here in the car park. Up at the dugout, there was another dead biker plus one crooked cop knocking on heaven's door when I left him. He may even be dead by now. I was so tired I didn't look forward to dealing with the pain-in-the-arse Inspector Hughes without some backup.

These cops all knew me, they would get me through the rest of the day. I would have to account for today's events to someone, but, hopefully, not right now.

Best of all I saw Greg Farrell, with his brother Rob, now standing over by the fire truck. I am sure if any big city cop gave me a hard time the Farrell brothers might sort them out on my behalf. A crooked cop would need more than his badge and uniform here and now.

We were a long way from civilisation.

Greg nodded in my direction, glad to see me alive among all this mayhem.

The medical team were busy.

The second of the two ambulances had clearly just arrived. The lights were still flashing, still telling the world they were here. The flashing lights switched to off as I approached.

Through the open rear doors of the first ambulance, I could see Jack Farrell and Jody Taggert attending to Ricky Chalmers. They were busy, efficient and focused. Whatever his condition may be, Ricky was in good hands.

The atmosphere amongst the various teams was sombre, dark, solemn. Heads down, focused and busy, no idle chit chat. Eyes on what you were doing, not wandering. No one looking at the centre of the tableau; the altar piece. A tribute to the unspeakable violence of the day.

Two dead men lying in a bloody pool, in the middle of the car park.

The two dead bikers. Dead as could be. Destroyed. Once human now nothing. No one else was looking at them. I couldn't look away, me, the perpetrator.

Their bodies lay as I had left them.

The one who had been on the right, now on his back, arms and legs flung about, his head half missing.

The one who had been in the middle still face down and zip tied, as I had left him, tied in case he tried to rise and fight again.

He would not be getting up. He was dead.

The area around the bodies was protected by police tape. The police forensics team would be here eventually to analyse the destruction.

More dead bodies on my watch, for the second time in a week. Prior to that there had never been a reason to call the forensics. Not once.

Flies had moved in, over their faces, on the wounds. That horrible low buzzing sound.

I called to an Albury cop I knew. "Mate, have we got a tent we can put up over here?"

"I am on it," he answered.

I left him to it.

Another officer from the Wodonga crew came over to me.

"Constable Taylor, would you be so kind as to help me with Sergeant Palmer. We can't get him into an ambulance?"

"What?" I said, "the Sarge is still here?"

"Yes unfortunately, he refused to go till he knew you were safe. He is sitting in the back of the van over here."

Over we went to the police station wagon.

There he was. The rear door was open, and he was sitting up, his bum on the floor of the van, his feet on the ground. He was in a semi argument with my girlfriend Wendy. She was now in full military nurse mode.

216

Sarge's rank held no meaning.

"No Sergeant Palmer, I don't care what you want to do," she said. "You are getting in that ambulance and heading back to hospital now."

The Sarge was pale as a ghost and obviously in a lot of pain.

"Oh Chris," he said looking at me, conveniently ignoring Wendy. "Thank God you are here, speak to this woman will you?"

"Me?" The notion that I could tell Wendy what to do was ridiculous. He was clearly out of his mind.

"Just let me give you this," said Wendy, preparing an injection. "It will ease the pain."

She grabbed his arm with a little bit of force, found a vein and was pumping the Sarge full of happy juice before he knew what hit him.

His eyes were already closing as he looked at me.

"I made some calls, all of this," said the Sarge, casting his eyes over the various teams now working around us.

Whatever narcotic Wendy had given him was starting to take effect.

"Good man that Barney - Plus - Yes - get on the front foot with this Chris. Front foot." His eyelids fluttered. "Hughes. Watch out for Hughes. Remember."

And that was as far as Sergeant Palmer made it into that conversation. His eyes closed and he floated away into slumber-land.

So, I had to watch out for Inspector Hughes, the bent cop. I knew that already. But what the hell was I supposed to remember?

"Grab the other side," said Wendy, snapping me back to the now. She grabbed one of Sarge's arms and I took the other. We gently lowered him backwards, onto the floor of the van. His feet were dangling out the end. He was out like a light. Blissfully medicated.

"Wendy," I asked, "what do you think I was supposed to remember?"

"Knowing you two I would guess he would want you to remember – don't be too hard on yourself."

Interesting.

"Jack, Jody," shouted Wendy to her number one paramedic team.

"Get me a stretcher over here please."

"Roger that," said Jack.

Jack Farrell and Jody Taggert were there in a heartbeat and the Sarge was stretchered away to the back of their ambulance, beside Ricky Chalmers, in barely a minute. Wendy had packed the two injured good guys in her A-team ambulance without a word to anyone. Just a natural born strategic thinker.

The backup ambulance would now be the conveyance for what remained of the biker gang, dead or alive.

I followed Jack and Jody back to their vehicle. They were all focus and efficiency. I could see through the open back doors that Ricky and Sarge were both out cold, anaesthetised. They were in good hands there was nothing for me to do. Jody was now starting up the engine, Jack hopped in the back between his two patients. As he was pulling the doors shut from within the ambulance he looked at me.

"Chris, I reckon they will both be all right."

"I hope so Jack."

"We're all glad you are OK mate," he added.

"Thanks mate, me too."

With a sudden clunk the rear doors were shut, and the ambulance drove away.

I felt a wave of relief, almost joy. The man I came with, and the man I came for, were both safe and alive.

The Sarge was more than my boss, he was my friend. As for Ricky, I don't know how I could face the town if I lost the footy coach on my watch. I was so glad they weren't dead I could have cried, which was probably the fatigue thinking for me.

Rob Farrell wandered over with two large mugs of steaming coffee. I was so desperate for caffeine I could have kissed him.

"Come over by the Fire truck and take a load off your feet mate," he said. "You look totally fucked."

He had changed his clothing.

"How come you've changed into your emergency gear?" I asked.

"Thought I might look obvious in my camo-gear with all your cop mates about the place. Swapped my coat and attached myself to the fire truck with Greg."

"Where did you stash your guns?"

"In the fire truck." He winked at me.

"I am pretty sure that is against State emergency Service regulations. You're supposed to save people, not shoot them."

"I would debate that," he said. "Anyway, who will ever know?" We both laughed.

We found ourselves two canvas chairs, set them beside the fire truck, and sat down to enjoy the coffee.

It was surreal.

It just needed Norma to kick start the barbeque and Greg to sell some raffle tickets.

Everything was calm, peaceful, almost tranquil.

Two young police officers were in the final stage of erecting a tent over the bodies of the dead bikies.

The remaining ambulance and the two paramedics were waiting beside their vehicle. They were talking to Wendy. looking like they had nothing to do. I wondered when they were heading back up the trail to rescue the wounded Detective Boofhead. They didn't seem to be in a hurry.

The little circle of police vehicles were a few meters further along the car park. Not much happening there. A couple of cops sitting in their vehicles, nursing their radio mikes. Doors open, waiting. A couple of cops standing by the police van, chatting.

Nothing urgent. Everyone waiting for the forensics team to show.

No one amongst the police team here seemed interested in talking to me about what the hell had happened at the other end of the trail.

I assumed the Sarge had given them a briefing, but even the Sarge didn't know I had shot a cop. Before I headed up-trail we had 'supposed' it might be Boofhead.

Now it was a fact.

It was self-defence and easily verified with my body cam, but I would still have to give my account. I would still be run through the hoops for discharging my weapon at a fellow officer. Who knew what bullshit could be thrown at me.

I didn't care, I was too tired.

I would have compulsory time off and counselling, but not today. It would happen eventually, just not now.

Sipping my coffee.

I could see the last living bikie cuffed and seated in the back of one of the police cars. He seemed subdued, probably wondering how this fun trip with his brother went so horribly wrong. Maybe hoping it would be over soon, and he could just go home to where he came from.

That would never happen.

Whether he realised it or not he was now 'in-the-system'. There would be no one in his immediate future much concerned about his welfare or comfort. No one would be worrying about his time or his freedom, he had lost control of both.

Tired as I was, I sensed opportunity.

"Robbie, could you give me your coffee mate?" He handed it over.

"I'll be back in a minute," I said.

"By which time you'll probably need more coffee I guess." Rob Farrell was a smart guy.

"Probably. Yes."

I stood and made my way over to the police car containing the biker. Everyone was busy, no one noticed, no one called out any objection. I checked my bodycam was still on. It was.

I hopped into the back seat beside my biker buddy.

"Remember me, mate?"

"Yeah."

"How they treating you?"

He gave a grunt of disapproval to that. I noticed the cable-ties I had put on his wrist were gone and he was now cuffed in front.

I handed him Rob Farrell's coffee.

"Can you manage this?" I asked.

He took it. "Thanks mate." Friends again. I had helped kill his brother but hey, no hard feelings.

"How is my brother?" he asked.

No one had told him his murderous brother had gone to God.

"Well, he is not looking too good right now. But he has the best possible people around him." All true, though even if it weren't I was under no legal obligation to tell him the truth. "They will let us know if there is any change."

I admired myself for such an artful lie.

"Coffee good?" I asked.

"Yep," he sipped some more.

"My name is Chris by the way, what's yours?" I thought we could move to the next level of buddy-dom.

"I should probably keep that to myself I think," he answered.

"Fair enough," I said. By all means, withhold the least incriminating thing about your current circumstance. Nice move.

"You blokes were on our trail quickly. Very impressive riding to catch us as quickly as you did. You are some seriously good road-riders." Shit on a bush trail but no need to go there.

"Yeah, we have done a few miles together," he answered to my praise.

"How did you manage to get up here so sharp?"

"We been waiting nearby for the last few days, waiting for the call."

"At the caravan park?" A calculated guess.

"Yeah, just keeping ourselves nice, did some fishing. Nice place."

"So, a call came in and you four blokes headed to the pizza shop?"

"No pizza shop mate, no. Butch got the call." Butch? That was AJ Davis's brother, the brother of my original Mister X. I didn't tell him that Butch was now dead at the other end of the Mitta Mitta Trail.

"Once he got the call we geared up and met up with the cop about ten kilometres south of the town and we all headed off together."

"You all headed off together?" I asked. "To here? Mitta Mitta? The five of you. You, your mates and the cop?"

"Yeah. Fat cunt could hardly keep up. Probably cost us half an hour. We'd have been done and dusted before you even got here if he hadn't dragged his fucking chain all the way. Fucking pig."

All I heard was that they hadn't been to the pizza shop.

"You didn't go through the town? You didn't go through Jarrajarra? You didn't stop at the pizza shop?"

"No way. Butch was told stay away. There was a fucking army of cops there. We went around, along the back roads. No way were going into town armed up and ready for action. This was all supposed to be on the quiet. Get in fast, get the cunt that killed AJ and then get out."

They hadn't been to the town and hadn't been to the pizza shop where Georgie had been murdered.

"You are sure you didn't go through the town of Jarrajarra?"

"Mate I have never been in the place, it's a shit hole from what I was told."

That was a bit rude, but I could let it pass in the circumstances.

"Who made the call to Butch?"

"The cop, what's-his-name? The fat Detective. Snow. Rude cunt."

"You sure it was Snow?"

"Course I'm sure. We were expecting a call today. We were sitting around outside the van. Call comes through, says, 'it's him' sorta thing. Butch always has his calls on speaker. He reckons you hold those things to your ear you get cancer of the brain."

"Could be some truth in that." The better part of Butch's brain was now spread over the bracken ferns at the other end of the Mitta Mitta trail. "You can't be too careful these days with your brain."

"It was Snow. I heard him clear and simple."

"You have heard Detective Snow before?"

"Yeah, on the phone and in the flesh, we've done heaps for him and his boss."

"You ever met his boss?"

"No, but you know, he mentions him like 'Boss wants this, Boss wants that sort of thing."

"You know his Boss's name?"

"No."

"You sure? Never heard his rank or his nickname anything like that?" I asked.

"No just 'Boss'. He wasn't my boss, so I didn't give a fuck."

We paused for a moment, both remembered our coffees and had a sip.

I couldn't think of a next question. Did this happen to Holmes? Poirot?

The door to the police car suddenly opened, on my side. It was Sergeant Will Walker. He leaned in.

"Chris, a word thanks."

I had been caught in the act of playing Homicide detective. Shit.

Walker led me around the back of the vehicle. I would most likely have to answer for talking to the suspect.

"Sorry Sergeant," what was I doing questioning the biker? "I know I should have reported in as soon as I got back here."

"Don't worry about that Chris, did you read him his rights?"

There was no mucking about with Sergeant Will Walker.

"Yes. I did."

"You are absolutely sure?"

"Positive." I tapped the camera on my vest. "It was on the whole time."

"He acknowledged you?"

"Yes."

He breathed a sigh of relief.

"Good work Constable. Good work, I was listening from behind the car. Heard it all. That was a bloody good interrogation. What did you think of him?"

"Me? Think? Well, he is a young kid really, way out of his depth. I think he was telling the truth."

"Exactly, plus he is probably still in shock, so I thought you had all we needed. Best to stop you there."

My God, he was just a clone of the Sarge, arrest was only half the job, we want convictions as well. No wonder they worked so closely together. If he started calling me son, I would probably hug him.

"Excellent work son, excellent."

I didn't hug him. I chickened out, plus I was suddenly exhausted again.

"Goodness, look at you. For heavens' sake Chris, let's get back over there by the fire truck. You have a rest. Take a seat on the bench, son, you've earned it."

I went to the bench. Actually, it was a folding canvas seat, but it felt like an armchair. I was so tired.

Not much else was happening in the Mitta Mitta trail car park.

It had all happened. Done and, mostly, dusted.

The rest would be just the clean-up and accountability. Who killed who, who gets to go home and sleep in their own bed. Who gets to go to prison for a long time.

Robbie provided more mugs full of coffee and some sandwiches. I enjoyed it all, relaxing for a moment. Taking a rest because, for the first time today, I could.

God I was exhausted. My head kept dropping. I had pretty much run a full marathon over the course of the day, been in two firefights, carried my wounded mate down a hill trail on his dirt bike. Somewhere in all of that I had manage to kill three rogue bikers and maybe a fellow police officer, another rogue.

Along the way, I had lost another citizen of Jarrajarra, Georgie Golino. Another person I had sworn to protect.

Hell of a day really.

Wendy had finished chatting with the second team of ambos and was walking over to me and the two Farrell brothers.

She spoke to Greg.

"OK where are those quad bikes?"

"Should be here in another five to ten minutes."

"Quad bikes?" I asked.

Rob Farrell answered on behalf of the trio.

"Your mate over there," said Rob, nodding toward Sergeant Will Walker.

"Sergeant Walker?" I asked.

"Yeah him," said Greg. "He saw the trail and ordered up some quad bikes, had to get them sent from Rob's garage. We don't have any in the Fire station."

Greg looked embarrassed. Here was a piece of useful equipment that the Jarrajarra Fire Brigade had not purchased via raffle. He looked away from Rob who was smirking.

"Norma banned them," chimed in Rob. "The boys being the boys, kept fucking around on them. I was making a fortune in quad bike maintenance at the garage."

"She made you sell them?" I asked Greg.

"Made is a strong word Chris. More that we 'Discussed' the matter. What with the cost."

"Yeah, Greg discussed," said Rob, "then Norma made him sell them to me."

"So now, whenever the Jarrajarra Emergency Services need quad bikes, they borrow yours?" I asked.

"Indeed, they do," said Rob, "and I now own six perfectly useless quad bikes which Scotty now fucks around on."

While I was talking shit with the Farrell brothers, Wendy had left our little group and was now over in the circle of police vehicles, talking to Sergeant Walker.

I had been watching that conversation.

They were deciding something.

Wendy had that hands on hips stance and, from what I could gather, she was laying down the law, to the law.

Wendy and Walker both turned, looking at me, they walked over to our little coffee circle.

Walker spoke first.

"Chris."

"Sergeant."

"Chris, son, you have done a great job here today, but ... well, Nurse Acheson here thinks it is time we moved you back to the hospital, and I agree."

Nurse Atcheson had laid a loving hand on my shoulder and was nodding in agreement with everything Walker was saying.

Walker finished and they both waited for me to agree, and I didn't.

"You can sit out the rest of the game lad. You've done well," he added.

Fuck that. I wasn't going home now.

"I am still good to go Sergeant Walker. There is a lot left here to do. There is a dead body back at the hide out and a wounded policeman who needs to be recovered."

"That would be Detective Constable Snow?"

"Yes, sergeant."

"Well, we know about Snow don't we. Tell me, is he likely to be a threat?"

"I don't think so Sarge, sorry Sergeant. I left him wounded but restrained, after he attempted to shoot me."

"Tried to shoot you, and now he is wounded?"

"Yes Sergeant."

"OK. Well Chris don't you worry about him. I think we have the manpower to handle him once those quad bikes arrive."

"Sergeant this hideout is very hard to find."

"No Constable, we have the GPS we will find it. The Nurse wants you back in the hospital, that's settled."

I was pissed off, this was stupid, I needed to show them the way, make sure that Boofhead wasn't a threat. The job was not done.

"Chris, I think we still need the ambulance so I will send you back in one of our cars. Is that alright?"

It wasn't really a question.

"Good then," he said, "all settled".

Wait a minute; he'd answered his own question.

He waved back to the posse of police vehicles parked further along the car park. It was a summons. Pre-arranged.

The young Wodonga lad, who had met me on the trail, now drove over in one of the Wodonga police cars. I finished my coffee defiantly. Sulking really, but too tired to put on a show of it. I slid into the passenger seat, belted up, and we pulled out of the park, heading back to Jarrajarra.

Benched, just like that.

We were just at the exit from the car park when Rob's son, Scotty Farrell, arrived in the Jarrajarra garage truck. I counted four quad bikes parked and tied down on the tray. He waved and smiled as we passed each other.

He was a good lad Scotty, I thought.

I was sound asleep within sixty seconds.

I don't remember anything of the drive home, getting out of the car, getting into a hospital bed.

I just slept.

12

SUNDAY, MARCH 18, 2018

Jarrajarra, Toowong District, Victoria, Australia.

I woke up at 7.00 am in a Jarrajarra hospital bed. Private room 1B, I knew the bed. I had been in this bed, in this room, before with Wendy. Sadly, she wasn't here now.

Sat up, feeling sore all over. This was the longest I had over-slept in all the years I had been on the police force. I was going to miss my morning run, too tired. The end of a 103-day consecutive days of morning run. I could start again tomorrow. It wasn't the number that was important, just the counting, and the discipline that came with the counting.

Yes, tomorrow I would start a new streak, just not today.

My glass-shredded uniform had gone but someone had delivered a full change of clothes from my home. Casuals, not a uniform. Was that a hint I had the day off? I was due.

The hot water in the shower stung just about everywhere. Those glass shreds had cut me all over. I had stitches on my face and chin. Neat and tight, a good job, Wendy's work for sure. I showered and dressed then went to find her.

The hospital was quiet. If there were other patients in our tiny little nursing centre they were still asleep.

Wendy was in the reception area talking through paperwork with another nurse. Big smiles all-round.

"You're awake."

"I am." We were brilliant at self-evident conversation.

"How are you feeling after your ordeal?"

"Ordeal?" I smiled; she always made me smile. "I feel pretty good now. Would love some . . ."

"Coffee," she finished the sentence. "Let's get you some."

She left the other nurse to the paperwork and led me to the kitchen. As we moved away from the reception area she put her arm around me and gave me a gentle squeeze.

"That's very nice," I said.

"Better than getting shot at I bet."

We made our coffees in the kitchen and went outside to the sunny seated area at the back of the hospital. We grabbed one of the tables. We had the area to ourselves, the sun was shining, there was not a breath of wind, it was morning cool, not cold.

It was a totally beautiful day.

Good to be alive.

"Great to be alive hey?" She said, reading my mind as ever.

I raised my coffee to her and then took a sip. She smiled and a few tears formed in her eyes. Happy tears. Relieved tears.

She grabbed my spare hand, and we sat like that for a while.

"No gunfights today Corporal, OK? That's an order."

"Yes Ma'am. I will do my best."

"Do that," she said.

"What if Barney acts up?"

"If Barney acts up, well you just talk it through OK. Don't shoot him."

"I'll try."

"Did someone mention my name?" Walking through the door with a bunch of flowers was Barney himself. "It was a good mention I hope."

"Yes Barney," Wendy smiled at him.

Joanne Farrell, Barney's new part time assistant, followed Barney through the door. She had her hands full with two large takeaway coffees.

"For me?" I asked.

"For whoever," said Jo, setting both coffees down in front of me. This was good.

Barney handed the flowers to Wendy. "For saving all the good men," he said as she took the flowers.

The new arrivals at our little picnic sat either side of Wendy, all three facing me like a job interview.

I could handle that, I had a ton of hot caffeine in front of me, I could handle anything.

"Chris," Barney paused a moment, looking for words then. "I am just so glad you're alive." Then he burst out crying.

Another one in tears.

Floods of tears.

This never happened in the army.

Wendy put her arm around his shoulders while he had his weep.

"Oh god I am sorry," he said. "How embarrassing."

Barney wiped his face and sniffed, "I was so worried, can you imagine having to train a new local cop? I couldn't bear it."

We all settled our emotions and, while I enjoyed all the coffee, Barney filled us in on all the overnight police activity.

The short version.

Our much-loved Boss, Sergeant Bruce Palmer, the Sarge, was in the Wodonga Hospital and recovering well. The piece of metal that had embedded under his shoulder had not cut any arteries, but he had managed to fracture two of his higher ribs. He would be uncomfortable and out of action for a few weeks but was otherwise all good.

What a guy.

My friend and number one murder suspect, Ricky Chalmers, had been airlifted to the Alfred Hospital in Melbourne. The big city to us regional folk.

Ricky had been shot up badly. Shotgun pellets everywhere. The damage list included, from the top, a broken collarbone, broken ribs, a punctured lung, shotgun pellets in his liver, kidney and intestines. It was remarkable that he was still alive, even more remarkable that he had made it down the mountain. A journey made without a single complaint, I thought. My God he was a seriously rugged individual. Still alive, back in custody, and now safe under the protection of real policemen, according to Barney.

Detective Constable Peter Snow, the 'Boofhead', was alive and expected to live. The paramedics had saved his life. By the time they found him, he had been in serious danger of bleeding out. Fortunately for him, our own ambulance-driving wonder-woman Jody Taggart had pumped him full of some 'neutral' O-negative blood and had kept him afloat. Waste of good blood in my opinion, but not my call, and who could be angry at Jody?

Boofhead was also under arrest, being held under police supervision, while in Wodonga hospital. He was currently charged with the murder of Georgie Golino. Just the statement of that crime made me want to go and find him in his comfortable hospital bed and have another go at killing him.

It was wishful thinking I knew.

Barney's list went on.

Superintendent Hughes, Boofhead's boss, was also in custody. Holy Hell, an inspector was taken down while I slept. He had been dismissed from the force and then arrested when the search team returned to base. He had then been shipped in the back of a divisional van to the Melbourne Watch-house. He would be there for quite a while. He was facing the same charges as Boofhead with a lot more to come. According to Barney's report, there was evidence aplenty of serious corruption.

Hughes was gone and not coming back.

Both of these crooked cops had been arrested by Detective Pete.

Detective Sergeant Peter Jordan had been quite the hero. It sounded to me that he had stepped into the pits of corruption and bravely arrested two corrupt, murderous, Victorian policemen. Plus, he had recaptured the suspected killer of Joey Golino and Azzolino Pisano and that suspect, my mate Ricky, was now safely in police custody.

Just to show what a serious policeman he was, he had already done a live TV interview with Angela Adams to humbly confirm all of his accomplishments. Miss Adams had flown to Jarrajarra in a helicopter only this morning for the interview. A bloody helicopter no less, would have been nice to have had one yesterday.

The Sarge's second-in-command, Wodonga's Sergeant Will Walker, had stepped up magnificently and managed all of the human damage at the Mitta Mitta Car Park most admirably. This was according to our own Wendy and the Farrell brothers, all of them stern critics of any ineptitude.

The forensics team, Carole and Glenda, had come and gone. The same two wonderful policewomen that had done the job at the Jarrajarra caravan park barely a week ago. Any more murders in our region and they would need a caravan of their own.

Best of all, I had a week off, courtesy of Sergeant Walker and a message of "Well done" that he sent via Barney.

Barney sat there reporting all of this, while we all sipped our various beverages and nodded. The morning sun was beautiful, Wendy was there, no one was shooting at me. It was just so damn good to be alive, my cuts and stitches barely registered.

My anger towards the shit cops who had infected our lovely town was not enough to ruin the morning. I had enough friends and good cops around me to isolate me from that corruption and misery.

Inevitably Barney dragged out his mobile and we found Detective Pete's morning interview on the internet. It actually wasn't too bad, not too far down the self-serving track, not too much of the glory hound. Perhaps I was just biased against him.

He had given a succinct rundown of the day's events. Not too much detail and a solid acknowledgement of the major part that the local police had played in the various arrests.

There was no mention that Boofhead had been seriously wounded. The fact that I had shot him in his fat bum was completely passed over.

Great result for me.

What was mentioned was that Boofhead and Hughes had been arrested after a lengthy investigation involving the Victorian Anti-

Corruption Commission and the Royal Commission into the murder of the politician Gary Rogers back in 2010. The very same commission that was currently playing out in the New South Wales Supreme Court.

As for the three dead bikers, from the little that was revealed to the television reporter, they may well have shot themselves. No doubt their demise would be discussed in more detail in time to come.

Dead bikers, corrupt cops, wounded cops, three murders, then a murdered mother and a still-missing drug lord. Quite the list.

Jarrajarra was in the big time.

Eventually Wendy, Barney and Joanne drifted off to their various Sunday ventures, leaving me to sit in the morning sun and ponder.

I thought of all the things I might do that day, but after I left the hospital car park, I walked home, lay down and went back to sleep for another twenty hours.

You can't beat your own bed.

13

MONDAY, MARCH 19, 2018

Wodonga Hospital, Victoria, Australia.

"So, if your mate is innocent as you insist, then we still have no idea who killed Joey Golino." Sarge was speaking from his hospital bed. Banged-up, bed-ridden, but still on the case.

Monday morning, I had gone to Rob Farrell's garage to inspect the remains of my once beautiful truck. Sitting on the back of a trailer, it was as far beyond repair as could be. Totally and utterly buggered, my Nan might have said. Rob lent me one of his 'For Sale' trucks. I could use that, he said, till the police department could provide me a new vehicle.

I had driven over to Wodonga Hospital to check on the Sarge. He was there chatting with his wife Vilma when I arrived in his hospital room.

More happy tears, this time from Vilma. My appearance was making everyone cry. Vilma thanked me and hugged me profusely.

"You saved his life Chris," she said, hugging me as we spoke. "The silly old goat going after bikers in the bush at his age. Honestly I despair. Thank God you were there."

"It was a team effort, Mrs. Palmer," I had insisted. "We kept each other alive really." The boss's wife was having none of that and just kept on hugging me.

Eventually she left us alone to get down to cop talk.

"So," said Sarge, "you're telling me our remaining biker insisted they had come after Ricky Chalmers to avenge the death of our Mister X, this AJ Davies fellow, and nothing else whatsoever."

"Yes. Plus, I like your use of the term remaining-biker, as opposed to the only not-dead-biker."

The Sarge was never impressed by my sense of humour. He ignored that one.

"So why was Snow with them, and why was he intent on killing Ricky, if he didn't care about our dead biker Mister Davies?"

"Why? I don't know really. Maybe Barney was right, this is just some front-foot cover-up action. Maybe Ricky was just an excuse for Hughes and Boofhead to get the bikers together then kill them all."

"It's a bit of a stretch." Sarge was not convinced.

"Well," I said, "I saw Snow kill the biker at the hide-out, so I know for a fact they wanted him gone. Perhaps he left the other three behind at the car park to make killing them easier when he got back."

"Maybe."

"You saw them," I said, "they were incompetent. Big and scary looking if that frightened you but we both saw them squander a huge advantage over us."

"True."

"Remember Barney's theory, Hughes and Boofhead are cleaning house. According to our remaining biker, they had worked together before. Maybe they tie Hughes to Folliero. Maybe we were just a surprise, which is why they weren't ready and waiting for us."

"I don't think those three would ever be ready for you son. Not in this, or any other, lifetime."

I shrugged at that.

"Nothing to boast about Sarge. I was well trained, better trained than them."

"Son, didn't your Nan ever teach you to accept a compliment?"

"Nan wasn't huge on compliments. She was more focused on your basic essentials."

"OK. Hughes and Snow on a cover-up, it would explain why Boof-head kills Georgie Golino. Maybe even make it look like Georgie and Chalmers were complicit in the original murders."

"Just a theory."

"And in that theory," said Sarge, "both the crooked cops and the biker gang all think Chalmers committed the original murders."

"Yes, that's what they really think. Ricky murdered Mister X."

"But you don't think he did it, apart from the fist fight with Davies."

"No."

"Why?"

"Originally it was a personal assessment, I just don't think he is a killer. And then I spoke to Georgie, and I believe what she told me. I mean, she correctly told us where to find Ricky. Right?"

"Yes," said the Sarge.

"So then, it is not too big a stretch to believe the rest of her story."

"Yes true. But Chris, if it isn't Chalmers, who was it?"

"I have absolutely no idea, I just know it wasn't Ricky. I believe Georgie Golino. Ricky was in her house asking for favours while Joey was still alive, on the phone, talking to her, husband to wife, from the pizza place. She is, sorry was, sure she heard the killer enter the shop."

"Over the phone?"

"Yes. Over the phone. She hears the doorbell ding, a few words from Joey, then footsteps then whack, whack, whack."

Not the greatest crime summary, but it was what I knew, in as few words as possible. The Sarge knew it too.

"Well Georgie Golino is not much help to your mate Ricky Chalmers now."

"No boss, she's not."

We sat and thought for a while.

"Not even her phone records help him," said Sarge.

"No," I said, "they just prove she was on the phone, doesn't prove who she had with her in her home."

"A good prosecutor will argue that she and Ricky were conspirators in the murder."

That was absolutely true.

We sat in silence a while longer. Stumped.

"Sarge, I think I should give our forensic ladies a call. Go back over the murder weapon. If it was a local that killed Joey, maybe we could find the weapon around here."

"Good luck with that son, but yes, worth a try. But we don't even know what the weapon was yet, do we?"

"No."

"Well, that will add some degree of difficulty."

The Sarge could do sarcasm as well as anyone.

The silence resumed; it was comfortable. I was just glad he was OK. One of the best people I had ever known and despite what Vilma said, he was a very strong and capable cop, even at his age. Whatever it was.

The Sarge had something he wanted to say.

"Chris you remember when you applied for the job up here."

"Yes, didn't think I had a chance, one man station, hardly any experience."

"I know, but Wendy gave you a strong push son, ex-army and all of that. She can be very persuasive. Then I looked up your war records and I realised what we were getting. The full package."

I didn't say anything to that.

"I am not saying I hired you as part of a secret plan or anything like that, but it did occur to me that it would not be a bad thing have our own sort of lethal weapon in the district. One who was on our side."

"Lethal Weapon? Really?"

"Bad description son, I mean someone who was hyper capable in these sort of violent situations. Didn't back away in confrontation."

"Well, I have seen a bit of that along the way. Bullets find you just as quick, whichever way you run."

"Yes indeed."

He hadn't finished.

"A long time ago, before my army stint, I was a young cop in Mirboo North, down south from here. I went out in the van with another Constable to check on a local farmer that had been stealing his neighbour's petrol, in broad daylight no less.

This fellow takes a shotgun onto his neighbour's property and just filled up his jerry-cans from the petrol tank at the neighbour's shed. The neighbour came out, this fellow fires a shot in his general direction. Just takes the next-door neighbour's petrol as if it is his, by right of the weapon. Outrageous."

"Kind of like our own Mellish bothers? Do as you please and serve yourself wherever," I added.

"Exactly, exactly. Just like the Mellish boys. Anyway, I won't go into too much embarrassing detail but before we could arrest him, get him in custody, my partner and I ended up in the local hospital. Badly beaten up and very lucky to be alive. Took another week and a team from the Special Operations Group from Melbourne to get him into a cell. I tell you, directing that SOG team to this fellow's farm, I have never been so embarrassed in all my life."

"But you survived."

"Yes, with not much dignity in that case, but my point is, when I saw your war experience, your training, the bunch of medals and commendations, it did occur to me we won't be needing that special team from Melbourne to come visit Jarrajarra. Not while you were the officer in charge."

"Well thanks boss, I suppose."

"It never occurred to me though that we would end up with something like this, or that I would owe you my life."

He struggled on the last bit.

"Fair go Sarge, I thought we worked pretty well together out there, all our army business came together pretty well. We were a team, we saved each other."

"Son, listen, I was there, I was the only one who saw, and, well, I only saw half of it, but what you did was incredible. If you hadn't been with me, I would be dead."

"Sarge, stop, please, I was with you. Without each other we might both be dead."

"Son, there are not many people in civilian life who will advance on a gunman, especially one with a machine gun, actually three with machine guns. I was there, I saw it all, alright?"

"Boss, it wasn't that brave really, I had no choice, and they had no clue. Bloody hell, they stood in a straight line, firing in tandem with all their ammunition in one shoulder bag. I am glad you were the only one who saw it, anyone else I might be charged with idiot abuse."

"Stop it, you're downplaying it as usual."

"OK. Sarge, the only thing we couldn't do was lay down and wait for them to work out their arseholes from their elbows. If we had done nothing we definitely would be dead. Both of us."

"Chris, what did I tell you? You need to learn to accept a compliment."

"I'll work on it."

"Good. So go and speak to those forensic ladies."

"I will."

I got to the door, and he said, "Well done, son."

I nearly teared up myself.

The Road to Jarrajarra, Victoria, Australia.

"My oh my, heavens above what a mess you made you naughty boy."

I was speaking on the phone to Senior Constable Carole Johnston.

"Glenda, get over here," shouted Carole. "It's the killer Constable from Jarrajarra, the man himself. Hang on Chris, I'll put you on speaker."

I was on the drive home from Wodonga Hospital. My flash-new borrowed truck had a blue-tooth connection that allowed me to use my mobile in hands free mode. The truck also had a reversing camera and a key you could leave in your pocket the whole time. I didn't trust myself not to lose the key and I felt unfaithful to my old dead truck but hey, life was for the living, even if you are a truck. I was loving the modern convenience of my new machine.

"Hello Killer, it's Glenda, thanks for all the overtime. You're paying for my new kitchen mate."

"Killer?" I asked. There would clearly be no tears of sympathy from these two, just pitch-black cop humour to get us through the day.

"Used with affection," said Carole. "We are loving your work. Thinking of a fan page."

"Well hold off the fan page OK. I hope that is the end of it actually." I answered with no great certainty. "It is all too exciting for my little town.

"Who did the head shot on the biker in the car park?" asked Glenda.

"That was the Sarge," I answered.

"Nasty," she answered in admiration. "Very nasty."

"One in the belly from you and a head shot from Sergeant Palmer," said Glenda.

"Nice work," added Carole.

"Who did the facial on the biker up near the hideout?" That was Carole asking this time.

"Facial?" There was no end to their gory curiosity. "Boy, you two have landed the perfect job."

They loved that and both burst out laughing.

"Professional interest," said one.

"Research," added the other.

"Well, the head shot at the hide-out, that was the biker's hiking buddy, Detective Constable Peter Snow. I shot the biker in the body. Then Boofhead, between shooting at me and my fugitive Chalmers, turned around and shot his mate, the biker, in the face, from about two metres."

"Way to go," came through my phone.

"Why the hell why?" Asked Carole.

"Well Snow shot him to shut him up I guess. Snow was riding with the bikers trying to kill the current suspect in the Golino murder."

"Wow, so you have hit biker in the gut and Snow in the bum with the Steyr rifle, probably going to kill the biker eventually, but then our injured Snow ends biker guy's misery by shooting him in the head," spoke Carole in summation.

"Complicated," added Glenda.

"I know," I answered. "Not so complicated for the biker."

"What's all this got to do with finding the killer of your mate Golino?" Carole Asked.

"Nothing," I said, "I don't think Snow, or Hughes, had anything to do with Golino. Barney reckons they were trying to wriggle out of being under Folliero's thumb. Had accepted bribes most likely. Careers over maybe."

"He is a smart lad cousin Barney," said Carole.

There was a small gap in the conversation, as we all contemplated Barney's theory on Snow and Hughes. It was a good one.

"Anyway," said Glenda, "next time can you shoot the baddies closer to the town. It was a long night, and we missed the BBQ and the applauding fans."

"I'll try."

"Oh, and the Steyr rifle," I had to ask for Rob's sake, that belongs to a concerned citizen, any idea when he might get that back."

"Oh dear," said Carole.

"The wheels of justice can be slow Chris," added Glenda.

"So maybe never?"

"Hard to say really, but yeah about then."

"We'll see what we can do," added Carole.

"Anyway, enough frivolity. You called us. What's the go Constable?" Carole had gone all official now.

"I wanted to ask you about the weapon that was used in the murder of Joey Golino and the other two blokes."

"Let me see, Joey Golino from the pizza shop, AJ Davies from the roadside and Azzolino Pisano from the caravan park?"

"Yes."

"Well, I can tell you this they all copped at least one whack on the head from the same thing. But what that whacking thing was, well that's the unanswered question. I don't think it was any kind of conventional weapon."

"Davies was stabbed as well, right?"

"Yes. Davies also had a knife wound in his thigh which caused him to bleed out. Otherwise, amazingly, he may have survived, with the emphasis on 'may have'. My estimate is it was a pretty standard carving knife. Could have been one in a hundred, maybe just taken from the pizza place in the moment. So, unless you can find the one with Davies blood all over it, possession of a similar knife won't prove anything."

"OK, I won't go looking for knives unless they have blood."

"Now the heavy object, our blunt force killing thing, that thing has me intrigued."

"Intrigued?"

"Yes. I heard someone suggest it could be the blunt side of an axe."

"That might have been me."

"Well, it's definitely not an axe."

"Then again, maybe someone else said that."

"Ha-ha funny man. But no, it can't be the blunt side of an axe because, the metal parts that struck the victims are in perfect parallel. When you magnify the strikes on the victims, you can see they landed in patterns of two. Perfectly parallel pairs. The blows are so parallel the weapon must have been made that way. So, it is some sort of heavy tool that can be swung easily, and the heavy end is actually two shafts each about half an inch wide, fifteen inches long perhaps."

"How did you work out the length?"

"Well, we are not just wonderful people, mate, we are also highly intelligent," said Glenda.

"Highly intelligent, and technical," added Carole. "We actually took shots of all the various blows and then we put together a composite picture of the imprint of the full double blade thing."

"Goodness me."

"Fifteen inches. 375 millimetres or there-about."

Glenda continued the description. "Two thick blades in parallel and heavy. Heavy enough to kill Joey Golino with a single hit to the front of his head."

"Two blades?".

"Yes, and the two parallel arms of this weapon come together at their base, into one arm, and I believe the single arm was used as the handle."

"It sounds like you are describing a big heavy tuning fork, like those things musicians use. My Nan had one. You hit it and it hums at a certain pitch."

"Yes, except when you hit with this thing, it makes big holes in people's skulls, kills them right quick. But, yes, I suppose, it might look like a humungous tuning fork."

"So, a handle of yet to be determined size and then two heavy parallel arms, the arms being about fifteen inches long."

"Yes, and there is a little thing we found that may help you. Davies raised his arm to protect himself on possibly the first whack. You remember he had big arms?"

"Yes, I'd say steroid type big."

"Steroids and the rest of it from his blood. Anyway, what may help us is that his arm didn't break. Just a massive ugly bruise. It would have hurt like hell. The bruise looks like it was caused by the point where the single handle separates into the two forks. I will send you a picture. You can clearly see the shape of the handle and the forks in the bruise. You can also see, if you look carefully enough some sort of printing that must have come from the weapon fork bashing thing."

"What does it say?"

"G dash F, and when I say dash that is what you see, a dash. G dash F in reverse of course, being a bruise."

"OK, I get it. G-F in reverse. Would you be able to send me a picture of that please, Carole?"

"Sure. I will do it now. Anything for you, Killer."

"I would much appreciate that and thanks for your time."

"My pleasure Chris, and seriously mate, great work on the week-end. The word from the top is you are a hero."

"Not sure about hero Carole, just happy to be alive really."

"Well, we were given the over-view by Detective Sergeant Jordan, he said what you did was unbelievable. I just saw the afters and looks like you went through that mob like a hot knife through butter."

Jordan? Detective Pete? Saying nice things about me, that sounded weird.

. . .

Carole, Glenda and I finished our phone call with just a little nasty banter, making dark jokes out of everything to do with shooting up the Mitta Mitta Car Park.

Make a joke, keep it light, the cop way.

A few moments after we disconnected, my phone dinged. Carole had sent the photo, so I pulled over to the side of the road to take a look at my dead Mister X's badly bruised arm.

It was huge and muscular, as I remembered, and there in the middle of the massive bicep was a bruise in the shape of a two-pronged fork. Right at the point where the handle meets the fork, just as Carole from forensics had said.

Right there in the centre of the bruise, clearly visible through a sleeve of faded tattoos, was a deeper darker imprint with clear letters that spelled out 'G-F', in reverse of course.

G-F.

What on earth did that mean?

Jarrajarra, Victoria, Australia.

"Well, it's not anything of mine." Greg Farrell was looking at the photo of the bruise from Mister X's dead arm.

He looked at me.

"You think I murdered Joey Golino?" Greg Farrell was not impressed.

"No mate no, bloody hell, no way."

Greg and I were sharing some of his superb coffee, sitting in the sun, out the back of the C.F.A. building. I had shown him the photo of the 'G-F' bruise on Mister X's arm.

"Even if I did think you did it, I would probably be working my bum off to get you off the charges. You can't get coffee this good every-where you go."

"That's true."

"Plus, if I got you sent away I'd have Norma after me."

"You would."

"So, say no more."

Greg had a longer look at the photograph.

"It looks like someone has dropped some weld on it. Marking a name, or an initial. I know it's a bruise, but it doesn't look machine made, it looks like someone has sort of done some raised-hot-metal writing on it. Doesn't look like the writing is factory made."

I had another look.

"Something home-made," added Greg. "Who makes their own tools around here?"

We both knew there were only two people in town that had the hot-iron skills and the equipment, plus the ability, to make their own heavy tools.

Only two.

Rob Farrell and Ricky Chalmers.

"Well, you know Rob didn't do it," added Greg, reading my mind as ever. "He was down in Melbourne dragging his wayward daughter back here."

He was, indeed, which left Ricky.

Still the only suspect in the village.

14

TUESDAY, MARCH 20, 2018

Jarrajarra, Victoria, Australia.

On the second day of my gifted holiday, I resumed running. My new streak was now one day old. I ran to the mighty Murray River then a few kilometres along the trail. Then back to town and the cafe.

I was all sweaty, so I sat outside in the sun for my morning dose of caffeine.

I needed to see Ricky Chalmers. I knew he was in some form of hospitalised incarceration in the Alfred Hospital in Melbourne. But that was a massive facility. I had no idea exactly where he was or how I could get in. The Sarge had told me to take the week off, plus he was in hospital himself. I really had no one to turn to.

Reluctantly, I called Detective Sergeant Pete Jordan, he answered immediately.

"Here he is, the hero."

Detective Pete was his usual charming self, my problem was after a week of it, I had stopped believing. The closer I got to the charm, the more it seemed fake.

"What can I do for you Chris?"

"Just one thing Pete. I would like to see Ricky Chalmers."

"You want to see my murder suspect?" He thought about it a bit.

"That could work. What about coming down to Melbourne and having a chat with me first and after that I will see what I can do."

I didn't like the 'see what I can do' bit. Sounded like he had a trade in mind.

"Is that OK?" he asked.

"OK." I agreed.

He gave me the where and when, so I jumped into my flash new marvellous driving machine and drove to Melbourne.

Melbourne, Victoria, Australia.

"Nice stitches on your chin Constable. Good work by Nurse Wendy, I assume."

Detective Sergeant Pete Jordan and I were sitting in a small booth in a coffee and breakfast place around the corner from Police Head-quarters in St. Kilda Road, Melbourne.

I couldn't help feeling a tickle in my chin at mention of my recent battle scar. Hadn't thought of it all day. Trust this smarmy bastard to make me twitch. I didn't like him mentioning Wendy either.

"Let me give you the good news," he said. "You can see your mate; you can see him this afternoon. OK?"

"Great."

"But I do need to ask you a favour. I think you owe me that much," he said.

"Sorry? I owe you?"

"Well, let me count. You shot a fellow cop. Is anyone chasing you down for that?"

"Not yet."

"And they won't, trust me."

"OK."

"Also," he was speaking as though he had rehearsed the reasons I owed him a favour. "You, and your Sergeant Palmer, were being hounded by former Inspector Hughes. He was going to have you both dismissed from the force as I remember. Feel free to correct me if I am wrong."

"You're not wrong."

"And, as of this morning, your nemesis Hughes, and his lackey Snow are both under arrest? Correct?"

"Yes, that's correct." This list was getting rather long.

"Who do you think did all that while you were sleeping off your big adventure?"

"Let me guess. You." I hated to admit he was right, but I was, by default, unimpressed by him and all the big city cops that he came with.

"Come on Chris," he continued, "I get it; I came to your town with Snow and Hughes, I was one of them. Part of the package. Another outsider. We all came on the same train as far as you're concerned. I understand. Just hear me out."

I gave in. I might as well listen. I had to wait for my coffee anyway.

"Alright, let me hear it," I said, and he did.

"I have been tracking Hughes and Snow for over a year," he said. "I have been working with the Royal Commission into the Rogers' murder, currently running in the Supreme Court in New South Wales."

"The commission investigating Michelle Folliero?"

"Yes, the very same. The Federal Police are very keen to tidy up. They tend to persist in the case of political assassinations. They are also extremely keen to locate Folliero and his dirty money."

"Which everyone thinks is a lot."

"Yes, quite a lot. So right now, I have a bit of grunt, you might say, some clout."

"How did you, a Victorian cop, end up working with the Federal Police and the New South Wales Supreme Court."

"Connections. Mutually beneficial arrests, you might say. I've worked with the Crown Prosecutor for the Commission, Ms. Berlic. You might have seen her on television."

"Yes."

"Anyway, Berlic and I have worked cases before. She used to work in Victoria before she moved up north to the federals."

"OK, you know people."

"And they know me, and they know I am not corrupt. So, when Hughes first came under their radar, they came to me."

"How did that happen?"

"Well, your first victim Mister X, AJ Davies, was picked up by New South Wales police on a rape charge two years ago. It was not his first rape, nowhere near it. But this time, the victim was fourteen years old, and we had him dead to rights, DNA, cooperative witnesses, you name it."

"So, he was going to jail?"

"Yes, what with his priors, Davies was heading to jail for a long stint. Given the age of the victim, it was likely to be very unpleasant for him."

"They don't like child rapists in prison, even big tough ones with bad reputations."

"No, they don't, and no matter how tough you are, there is always someone tougher. Like your footy coach, for example."

"Funny, my Nan used to say that when I got in trouble. Be careful; there's always someone bigger and meaner than you."

"She sounds like a fine lady."

I didn't respond to that. Why did I mention my Nan to this bloke? Jesus, he was a charmer.

"Anyway, in exchange for his freedom, Davies offered up several other offenders and information on other matters of interest."

"He gave you Hughes?"

"Yes, Hughes and his puppy Snow. Also, even more valuable, he knew where the body of Gary Rogers was buried, and he knew the who, the how and the why. With regard to the who, Davies was able to tell us that Jack Hayes murdered Rogers, that Alexander Sheahan was the driver, and Michelle Folliero was the employer.

"Once they had all those names, Berlic contacted me, since the Rogers' burial site was in my state. Together, we got Sheahan to roll over and confirm what Davies had given us. So, after we found Rogers' body and his phone, we were able to put together enough evidence to nail Folliero and his henchman Pisano, without giving away Davies as a source."

"So," I said, "you fire up a Royal Commission, and all the world thinks Sheahan had been the one to inform?"

"Yes, which was convenient, because this left Davies as a very

248

valuable inside asset for our team. Our plan was to leave Davies out there to continue our hunt for more evidence. We needed more than just the testimony of a couple of crooks to nail someone like Hughes and all the other corrupted officers in his cohort. We wanted arrests and convictions on all the names that Davies gave us."

"Bullshit, what you wanted was Folliero's money," I said, "and to get that, you left Davies out there in the wind despite the fact that he had raped a fourteen-year-old."

"Yes, well, that is true, I guess," he said, hardly embarrassed at all.

"Anyway," continued Detective Pete, "once Pisano and Folliero were actually named in the Royal Commission, they took flight, and somehow Davies went with them."

He'd barely registered my mention of the child rape. He was clearly comfortable with collateral damage.

"How did you let Davies, a serial rapist, run free in the community?" I asked. "Weren't you keeping tabs on him, for fuck's sake?"

"We were, we were! But we weren't living with the guy. He was undercover with the worst crooks in the country. You have to give him some rope."

"So, they all disappear after being named?"

"Yes, they disappear. Then somehow Pisano ends up in your little town, along with Davies and their local connection, your mate, Joey Golino."

"Folliero's nephew?" I said.

"Yes, as we all know now," said Pete. "Most likely, they were all trying to escape the country with Folliero and his money."

"In a very big bag," I said.

"Maybe a truck load of bags," said Pete.

"And Davies ends up in the pizza shop?"

"Yes, and then, God only knows why, along comes your footy coach, Mister Ricky Chalmers, all 6'3" and 250 pounds of muscle and hard edges, who, for some unknown reason, maybe he didn't like the Capriccioso, I don't know. But, for some reason, starting at the pizza place and systematically, over the next hour or so, he beats three men to death, one-by-fucking-one. Quite a guy, your coach. I can see why you won a premiership with him at the helm."

"Ricky didn't do it," I couldn't let it pass.

"Well, Constable, I beg to differ. We have his admission to the location, which he made to you and me. We have an admission to the fighting, and we have his DNA evidence on the body of his first two victims, Golino and Davies."

I was shaking my head. "Give me time, and I will prove he didn't do it."

"Sorry, Chris, I know he is the town hero, but I think he did it."

"So," I asked, "how were you able to arrest the two cops for murder? What evidence do you suddenly have for that?"

"I had people listening while you were there talking to Georgie, and after that, the same people were listening while Snow was there talking to her."

"You had the pizza place bugged?"

"Yes. The bugs were placed the day we identified Davies' body."

"So, you were listening to Georgie and me?"

"Yes, and I must say you did a pretty good job of interrogation. Not so good on the real estate sale." That smarmy smile again.

"What?"

"Selling the pizza shop for Georgie to what's-his-name at the caravan park."

"Oh, God. That." Bugged conversations could be embarrassing. I had forgotten the Wally part of the chat with Georgie.

"Wait a minute," I said, "you said you heard Boofhead there, so you heard Georgie Golino getting beaten to death. You did nothing."

"No, no! Jesus no. I didn't sit back waiting while she was killed, nothing like that. The listening post is in Canberra. It is a Federal Police investigation. Round the clock. Someone with a pair of head-phones in a room somewhere heard what was happening to Georgie Golino. By the time it got to me, and I got to her, it was all over."

He could tell from my face; I did not fully believe him.

"My God, Chris, you do have bad thoughts about me. I am not so ruthless that I would let someone die just to collect evidence."

I was not sure I believed that. He, or someone in his team, gave Davies a free pass on the rape of a teenager.

"I got there as soon as I could," he continued. "I was too late; she was dead, and they were gone. I am truly sorry."

I stared at him, wondering what Georgie's last minutes must have felt like. Wishing I had killed Boofhead while I had the chance. There was more, something he hadn't told me. There had to be.

"So, you heard something on a tape," I asked, "a bashing, presumably a couple of voices. How is that enough to arrest and charge two senior policemen? From what I know, Hughes wasn't even there. It was just Boofhead on his own."

"Georgie Golino," he sighed. He actually looked genuinely sad, if only for a moment. "Let me say, under very severe duress; she gave him Chalmers' location. She gave him the GPS coordinates that she gave you. Also, she gave him the evidence that she had against both Hughes and Snow, or Boofhead, as you call him. It was that evidence that is the basis of the charges against them."

"If Georgie gave Boofhead the evidence she had promised to give me. How did you end up with it?"

"Well, mate, you got it for us. Snow was carrying it when you shot him. I found it in his things at the hospital while he was being operated on. He was actually carrying it with him. Thank God you didn't put a bullet in it."

"What was it?"

"Two things, a ledger in a small red notebook, not large, would fit in a pocket. Tucked in the notebook was a thumb drive with a couple of videos stored on it."

"Notebook and videos?"

"Yes, your mate Joey Golino was paying off a few Melbourne-based cops on behalf of his uncle. He kept a ledger of payments, names, dates and amounts. He also took videos of the money handovers if and when they were stupid enough to collect in Golino's car. He actually copied the police playbook on that one. We have done it ourselves. Smile, you're on candid camera. Camera under the dash."

"If the evidence was all they wanted," I asked, "why go chasing Ricky Chalmers into the bush?"

"My guess," he said, "they were cleaning house, as well as chasing money."

"Think about it from Snow's point of view," he said, "for one brief moment, he has half of it all nailed down. He has Chalmers, a worthy murder suspect, cornered. He has all of that incriminating evidence against himself and Hughes safe in his very own pocket. He is probably up there on the Mitta Mitta, ready to finish off Ricky Chalmers, assuming his cohort had killed you and Sergeant Palmer back at the car park. He has left a long trail of mayhem, all of which he can blame on Chalmers, especially if Chalmers is conveniently dead."

"He very nearly pulled it off, Chris. He would have travelled back to Melbourne a hero."

He was right.

"But they didn't do their homework on you, did they?"

I laughed at that. "Boofhead was offended that I had beat him up there in the bush. The local plod, he called me."

"They didn't check you out, but I did. You have done stuff like this back in your army days. SASR, my God, they were just a bunch of bush league bullies next to someone with your training."

He waited for a response, but I couldn't think of one. Boofhead and his band of bikers were, indeed, bush league, but playing serious games with big guns.

"So anyway," he continued. "You come along, and down they go like nine pins. Well done, Constable."

I wasn't feeling triumphant. They weren't much opposition, and yet the carnage these people had wrought would stain our town forever.

Murders everywhere, and now poor sad Georgie Golino, the shining golden girl of her high school years beaten to death by a crooked cop. All because she married the wrong guy.

I hated all this Machiavellian bullshit. I was glad Ricky had stepped up and beaten the shit out of Davies. I wished he'd found the chance to do over Snow and Hughes as well.

I was sick of it.

"What's this favour you want?" I asked.

"My favour is this. Go and meet your mate Ricky Chalmers in

hospital and tell him for me that there is a deal on the table. He can be free tomorrow if he has the information I want."

"Let me guess, where are Folliero and his money?"

"That would be good, or anything he knows on either subject."

"Wait a moment," it just occurred to me. "If you were listening to my conversation with Georgie Golino, you heard her tell me that Ricky Chalmers could not have been the murderer."

"Chris," he was exasperated now. "Yes, I heard it, but that's the word of a dead woman. She may have been manipulating you. Saying what she wanted you to hear, to get you to rescue her lover. That's not evidence."

"Bullshit. It most certainly is evidence. You're not the judge here, remember. Her voice is on tape. We both know it is her. You can verify the timing of the phone calls she mentioned. We can play the tape and let a judge and jury decide if she was truthful."

"Well, I suppose Chalmers' defence lawyer could do that. The jury might believe it. If it went to trial."

"If?" I finally caught on. He was after the money and the glory. He knew Ricky was innocent and didn't care. His carefree attitude to collateral damage, again.

"Yes, if," he said. "Just say for a moment your beloved football coach did commit the crime. Just say for a moment he knew where Folliero was hiding, and maybe he even knows where all of that missing Folliero cash happens to be. A man with that much information would have a lot of leverage. He might be able to swing a very good deal for himself."

"So, you're saying if Ricky can locate Folliero and his money, you will get him off a triple murder charge? Even when you already know he is innocent."

"He is not innocent, Chris. We have him at the scene. We have him beating Davies. He knows a lot more than he is telling."

"So, you charged him with murder just to leverage him?"

"Deals can be made, Chris. It is never too late to talk."

"But you know from your bugs he didn't do it."

"Maybe, but maybe he knows more than I know about Folliero. I want everything he knows."

"And you don't care how you get it. Just let an innocent guy linger in jail till you get what you want."

"Getting this to trial could end up taking a few years. Alternatively, your mate could be out tomorrow. Footy season starts soon. He could be back at training as soon as he gets out of the hospital."

I felt like punching him in his charming face and getting blood on his perfect suit.

He just shrugged, and now I knew why I hated the prick. He wanted the big name; he would trade everyone for Folliero and his money. The murder victims were just a side issue. He was almost as bad as Boofhead and Hughes.

And I still hadn't ruled out killing Boofhead.

Alfred Hospital, Melbourne, Victoria, Australia.

Detective Pete Jordan fulfilled the first part of his deal. I was allowed to see Ricky Chalmers.

I was waiting in the Detention Ward in the Alfred Hospital, the main casualty centre in the city of Melbourne.

The Detention Ward was really just a few rooms where they imprisoned patients for any one of a million reasons. Most hospital patients were content to be sick and cared for and leave it at that.

Some patients found a reason to be restrained or contained as well as sick. If that was their preference, then this was where they ended up.

It held nut-jobs who acted up in the emergency ward. Patients who are too angry to manage and criminals who are too badly injured to be put directly into prison. This is where they went, a few bleak, secure rooms in the bowels of a huge city hospital. This is where they remained until they were well enough to ship off to jail or throw back into the world.

I was sitting outside Ricky Chalmers' locked room with his sister Kate. She was looking better than the last time I saw her in her own detention ward at the Jarrajarra Nursing Centre. She looked pretty good, in fact. She was a tall and striking woman. Now healthy again, you could clearly see she was Ricky's sister.

"No need to ask," she said. "I am totally off the oxy, I have given up the cigarettes, and I haven't entertained any gentlemen at my farm since I got out of your girlfriend's hospital," she said with a smile.

"None of my business what you do, Kate. I'm just here to check on Ricky. Here as a friend, not a cop."

"Well, then you just missed the good-news-doctor by a minute." She took a huge breath and let out a long sigh of relief. "The operations were a success. We can see him when he wakes up. It could be a few hours yet, but he is going to be fine, they told me. Going to be just fine. Fine." Another deep breath and a huge sigh. "He is not going to die."

Then her smile vanished, and she burst out crying. She buried her face in her hands, her elbows on her knees, and she howled.

"Oh shit," she sobbed. Crying was not part of the Kate I knew. "Oh fuck," she went on.

She wailed almost, then stopped for long enough to squeeze out, "Sorry, Chris." Then she wailed some more for a good two minutes.

Battling for control, she grabbed a tissue and sniffed and wiped and moaned.

"I'll be right," she said. "Just saying it out loud to someone set me off."

"Saying what?" Fuck, I could ask some truly dumb questions.

Her bottom lip quivered again, but she held back a second flood burst. "The not dying bit, I mean."

She looked away, determined not to cry again.

"Do you want a coke?" I asked eventually.

"Coke?" It was almost an exclamation.

"The drinking kind. Diet coke with all the good stuff in it, pheno, keno, beno, and so on."

"Sounds great." she sniffed and wiped.

While she cleaned up her distraught face, I went and found a machine. I came back to our seats with two Diet Cokes. Then, the beautiful click of the can opening and that first magnificent sip. We did it in perfect harmony.

"You should get back into running, Kate and reward yourself with one Diet Coke a month. Positive addictions are the go, in my book."

"You think so?"

"Works for me. I was hooked on oxy myself a few years back."

"You? No?"

"Me? Yes!"

"How did you get off it?"

"I was fixed by the same hard bitch that fixed you. Nurse Wendy has form in this area. Good form."

"Bugger me," she said. Her smile was back. That was good.

We sat and contemplated our cokes.

"I looked up oxy withdrawal on the internet," she said. "Those few days in the hospital really helped. The first seventy-two hours of cold turkey is the worst, apparently. I was about eighty hours in when you showed up during my, ah, altercation."

"Altercation, was it?" Had to laugh at that.

"Anyway, I am over a week now. So, I am supposed to be actually over the physical dependency."

"So, how does it feel? Do you still want it?"

"I could kill for it. But I won't. Need to stay straight for my idiot brother."

"Good reason," I said.

"You saved me, and now you have saved Ricky," she said. "I owe you."

She was the opposite of Detective Pete, who, somehow, felt I owed him.

"You mostly saved yourself, Kate, and, as for Ricky, well, you know, I was in the right place at the right time. With a big gun and some very huge targets."

"You carried him down the mountain, for heaven's sake."

I had to laugh. "Carried is far too dignified a word to describe our progress down the Mitta Mitta trail. Dragged, tumbled maybe, boon-doggled perhaps. But I did get him down to that other person, that person who really saved you and was really the one who saved your brother."

"Your bossy girlfriend?"

"That's the one."

She laughed. The relief on her face was obvious. It felt good.

Ricky would live according to his doctor. That was our first hurdle. Next, I needed to get him out from under these murder charges.

I pushed very gently in another direction.

"That was an amazing dug-out he had created up there. Completely invisible if you don't have a GPS. I know he built it for Joey Golino."

She looked at me but gave me nothing.

"How did he get into building dugouts?" I asked.

She did a tiny jolt of her head backwards, like a note of surprise, almost imperceptible. "You know about him doing underground dugouts?"

"Yes," I said.

"It's no crime to build a dug-out, you know. Not my business how people use them."

"That's true," I answered. "Though to be legal, you'd probably need to ask the council for a building permit at least."

Then the penny dropped.

"Oh Jesus," I said. "He built them for the Mellish brothers for their dope growing?" It was half question, half a statement of the totally obvious.

She nodded her head, just a tiny tilt to the side. It was a 'yes'. "I never said a word," she added, sipping her coke.

"I thought the Mellish boys built them by themselves."

"Ha," she laughed. "Just like they fix their own cars that don't run till they get Ricky or Rob Farrell to take a look."

"Oh," I said.

"They'd like you to believe they do the man-stuff themselves," she said. "Little boys, playing as grown-ups."

"Oh."

"You've lived in Jarrajarra long enough, Chris. Have you ever seen a Mellish fix anything, ever? Did a Mellish ever make anything better? They're a family of inbred fuckups, and those two brothers are the worst, especially the younger one."

"Jason?"

"Yeah, him."

"Oh," I said again. This was called leading the interrogation.

"They tried making their own little underground man caves, but all they ended up with was collapsed mud-holes in the ground. Their caves kept caving in. Couldn't stay erect, probably why they can't keep their girlfriends."

"You don't like the Mellish clan."

"Wally's alright I guess, harmless, friendly. The rest of them, the uncles and aunties and those two brothers, not worth twenty cents. Permanently angry pack of shits all of them. Apart from Wally."

"What about the Mellish girls."

"Georgie? May she rest in peace. Georgie and Sue, we were never friends. Leave it at that mate."

"So, Ricky made the underground Mellish dope farms," I summarised. "The Mellish brothers grew the dope, then sold it to Joey Golino. Joey learns about the dug-outs and ends up hiring Ricky to make him one. A special one that no one can find."

"Making a hole in the ground is not a crime," she said. "How that person uses it is their business."

"That's true."

Another thought occurred. Ricky was the town gardener, curator of the bowling club, the football and cricket fields, all the outdoor assets that the town controlled.

"Oh Kate! Please don't tell me he used the town council's excavation equipment."

Normally that was a question I know she would not answer, she was not one to tell tales against her brother, but the wicked smile on her face gave her away. She had a thought and couldn't hold it in.

"Let me put it this way Chris, if the town council found out what machinery went into those constructions, well, how can I put it?" She was close to laughing out loud. "I don't think Norma Farrell would be too pleased."

Then she did laugh out loud, and I joined in.

"Well, I guess what Norma doesn't know can't hurt her," I said. Could I possibly keep a secret from Norma Farrell or was I deluding myself.

"If Norma ever finds out," Kate said. "I'll know it was you."

. . .

We waited there a few more hours, together, until Ricky woke up. We were allowed in to see him, but he was mostly out of it. He knew I was there and briefly gripped my hand.

"Thanks brother," he whispered, before falling back to sleep.

That felt good.

～

Kate walked me to my new truck.

"Can I give you a lift anywhere, Kate?"

"No thanks, no need. I am staying in a motel around the corner. I will probably keep a room in there and hang around till he is released."

"When he is released from here, they will probably move him to jail."

"Well, I intend to get him a good lawyer and see about bail."

"Kate, he has no chance of obtaining bail. A triple murder usually means you wait behind bars for your trial."

"I can only try; he would try for me."

"I know he is innocent, Kate. I believe there is stuff he is holding back. I am hoping he knows more about those three blokes that are dead than he has admitted to me."

"Why?"

"Because" this was the time to float the bargain. "I am very sure that Detective Jordan, the Homicide guy, would trade for anything Ricky knew about Folliero and his money and his whereabouts."

"Trade?"

"They know that a good defence lawyer will likely get him off. But even getting a not guilty could take Ricky as long as a year, more likely two. They can drag the chain, string it out, take forever. All that time he would be in jail."

She was thinking. Looking into the dark horizon.

"Information is gold Kate, but only for a while. If Ricky knows anything, he needs to horse trade now. If you know anything you should start work on his behalf now."

"What would I do?"

"Start haggling. Jesus Christ, who would know more about nego-tiating than you."

"Me, the hooker?"

"I mean you, the caring sister." She didn't buy that.

"But yes, as for your working experience, I reckon your last customer would say you drove a hard bargain, definitely."

I got that world-weary smile again. She didn't take offence at my lame joke.

"I will talk to Ricky when he wakes up properly," she said.

As much as I hated Detective Pete for pushing the charges against Ricky, I still hoped Ricky might have some worthwhile information to trade for his freedom.

"It's all just trade Kate, you can do that."

She gave me that shrug again.

"I will talk to Ricky," she said again, with some finality this time, and we left it at that.

I hopped into my brand-new special truck with all its new and wonderful gadgetry. I was already loving it more than the dead one. I turned the key and away I went. On the five-hour trip back home I tried one of these blue-tooth podcasts. It was mind boggling, like a documentary for drivers. Who had ever heard of such a thing.

I was home before I knew it.

15

WEDNESDAY, MARCH 21, 2018

Jarrajarra, Victoria, Australia.

"Christopher," shouted Sarge. "You're supposed to be on a break for at least two weeks."

Two? I thought it was one.

I was sitting in the Jarrajarra cafe waiting for a coffee, speaking, by phone, to the Sarge. He was still in Wodonga hospital. Actually, I was more listening than speaking, he was not happy and was doing all the talking.

"I told Will Walker to tell you to take time off. It wasn't a suggestion, Constable."

"He did Sarge, but he doesn't have that same air of authority that you have. He is really friendly and nice. I felt compelled to try him on."

"Yes, well I am telling you now, take two weeks off, that's an order."

"Well boss you are off duty so I don't know that you can give orders from a hospital bed. Is that even legal?"

He was injured and in hospital, I was sure he would love being revved up. Normally he ate stress for breakfast.

"Don't play the goose with me son. Did you call me just to see how far you could raise my stress levels. Holy Mother of God."

"Sarge, do you want to hear my question or not?"

He took a long pause, pretending to be angry. Of course, he wanted to hear my question. I waited.

"OK, go ahead."

"Well, I have been to see Detective Pete. After that I visited Ricky Chalmers in hospital, and I also spoke to his sister Kate. Let me fill you in with what I've found."

I told Sarge about Davies being a police informer, about the bug in the pizza shop, how Boofhead was caught, on tape, in the act of murdering Georgie Golino.

Some of this he already knew from his own team. Sergeant Will Walker had visited him and brought him up to date.

Some he didn't know about the video evidence against Inspector Hughes and others, how I had obtained that evidence inadvertently by shooting Boofhead.

"Lucky he didn't have it in his back pocket," said the Sarge, aware I had shot the Boof in his massive arse.

Finally, I related Detective Pete's request that I extract a deal from Ricky Chalmers if I could.

"What kind of deal?"

"All charges dropped in exchange for whatever Ricky knows about the location of Folliero and his money."

"Well, if Chalmers is innocent as you insist, how on earth will he know any of that?"

"I don't know boss, but I can only ask, so I did. Actually, I asked his sister and she said she would get back to me."

"Alright then," he said. "So then, what is your question?"

"OK, this is what's bothering me. If both of the crooked cops, Boofhead and Inspector Hughes, had no knowledge of the bug in the pizza shop, or my conversation with Georgie. If it was only Detective Pete who knew about the bug, then how did Boofhead manage to turn up at the pizza shop only a few minutes after I left?"

The Sarge had to think about that one for quite a while.

"OK, very good question. Clearly Snow didn't know about the

bug, else he would not have murdered Georgie Golino in the pizza shop."

"Correct."

"Whoever got him there didn't know or didn't tell him about the bug."

"Correct."

"I can only think of two answers."

"Only two?"

"Two that make sense to me."

"And what would they be?"

"Well," he said. "Either Detective Pete told Boof, which means all of them are working together and Jordan has now turned against Hughes and Snow. Maybe he wants all that money for himself. The other possibility is someone higher up Pete Jordan's chain of crusading crime fighters told Hughes and then Hughes told Snow."

"So, either Detective Pete is corrupt or there is another crooked cop lurking in the mix somewhere?" I asked.

"Maybe," replied the Sarge.

We both thought about that for a long moment.

"Chris," said Sarge eventually, "it's not mind reading. Detective Boofhead is right here, in custody, in Wodonga hospital. I might get Sergeant Will Walker to pay him a visit and ask him your question."

"Will Walker?" I asked. "What about me?"

"Well son, you're on holiday remember. Plus, even if you weren't on holiday, you are not a member of the integrity unit. You are the local plod, and you have four local murders now, counting poor Georgie. Why don't you focus on those and let the police force sort out their bad eggs?"

Police investigating police. I had to hold back a laugh at that. But he had a good point about my priorities.

"Forget which side of the fence Jordan is on," said Sarge. "Forget about the cops who are already in custody. If you think Chalmers is innocent well get out and prove it. If he is guilty, then get him to take this deal. Either way, you need to find out who did it."

He made a lot of very good points. Ricky was still in cuffs, and I still hadn't found the real killer.

We paused while we both thought it all over.

I didn't want to aggravate Sarge, but I knew down deep I was determined to solve it all, the murders, the money, and the crooked cops. Who brought all this evil garbage to my town? What did they want? Why did they do whatever they did?"

"You are not really listening to me are you?" said Sarge.

"No Boss, not really. Sorry I bothered you during your long journey back to health."

"You know son, my Wodonga crew is leaving me alone; it is only junior constables from Jarrajarra interrupting my rest. I am supposed to be recuperating from these terrible wounds I have suffered. Should have been fatal, or worse, according to the doctors."

"Some of the worst wounds I've ever seen, Boss. It's amazing you lived."

"I know son, incredible really. A lesser man would have perished."

"Expired even."

"I'm a walking miracle."

"Is it too early to be talking Sainthood?" I asked.

"Not for me to say Chris, not for me to say."

Sarge's sense of humour was intact. All would be well.

"Sainthood would be nice," he added before ending the call.

I finished my coffee then ordered some more, three take-aways this time. One for me, and the other two for Barney and Joanne. Delivering coffee was a good excuse to visit the station and see what was happening in my enforced absence. When I went to pay, Leanne who owned the cafe refused to take any money from me, which was unusual. I always paid at the cafe.

"It is a glad-you're-alive-gift, Chris. We were all so relieved you didn't get shot."

"Me too," I answered. "I'm very glad myself. That's very kind, thank you." It was three days since the shoot-out, I should have known it would have been totally dissected and distributed across the

Jarrajarra gossip network. I couldn't guess how it would have all been described.

"More important, where would we be without our footy coach?" said Leanne, smiling, reminding me of the town's priority.

"Absolutely."

Priorities. Always priorities.

I took the coffee gift over to the station. Barney and Joanne were busy behind the front desk. Joanne was doing some work on the 'Welcome to Jarrajarra' website. Barney was organising a small stack of post-it notes. I was delighted to see the little yellow stack of jobs to do.

"Coffee for you guys and work for me, great."

"Chris," they said in surprise unison.

"You're not supposed to be here." Barney looked and sounded quite stern. "These are for Tim," he said holding up the post-its. "You are supposed to be home resting."

Who the fuck was Tim?

"Hi Chris," I turned to the cheery voice behind me, this was Tim. Tim who had met me, and Ricky, on the trail, with Wendy and the gang, after the shoot-out. Tim who drove me home from Mitta Mitta back to the bed in the Jarrajarra Nursing Centre. The Tim who got me from the police car to the bed without waking me. That Tim.

"G'day Tim," I smiled confidently, as though I had always known his name. "Good to see you mate."

No, it wasn't, he had just come out of my office. He was taking jobs from Barney. It wasn't good to see him at all.

I was the only cop in Jarrajarra. Not Tim.

"Sergeant Walker posted me down here for three weeks while you took your break," said Tim. "Help Barney and Jo keep things under control till you're back on deck."

Three weeks now! If my holiday extended any further, I would be retired.

"OK," I said. Not OK, I thought.

"Actually, there is one job for you Chris," Barney smiled as he held up one of his yellow notes. "Mrs. Gillespie called; she has baked you some chocolate cake."

"For me? Not for her granddaughter?"

"No definitely for you this time, she felt you might need a sugar hit after your ordeal in the wilderness. She was worried about you; thought you could do with some care and attention."

From anyone else in town this might have sounded cynical, or playful at least. But from Mrs. Gillespie, I had no doubt she was sincerely concerned for me.

"I'll do it now," I said, and grabbed the yellow ticket from Barney before Tim stole that and Mrs. Gillespie's affections as well. Not that I was the jealous type, of course.

But Tim was not looking at Barney's job tickets, he was looking at the fresh take-away coffees on the main desk.

"Any of these for me?" he asked with an expectant smile on his face.

"No," I said, sounding like a grumpy local.

I left him to find his own coffee and headed off to more tea and cake with my other true love.

As I was leaving, I heard the voice of Joanne Farrell. "Here you go Tim, you can have mine."

Sabotage.

Mrs. Gillespie's home was a neat white 1950's weatherboard, built by her husband as a home for their growing family. Still impeccably maintained, the garden perfect even in the early stage of autumn.

The only imperfection in the whole house was her squeaky front gate. I suspect that was deliberate. Normally Mrs. Gillespie would be at her front door waiting a few seconds after I opened and shut the gate. It was an early warning system, I never had to knock, but today I did.

I knocked on the front door and waited. Above the door was a plate inscribed as follows 'January 6, 2000. Fifty years of love and family. Happy anniversary to Doris and Bert, our wonderful Mum and Dad. From your loving children Roland, Vilma, Anne and Marjorie. May there be many more happy years to come.'

I didn't know the others, but I knew Vilma Gillespie, she was now Vilma Palmer, my boss's wife, Mrs Sarge. It was standard operating procedure for the wives back then, get married and change your surname to somebody else's. Great time for men, not so good for women. Terrible for everybody in my own family. The adult men I knew contributed nothing but alcohol, debt, violence and fear. Not something to worry about during cake and tea with Mrs. G.

I knocked again but no answer. She was 95 years old. She had invited me over; I knew she would wait till I arrived to weave her magic. She would not have forgotten and gone on a shopping trip. I was very worried, very quickly.

I went to the back door, it was open. I went in, calling out 'Hello' and 'Anybody home?' several times. I followed the lovely smell of just-brewed tea and freshly baked chocolate cake into the living room. There it was, the morning tea, mostly for me, all beautifully prepped and laid out for my enjoyment.

There, beside the food, sitting quietly in her armchair was Mrs. Gillespie, eyes open, smiling peacefully as she gazed out the window.

I sat beside her and spoke quietly but there was no response. I took her wrist very gently and felt for her pulse. There wasn't one to find.

She was dead.

I called Jack Farrell. He was at the Ambulance depot at the back of the Nursing Centre. So far, he had been having a quiet day.

He ran over, it was less than one hundred metres as the crow flew. He was there, with his gear, by her side in less than one minute. Jack did a slightly more professional examination than I did. Same result.

We looked at her and both let out sad, genuine sighs.

We simultaneously looked at the chocolate cake. Then we looked at each other.

"I can't," I said.

"It looks pretty good," said Jack. "She would probably want us to have it.

"I know she would," I replied. "But I can't."

"OK," he said, rather sadly.

Jody Taggart walked in with the heart starter thing they usually carry in the back of the ambulance.

"Found it," she said waving the heart starter.

"No need," said Jack.

"Yum-yum cake," said Jody and grabbed an end slice, a slice that I knew was meant for me. She took a large bite. She saw us both looking at her.

"What? What?" Pause. "I am sure Mrs. Gillespie would want me to have it."

She would indeed.

"Natural causes?" I asked.

"Yes," said Jack. "I'd reckon so."

I stepped outside and called Vilma Palmer, my boss's wife. I told her as gently as I could that her Mum had died, and she was understandably sad.

"It is strange Chris," she said. "Here I am age sixty-five, suddenly I am an orphan."

"Orphan? It's just a word Mrs P," I said, wanting to cheer her up. "You've had a beautiful mother and a wonderful father who loved you all your life. You are, and always will be, a part of a beautiful family, plus you have gone and made your own family. I wouldn't think of yourself as an orphan."

She burst out crying.

I hadn't lost the magic touch. Maybe she wanted to be an orphan.

I really should have left that bit to Barney.

Jack Farrell called and spoke to Vilma Palmer, and they organised the local funeral company to come and handle Mrs Gillespie's body. The funeral team showed up in their hearse, and after they left, I collected the remaining cake, locked up the house and headed back to the police station. Barney would know what paperwork was required with death by natural cause.

Once that was out of the way, Barney and I went to the cafe for more coffee and a chance to review our murder inquiry.

"G-F?" asked Barney. "A weapon that looks like a large, heavy tuning fork?"

"Yes," I answered. "G-F, in reverse, like a photo negative, bruised into the arm of our Mister X."

We were sitting in the afternoon sun outside the cafe.

"I can't think of any 'G-F's in town other than Greg Farrell," I said. "I am not ready to contemplate one of my best mates, not to mention Norma's husband, as a murderer."

"Right, yes," said Barney. He was looking at my phone, only half listening to me. He was staring at the photo of AJ Davies' battered arm. "There is a sleeve tattoo on the arm here, makes it hard to see the bruise."

"It does." I was wondering about that tattoo. It was hard to tell exactly what shape it was. The little bit I could see looked very artistic, not a scratchy prison job at all.

While Barney was still thinking I took back my phone and called my favourite forensic cops, Carole and Glenda.

"Hey, Killer," Carole answered the phone. "Have you found my murder weapon yet?"

"Working on it, I have the best criminal mind in the district on it at this very moment."

"Hi Barney," she shouted in my ear.

"Hello Carole," he answered, still thinking about G and F and what the hell that meant.

"Caz," I asked. "Could you send me a full picture of AJ Davies' arm. I want to check that tattoo.

"No worries, will do, anything else?"

There was nothing else and we signed off quickly.

I watched Barney in his deep thought process. I guessed from his rapidly darting eyes he was running a catalogue of every family in town whose surname started with F then skimming through the first names for a G. He buzzed and whirred for another minute. Finally, he spoke.

"No, there aren't any G-Fs in town, but -"

"But what?"

"But, Christopher, who says they are initials?"

"Well, no one says anything of the sort, Barn. I was just starting with initials." If I sounded defensive it was because I was supposed to be the professional sleuth, but Barney had dived deeper yet again.

"This is a farming area," he said, "there could be any number of incomprehensible tools in the area with a G-F welded onto them."

"Possibly. Maybe. Massey Ferguson has a G and an F," I said.

"Really?" Barney sounded scornful.

"I am going to have to look, aren't I?"

"Yes, I am afraid so. I could do some internet sleuthing for you, but it won't beat the search capabilities of a real policeman." Barney clearly had no intention of wading through the vast stores of metallic rubbish that lived in the grotty farm sheds surrounding the town.

My phone dinged; Carole had sent me a picture. It was a photo of the dead tattooed arm of AJ Davies, plus the now famous G-F bruise. I knew that tattoo. I had seen one just like it very recently.

"What is it, Chris?"

"It is a Ta Moko, is what it is Barn, and a familiar one at that."

Very familiar.

"You can't just come into my workplace and demand I go to the police station."

"It is a request Jen, not a demand. I am sure the bakery can cope for half an hour or so." The usual policeman's fib, "this won't take long". Actually, I was thinking this could take her the next few years of her life.

Once I had told Barney who owned the other Kiwi Ta Moko in town, he pointed me to the Bakery. Justin Mellish's new girlfriend Jenny had been working there for the last few weeks, basically since she arrived in town. I couldn't remember her surname. Barney made a guess that it was McClain.

Here she was, Jennifer McClain, working every day in the Bakery.

The Bakery, the centre point of the town, where she could see the police station, the police yards, and the pizza shop. The whole main street of town for heaven's sake.

I never went there myself, the Bakery. It was pre-emptive discipline, to avoid the irresistible array of sugar-laden cakes they had on display, plus their coffee wasn't quite as good as the cafe. I hadn't been inside the place in a year.

Was she my missing link? How did Boofhead know to go to visit Georgie Golino in the pizza shop so soon after I left there last Saturday? If Boof was unaware of the bug and if Detective Pete didn't tell him then who did? Here was my answer, maybe.

After speaking to her Bakery boss, Jen came with me to the station without making a scene. As we exited, I stood momentarily at the door. She could have seen everything. Me, leaving the pizza shop after speaking to Georgie. Me again, gearing up in the yards out back of the station ready to go find Ricky. The Sarge, planning, joining me. Rob Farrell delivering his Steyr rifle. She would have seen all of it.

As we walked to the station, I texted Carole and Glenda, the dynamic forensics team, and asked then to send me head shots, and tattoo pics, of all the dead bikers, AJ Davies and his two mates who had died at Mitta Mitta. I put an ASAP on the end of that.

"Jen, you don't have to say anything. I am not recording you here, and if you want a lawyer present you are entitled have one. Eddie Doolan could probably be here in half an hour if that's what you want."

"Tell me why I am here," she said, "then I'll decide if I need a lawyer."

Fair enough. I told her.

"I am investigating the murder of Georgie Golino and I suspect you may be indirectly involved."

I was watching her as I spoke. Her whole body gave this small involuntary retraction, as though gravity had grabbed the back of her shirt and pulled her back a fraction of an inch, against her will.

"OK," she said.

"So, OK?" I said, "meaning you don't need a lawyer present and I can question you?"

"OK as in ask your questions. Doesn't mean I will answer."

"Alright," I said, confident this would pass the warning test in court. "You don't have to say a word, just listen, nod if you feel like it. You can't be hung for nodding, alright?"

She gave another little start. Maybe I shouldn't have mentioned hanging.

"Sorry," I said. "Bad choice of words."

My phone dinged. I checked. Caz and Glenda had come through again. Oh my God, how they had come through. Twenty photos of heads and tattoos, in a gory sequence from the only not-dead-biker, the one who remained alive, to the merely dead, to the massively-devastated-dead. I noted the various positions of AJ Davies in the slide show.

Picture number seven showed the Davies Ta Moko, the authentic Kiwi tattoo, the near identical one Jen had on her own arm. It may have differed from Davies' for tribal reasons or gender reasons, I didn't really know, but I was damn sure it had been done by the same highly skilled tattooist. They were too good and too alike not to be.

The last picture was Davies' battered head, and it was just bloody gruesome.

I set up on number one, the guy who had been in the middle, Davies' brother, killed by me in a nice clean belly shot. Horrible way to die, but a lot less messy.

"I believe you know these guys. In fact, I think you know all of them pretty well."

She looked at the first photo. She knew them. She was trying not to say anything, but she knew them.

She got to number seven, and her bottom lip started to shake. She knew who it was, she was close to tears but still checking photographs, skipping faster till arriving at the last. Davies' battered head, beaten down, his skull fractured, dying bruises filling the whole side of his face. With all of the dried blood cleaned away by forensics, his swollen, misshapen skull looked grotesque.

She started to cry, flipped the phone across the desk to me, lowered her head and continued crying.

"Don't say anything OK?" I said. "Just take your time and don't say anything. What you don't say can't hurt you."

I let her cry for a bit, regain her composure.

"Here is what I think. I think you and AJ Davies had some sort of relationship before all this."

She looked up at me, still crying. Listening.

"If that's the case, then I am sorry for your loss." Was I sorry? Probably not.

"I think sometime after police discovered the body of the politician Gary Rogers, on February 15th, your friend Davies asked you to come to this town and keep an eye on Joey Golino."

She looked at me with not much reaction at all. That was OK.

"I don't know if you even know, or even care, who Rogers was, who Joey Golino was? It was probably enough that Davies asked you to come here and watch Joey Golino. He asked you and you said yes. He was your friend perhaps, maybe your lover, for all I know."

That hit a nerve.

"I think AJ Davies knew Joey Golino and he knew Golino's relationship with Michelle Folliero."

"Whatever the reason, you get yourself a job at the bakery, from where you can keep an eye on what happens around town. You hook-up with Justin Mellish who gives you a bed for the night at no extra cost. I suspect you are doing all of this out of love for Davies, and Davies is not a jealous type and doesn't give you much money to play with. He just asks you to do things and you do them."

That was true too. Her body language read like a book.

"I believe Davies gave you a phone number to call if you saw anything, out of the ordinary, going on with Golino. So that's your real job and that is what you do while working at the bakery."

So far, so good.

"Then of course Golino and Davies get themselves killed." I checked my calendar. "They are murdered here in town, twelve days ago."

She was listening very intently now.

"That leaves you stranded in Jarrajarra with no cash and no one to turn to."

She had tried a poker face, but it was terrible, the fractional body shifts were getting worse. Small, involuntary inhales and bum shuffles on her seat.

"So, you try the little cash play on the owner of the Warrangatha pub. You had a car, you had fifteen thousand dollars of the Mellish boys' cash. You try squeezing the publican for an extra fifteen. If that had worked you would have been gone. Never to be seen again. Goodbye Jarrajarra. Goodbye Justin Mellish."

I was right again, certain of it.

"But the Warrangatha publican calls me, and you end up with nothing. Still stuck in Jarrajarra. Still sharing a bed with a Mellish but the man you really love is dead."

She had followed at least one instruction I gave her. She wasn't saying a word.

"So, you are stuck here. But then someone else contacts you, using the phone number you were given by Davies. Someone who doesn't identify themselves, but someone who knows why you are in Jarrajarra and what you are doing. That person encourages you to keep doing what you are doing and contact him if you see anything."

So far so good.

"And yes, it was a him, not a her. I suspect you eventually worked out who it was who'd replaced AJ on the end of that line."

She was getting very tense.

"Then, around Tuesday, life got a little bit easier for you when Davies' brother turned up with a couple of his biker mates. Parked themselves in the caravan park and waited. Waited for a call. You might have even crept away from the Mellish boys and had a drink with them while they waited."

"I don't creep away from any man," she said. "I go where I please, when I please, with whoever I fucking please."

"OK. Well maybe it was just nice to get down there with Davies' brother, Butch, I think his name was. You and Butch and the two muscle bound kids he carted along, barely adults really. You all just sit and drink and plan some serious revenge on whoever killed AJ.

Back to tight lipped silence. Lips like string, my Nan would have said.

"Maybe you did that and maybe you didn't. But day to day, you went on doing what AJ had told you to do. You kept your promise, and eventually you saw me visit Georgie Golino at the pizza shop. Saturday. You saw me gear up in the back of the police station, guns, vests, the works. You saw me head out of town, going south."

That was exactly what she had done. Her body screamed 'guilty'.

"So, you made a call, and whether you knew in advance you certainly know now, the man you called was Detective Constable Snow. You know that because you saw him arrive at the pizza shop only minutes after you spoke to him. You were working with a cop. You were a cop's snitch."

It was true, I had it exactly right, her movements were no longer fractional. She had her arms around her waist, and she was rocking in her chair. She looked like a pending eruption, her face was getting redder, the tears were rolling again.

She looked away. Trying to control herself.

"Then of course Snow gets shot and he is now in custody, no doubt he will give you up without even thinking. We have him dead to rights for the murder of Georgie Golino. You can actually listen to it on tape if you want. He will trade anybody for a few years off his sentence. He might even put you forward for the murder of Joey Golino and your boyfriend AJ."

Her face was getting redder, and she was rocking harder.

"What really hurts is that Davies' brother Butch is dead now as well. So, he is not going to get you out of here. I bet you are wishing you never heard of Jarrajarra. It has not been a happy town for the Davies clan. Not at all."

She was back to looking at me, still rocking, still weeping, but trying to work out my angle here.

"What I wonder is this, once you worked out that you were calling Detective Snow, did you ever ask yourself how and why he was in the act. Did you ever ask yourself, why was AJ working with him?"

I had her attention.

"I'll tell you. Here is your answer. Your boyfriend AJ didn't work WITH ex-Detective Snow, he worked FOR him. Snow said jump and your beloved AJ said how high Sir? AJ Davies is what cops call a CI, a confidential informant. What you might call a snitch, a dog."

Bingo. She erupted. Oh, my goodness did she erupt.

"You fucking pig cunt!" she screamed. "AJ was no dog you fucking cunt! You Cunt! Cunt! Cunt!"

"I hate to burst your little picture of your boyfriend, Jen but that was exactly what he was."

That landed right on the button.

"AJ wasn't my boyfriend alright," she shouted, "he was my husband, you fucking prick."

Oh. Oh dear. That was a surprise.

"Lots of women murder their husband, Jen. Maybe you and Detective Snow were working together." I didn't really believe that, why did I say it? Pretending to be a homicide detective, again.

She looked at me, ready to murder me, right then and there. I could see her mental wheels spinning.

"I couldn't have killed anyone on the Saturday night, you fucking dumb pig. I had an alibi; I was in a motel in Tumbarumba with Justin. Go ahead, ask him you fuck!"

Well, bloody hell, there was a trifecta guaranteed to convince a jury of a women's innocence. She couldn't have murdered her husband on Saturday night because she was at a motel fucking her boyfriend at her husband's request. There was a defence. The things you do for love.

Wow.

It was confused but I believed her, I believed every word.

She was rocking again, head down, crying. Bloody hell, who would be a woman in love, especially one in love with a fucking A-grade arsehole like AJ Davies?

My door opened. The ever-reliable Constable Tim from Wodonga leaned in to lend support.

"Everything OK?" asked Tim.

You had to admire a young cop who stepped up to assist before he knew where he was stepping. I couldn't help noticing the smudge of Doris Gillespie's chocolate cake on his chin and a few crumbs on his shirt front. Mrs. G would have loved it.

"It's OK Tim. All good. All clear. Maybe a glass of water from the kitchen would help."

He retreated, leaving me alone again with the biker-girl Jen, back to silent sobbing.

I passed her a tissue from my drawer, and she took it. Tim returned with her glass of water from the kitchen, and she took that too. Then he left us alone.

I now had the answer to my little riddle. How did Boofhead get to Georgie when he did, without knowing that the pizza shop was being bugged, that he was being recorded as he went about bashing Georgie to death.

Jennifer McLain told him, that's how. Faithfully fulfilling her duties to her dead husband AJ Davis, serial rapist, snitch and scumbag.

What did it mean? It meant that smarmy fucking Detective Pete was, probably, one of the good guys.

I still didn't know who killed Joey Golino, or even AJ Davies for that matter. But it was looking less like a rogue cop by the minute.

What else did I want from Jen? Nothing really. I felt sorry for her.

"Jen," I asked. "How much cash have you got on you?"

She sniffed, regained control, looked suspicious, expecting maybe I'd ask for a bribe.

"Just over a thousand."

"Are you in town with a car?"

"I have Jason's little run about thing."

Jason's, not Justin's? That was interesting.

"Don't go back to the Mellish farm," I said. "Don't go to the caravan park. Just get in that car and go. No one is looking for you and they probably never will. If they ever do, it will be for conspiracy to murder Georgie Golino."

"I had nothing to do with any of these murders. I didn't even know the Golino woman." Her tone was pleading now, softer, almost gentle.

"Stop, stop," I said. "It doesn't matter what you say or what I think. Save it. No one is thinking about you right now, no one is looking for you."

Which wasn't entirely true, as I would find out soon enough.

"Listen," I said. "You are caught up in the edge of something way bigger than AJ Davies and his biker mates. There are people involved who will put you in prison for years. But right now, this minute, you are not even on their radar. Do yourself a favour and keep it that way. Take the car, take the cash, get in the car and go. OK? Just leave. Leave this town, leave the Mellish brothers, just go and don't come back."

This was the best deal she would ever get from a policeman.

Why let her go? I really didn't know, but, if I locked her up now and called Detective Pete, I was sure she would be tied up in this case, and the legal machinery that surrounded it, for years. For what purpose?

Maybe she reminded me of my own mother. Tough, pretty but not tough enough for the problems bought by her choice in men.

She was extremely suspicious of me, very wary, but weighing up my offer.

Then, before Jen had decided what to do next, as if to remind us that not all of Jarrajarra's troubles were imported, we had our own little Mellish moment.

"Where is she? Where the fuck is she?"

I heard screaming from the direction of reception. I knew the tone and the voice. I moved quickly, but I was seated behind a desk, with another person seated opposite, between me and the door. Not exactly the defence ready position.

By the time I made it out of my office, past the kitchen, into the reception area, serious damage had been done.

Constable Tim from Wodonga was flat on his back unconscious.

Barney was still standing behind the reception desk. He had his hands to his face, trying to capture the river of blood spurting through his fingers, from his nose.

Joanne Farrell was still on her feet, in action. She was coming around from the tall reception desk, a police baton held expertly in her hands and swinging quite skilfully at our visitor.

There in the reception area, Jason Mellish, drugged up and angry. Not Justin, but Jason, bloody hell.

"Jenny!" He screamed. "Jenny."

"Hey!" I shouted even louder than he screamed.

That got his attention, and he turned his reddened, weepy eyes to me.

"Where is she you fucking pig?"

I might have answered had he given me a chance. So might have Tim, or even Barney, had Jason been inclined to listen. But he wasn't and he charged.

The problem for a guy like Jason was that his size determines most fights before they even start. People are scared by his massive muscles and angry demeanour. They go into a defensive shell, and he is so big, and he punches so well, they get beaten up without even fighting back.

His second problem was that his skills are limited to boxing. He has trained a bit and can box a bit. This was street-fighting, and the Marquis of Queensberry was not around. None of this was good for Jason.

Finally, His major problem was his total ignorance of his own limitations.

So, then Jason charges me and, it appears, it is now my turn in the Mellish barrel of brutality.

Not to sound too smug, but, at that moment I performed a semi-perfect execution of a combination I had seen on a Bas Rutten self-defence video.

Bas Rutten is a former world champion heavyweight MMA champion and a very eloquent man. What he doesn't know about street fighting is not worth knowing. I highly recommend his instruction.

Jason steps toward me, screaming something, but I had stopped listening. His right hand is up, he is leading with his right, from a distance, which is a really dumb move. He sprints forward, but before he is close enough to launch, I kick him in the balls hard, wearing steel tipped hiking boots, it landed perfectly.

I have done it before.

He commenced leaning forward. My steel-tipped boots had landed perfectly, and Justin started leaning slowly downward toward a painful collapse.

His right hand is still in the air. The limb that Jase forgot, just hanging up there as he folds.

I switch feet, for Bas Step two. I next do a left, steel tipped, round kick to his liver area. I've done that before as well, it landed very nicely. At this point Jason is toast, a good liver shot is a finisher, but I still had a step to go. You don't often get a chance to execute a three step Bas Rutten lesson on a live volunteer.

My left kick is complete, so my left foot lands, and is now my lead foot. Next, I am stepping in to execute a textbook Rutten-Right elbow to the face of the younger Mellish. Like all great elbow-ers I had stepped a fraction to the left side of my opponent, allowing room for my right elbow to land and to gain maximum leverage at the point of impact.

Just as I had been taught, just as I had trained.

I was flowing like water through the defences of my enemy.

I was almost smiling; such is my love of justified, relatively harmless violence perpetrated on people like Jason Mellish.

I was too cocky by half.

I caught a glimpse on my left side of an incoming police baton. Swung hard, travelling fast, towards the temple of the same head I was aiming at. In the micro moment I had to react, I pulled back a little, twisted my chin away a little, but it was not enough.

The end of the baton clipped me on the temple, then rocketed on relatively unimpeded by my skull, into the head of Jason the invader. At the same time my own distracted elbow rolled with some leftover force into Jason's cheekbone.

Jason and I collapsed in unison.

In my last moment of consciousness, I caught a flash of Joanne Farrell both hands on the baton. Her eyes were widening as her focus swung from the back of Jason's head to the side of mine. She might have said "Whoops," or that might have been me. There was definitely a sense of 'Whoops' about the whole collision.

If it had been a fight in the boxing ring, with a referee I would not have made the ten count. I would have been disqualified anyway for kicking Jason in the testicles. But it was the Police Station reception area and there was no referee.

I was out cold for a moment, then I regained my faculties within about twenty or thirty seconds. Maybe it was longer than that, there is a good reason the unconscious boxer does not conduct the count.

I had been knocked out before and it is never fun, but I was confident I would survive.

I sat up and looked around.

Joanne was attending to Constable Tim from Wodonga who was also sitting up. He was leaning against the reception desk as Joanne wiped his bloody nose with a cloth. His eyes were closed but he was breathing and conscious. He would need checking. But he was coherent, making thanks to Joanne and offering apologies to Barney for not defending him better.

"Don't be silly," said Barney a couple of times.

Barney had done a summary wipe of his own bloodied face and jammed some cotton balls up his nostrils. It did little to stem the flow of blood from his nose, but he didn't seem to notice. He was busy with Jason Mellish.

Jason was now face down and groaning loudly, he sounded traumatised. Barney had managed to get Jason's hands behind his back and had cuffed him, just like a real cop should. He was currently zip-tying Jason's feet together. Our wild Mellish was going nowhere, taken down by my two admin assistants. They grow them tough in Jarrajarra.

I got to my feet and walked over to help Barney. My head hurt a bit, but I had managed worse.

"Have we called an ambulance?" I asked.

"On their way," said Barney, sounding very nasal with his nose stuffed full of cotton wool.

"Chris I am so sorry," said Joanne. I noticed she was crying as she looked at me. "Chris, I can't believe I hit you with the baton. I am so sorry."

"Forget it Jo, great job really, you pair didn't need any help from me. I should have left him to the both of you."

"I'm sorry." She said it again.

"Forget it, welcome to the team. You are now an official-un-official cop. You took down your first perpetrator. A Mellish, no less. Good job."

It hurt to talk actually but I faked it well enough. Couldn't have the poor kid worried.

"Good job Barn," I whispered.

"Thank you Chris, it has been quite distressing, but we managed." He gave me a smile through the cotton balls and blood. "I feel like the bride of Dracula."

"No, mate, she looked much better."

That got a laugh, but he was still a bit weepy. My mate Barney was not built for the sort of hatred that Jason Mellish carried around like a wallet in his pocket.

I grabbed a handhold on the zip ties around Jason Mellish's feet and dragged him across the floor, down the hall, past the kitchen and past the office into the cell. His head bumped the wall a few times along the way, my bad. I shut the door of the cell and locked him in.

"Jason Mellish you are under arrest for being a total prick. If you are lucky, we might get a doctor to attend your wounds sometime this year."

He groaned and moaned, but the fight had gone out of him.

Just as I finished my nasty little spiel, Jody Taggart arrived at the cell door and looked at Jason.

"I think we need to get him to hospital Chris."

"You can tell just by looking?"

"Yes I can tell just by looking, and by listening."

I had to admit he was groaning a lot, and he may have been coming down from some sort of drug thing. His cheek and temple were both swollen and bruised. Blood around the eye suggested his cheek might be broken. Every few seconds he was doing a large involuntary shiver, a borderline convulsion maybe. He did not look or sound a well man.

"Hospital it is then," I sighed. I opened the cell door and Jody went to work.

In the next fifteen minutes, we agreed it was safest to ship Jason to the detention ward at Wodonga Hospital. He could share a ward with Detective Boofhead. They'd get on well. For safety's sake, I called my temporary boss Sergeant Will Walker at Wodonga Station. He arranged to send a police car and a couple of officers to meet the ambulance on its way to Wodonga Hospital. The officers would ensure Jase did not get out of control again. That would be hard considering his condition and his restraints but safest is best.

I would remain at Jarrajarra station, officially back at work for the rest of the day, to guard the fort in case the remaining Mellish clan decided to stage a second rescue attempt. This was highly unlikely as the only candidates were Justin, who was too smart, and Wally, who was too old and still on his quadrella bender. In the unlikely event either of them attacked anyone this afternoon, I would shoot them in the leg, like in the movies, then send them home with a warning. I was done fucking around.

Joanne and I managed to get both Barney and Constable Tim over to the Bush Nursing Centre. First impressions were that they would both be OK. Barney was as resilient as hell and Tim was a young, tough, country cop, I decided I would have to like him, be his friend, though not as friendly as Joanne who seemed to like him a lot. Young love, maybe? I don't know, my head was hurting, I could be imagining it.

While I was at the Nursing Centre, Wendy found the time to check my concussion status. She declared me no dumber than usual and allowed me to continue on with my day. She was busier, and far more concerned with Barney and Tim.

After all that I went back to the station and checked on the status of Jennifer McClain. I had left her alone in my office at the start of the battle.

She was gone.

I hoped it was permanent. I hoped, for her sake, it was goodbye Jarrajarra. She, and her steroid-loaded colleague locked away in a Wodonga cell, were the only members of the biker team still alive. She was the only member of her gang to walk out of our town under her own steam. She was free to leave, and she had taken the opportunity.

Good luck to her.

After all the sad and violent events of the day I came to the same question I had been struggling with for the last eleven days.

Who the bloody hell killed Joey Golino?

I decided to lock up the station and go home to sleep on it. If Justin and Wally Mellish decided to lay siege to the station, for the release of their boy, they could do it on their own. They would not be getting Jason back home in a while. He was going to prison for his effort today. I would see to it.

16

THURSDAY, MARCH 22, 2018

Jarrajarra, Victoria, Australia.

Wendy made it home around 1 a.m. She crawled in beside me and I quickly learned that Barney and Tim were all good. Tim had a broken nose, but it wasn't anything requiring surgery, Wendy had wrenched it back into place with very little sulking from Tim. Barney just had a black eye and a sore nose.

All good.

Wendy then declared she couldn't sleep, and it was my turn to make the midnight cup of tea. Sitting up in bed drinking our cuppas, I described the mystery murder weapon I was looking for. A 375-centimetre, 15-inch, ten-kilogram-ish, tuning-fork-type metallic thing.

Heavy enough to fracture skulls with one whack.

I showed Wendy the bruise photos, from my phone. All of the bruises and breaks the weapon had caused. I also showed her Carole's composite drawing of what the weapon would look like.

"It's a drop bar," she said, simple as that.

"A drop bar?"

She laughed. "Haven't you ever driven a tractor in all your adventures? Slashed a paddock? Made some hay? Dug a hole? Smoothed some ground?"

"Yeah, well, no, actually. No, I am not what you would call a tractor driver of any experience. No, ma'am, not me."

She loved it, my ineptitude. I loved her laugh, even when it was directed at me.

"You and the Sarge, both city boys, and Barney, a town boy, lives in the country all his life but has never set foot in a paddock." She laughed some more.

"OK" she continued, "so, you're a farmer, right, and you're driving the tractor."

"I am a farmer, yes indeed."

"Well, you need to transfer the power of the tractor engine to the devices you have hooked up to the tractor. Say, for instance, the grass slasher."

"That is exactly and precisely what I want to do. Right now. Slash a paddock by transferring the power."

"Well mister farmer, you do that through the PTO, which is the Power Take Off."

"Yes," I said, "the PTO. Exactly. Everyone knows that."

"And the PTO is hooked up to the various devices through the hitching mechanism, which is just a lot of joining steel, with arms and bars and lengths of steel, and lots of bolts. Then there are the two drop bars, one on each side of the hitching mechanism to stop the whole thing swinging sideways while you're doing what you do, like slashing your paddock."

I had absolutely no idea what Wendy was talking about.

Not a single solitary clue.

She grabbed my phone and looked it all up on the internet. She found a photo with arrows and labels. There it was, just as she described, a big hitching mechanism, and on each side, joining the mechanism to a fixed point on the tractor was a detachable piece that was a perfect simile of my drop bar. A 375-centimetre, 15-inch, steel tuning-fork-thing, looking as lethal as hell.

"There you go," she said.

"Wow," I said. "It's a stabilizer."

"Exactly, " said Wendy. "A stabiliser that would put a hole in anyone's head, I reckon,

"So, my 'G-F' is either the maker's name or the owner's name, or a part thereof, or even the initials."

"I would say so, city boy."

"Thank you, Dolly Parton."

We finished our tea and had a beautiful night together, including some sleep. Somewhere during the night, my baton-induced headache disappeared.

~

I had always thought crime investigation was supposed to be glamorous. I bet the Sarge never saw Tony Bonner in Homicide searching through spare parts buckets in grungy farmyard tool sheds, especially on his three-week recuperation holiday from work.

The Jason Mellish drama had allowed me back on the job for a brief period yesterday, but that was all over now. The valiant Constable Tim from Wodonga was back on deck, in my office, broken nose and all, and I was officially back on leave. I was being forced on a holiday whether I liked it or not.

With nothing else to do, I went off to search for my murder weapon, which I now strongly suspected was a thing called a drop bar. What a miserable, fruitless experience my search turned out to be.

What did the US politician, Donald Rumsfeld, say about 'know-unknowns and unknown-unknowns and knowing what we don't know." He didn't mention my Nan's favourite, N.F.I. No-Fucking-Idea.

What person in the Melbourne Housing Commission high-rise slums had ever heard of a drop bar? I hadn't stood on green grass till I joined the army. Never mind about paddocks and farms.

Drop-bars hey?

I visited all the farms in the immediate area. At each of them, I asked permission to look in their shed, and everyone said yes; some wanted to question me about the big gun fight on the weekend, and others wanted to know about the punch-up with Jason Mellish. I spoke politely without saying too much.

While searching the local farms and speaking to the owners, I found drop bars of every description. Some were on tractors, some rusted and broken and stuck in oil drums full of similar dead and rusting gear. Some of them were brand new and unused and waiting for the call.

But none of them had a G-F emblazoned on the side.

Sometime after noon, I paused my search and retired to the cafe for a coffee and sandwich.

After lunch, I put my runners on and jogged out past the caravan park and along the river to Ricky Chalmers' farm.

I checked his tool shed and garage. There was no one to ask permission, and I did not have a warrant. If I found what I was looking for, I would have to come back and do it again, legally.

I searched the shed; it was as clean and impeccable as everything managed by Ricky. But the murderous drop bar was not there.

I quit looking.

It would take the spiritual intervention of my good friend, the dearly departed Doris Gillespie, to reach out from the other side of the grave and deliver me my drop bar.

17

FRIDAY, MARCH 23, 2018

Jarrajarra, Victoria, Australia.

Doris Gillespie's funeral service was at the local Anglican church. There were more people in attendance than the church had seen in a long time.

It was a good farewell; the young minister did not seem to know Doris all that well, so he held back on the rhetoric and acted more as a master of ceremony.

Alf Longmuir, the pompous old president of the R.S.L., made a lovely speech about Doris and her husband, Bert. He said some well-researched words about Bert's war career and referred to the couple's early years in Jarrajarra.

Vilma Palmer and her sisters stood up together, and, in a team effort, they made a lovely little farewell to their mother.

After that, the priest ran a short video of Doris's life in pictures. While the photos shuffled across the screen, Doris' favourite music played in the background. Who would have guessed Doris was an Elvis fan?

Toward the end, we reached that awkward point where the priest asked if anyone would like to share a few words on their memory of the deceased. I had a lot of good thoughts about Doris, but I could never stand up in a place like this to recite them. They would just have to exist between Doris and me.

There was an uncomfortable moment when it seemed no one was prepared to speak, but then the ice was broken by Justin Mellish, of all people. He stood up in a clean suit, his long hair freshly groomed and said his words for Doris.

"When me mum dies," said Justin, "Dad wasn't too flash on the home front. Old Doris took to inviting me and my brother Jason into her house for a feed after school. Doris' cooking was so good, and there was so much of it. Jase and me took to wandering past her home whenever we got hungry on the weekends, even though we hadn't been to school. Not that we went to school much on weekdays either."

The assembly all laughed at that.

"We were always hoping for an invite," Justin added. "She hardly let us down. We didn't even have to knock and ask. She seemed to sense we were around and hungry. She'd come out and drag us in and feed us up. Doris didn't ask for anything ever for herself, we didn't have to mow the lawns, put out the garbage, or anything, but we did. I am pretty sure it was all just for us and not like she was making a widow's move on old Wally."

The comment about Wally brought the house down. People laughed for a good minute. Even Wendy laughed at a Mellish joke. There was hope for Justin yet.

"She was a real good lady Doris, the best," he concluded.

If Justin Mellish surprised me, I practically fell off my pew when Saxon Tyson-Howard stood up to speak. Our local graffiti king had something to say and something to show.

"I am really sad Mrs Gillespie died," said Saxon. "She was a really nice old lady and made great chocolate cakes that she always gave me. I thought other people might be sad too, so I did a drawing of her to remind me of what she looked like when she was happy and feeling better. Thank you."

His words complete, he unfurled the rolled-up paper he had been holding in his hand. The assembly let out a collective gasp. We had an artistic genius in our midst.

The black-ink-on-white-paper portrait was perfect, incredible, really. Those people who had been weeping during the service all started up again. The portrait was that good. Photo-authentic in execution but a sort of hyper-reality to Doris' eyes and her smile that made it seem she was right there before us. Alive and happy to see us.

From the many people who attended her farewell and from the stories told by those who stood up to reminisce, I realised Doris, and I hadn't been a mutual salvation friendship at all. I was just one small part of her busy schedule, one of many whose life she deliberately set out to improve.

How does a person become so selfless and kind? It has to be something you're born with.

I didn't know then, but Doris still had one more surprise waiting, and this one was just for me.

~

At the end of the funeral service, everyone left the church and headed to their cars, or they just walked away, like Wendy heading back to work.

For those of us in cars, there was the usual shuffle at the car park exit as people jockeyed to be next in the outbound line. Being a cop has its advantages, and I hustled through.

There was a line heading to the cemetery, and I joined that right behind Justin Mellish, who was driving the town's red tractor. This was a multi-purpose tractor with power connections front and back that was normally the tool-in-trade of Ricky Chalmers in his role as Jarrajarra's gardener and curator. The town tractor could be used for digging, levelling, mowing, slashing, and trenching. I had never driven a machine like that in my life, but whenever there was a town project in progress, Ricky and the tractor were usually present and busy.

This tractor was the same one that Justin and I had retrieved from Ricky's shed on Justin's first day of community service a week ago. On that day, it had been caked in mud. Very unlike Ricky to leave it in that condition. Normally, any tool that Ricky used was pristine, clean, working and always mechanically perfect. Today it was totally perfect, as clean as the sky above, which must have been Justin's handiwork.

Today the town tractor was linked up with the front-end loader, which meant there was nothing attached to the rear of the tractor, so I got to watch two perfect, clean, unattached drop bars swinging to the rhythm of the tractor as we drove the kilometre out of town to the cemetery.

So, we drove at a funeral pace, in procession, along one of those perfectly pragmatic country roads. Dead straight and dusty, from the centre of town until we reached our target, the Jarrajarra cemetery, Doris' final resting place, the plot next to her husband, Bert.

We arrived, and Justin made the left turn into the graveyard, just a few vehicles behind the funeral car, directly in front of me, slow and respectful.

There in the perfect sunshine of our final goodbye, Doris Gillespie shined her wonderful light on me for one last time.

Maybe I hadn't noticed the brand name of our town tractor before because it was caked in mud, the first time I really looked at it. Maybe it wasn't covered in mud, and the name of the tractor simply meant nothing to me. But there it was now.

The name of the Chinese tractor.

'DONG-FENG'. The middle letters of which formed my previously unidentified 'G-F'.

The hearse had parked with the rear door pointed toward a perfectly rectangular hole. I would guess that was one Jason dug earlier today.

Justin pulled up to the side of the road near the burial site. I parked behind Justin. He gave me a wary nod. Was that a suggestion that I had locked up his brother yesterday, and we would have angry words later?

I really didn't care. I just nodded back.

I went to the back of the DONG-FENG and reached out for the drop bar. It was still attached to the tractor's hoist at one end, but it had heaps of swing room at the free end. I turned it in my hand, and there on the double fork, emblazoned in hardened solder, was the label of the tractor. The word DONG-FENG was written along the thick edge of the double blade. The word was centred where the double blade joined the single arm. Right at the pivot. The very point that struck AJ Davies on the arm, leaving a bruise that would last till his flesh rotted from his dead arm.

'G-F'

Bloody hell.

Here I was trying to help Ricky get off a murder charge, had I just proved he was as guilty as hell. Great detectives work in the weirdest ways.

"What are you looking at?" Justin's voice interrupted my reverie.

"What's this label here, Juz?"

"That? Ricky does it on the parts for this machine. These imported tractors are not bad machines, and they're cheap as chips, but all their add-ons are shit. Fucked. They break all the time, plus they're non-standard size. So, Ricky either makes 'em himself or stiffens 'em up. He puts the label on 'em, so you know it doesn't go on any of the other machines. Wouldn't fit if you tried."

"He makes them himself?"

"Fucking Ricky, hey, mister freakin perfect."

"Amazing."

I took a photo of the pivot point on the drop bar and sent the photo to Carole and Glenda, the forensic superstars from Seymour Crime Services.

About ten seconds later, I received their reply.

"OH, MY GOD! BINGO! BINGO! BINGO!" all capitals. "Glenda and I are in the car and on our way to you. Set up the BBQ, hold that thing, whatever it is. Be there in a couple of hours. Well done, Killer!!!"

I didn't think I literally had to hold the drop bar in my hands. It wasn't going anywhere. It was firmly attached to the digger on one end, and Justin would need the machine when the burial was over.

I left the drop bar where it hung and turned my attention to Doris' burial. Once she was in the ground and the mourners had left the cemetery, Justin drove forward in the town's digger and replaced the soil over the coffin, then smoothed it out rather nicely. He was quite a capable worker. He was thorough and careful, meticulous even. It was easy to forget he was on voluntary community service for busting up a hotel.

With Doris buried, I accompanied Justin and the digger and the suspect drop bar back to the council shed. It seemed a good chance to get Justin to chat and maybe confirm his alibi for my murders.

We parked at the council shed.

"Hang here, Juz, and I will get you a coffee." I went to the fire station next door and used their fabulous machine to make two perfect lattes.

"Tell me about this drop bar," I asked, "Why do you leave it dangling here when it is not being used?"

"Just one less thing to fiddle with when you change devices on the PTO. Most tools that go there need the drop bar."

"So, this one was here when we saw it the other day in Ricky's shed, all covered in mud."

"Yep."

"Well, you have done a marvellous job cleaning it all up." Which he had, and that was a pain. If this had been the murder weapon, it would have been polished clean of prints by now.

"Are there any spares for these parts?" I asked.

"Yeah, Ricky keeps a shit load of spares for this machine. He has made a heap of the accessories. The originals break all the time. He makes them thicker, so they won't break and yet the same size at the connection, so they fit. Come, and I'll show ya."

With that, he turned and led me inside the town's work shed. We approached a wall of implements. One section had various tractor accessories hanging from pegs and nails. There seemed to be hundreds of various implements. All clean, like the shed itself. No rust or dust anywhere. Typical Ricky Chalmers workspace.

"You've kept it the way he likes it, all tidy."

"Yeah," said Justin. "Wouldn't like him coming back to work and cracking the shits with me. He's a good bloke Ricky, one of the few."

"There are a lot of parts. How do you know what each of them is for?"

"You just learn by usin' them. He grabbed a strange piece that also had the 'DONG-FENG' labelled on it.

"See," he said as she showed me the soldered label. "The Dong bits are all non-standard size. Most of the other attachments can be used on any of the tractors, but the DONG gets its own pieces, so Ricky usually solders the label on like this, so you know who-is-who-in-the-zoo, so to speak."

"And where are the drop bars?"

"They're along here," he said as he moved along the rows of hanging pieces. He came to a section with about a dozen drop bars. He flipped through them.

"Funny. The spare Dong bar is not here."

"You sure?"

"Unless he didn't make one," Justin kept looking as he spoke. "There was definitely one here last time I helped out. Maybe he broke one and hasn't made a new spare."

"Or maybe someone took it. Your brother Jason maybe?"

"Jase hasn't got a key. I've got the key Greg Farrell gave me. The only others I know of are on Ricky's key chain."

"Would Jason or Jenny have access to your keys?"

"Nah, mate, they took off after the Warrangatha pub thing."

"They went together?"

"Yep, she was pissed off with me after I told her to give that publican his money. So, I got the flick, and Jase stepped in."

"Where did they go?"

Justin smirked his answer. "Where he always goes when he cracks it with me. Bums a cabin from Wally down the caravan park.

"They went to the caravan park?"

"Yeah, with a bunch of her bikie mates that blew into town, sniffin' anything they can get their hands on since last week."

"Jason on cocaine? That explains a bit."

"Yeah, you saw yesterday what that shit does to him."

"I did."

Jason had been sniffing cocaine with the mostly dead bikies. That would help explain the impressive degree of ineptitude they showed in the Mitta Mitta gunfight.

"That stuff makes you crazy. That's why I always stay on the weed, mate. Mellow."

"Justin, your brother is in trouble. Assaulting a police officer and two public servants while on drugs. That's a possible five years."

He was rubbing his eyes, weary of his brother, as far as I could tell.

"Well mate, I am sick of bein' Mummy and Daddy for the dumb cunt."

Justin just looked sad. Big, hard, tough, but very sad.

We stood in the sun, sipping our coffee. Strangely Justin was still in the suit he had worn to Doris' funeral.

I tried to say it as gently as I could,

"You know, Juz, once they start totting up the charges for yesterday, they could take a look at Jason for Joey Golino's murder."

That made him stop and look at me very carefully.

"Please tell me you guys have a rock-solid alibi for that Saturday night?"

"Saturday?"

"Saturday the 10th. Two weeks ago."

"I spent the afternoon watchin' Jason get himself shitfaced in the Tumbarumba pub. I won myself some money on the pool."

Great, he had an alibi that was easily checked and lined up with his now-departed girlfriend, Jen. That was good.

"Why were you in Tumbarumba?"

I could see him weighing up whether to answer or not. He looked at me a bit longer.

"Sold all our remaining weed to a new bloke from Sydney for a big wad of cash. Which I will I deny I ever said."

"Remaining? To Sydney? I thought Joey was your only customer?"

"We had a falling out with Joey. Haven't sold to him for a couple of months, and, for your info, I am now out of the dope-growing business."

"Wow. Out?"

"Yep. Look at Joey, stay in that world too long, and there ya go."

"Can I ask, did Jen go with you? On that trip?"

"Yeah," he smiled at the memory. "Spent the night in the motel there with her. Fucked ourselves silly, shit, thought I'd found the girl I might marry. Can you believe that?"

"Mate, I hate to tell you this, but she is already married. Or she was."

"Married?"

I nodded.

"Who's the lucky guy?"

"Not so lucky. He was the bloke that got murdered with Joey."

"AJ Davies? She was married to AJ Davies?"

"Yes."

"Fuck. A low-life scumbag like Davies? Jesus Christ, I had her wrong."

"You knew him?"

"Yeah, I knew him. Didn't know he was married. Didn't act like he was married."

"So, you spent time with him?"

"No more than I had to. I met him with Joey. Chris mate, the world is a safer place now that cunt is dead, believe me."

"I do." I thought a moment. "What did Davies have to do with Joey Golino?"

"He supplied Joey with his oxy."

"Joey sold oxy? I thought he just stuck to the dope." I was lagging behind in my knowledge of the local drug scene.

"Nah, Joey was convinced Oxy was easy money. He started selling a few months ago. His big idea was AJ Davies would be the oxy man and me and Jase would be the grass guys."

"We bumped into Davies a few times," said Justin, "he's always up for a party, but then there's always some fucking thing, or some poor cunt, upsets him, and he turns nasty. I was always tryin' to keep away from the fuckwit. If you're selling drugs, why the fuck do you wanna be beating up people in clubs? Just bring the cops down on yourself. It's stupid."

"You saw this?"

"Mate, that shit happened every fucking time he stepped out the door. I told Joey we didn't want to be doin' grass with him if he was doin' the other shit with Davies, didn't want any part of it. Davies was trouble."

"You quit because of Davies?"

"Yep."

"What did Joey say to that?"

"He just said, 'fine, suit yourselves. I'll get it off Davies."

"Just like that?"

"Yeah, just like that. I tried to tell him your junkies were not like your dope smokers. He'd have cops all over him."

Georgie Golino had told me about her distaste for the junkies who were recently harassing the pizza shop. It was the oxy users. Suddenly her reference to 'junkies' made sense.

Justin continued. "Joey said you'd be no problem; he could handle you. I told him you were not like that. He told me Davies had connections higher up, so there was no worry."

"He did have connections. Not anymore."

"Anyway," Justin continued, "once you're in with Davies, the cops are the least of your problems. Davies becomes the problem. He was a real fucking handful, huge and nasty. I wouldn't take him on."

"Someone did."

"Yeah, true." He paused to think a moment. "You need to be careful, Chris. You know he had a brother who is half the size, half the brains and twice as fucking nasty."

"Yes, I know about the brother. Butch Davies. Met him already."

"Where?"

"Up at Mitta Mitta last Saturday."

"Fuck, is he the one in jail?"

"No."

"No?"

"No, mate, he was one of the others."

"The others? Fuck me. You killed him?"

What could I say to that? Technically Boofhead had killed him. I'd just set him on the path. I shrugged a non-verbal kind of 'yes'.

"Well, score one for humanity," said Justin.

We returned our attention to our coffees. I didn't think either Justin or I would be attending the Davies' brother's funeral.

Oxy users in Jarrajarra? I was sure there were a few, but I only knew of one.

~

I was doing too many illegal searches.

I promised myself I'd stop once I knew who murdered Joey Golino.

I had waited at the Council shed until my forensics buddies, Constables Carole and Glenda, arrived to take charge of the suspicious drop bar. It was a promising find, but we were all doubtful it was the actual murder weapon. It had most likely been attached to the Council's DONG-FENG while the murders were happening.

Carole bagged it anyway, which left Justin Mellish and Jarrajarra short one drop bar. Two short, really, if the murder weapon was out there somewhere. Justin complained he wouldn't be able to use the tractor's mowers, but Constable Carole was not deflected.

"Them's the breaks," she had said. "Sometimes the pursuit of truth and justice can lead to discomfort."

Justin was puzzled. I don't think he appreciated Carole's warped sense of humour or her passion for her job.

I also realised that Carole and Glenda knew as much about PTOs and power take-off apparatus as I did. The purpose of a drop bar was as much a mystery to them as it was to me.

The girls left disheartened. We thought the real murder weapon was still out there, hidden and hopefully still encrusted with the blood of its victims.

I had gone home to wait for dark. By 9.00 P.M., it was not just dark but cloudy as well, which was good for me. I put on my black tracksuit and found a black beanie that I never wore in public. It was close as I could dress to full ninja. I also donned my spare headlamp.

Dressed for invisible, I set off on a not-so-innocent run, out along Town road to the caravan park, through the caravan park and then past cabin 143, now looking clean and innocent and ready for unwitting customers.

I ran along the river trail. The run so far had been adjacent to houses and farms and then caravans. There had been just enough light to make my way. Along the river, it was pitch black, and I needed the headlamp.

I was heading back to the Chalmers' farms. Ricky and Kate had inherited their father's dairy farm and split it into two, one for each of them. I had already had an illegal and unsuccessful search at Ricky's place. This time I was heading to Kate's.

I was about to break the law again. Illegal searches, with no warrants and no immediate cause, were becoming a habit. I hoped none of this would cost me a court case.

I turned off the trail and walked past Ricky's place to get to Kate's. With Ricky in a Melbourne hospital and Kate by his side, I was confident both places would be empty.

Kate could, theoretically, have had access to Ricky's keys, and that meant she could have had access to the council's equipment shed. That gave her, theoretically, access to the drop bar, lots of drop bars. Plus, at the time of the murders, she had been an oxy addict, which made her a potential customer of both Golino and Davies. There were a lot of 'theoreticals' in my theory, but Kate Chalmers was the constant.

I had seen what she had done with the baseball bat on her hapless client's truck. Could she make that violence work on a guy like Davies? Could she have done it to Azzolino Pisano, back at cabin 143? Pisano was Michelle Folliero's bodyguard, and he was almost as big and, by reputation, every bit as mean as Davies.

I had been inside Kate's house when I was called here the other day. I had done a fairly thorough search. While looking for her patron's cash, I stumbled on her pile of empty oxy containers. I hadn't stumbled on a murder weapon, but on that day, I hadn't looked in her shed.

I was going to sneak a look in there now while I could.

I made it to the shed door and observed that it was locked. I was looking for a hidden key when I saw, through the trees, a car swing into Kate's drive. I switched off my headlamp and quickly stepped back into the darkness behind a clump of trees beside the shed. I watched the car lights shine their way along the curving drive toward the house, hoping I had not been seen.

The biggest problem with any crime, including illegal search, is typically getting caught. If it was Kate, I could hardly step out of the darkness, dressed like a ninja, and cover myself with 'G'day mate'. There would be questions. None of which I could answer without admitting to breaking the law. The Sarge would not be pleased. Barney would be mortified.

I stood still and quiet in the darkness and waited till I could exit safely.

Kate got out of her car. She was alone. She locked her car and went into her house.

I took the opportunity to move around the perimeter of her parking area. Still in the darkness, covered by trees and my own black running clothes, I found a spot where I could observe both the house and the shed. It was a good hiding spot. I stepped back, deeper into the darkness and waited.

Exterior lights came on, and the area around the car park was now lit like the day. After a few more minutes, Kate came out of the house and headed towards her shed. She unlocked it and went inside.

I waited, confident I was near invisible.

I was close enough to hear Kate moving about in the shed, moving stuff around, and then perhaps the opening and closing of a door. Then there was silence.

The shed just had the entry door she had used and a roller door for vehicles. There were various vents but no windows. I couldn't take a peek inside. Not sure it would have been a smart move, considering the dubious legality of my presence.

I waited.

Nothing. No sound, no movement, nothing, for at least thirty minutes.

Thirty minutes is a long time to do nothing in a shed. Did I hallucinate her arrival? Was my baton-induced concussion giving me fantasies?

Had Kate seen me, was she there on the other side of the wall, like me, wondering what to do next? Stalemate.

Eventually, I could hear the sound of movement from inside the shed, the closing of a door, more furniture being moved around, pushed along the floor. Then the shed door opened. Kate came out, locked the shed then returned to her house.

I could see in her hand she was carrying a red and white plastic shopping bag. From her grip and the way the bag hung, it was obvious that the contents were reasonably heavy. It was impossible to see what those contents were.

I waited.

After another ten minutes, I could hear her talking. It must surely have been a phone call; I was confident she was the only person in the house. I couldn't hear what she was saying or determine who she was talking to. I could risk getting closer to listen. I could even risk breaking into the shed, trying to work out what she had been doing. But I didn't. Discretion won the day, which is what I always tell myself when I chicken out.

I pulled back further into the bush and the darkness. I walked along the track, beyond Kate's property, past Ricky Chalmers' place, and back to the river trail. I walked about half a kilometre along the trail until I felt safe enough to use the headlamp. Once that was on, my ground was lit up like daytime. I ran back home and went to bed.

What had I just seen? Why did she take so long in total silence? What was in the plastic bag? The what and the why?

I had no idea.

I fell asleep before Wendy made it home. I had a dozen guilty dreams of Kate turning at her shed door and seeing me there, lurking in the bushes. Each time I woke, I was glad it was a dream and I didn't need to explain.

18

SATURDAY, MARCH 24, 2018

Jarrajarra, Victoria, Australia.

My phone rang at 5.00 A.M.

Wendy had worked even later than I did, so we had put off our early morning run. We'd go later and make a morning of our day off work. We were still blissfully asleep when the mobile sounded.

It was Detective Pete.

"Chris, mate, you've done it again. You are a shoo-in for cop of the year."

Detective Peter Jordan was ecstatic.

"Cop of the year? Is that even a thing?" I asked.

"Probably not, but it should be." Why was he so bright and cheerful? Why was I mumbling?

"Did I wake you up?" He asked.

"Late night." I had tried to fake being up and about; clearly, I'd failed.

"Sorry, Chris, I thought you were always up early for a run. I thought I'd catch you early with the good news."

"Not today. So, what's the good news?" I was about half a sentence behind the conversation.

"I have a message from the Jarrajarra lawyer."

"Eddie Doolan?"

"That's the one. I think we have a deal, thanks to you."

"Thanks to me?"

"Yes, after you spoke to the sister Kate, suddenly Ricky is willing to talk in exchange for his freedom. Well done, Constable."

"OK," I was still trying to wake up. "What do we get?"

"We have been offered statements on the circumstances around the deaths of the three Jarrajarra murder victims, Golino, Davies, and Pisano. We have been offered the location of the Folliero assets, including his cash, all the money the three victims were carrying at the time of their murders."

"What about Folliero," I asked. "Where is he?"

"According to the Chalmers' lawyer," said Pete, "they don't know."

"Hang on," I said. "If Ricky knows where Folliero's money is, but he doesn't know where Folliero is, what does that mean?" I asked. "Is he dead?"

"Most likely," said Pete.

Folliero dead? We both went quiet and had a think about that.

"Ok," I said, "what does Ricky get for all this?"

"Ricky and Kate," he emphasised the 'and Kate'.

"Why Kate?"

"Why not Kate? She is probably an accessory. She wants immunity for herself as well."

"OK." I thought Kate Chalmers could be guilty of a lot worse than 'just an accessory'. I had seen what she could do in anger.

"Anyway," said Pete, "they both get immunity for any criminal charges that might arise from their statements. If they lie in their statements, the deal is off."

"That's it?"

"Plus, your footy coach gets his freedom immediately. He is being moved by ambulance to Jarrajarra Hospital today as we speak."

"It's not a hospital; it's a Nursing Centre."

"Yes, of course, sorry, Nursing Centre."

"He is on his way, and you haven't even spoken to them yet?"

I knew he hadn't bothered to ask Wendy since she was lying in bed next to me. I was angry at him again.

304

"Well, I am hoping we might get a favour from your very close friend, the lady in charge. Hoping she can find a room for us."

"I don't know. Ricky Chalmers doesn't qualify as a nursing mother," I said. "Give me a moment, and I'll see what I can do."

I put the call on hold.

I turned to look at Wendy.

"Did you hear all of that?" I asked.

"Yes, I heard."

"So, is it OK, Nurse Practitioner Atcheson? Can we put Ricky in one of your wards?"

"Yes, of course, it's OK. I'd love to have him. I don't think Ricky will murder me while I am trying to make him better."

"I don't think Ricky murdered anyone ever."

"Well, what is he confessing to?"

"Not much, I reckon. I have a feeling most of the confession will come from Kate."

There, I said it out loud. I thought Kate Chalmers could be my triple murderer. Possible access to the shed and the murder weapon, definitely an oxy addict, supplied by Golino. But why murder?

"Chris," Wendy interrupted my mental sleuthing. "You need to pull your head in with this bloke Jordan, just a bit. If you get all testy with him on these small matters, he will go around you on the big ones. Just roll with it till you solve your case."

I got the look. Wendy had spoken.

I took the call off hold and faked friendly.

"All good," I said. "They have exactly the right ward to accommodate a patient and a conference."

"Great," said Pete.

"How exactly does this happen?" I asked.

"Well," said Pete, "Ricky and Kate will offer their unsigned statements for Berlic and me to read. We offer them an immunity document that applies to any crimes described in the statements. We get to question them about the contents of their statements. If they're telling the truth, if we believe them, then we sign their immunity, and they sign their statements, and they hand over significant Folliero assets, and we all shake hands and go our separate ways.

"So, even if they are the murderers, they walk?" I asked. "All in exchange for Folliero's money?"

My best buddy Detective Pete laughed out loud.

"Well, mate," he said, "it sounds like you have finally woken up today because that's about it. Money won't buy you love, but Folliero money will get you just about anything else, including your freedom."

I couldn't even speak to that. Big-time crime had come to Jarrajarra and all the bullshit that went with it.

"There is another tiny wrinkle," said Pete.

"What's that?"

"The Chalmers, Ricky and Kate, both want you there at the meeting."

"Me? Why?"

"Chris, mate, I wouldn't have a fucking clue. The way you small town communities operate is like another planet. But you know what? I think it will be good for both of us."

"Why?"

"Well, you deserve to hear it all first-hand. Plus, I get to borrow your army-trained interrogation skills."

I didn't know what to make of that. I never trusted compliments, especially from a charmer like Detective Pete.

Jarrajarra Nursing Centre.

The team of cops and lawyers sat outside Ricky's room while the prosecution team read the two separate Chalmers' statements.

I guessed that on the other side of the door, Ricky, Kate and their legal team were going through their unsigned freedom agreements.

Meanwhile, I stood with my forensic buddies, Carole and Glenda, waiting.

Eventually, everyone's reading was completed, the ward door opened, and Eddie Doolan invited us all into Ricky Chalmer's ward.

Ricky was sitting up in a hospital bed in what was, normally, a two-bed ward in the Nursing Centre. He looked a lot better than when I had last seen him, barely conscious, in a Melbourne hospital only five days ago. He was recovering quickly.

His sister Kate was sitting beside him in one of the many plastic chairs squeezed into the room.

Eddie Doolan, our local solicitor, was seated beside Kate. Seated next to Eddie was a barrister from Melbourne, Jeremy Oakley. They were the Chalmers' team.

The four of them had their backs to the wall facing their interrogators.

We all filed into the ward behind Ms Jessica Berlic QC, chief prosecutor of the New South Wales Royal Commission, into the murder of Gary Rogers. Berlic took the front chair while the rest of us sorted ourselves onto the remaining plastic.

Seated around Berlic were Detective Pete Jordan and a bunch of legal support types who had all flown down by chopper from Sydney with Berlic for the event. It was quite the team.

I was there because Kate and Ricky had demanded my presence. I had no idea why. I was back in uniform, my holiday cancelled, and my concussion suddenly and miraculously cured in the eyes of police HQ. No doubt assisted by the extraordinary circumstance and ad hoc convenience. I was part of the show.

Sitting beside me, along the naughty boy's row on the back wall, was the fearless forensics team from Seymour Police Crime Services, Carole and Glenda. Happy as ever and ready to collect whatever artefacts, used weapons or DNA required by the agreement.

There were no desks, and everyone with computers or papers and briefcases had them laid out on the floor, in their laps or on a spare chair.

~

"Kate, you say in your statement that you were raped," said Ms Berlic, starting the show. "Exactly who raped you?"

"All four of them," answered Kate. "Golino, Davies, Pisano and Folliero."

"When did this rape occur?"

"Rapes, plural, there was a bunch of them." Kate looked at me as though daring me to laugh at her twist on the old joke.

"Sorry, when did these rapes occur?"

Eddie Doolan answered on Kate's behalf. "That question is covered in detail in the statement which you have in your possession." said our local solicitor.

"Our agreement is pretty clear, Mr Doolan," said Berlic. "We have the option of questioning both of your clients on any matter raised in their statement."

The Chalmers' team, Doolan and Oakley, leaned into each other, mumbled a bit then nodded at Kate. Kate continued.

"About a year ago, I got a call from Joey Golino. He said he had some friends staying over in the caravan park. Fishing buddies. Would I be interested in a party? I said Yes."

"You were invited to attend in your professional capacity? As a paid escort?" Asked Berlic.

"Yes."

"Did you assume this would involve sexual relations with members of this fishing party?"

"Yes."

"How was that negotiated?"

"I gave Joey a price for the night, and I said no more than one go each. One time for each of his three mates. That did not include him."

Berlic and her team conferred for a few moments. They seemed to be reading Kate's statement. Berlic resumed.

"What happened at the caravan park that first time?"

"Well, they had booked three cabins at the far end of the caravan park, the more private end. The last one, cabin 143, was where the party was."

"These are cabins, not caravans."

"Yes, cabins. They have two bedrooms, a toilet, a shower, a kitchen, dining area. They are like small homes.

"You have entertained clients at the caravan park before?"

"Yes."

"And this party was about a year ago."

"Yes, March 2017, a Monday night."

"At this party, you had sexual relations with three of the attendees at the Golino party."

"Yes. Joey Golino paid me in cash when I arrived. We all had a drink and got down to party."

"You say in your statement this did not go as you might have hoped?"

Kate snorted an angry laugh at that.

"That's one way of putting it. Yes."

"Can you explain that in more detail, please?"

"Well, first, they drugged me."

"Why do you think that?"

"Well, I don't get myself drunk when I hire my body out for a gang bang alright. It is not safe when you're sober, and it is fucking dangerous if you're drunk."

"How could you be sure you were drugged?"

"I had two glasses of beer, I pretended to drink with them, but I was only sipping."

At the word 'sipping', one of Berlic's team made a noise, probably innocent. She tried to cover it, but she'd caught Kate's attention.

"You think this is funny." Kate was angry. "You little cunt."

"I'm sorry, I wasn't laughing, honestly," said the aide.

"Bullshit," said Kate, "you can fuck off right now, you polished little turd. Fuck off in your fucking unblemished business suit! Fuck off!"

This was not a court room and there was no judge to call the witness to order. Kate's team leaned in to try and calm her down.

On the prosecution team, eyes darted back and forth. Shock was registered. Eventually, Berlic nodded toward the woman who, maybe laughed, maybe didn't, then nodded toward the door. The assistant administrative type gathered her things and left.

Kate now had her elbows on her knees and her face in her hands. Doolan was patting her back, being a friend. He was a good man, our town lawyer.

"I apologise, Kate," said Berlic. "Please continue when you are ready."

Kate took her time to recover herself. Through all this testimony, Ricky just lay in his bed looking at the roof, showing nothing beyond his improved health. Eventually Kate resumed.

"I only drank two beers but, by the end of the second, I could barely stand up, could hardly keep my eyes focused."

"How did you know you were raped?"

"I could still count. I was still aware of who was fucking me. Folliero went first. He took me to one of the bedrooms. He was the one who poured me the second beer. He stayed about twenty minutes. He was pretty harmless, like a rabbit, really, lasted about twenty seconds on the job. Probably stayed longer for appearances."

"Davies went second, and he was really rough. He hurt me and seemed to enjoy it. I tried to tell him to ease off a bit but, by then, I could barely talk from the spiked drink. While he was with me, he called the others the others to come in and watch."

Watching Kate, I could see she was reliving that night.

"He was too rough. He enjoyed hurting me. He enjoyed them all watching him."

She paused, Doolan offered her a glass of water and she drank it before continuing.

"Eventually, they all had their go, and they left me alone for a while. I might have slept. I don't know. Then my head cleared a bit. They were in the living area getting rowdy. I was still in the bedroom, and I wanted to get out of there before they decided to come back. I got dressed, gathered my stuff, and went to leave."

"In your statement you say that Davies wouldn't let you leave."

"No, he grabbed me before I made it to the door, said he wanted more party time with me and said he would give me more money, but I said no. I tried to get past him to go home but he insisted."

Jeremy Oakley, Kate's Barrister, interrupted.

"This is all described in detail in the statement. Davies beat my client severely. Punched and kicked her. In the main room in front of the other three men. None of whom intervened on her behalf. None of whom made any attempt to defend her. Then Davies took Ms. Chalmers back to the bedroom and raped her. During the rape he called the other men into the room to watch him perform anal sex upon her."

Oakley was red in the face with anger. If he was acting, he was bloody good.

"Is any of that not clear? Is there any part of that description that could be improved by asking my client for more detail? He demanded sex and she said no. Then he beat her and forced himself on her. That's rape."

Berlic's team conferred, then Berlic resumed.

"Tell me please, what happened after the second time with Davies, after the beating."

"After the beating I was in a bad way, but it had shaken off the drugs they gave me. I was awake but I really wished I wasn't."

"Davies got off me, then Joey Golino joined in. He was as drunk as the others, and he just took his chance I guess. I was too banged up to be surprised by anything at that stage."

"Then what happened?"

"Well Pisano tried to have another round, but he fumbled about, couldn't get it up, so he belted me a few times as though it was my fault he had a limp dick. Make himself feel like a man, I suppose."

Kate was getting visibly upset. Her barrister, Oakley, stepped up again.

"This is all made clear in the statement. After Mr Golino had sex with my client without her consent, Pisano tried again then Davies took all of Ms. Chalmers' money from her purse, including her agreed payment for the evening. Davies then threw her out of the cabin. Leaving her naked, in the caravan park, no money, badly beaten and alone. By taking back her payment he invalidated her consent to any sexual activity that evening. They effectively raped her by deception. What is the point of putting my client through all of this again?"

He was pretty good this bloke. I'd hire him.

Ms. Berlic had a think for a moment. Then continued in a slightly softer tone.

"Kate, you say in your statement that on that first occasion, apart from Joey Golino, you didn't know who these other men were."

"No, I didn't, they were just fishing mates of Joey for all I knew. I didn't even know Joey fished."

"When did you first put a name to these three men."

"Folliero and Pisano? Only last week, when their names and faces were broadcast on the news. During the inquest. Alongside you, Ms Berlic, if I recall."

Berlic gave no response to that.

"AJ Davies? I found out his name after I saw him at the pizza shop with Joey Golino two weeks ago."

"The night of the murder?"

"The night he died. Yes."

"Can I go back to your injuries please?

"OK."

"It was the injuries you received in the beating from Davies which led to your addiction to Oxy-Contin and other pain killers? Is that right?"

"Yes."

"Subsequently, about six months after the rape in the caravan park, your local doctor refused to prescribe you the dosage of Oxy-Contin that you wanted? He wanted to wean you off your dependence on the pain killing drugs."

"Yes, God bless him, he thought I should be trying to get clean."

"But rather than give up the drugs, you turned to your brother in the hope that he could find more of what you required?"

"Yes. I nagged the shit out of Ricky to be honest. He's my younger brother, I can still bully him when I want to. There was just no way I was ready to give up the drugs. I was hooked. Without the drugs I was just in too much pain."

"Mr Chalmers," Berlic turned her attention to Ricky. "Your sister asked you to get her some Oxy-Contin and you obtained these drugs from your connections in Sydney."

"Yes."

"And the man in charge of these connections, who eventually supplied you the Oxy-Contin, was in fact AJ Davies?"

"Yes."

So, Davies was the football connection that Ricky had told me about. The mad bad biker that had sold him the Oxy for his sister.

"Ricky, you did not know that Davies was the man who had raped and beaten your sister?"

"No. I had no idea," said Ricky

Ricky had barely spoken to this point. His voice sounded soft and tired. But he was alert. Berlic continued.

"How did you find out about the rape and the beating."

"Kate told me on the night. Two weeks ago."

"Kate, you had never discussed these matters with your brother before the night of March 10th, 2018?"

"No."

"Why not?"

"Are you serious?" Kate shook her head. "I don't discuss my business with my brother, not with anyone."

"I don't understand why you wouldn't tell your brother that you had been raped and beaten? Or even go to the police after."

Kate was shaking her head in disbelief. Her anger appeared ready to explode again.

"You're a city girl right?" Kate was getting annoyed at Ms. Berlic QC.

"Yes," said Berlic. "I am."

"Love your parents? Good to you, were they?"

"Yes, though I don't see what this has to do with my question."

"Well let me see, how do I say this to someone who wouldn't have a fucking clue? When you live in a small country town, everyone knows everyone, and they all know your business. We all know the good family men, the straight shooters. We all know some blokes that are mostly good, maybe just a bit off centre in one department. And then there is the one, in every country town, everyone knows about this bloke."

"The man who drinks himself shit-faced every night, who fucks his daughters and beats his sons and maybe fucks and beats his wife all on the same day.

"In any country town, I guarantee you, there is always one. In Jarrajarra that man was my father, the king of the wife-beating, kid-fucking, boozers, and his best-mate and drinking buddy was the local cop. There wasn't a man in town big enough or brave enough to stand up and stop him and that included your predecessor."

Kate looked at me as she made that remark. Everyone did a side glance at the same time to check who it was hiding in the corner.

She hadn't finished.

"When my brother tried to stand up for me, the first time, my dad put him in hospital. Ricky would have been ten, maybe. Dad beat him unconscious and kicked him while he was on the floor, screaming at me, 'I hope this teaches you a lesson'. Me! Teach ME a lesson? Not Ricky, ME!"

"Why me? Well mum was fucked, and my older sister had topped herself, hadn't she. Hung herself from a tree in the back yard. But you know life goes on. It had to be me didn't it?

"Then you grow up, the old man is dead, my mum's dead, my sister is just forgotten. And my brothers the local football hero, so fucking tough no one could even imagine him copping a hiding every single day of his childhood. And here am I the town whore."

"Who the fuck in this town do I turn to when I need help? The same people who left me in the care of that fucking monster. The same people who watched him put my brother and my mum in hospital so many fucking times I lost fucking count. Who fucked my sister till she hung herself. Who-the-fuck would help a slut like me anyway?"

"I know what they will say before they even think it. How the fuck does she get raped at the end of a paid gang bang for fuck's sake?"

"I am on my own in this shit. So yeah, I said nothing, and I wouldn't now except this cunt here," she was pointing directly at Detective Pete. "He wants to put my brother in jail for something, he knows he didn't do. He knows Ricky is innocent, don't you? You fuck!"

Detective Pete gave her nothing in return. He just looked at her without a flicker. If he had seen her with the baseball bat, he might have been a tad more worried.

The rest of us in the room seemed to take a moment of voluntary silence. Then Berlic resumed.

"So, at that stage, immediately after the rape, you told no one?

You didn't seek any help? Initially Oxy-Contin was supplied via doctor's prescription? Then when the Doctor wanted you to stop using Oxy, maybe consider rehabilitation, you then turned to your brother to continue your supply?"

"Yes."

"And you were unaware that the man who supplied Ricky was in fact the same man who raped you in the caravan park."

"Correct. I didn't know."

"But Ricky, Mr Chalmers, didn't get you very much Oxy did he? You say in your statement that he encouraged you to get off the drugs, just like your doctor."

"Yes. Ricky's supply only lasted maybe a month and he was crystal clear he was not going to get me anymore. So, I went and spoke to Joey Golino, I knew he sold dope to the kids around town. I told him I wanted Oxy. I was a junkie, I was desperate, I would do anything except stop."

"You went to him, even though he was one of the men that raped you?"

"Yes, he was a part of it, but I was desperate, and Joey was my best option."

"Did you threaten Mr Golino in any way?"

"Threaten him?"

"Yes, did you suggest to him, perhaps, that you would tell his wife about the night in the caravan park if he didn't supply you?"

"Tell his wife?" Kate shook her head and laughed at that idea. "No, I didn't threaten to tell his wife, I didn't have to threaten him with anything. It was just a straight business deal. I offered him cash and he took it."

"As simple as that?"

"Look, Joey Golino was a drug dealer, and I was a junkie with money, good clean cash money. By the time this all came to a head, I was spending just about everything I had on his shit. I didn't have to blackmail him. He probably thought it was funny, ironic, but he was too greedy to laugh."

"How did your arrangement with Golino operate?"

"I would ring up and order a pizza, the size of the pizza order told him how much Oxy I wanted, which usually meant how much I could afford. I would give it forty-five minutes and go in and pick it up, the Oxy and the pizza."

"How long did this arrangement last?"

"From when Ricky's Oxy ran out, till a fortnight ago."

"Till his death?"

"Actually, till just a few days before his death."

"So, about four to five months."

"Yes."

Kate's barrister, Mr Oakley, leaned forward to speak.

"Kate, would you say that during this time your addiction was increasing and the amount of money you were spending was going up accordingly and all of this was affecting your mental state?"

"Yes, absolutely. I was hooked, a full-blown junkie, it was all I could think of, every minute of the day. Look it up on the internet, that shit is worse than heroin and I was drowning in it. If I didn't have my shit, I was thinking how to get it. If I had it, I was using it till it ran out. I was off my head crazy."

The Berlic team didn't seem to object to Oakley doing some questions. It wasn't a trial just a review of the statement. Oakley's question had just re-emphasised a key point in her statement. On March the tenth, Kate was out of control.

I had seen it for myself not long after.

Eddie Doolan interrupted. "We would like to take a fifteen-minute break at this juncture."

Both teams mumbled, nodded, then agreed to a break in the meeting.

It was part of the deal that everything in the written statement from Kate and Ricky, and everything they discussed in this meeting, had to be true. Break that agreement and the deal was off.

So far, it seemed to me, Ricky and Kate had stuck to their end of the bargain. I believed everything they'd said. So far.

~

During the break, the opposite sides retreated to their respective ends of the Nursing Centre's car park while I showed Carole and Glenda the way to the kitchen where we made ourselves some awful coffee.

"Why all the questions?" Asked Carole.

"Didn't they write it all down in their statement?" Added Glenda.

"They have the statement, then they do the questions, they are looking for inconsistencies. Looking for lies," I said, trying to be helpful.

"They are getting immunity," said Carole.

"Why would they lie?" From Glenda.

"Why does anyone lie? Advantage, money, reputation, not hurting someone's feelings. I don't know."

"Makes no sense to lie if it buggers up your immunity," said Carole.

"None at all," added Glenda. "Unless you have to lie to achieve the immunity."

"Well, that's fucked," said Carole.

"You aren't getting bored are you?" I asked.

They looked at me like I was stupid.

"Fuck no," they answered in perfect harmony.

"Ms. Chalmers, can you tell me what happened on the night of Saturday, March the tenth."

We were all back in the wardroom. The meeting had resumed.

"I had been trying to buy some Oxy from Joey since about Thursday," said Kate. "I called him again, several times, on Friday. Friday afternoon I went around to the pizza shop, he said he was out of my stuff. I had to wait. Told me not to come around again till he was stocked. He was pretty angry, didn't want me there. I was just a fucking junkie and he had nothing for me."

She took a pause.

"After that, on Friday, I told myself I was going to get myself straight. I was going to do it on my own. Getting knocked back by Joey Golino, after begging him, Jesus, I felt I was probably as low as I could get. I don't know. So anyway, I tried cold turkey. I locked myself in my house, shut out the world and tried to ride it out."

"And that didn't work?" Asked Berlic.

"Not even close," said Kate with a sad laugh.

"By Saturday I was climbing up the wall, I was aching all over, God the pain. I gave up on the idea of going straight. I rang Joey, Saturday about seven P.M. I'd lasted 24 hours. I was ready to beg him again when he just said come over, he had some stuff, come in the back way. He was all stocked up, so I drove into town, to the pizza shop."

"When I got there, I went in the back way, as Joey asked me, and I ran into AJ Davies who was waiting for me. I had my money for my Oxy. Davies took that, then grabbed me, and took me into the back room of the shop, where he raped me again. Pretty much the same story as the first time. He called Joey in to watch, he fucked me in the arse, again, and he was rough as hell, again."

"Did you try and fight back?" The question came from one of the admin types in Berlic's crew. It seemed like a question that had slipped out.

Kate let out a sigh, and then her barrister and solicitor both intervened.

"My God!" Doolan said. "Is that a serious question? This man Davies was a giant, he caught Kate by surprise, after she was lured to the pizza shop by Golino. What is the point of these questions? You have accepted the agreement, you have our statement, what is this about? Your morbid curiosity?"

"Our agreement entitles us to question your clients on everything raised in their statements." Berlic was not very happy with her assistant, but she was not backing off. "We will question your clients till we are satisfied. We've been through this already Mr Doolan. Do you want to withdraw the statements and we will withdraw the offer of immunity? Your choice."

Kate put her hand on her solicitor's arm. She was ready to go on.

"Yes, I tried to resist, he just ignored that and choked me till I almost passed out, unconscious. After that I didn't resist much, I just wanted to get it over quickly. I really didn't care if he killed me at that stage. I was pretty sure they weren't going to offer me any Oxy. After he finished, he just told me to get dressed and get out."

"Do you think he and Mr Golino were working together to lure you there for the purpose of the rape."

"For heaven's sake," interrupted Oakley, the Barrister, "Of course they were working together. Kate calls Golino, he tells her to come over on the false promise of Oxy-Contin. He directs her to the back door where Davies is waiting for her. Davies rapes her and Golino watches. They are both complicit in the second rape."

"Ms. Chalmers, anything to add?"

Kate thought for a moment.

"I think Joey was scared of Davies; I had the feeling Davies was the man in charge."

Berlic stopped to confer with her team, they read a page from the statement amongst themselves, then Berlic resumed.

"So, at this stage, you go home, you rest there and then your brother Ricky appears at your door."

"My bedroom door actually, he never knocks."

"Yes, OK. So, Mr Chalmers what happens then."

It was Ricky's turn in the barrel.

"I hadn't seen Kate for probably two months, I knew the drugs I provided would have run out. I was worried. Plus, I heard her driving into her farm and she was driving crazy, even faster than usual. What with the noise she made, I thought she had crashed into her shed. I went and checked."

"When I found her, she was in a bad state, in withdrawal, she'd obviously been on the stuff recently and she had bruising on her throat. She just looked terrible."

"Did this trigger any bad memories?" Asked Oakley.

"Yeah, well it sort of reminded me of when we were kids, Katie copping the brunt of everything, but I was angry at her as well. For being on the drugs, hiding from me. I asked her who had been supplying her, I asked her pretty firmly, and eventually she told me it was Joey Golino."

"I asked her who had choked her, and she told me it was this bikie mate of Joey's. He'd raped her that night and he'd raped her before, at the caravan park."

"And you were angry?"

"Yes. Damn right I was angry."

"And you decided to do something about it?

"I decided to go and speak to Joey. Tell him to stop supplying Kate with drugs."

"Were you meaning to speak to the biker as well?"

"Yeah, he was definitely on the shit list. We were going to have a different conversation."

"So, you headed off to the pizza place."

"I did, and Kate said she was coming with me."

"But wasn't your sister in a bad way at this point?"

"Yes, she was. But my sister is a very determined woman. She was probably worried about me getting in a fight, she'd seen the opposition so to speak.

"You didn't know that you would encounter AJ Davies?"

"No."

"You didn't think to talk Kate out of coming with you."

"Me? Talk Kate out of doing what she wanted?" Ricky laughed at the suggestion. "That's just not going to happen. She got in the car and came with me. End of story."

"What happened once you arrived at the pizza shop?"

"We get there, Joey is closing up, shutting curtains, we see him through the window and Kate tells me the guy in the background is the bloke who raped her."

"You recognised him immediately?"

"Yes. AJ Davies, the worst stand-over man in Sydney probably."

"Were you scared? Did you think about not going in?"

Ricky had to think about that.

"I wasn't scared, I was angry. He was just one more prick who had abused my sister. She has not had the easiest life and pricks like this just made it harder."

"So no, I wasn't scared, but I wasn't stupid either, I suspected he may have a gun and I knew he would use it if I gave him a chance, so I guess I just decided to go in hard and fast. That's what I did. I went through the door, across the floor and hit him before he even knew what was happening."

I had seen Ricky play football, and that was probably the truest thing I'd heard today.

"What happened then?" continued Berlic.

"He didn't go straight down that's for sure. He is a big guy and steroid strong and, I'd guess, he had done a bit of martial arts but maybe not as much as me, and he didn't have a gun."

"How do you know that?"

"Well, we fought for a while, he had a few good moments, if he had a gun I reckon he would have used it. I had the better of it. So yeah, he didn't have a gun. Not on him at least."

"And you won the fight?"

"Yes, at the end, I was on my feet and still conscious and he wasn't, so yeah, I won."

"And then you left the pizza shop, and once you were outside, you found that Kate had gone?"

"Yes. I gave Joey the hard word about no more drugs for Kate or else I would be back for him. Then I left, went outside, and Kate and my truck had already gone."

With Kate gone, I knew that Ricky, badly bruised from his fight, had gone to Georgie Golino to seek help. She had rejected him, sent him away. I wondered if they were going to talk about Georgie now. They didn't. Georgie wasn't the target here.

"So, Kate," continued Berlic, "where were you?"

"Ricky was in there fighting, they were at it so long, I was worried, I wanted to help him, so I took his car and drove to the council shed and grabbed a bar from his work desk there."

"Why do that, why not grab a tyre lever from the truck?"

"I couldn't see anything heavy enough. Davies was a monster. I had been to the shed with Ricky before, it was only about fifty metres down the road and around the corner. I had the keys, so I drove down and got a drop-bar. A tyre lever wouldn't have been big enough to stop Davies."

"You took the drop-bar and went back to the pizza shop?"

"Yes, and when I got there, I couldn't see Ricky or Davies. I went in. I could see Joey on the phone. When he saw me, he put his hand over the phone and told me to get out, go away. I asked him, where is Ricky? Where is my brother? I tried to go down the passage to the back to look for him."

"Mr Golino tried to stop you?"

"Yes. He was shouting at me, telling me to get out. Saying I didn't know what I was getting myself into. Ricky and I were dead meat. All that tough guy shit-talk men go on with. None of them half the man my brother is. Anyway, I was looking for Ricky and Joey was getting in my way. Just shouting at me, then he grabs my arm, to drag me out, and I just hit him with the drop bar. Just like that. Once."

"You weren't trying to kill him?" Asked Oakley.

"No. I was just trying to get him off me, not even thinking of hurting him, just wanted him to stay out of it. I just wanted to find Ricky. I didn't even look at Joey."

"You found Davies in one of the back rooms?"

"Yes. He was in a back kitchen, off the main passage, he was on his own, sitting in a chair next to a sink, washing himself, washing the bruises and the blood, he was a mess. Looked like he had been beaten up really badly which, I admit, I found very pleasing."

"I asked him, where's Ricky? He told me to piss-off, or words to that effect. I don't recall exactly but something in his typical manner, something offensive, and I hit him, and screamed at him, 'Where's my brother? Where's Ricky?' He said that Ricky had left, and he didn't know where he was. Then I thought of the money this pig had taken from me, the times he had raped me, I thought of what he had done, and I got very angry at that point, and I hit him several times with the drop bar. I hit him really hard, he fell on the floor, and he was trying to defend himself. I Kept hitting his arms when I was trying to hit his head, I was so angry I just wanted to make him feel how I felt, help-less. I grabbed one of the chopping knives out of the sink there and stabbed him with it, hard in the thigh. He screamed as I stabbed him and he dropped his arms and grabbed his thigh, crying like a baby the fucking coward. I then hit him in the head again a few times till he just went limp."

Kate's Barrister, Mr Oakley, asked a question.

"Kate, did you go to the pizza place with the intention of killing anyone?"

"No," said Kate, "I went there to find and to help my brother. He had been in there so long I was worried for his life. I go in there and I realised I was alone with two guys, one who'd already raped me that day. I guess I feared for my own life, plus I was still so angry about what they had done. I hadn't planned anything. Nothing."

"But, before you left, you took the money from their wallets?" Asked Berlic.

"Yes."

"Were you taking a late payment for your services?"

"No," said Kate, shaking her head, "Allowing a pig like Davies to punch out my chocolate starfish is not on the menu. Straight down the birth canal is all I offer."

Carole and Glenda both snorted with laughter beside me, then blushed and tried to hide. Kate didn't mind them laughing as she had made the joke, she looked chuffed actually.

The junior aides around Berlic looked totally confused by Kate's vernacular.

"Why did you take the money Kate?" asked her Barrister, Mr Oakley QC.

"It was the caravan park in reverse. They were unconscious just like I was that night. So, I treated them like they treated me. Payback. I went through their wallets, and I took all their cash. Joey had about a thousand and Davies had about five thousand. I took it all, left them nothing. Same as they left me."

"Then I thought fuck it, I decided to take Davies' pants. To strip him like he stripped me, try finding your way back to the caravan park naked you animal. See how that feels. Then I thought might as well do Joey as well, he had stood there doing nothing while I was humiliated, I might as well include him in the strip show."

"Why did you leave Golino's shoes and socks on?"

Kate looked a bit confused by that, then thinking back, she remembered.

"I never took them off. They stayed on. I cut his pants off with the knife from the kitchen. It was easier, and I was in a hurry."

"You also found a set of keys to cabin 143 at the caravan park," said Berlic.

"Yes. They fell out of Joey's pants as I was cutting them off. I looked at those keys and, I was still so angry, that's when I decided to go and see if his mates were there."

"It didn't occur to you that you had injured both men fatally?"

"No, it didn't."

Bingo! There it was. I saw that tiny, fractional pull back of the head, that ever-so-slight jut of the jaw. I had seen Kate do that before, at the hospital. I thought I had noticed it earlier. It was barely visible, but it was a tell. This time it was definite.

She had just lied. Now she was thinking of her next words, and then she did it again, the backward shrug, the pointing chin. Whatever she said next would also be a lie.

"I've never killed anyone before, Ms. Berlic."

Oh dear, another lie.

Did anyone else notice? It didn't seem so.

Did they believe her? I think they did.

Berlic's team conferred amongst themselves, looking at their copies of the statement, whispering. They literally turned the page of their statement in unison, their very own tell. They had accepted what Kate had told them and were moving on.

Eventually, Berlic continued the questioning.

"Can you explain for us what happened at cabin 143?"

"I drove Ricky's truck to the caravan park. I stopped near the public toilets there and cleaned myself up as much as I could. Tarted myself up you could say."

Kate was calmer now, it had been a roller coaster of a meeting, tears, rage, sadness, and pain. Her body language suggested she was remembering what actually happened. Not making it up, either that or it was all bullshit, and my lie detection skills were a figment of my own imagination.

"I had a shirt on, and it was covered in Davies blood, so I took that off, under that I was just wearing a low-cut singlet, so I pushed up my boobs, made a show of it and walked up to the cabin door and knocked."

"Who answered the door?"

"Pisano."

"Where was your weapon, the drop bar?"

"In my hand."

"Didn't he see it there in your hand."

"Well first off he was as pissed as a fart, drunk as the skunk he was. Second, all he saw was my tits. I had my left hand against the door frame, so I could lean in and give him a front row view of the merchandise. I had my right hand hanging out of sight just enough, so the bar was hidden behind my leg."

"Did he recognise you?"

"No, he didn't appear to."

"What did you say?"

"I said 'Joey sent me, said you should have some fun while you were waiting.' Something like that. I was implying I was paid for, and he should get some action courtesy of Joey."

"What did he say to that?"

"What did he ever say, I only met him twice and I only ever heard him grunt. He was just a lap dog, looked scary if blokes like that scared you. I was past fear by then."

"What happened next?"

"Really he made it easy for me, he just grunted and turned to walk inside, left the door open. I guess he assumed I would follow like his little puppy, get on the bed, and spread my legs."

She paused for a moment, remembering.

"I just stepped into the cabin behind him and hit him in the back of the head with the drop-bar."

"How many times did you strike Mr Pisano?"

"I don't really remember, I was in a hurry, I thought Folliero would be in there somewhere and I wanted to move quickly and as quietly as I could. I think I only hit him once."

"What were you thinking at this stage?"

"Thinking? Jesus Christ? Whatever was going through my head, I don't reckon you'd call it thinking."

She paused. She was definitely 'thinking' now.

"When I left all the drama at the pizza shop my plan was 'get the

325

others, make them pay'. When I got to the cabin I was wondering 'how the hell do I do this'? It wasn't like the pizza shop where I was going to help Ricky and I just barged in ready for whatever. At the caravan park I wanted payback, they hurt me I will hurt them, they took my money I will take theirs. My plan was to get them before they could stop me?"

"When you struck Pisano," said Oakley, "did you intend to kill him?"

"No, shit no, I thought it was like the movies, hit them on the head, they fall over unconscious, later on, they get up good as gold. By then I needed to be somewhere else."

"Let's move on to Mr Folliero." It was Ms. Berlic directing traffic. Even in the review of his murder Pisano was just a second banana.

"How did you deal with Mr Folliero?"

"I didn't deal with him in any way. He wasn't there."

"Not there in the cabin?"

"Not anywhere, there was only one bike outside that I saw. I don't know how they got there, by car or whatever, but Folliero was not in the cabin, and I looked everywhere, he was gone."

Berlic's team had another one of their lean-in-and-whisper type conferences.

Kate interrupted them.

"I think they had murdered him."

"Pardon?" Asked Berlic.

"The three of them Joey, Davies and Pisano had killed him, and I assume they had buried him somewhere. But from what I have read of Folliero and his love of money I am pretty sure he is dead, and I am sure he was dead by the time I got to the cabin."

"Why are you so sure?"

"I am sure he is dead because when I went to take Pisano's cash, he had two wallets, one of them was Folliero's."

"He could have been holding it for Folliero."

"No, all the cash was in Pisano's wallet and pockets, over ten thousand. Folliero's wallet was empty except for his credit cards."

"Folliero had a gun tucked in his belt, which I took in case he woke up and decided to use it. He also had a really thick ugly crucifix in his pocket which Folliero had been wearing when he raped me that first time a year ago. It had diamonds set in in such a horrible design you couldn't forget it."

"You saw it once and you remembered it as definitely belonging to Folliero."

"I saw it once, while its owner, Folliero, was boring me to tears with his limp dick half inside me. You tend to remember the little things at special moments. Then there is his name Michelle Folliero which I take to be 'indicative of ownership' which is inscribed on the back of the thing. So yeah, I'd say it was 'definitely belonging' to him as you put it."

Kate was getting defiant and angry again. It was never dull at a murder confession, or so I assumed here at my first.

Both of Kate's legals did their own forward-leaning-head and whispering thing, then Oakley spoke.

"Neither of my clients possess any further information on the whereabouts of Mr Folliero. I believe now is the time to address the assets of these men that Ms. Chalmers acquired on the night of the tenth. This will also clear up her opinions on Mr Folliero's death."

The Berlic team conferred and reached an agreement.

"Please, yes, go ahead," said Berlic.

Oakley responded by handing over a large envelope.

"As a sign of good faith, here is all the cash and money taken by Ms. Chalmers from the three men on the night. There is a summary page inside the envelope detailing the amount of money taken from each victim, for a total of sixteen thousand dollars."

He handed over a second smaller envelope. "Here is Mr Folliero's wallet and credit cards."

Berlic turned and nodded to Carole beside me. Carole and Glenda stepped forward with their own bags and started taking possession of what was being handed over. The tagging and bagging slowed things down even further.

It had been a marathon. Ricky and Kate were both sitting quietly, waiting. Eventually Carole and Glenda were ready for the next offering.

Oakley pushed forward a small suitcase on wheels which I thought had just been part of his big-city-barrister baggage.

"As a further sign of good faith, this case contains one million dollars in cash that Ms Chalmers found in cabin 143."

You could see a group reaction from Berlic's team. They took the case, quickly checked the contents, and then conferred yet again.

"We believe Folliero was worth a lot more than that," said Berlic. "If he was on the run with no intention of returning, surely he would have had more than one million?"

"He did," said Oakley. "Substantially more."

Oakley handed several photographs to Ms Berlic.

"This first photograph shows the crucifix Ms Chalmers recognised as belonging to Michelle Folliero," said Oakley. He held up an A4 copy of the photograph for the rest of us to inspect. The crucifix really was thick and ugly as Kate described. You'd need to be a religious nut to wear it everywhere. It was gross.

"Ms. Chalmers found this in Pisano's pocket along with Folliero's wallet."

He lifted a second A4 photo to show the other side of the crucifix.

"You can see here the name inscribed 'Michelle Folliero'.

We all nodded and mumbled approval.

He then held up a third photo.

"Now, you see here, the crucifix separates into two separate pieces. The top end is a cleverly disguised USB stick. The data end has been hidden in the base. It is a USB stick, but it is also a wallet. It is what crypto currency investors call a hardware wallet; this stores all Folliero's private crypto keys securely offline. In layman's terms this is a secure method of owning bitcoins and other such currencies.

"It appears Michelle Folliero has been investing in various crypto currencies since 2012. His biggest investment is in Bitcoin, but he has invested in others. He was a dedicated student. We have had the contents of this hardware wallet evaluated by crypto specialists working with the Commonwealth Bank of Australia and verified by a company called CoinBuyer which is considered one of Australia's safest exchanges."

He stopped talking while everyone in the room caught up.

"And?" said Berlic on behalf of everyone.

Oakley passed her a printed sheet of paper.

"This is a statement showing the current value Mr Folliero's investment in crypto currencies. The value contained in that hardware wallet is three billion dollars and rising."

"Bullshit," said Berlic in disbelief.

The room stopped for a moment. Silence. Three Billion Dollars? That could not be correct.

"Fucking hell," whispered Carole and Glenda in unison again.

"Mr Folliero was, prior to his disappearance, probably the biggest holder of crypto currency value in the country. You don't have to believe me, you can work it out for yourself," he said. "Once you have signed the immunity."

Berlic seemed to pull back. She looked right then handed the statement to one of her offsiders.

"Mat?" asked Berlic. "Is there even that much Bitcoin value in the country?"

"Bitcoin?" He said, "I've heard reports of over ten billion, plus, if he had upwards of a million to invest, from 2012 till now, and he spread it around to other coins? I can't say exactly but three billion is definitely possible. Believable. Yes."

"OK," said Berlic.

"Won't take long to verify," added Matthew. "Once we had the wallet."

We all sat in silence. Stunned I think. I know I was. I'd have murdered the lot of them for half of that. I'd already done the remainder of their gang for free. Don't think like that said my Nan in the back of my head. Money doesn't buy happiness.

Silence remained.

"And the weapons?" Asked Ms. Berlic QC, her final question in a marathon event.

"All of the weapons used, once we have the signed immunity," said Oakley.

"What about a photo?"

"No photos, just the weapons, once we have the signatures."

"OK, I get it," said Berlic.

"Give me five minutes please." Berlic stood up, looked at Detective Pete. Gave him the nod to the door and he stood up to follow her out.

"Chris," he said and nodded at me to go along, so I did.

We stepped out to the lovely sunny little rest area at the back of the Centre facing the car park.

Ms. Jessica Berlic QC was a different person away from the show, more Carole and Glenda than Perry Mason. She reached out to shake my hand.

"G'day Chris, nice to meet you at last."

"Nice to meet you too," I said.

"What do you cops think? Are they telling the truth?"

Pete wobbled his head, in a kind of nonverbal, half-hearted no, but mostly yes.

"Chris, you go first," said Pete.

"Well, only my opinion, it is mostly true. But Kate lied twice. Ricky was straight all the way."

"I agree," said Pete. "Kate two, Ricky zip".

"What were the lies?" She was looking at me.

"She has killed someone before."

Berlic's eyes widened.

"Agreed," said Pete. "I reckon it would be her father, supposed to have been a tractor accident. Sounds suss to me. They might have done him together, but Ricky didn't speak about it, so he didn't have to lie."

I was impressed Pete had done some work of his own.

"Does it matter if they killed their dad?" Asked Berlic.

"Well, yes, it matters, but not to us," said Pete. "Not now."

What was the second lie?

I looked at Pete. "Your turn."

"She meant to kill them," he said.

"Absolutely," I agreed.

"And Folliero?"

"I think," I said, "that they both think he is dead. How he got that way who knows?"

"Well, we have a million and change in cash," said Berlic, "and three billion and the weapons once we sign the immunity. My bosses would love that money."

"Your call, Jessica," said Pete.

"Three Billion," she said. "It can't be true, can it?"

"I would trust Eddie Doolan's word every day of the week," I added.

"He's had it evaluated," said Pete. "He's an officer of the court. He won't be making it up."

"OK," she said. "Let's go."

She turned to go back to the meeting room.

"You're going with it?" Asked Detective Pete."

"Yes I'm going with it. I think it is safe to assume Folliero is dead. God knows how they all aligned against him. Maybe Davies was going to kill Joey anyway, or vice-versa, who knows. Maybe they were all in it. We know him well enough to say he wouldn't leave that sort of money behind."

"And now we have it," said Pete.

"Yes we do. We have all that money, three bloody billion" she rolled her eyes and flashed that beautiful smile.

We went back to the room, and Ms Jessica Berlic QC became the ice queen again.

∼

The meeting re-started.

Berlic pulled four pieces of paper out of her briefcase and signed them all, then handed them to Eddie Doolan.

"Thank you," said Eddie. He read the top document, quickly checked the others, witnessed them, handed a copy to Kate, a copy to Ricky, one back to Berlic and then put the fourth and final copy into his briefcase.

"The signed statements, thanks," said Berlic.

Eddie pulled out his own stack of documents from his case, they each looked to be about ten pages thick. Kate and Ricky each got their own pile. They were making separate statements.

Kate and Ricky then went through their own signing process.

When they finished, Doolan collected the separate statements and handed them to Berlic.

"These are identical to the unsigned draft statements you already have in your possession," said Eddie.

"Yes I know, just checking," said Berlic as she quickly re-read both statements. Finally, she put the signed Chalmers' statements into her briefcase. The deal was almost done.

"So, the crucifix please," asked Berlic, there was a hint of excitement in her voice. Was it nerves?

Doolan reached into his brief case again and took out a small plastic zip bag. He held it up so we could all see it contained the ugly wooden, diamond-studded crucifix. He went to hand it to Berlic, but she indicated he should hand it to her senior assistant Matthew. The crypto money expert. He took it and immediately separated it and plugged it into his laptop. You could see his brain disappear from the room, into cyberworld. Berlic watched him then returned her attention to the Chalmers' team.

"You have some clothing for us I believe, Mr Doolan?"

Eddie Doolan opened the small travel case he had arrived with, similar to the one Oakley used, to hold the million in cash. Doolan extracted a paper parcel and handed it toward Berlic.

"This parcel contains the clothes taken from the victims at the pizza shop and the caravan park," said Doolan.

Berlic nodded towards Carole and Glenda, the forensics team. Carole stepped forward and took the parcel, and remained standing beside Berlic.

"And the weapons," said Berlic.

Eddie lifted a red and white plastic bag from the case. I was certain it was the same supermarket bag I had seen Kate remove from her shed when she gate-crashed my illegal search last night. It certainly looked the same.

"This bag contains Pisano's gun. The drop-bar, referred to in the statement and the knife that she used in her interaction with Mr Davies and on Mr Golino."

He held the bag out and Carole took it. Stepping back to her seat she opened it, in such a way that she and Glenda could look in together. Their eyes widened and they looked like they had to restrain themselves from sharing a happy hug.

With her back turned to the rest of the group Glenda looked at me and smiled then theatrically mouthed the word - "BLOOD". Together they quickly bagged and tagged the contents of the shopping bag and the bag itself.

We had reached the end, Berlic spoke.

"I think we will end it there; thank you, Mr Doolan. We will be in touch. Meanwhile, if you wish to speak to me privately, I am available with the rest of my team down at the Community Centre for the next day or so."

"Here in town?" asked Oakley.

"Yes, Jeremy, here in town. We will be verifying some elements of the statements."

Mr Jeremy Oakley QC seemed not too pleased with the notion of an overnighter in Jarrajarra.

"For the sake of my clients Ms Berlic," he said, "will you confirm we have an agreement?"

"Yes. We have an agreement, yes. If we find any deliberate lies on either statement, then immunity is cancelled for that person." said Berlic.

With that said, she offered a handshake to Eddie Doolan, and he accepted.

If ever a meeting was over, this one was. We all shuffled around and then shuffled out.

"Stick with us, Killer," Carole whispered as we hit the door, heading out of the room together.

"I need some decent coffee," whispered Glenda.

"I need something stronger than that," from Carole.

"Come with me," I said. I felt a pleasant glow being part of a small team of cops who I liked; it was like the best of the army if only for a moment. I phoned Joanne Farrell, the town liaison officer, she of many talents and ill-defined purpose. I politely offered her our coffee orders and she was happy to oblige. I think she was still feeling guilty about knocking me out. I could probably trade off that for months.

We three mere Constables headed off to the police station to have a debrief and coffee. I am sure there was a beer in the fridge for Carole. Maybe I would even get to see the blood.

Jarrajarra Police Station

"Holy shit, what a woman," said Carole.

We were in the kitchen, back at the police station. It was about 6.30 P.M.

The forensics sisters, Carole and Glenda, were sitting around the table with Barney and Joanne Farrell, both keen to know everything about the meeting. I was leaning against the wall, enjoying my coffee, just happy to be watching and listening.

"You sound like you admire her," said Joanne.

"I think I do a bit," said Carole. God, she took down two of the worst bad guys in the country, AJ Davies and that shithead Pisano. No gun, just a bloody lump of steel. She did Pisano single-handed, and he had a gun. Fuck me, that is ballsy."

"Took no prisoners," added Glenda.

"Which is not even acceptable in a war zone," said Barney. "God knows how long it will take our little town to recover."

"Sounds like your little town let her down when she needed it, Barn," said Carole.

"And the cop before Chris was no help by the sounds of it," added Glenda.

Carole and Glenda were a double act, they were sisters, but they could have been the same person. Finishing each other's sentences.

"Kate Chalmers has been defending herself, by herself, for a long time." The new voice in the room was Detective Pete, come to join the party. He had obviously heard the conversation as he made his way to the kitchen.

A Detective Sergeant entering a room full of constables and police admins will always stop the party chat for a beat. But not much intimidated Carole or Glenda for very long.

"So, can anyone tell me how a man like Davies was not in jail?" Asked Carole while looking at Detective Pete.

Detective Pete put a hand up in surrender, "Mistakes were made," he said.

"And people died," answered Carole.

That took the wind out of the party for more than a moment. But Barney, always the good host, asked, "can I get you a beer, Sergeant?"

"Yes, thanks, I'd kill for a beer," said Pete. "But not in this town," he added after a pause, "I reckon I'd get caught."

That got a laugh and relaxed the gang. I slowly realized that without Boofhead and Hughes to sour everything around them, Detective Pete could be a charming fellow.

As he took the beer from Barney, he had another pleasant surprise for everyone, "In case you are interested, the computer expert on Berlic's team think three billion is an underestimate."

"What?" they all asked.

"How much?" Asked Glenda.

"Could be as high as five, he thinks. He is only halfway through. We'll know tomorrow." He raised his stubby of beer to the room. "So well done, you guys, good work Jarrajarra."

"Is that crypto stuff real money, though?" asked Joanne, the wise head in the room.

"Who the fuck knows," said Carole.

The party rolled on, and for the first time in two weeks, we all relaxed.

Carole and Glenda had decided to stay in town overnight. They were not getting paid overtime, and the case felt settled. Their three-hour drive back to Seymour could be done during work hours tomorrow.

They could have stayed overnight with Barney, who was their cousin, but they were both semi-pissed and opted for the motel rather than gate-crash on Barney's aged mum.

When the unplanned office party ended, we locked their truck in the police yard, and I drove them back to the Jarrajarra motel.

"Nice wheels, Killer," said Carole. "This what they give you after your truck got toasted by the bikers?"

"Just a loaner, sadly."

"Nice," she said.

I parked outside their motel room to let the girls out. Problem was, Glenda had fallen sound asleep during the two-minute drive. Not exactly snoring but not far off it.

We sat for a moment.

"Cutting off the trousers, leaving them naked, that is weird." Carole was fascinated by Kate Chalmers' actions on the night of the murder. "That is way beyond angry. It is psychotic."

"Any wonder? After what she lived through," I answered.

"Did you know her?"

"Well, I knew her a bit, I knew she was on the game, but you saw what she is like, get her talking and she is funny as hell, in a world-weary-jaded kind of way. No one ever complained to the station about how she made her living."

Not entirely true.

Her last client had complained vociferously a fortnight ago, but he was the only one. Plus, on that day, she was on the downside of a triple murder, so she might have been a bit stressed.

"She was always friendly to me," I added, "and her brother Ricky is the local football hero. That gets you a pass mark with most people in a small country town."

"You liked her?"

"Yes, I did. She always had a dark sense of humour. She was a runner like her brother and me. This Oxy-Contin thing was a real surprise."

"Oxy can happen to anyone," said Carole. "I reckon her problems go way deeper than the drugs."

"True."

"She is a big, tall girl, strong," continued Carole. "She would have put the wind-up Folliero if she had ever gotten her hands on him."

"Maybe she did."

"What?"

"How do we know she didn't? Like you say, stripping those guys and leaving them exposed is a weird punishment for her rapists. What if she took him?"

Carole was intrigued; I could see it.

336

"What if she took him?" said Carole. "So that she could punish him some more. He was the leader of the group, the father figure, maybe?"

"Would it need to be that psychological?"

"No, not at all. They raped her. She hated them, payback."

"Exactly, payback, she said it herself."

"Plus, the others," said Carole, "they were all huge guys, yes?"

"Yes."

"Folliero was a weedy little shit, right?"

"That's what I'm told. Never met him myself. Also, she had the drop bar, she had Pisano's gun. She had just killed Pisano. If Folliero saw that, he would be shitting himself."

"He would, most definitely," said Carole.

Silence in the front seat. We pondered.

"Where would she take him?" Asked Carole.

"I have an idea where she might."

"Where?"

"Let me ask you this." I paused for effect. I knew the fearless forensic was hooked. "How do you feel about illegal searches?"

Twenty minutes later, we were parked off the road, a few hundred metres short of Kate Chalmers' place. Glenda had woken up and was sober again. Carole was on her phone checking the internet.

"Lookup 'Victoria Police entry without permission'," said Glenda from the back seat.

"OK." Carole followed instructions and typed the search request into her phone. "Right, I've got one here. It's a beauty," she said. 'The police can enter your home without permission if they are in hot pursuit of someone whom they have the authority to arrest' – That'd work; we're in hot pursuit of Folliero."

"Hot pursuit? That's America, you idiot," said Glenda.

"Oh yeah," said Carole. "America, you're right."

Carole kept looking.

"Here we go," she said eventually. "This is the one - police can enter in urgent circumstances, such as when a person is seriously injured or about to be harmed or preventing domestic violence."

"That will do the job," said Glenda.

"OK, so what the hell are we doing here?" Asked Glenda.

"Well, Constable Killer and I want to examine the possibility that Michelle Folliero, or his corpse, is somewhere within Kate Chalmers' farm."

"Without any form of warrant or legal authority?"

"We have urgent circumstances."

Glenda had to think about that.

"It only works if she is not home. If she's home and she asks us, what are we doing? If she questions the 'urgency'? What do we do then?"

"We could fake our urgency," I said.

That got no response.

"That was a joke," I added for clarity.

"I know," said Carole.

"What would Barney advise," from Glenda.

"He would advise us to go home and get a warrant," said Carole.

We sat and pondered again. It was turning into a pondering mission. Finally, Carole spoke up.

"Why doesn't Constable Killer here ninja up and sneak around the property, ascertain if the house is empty."

"And if no one is home," I added, "I could declare the situation urgent."

"And if we go in, and it turns out not to be urgent, we could all go home."

"And never mention it to Barney."

"This sounds like a workable solution," said Glenda.

So, I ninja up and, in the pitch-black night, I snuck around Kate's place. The doors were unlocked. The curtains were all up. It was obvious very quickly that the house was empty.

The thing that clinched it for me was the front door. Not so much the door itself but the envelope pinned there, with writing on it. I shone my torch on it to see what the envelope said.

It said – 'Hi, Chris.'

I opened the envelope and read the contents.

Hi Chris

I saw you sneaking around outside. Not while you were doing it. You were too good for me there. I saw it when I checked my security video this morning. I have a camera hidden in the gum tree you were hiding behind. You didn't see that did you? Working girls can't be too careful.

I knew you'd be back for another sneaky look. You are so fucking persistent. You just don't give up, do you? Where were you twenty years ago when I needed a real cop?

Anyway, you are welcome to look around and find whatever you find. Hope it makes you happy. I'm glad we didn't confront each other last night. Not sure what I would have done with Pisano's gun right there in the bag. I like to think I would not shoot the man who saved my little brother, but, hey, we all know what I'm like when I lose me rag.

I guessed you would not tell anyone and still won't. "Illegal search," I think, is the term they use. That would put a dent in your hard-earned heroic reputation. Could even cost you your job in a case as big as this one. Can't have that, mate. Can we?

I will have to leave it up to you from here on to keep Ricky out of jail. I kept the statements separate, just in case you worked it all out. He didn't tell any lies, and he only guessed what happened next. By the time I had finished those three cunts, Ricky was long gone, hiding in the hills somewhere.

Thanks in advance for looking after him.

So goodbye, Constable Chris thanks for being an honest cop, not counting our little insurance scam we pulled.

Kate xx

PS I'd rip this up if I were you. Too much incriminating stuff. Just keep it between us, I reckon.

· · ·

Wow.

Kate was gone and gone for good. That was clear.

One sentence stood out - After she had "finished those three cunts". I took that as an admission, just for my benefit. She had meant to kill them.

She had also guessed correctly, I would be keeping this letter to myself. Illegal searches and insurance scams could stay our secret.

Time enough to think about it all later. Right now, I wanted to check if Michelle Folliero's corpse was on the property or not, and I only had one place in mind.

Before I started, I called the dynamic duo in for support.

"The coast is clear. The situation is urgent," I spoke into my mobile.

"Roger that Ninja 1, Ninjas 2 and 3 are in hot pursuit."

I heard my new ute start-up in the distance and listened as it drove the short trip down the road to Kate's front door.

By the time they arrived, Kate's letter was stashed in my wallet.

I had my steel boots on, and the garage door gave way after four solid push kicks. I think by five kicks, I might have lost my killer glow in the eyes of the two forensics. Number four did the trick and maintained my reputation.

We were inside, and the tall timber cupboard against the far wall looked like the only thing that could be moved single-handed and make the scraping sound I had heard. Everything else was attached to the walls or far too heavy.

I pushed, it scraped, and when I had pushed the cupboard far enough, a trapdoor in the concrete floor was revealed.

"How the hell did you go straight to that?" asked Carole.

"I might have been interrupted during a previous urgent search?"

"Might have?"

"Yeah, I can't remember exactly." When in doubt, fluff about.

I lifted the trapdoor, and it revealed a square concrete well descending into darkness, with a steel ladder against one wall. It was perfectly built. It had to be a Ricky Chalmers production.

340

We were working by torchlight.

"Can you see a light switch anywhere?" from Glenda.

Carole found two switches by the broken door. She tried each one. The first set on the main lights inside the shed, and the other set on the outside light. Neither of them lit up the dark tunnel below the trapdoor.

We stood around the trapdoor, torches shining down into nothing.

"Who goes first?" I asked.

"Not me," said Glenda, "I am just your forensic type. Post-crime analysis is me."

We looked at Carole.

"I just turned fifty. I'm supposed to avoid ladders at all costs," said Carole. "Especially ones going down."

"Yes, well then." Looked like it was me. "My turn, I suppose," I said.

"That's the spirit," said Glenda.

So down the ladder, I went, into the darkness, with my crappy little police-issue torch as my friend.

At the base of the ladder was a concrete floor. On the opposite wall from the ladder, there was a doorway with no door, just the opening into a tunnel. The tunnel went about thirty feet into more darkness. The direction would have taken it away from the shed, away from the house and car park.

I hadn't been in that direction before, above. I could not remember what the ground above looked like. More sheds? More dirt? I didn't know. Right now, it didn't matter.

I followed my flashlight to the end of the tunnel. This time, this end, there was a door. The door had two bars across it. When opened, it would open toward me. Fuck.

I hadn't thought of booby traps since the army.

Fuck.

"What are you doing?" Shouted one of the forensic sisters. From this position, I couldn't tell who. Whoever it was, the sudden noise frightened the shit out of me.

"I am sneaking up on a perpetrator as we speak."

"Good," said the voice. "We'll keep it down this end."

"That would be extremely fucking helpful," I answered.

I tried to remember my booby-trapped door protocols.

The approach? There couldn't be a pit or a pressure mat; the floor was uncovered concrete. It had been set a while since Ricky's dope growing days, I guessed.

The door? It opened out, so that meant a possible pressure release trigger. That seemed highly unlikely. The metal door would offer some protection.

The bars on the door? I checked. I even lifted them ever so slightly. Nothing.

The builder? Ricky Chalmers? No question it was Ricky's work. Would Ricky have an alarm on the door? Possibly. Would Ricky make a bomb that could kill someone? Highly unlikely. Very doubtful.

I lifted out the two bars.

I gripped the handle. It was just a handle, not a doorknob.

Fuck it. I held my breath and kept myself positioned behind the protective steel of the door. I put my faith in Ricky Chalmers not being a bombing kind of guy.

I pulled the handle hard.

An alarm screamed in the tunnel, almost loud enough to burst an ear drum.

"Aaaaaaaaaaargh" A collective scream came from the other end. The forensic sisters had jumped, and screamed, in harmony, scaring me almost as much as the alarm itself.

I looked around the tunnel. No alarm on this side. Just the horrible violent noise of it echoing from the hard concrete walls.

I flashed the light inside the door. There it was, on the wall, high up and fifteen inches long. An old-fashioned bell alarm with a battery driven hammer. The hammer going full speed, against the bell, screaming at me. Screaming.

I reached up and ripped out the battery. The alarm, thankfully, shut the fuck up. My ears thanked me, my stomach was still jumping hoops.

"All clear," I shouted to the valiant sisters at the other end of the hidey-hole.

"Holy fuck Chris," shouted Carole. "Whatever you did, don't do it again."

The door was open, and the alarm was off. I was in.

The concrete wall stopped about a metre beyond the door. Beyond that point was a muddy mess. It looked like a tin wall. Maybe the wall of a caravan dumped into the space beyond the door.

In the centre of the mud-caked tin wall, someone had smashed and cut a hole. Not as clean as sophisticated as the concrete entry that had delivered me here, but an entry, nonetheless.

I shone my torch through the hole. It was a caravan alright. An old one. The roof looked to be on the point of caving in. I guessed the weight of the earth above was pushing it down.

It was also a long one, thirty foot I'd guess. Not the sort you would tow around the country on the back of your pick-up truck. More like the one you buy second-hand and park in your backyard to house the kids. The sort of caravan that stays in the one spot forever, or till it falls apart.

It was falling apart now. Water was leaking in various parts. Dust was falling from the roof toward the centre. It was not a roof built to carry much weight.

Cave-in, just another tiny concern.

I had to walk under the sagging roof to get to the bedroom section at the far end of the caravan. The dirt from above and the water from the drips landed on me as I got closer.

Never mind the drips, I was overwhelmed by the smell. Disgusting.

Blood, piss, shit and rotting flesh.

Oh, dear.

I was scared to point the torch. Scared of what I would see.

There was a chain, wrapped around a bar near the door to the shower. Looked like one of those bars that old people used to get out of wheelchairs. The chain was looped and locked.

I followed the length of the chain, toward the end of the bed. There, on the bed, the chain ended. Looped, locked and taped for good measure, around two human legs. White and naked. The no-trousers thing was becoming a signature of Jarrajarra's first multiple murderer.

I shone my torch into the face of the corpse.

Michelle Folliero. Decidedly worse for wear.

Dead.

I had seen dead bodies before.

Not like this one. Beaten, burnt by cigarettes, battered, bruised, lying in a pile of his own dying shit, a puddle in the mattress of his last piss. I had seen a lot of corpses. But of all the dead bodies I had ever seen, this one was a first.

This one.

It opened its eyes and whispered, "Help me."

I jumped back so hard I hit my head on the sagging ceiling.

"Holy fuck."

"What? What?" Came the voices from the other end of the tunnel.

I might have screamed though I don't recall.

"Holy shit," I whispered. Time for the experts.

"Just wait right there," I said to what was left of Folliero and made my way back to the real world, back through the tunnel, up the ladder, and out into the fresh air. I found a nice spot leaning against my still shiny new truck.

"Don't tell me?" Said Carole.

"You found him," said Glenda.

"Yes" I said. "Alive."

Their eyes opened a mile wide. At least a mile, maybe more.

We all paused for a moment.

I called Wendy at the Nursing Centre and suggested she bring the ambulance, and Jack and Jody, and most importantly, herself.

I called Detective Pete and pin dropped the location, though I am sure he remembered it already.

I called Barney and begged him to bring coffee and sandwiches. God bless him, he agreed without hesitation.

Bloody hell.

I took a breath and went back down into Michelle Folliero's little corner of hell.

I wanted to do one more trip before the gang all arrived.

Down the ladder, along the tunnel, through the gaping hole in the steel wall, down the dripping dusty can to the bedroom.

I had seen it the first time but in my total fright and disgust it had not registered.

Another envelope.

I was worried it might contain more incriminating stuff that would embarrass me. But no.

On the outside of the envelope, it simply said –

"Yes, OK. Sorry, I lied."

Inside the envelope was another special crucifix and a short note saying – "The hypocritical cunt wore two crucifixes; can you believe that? Fucking Catholics, hey. xx"

I headed back outside. If there was anything else that made me look bad, I would rather leave it behind than spend another minute down here.

Within thirty minutes the ambulance and the medics had arrived. Wendy came with them.

Barney arrived with a thermos and a bag full of sandwiches.

Detective Pete arrived alone, and empty handed. He had gone down below with the ambos to see the situation himself. He quickly returned to the surface and the fresh air.

I handed him the note with the second crucifix, and he checked for himself, that it was the 'special' kind. Another detachable USB. He called the prosecution team.

Within the hour the gang was all here, the prosecutor Berlic, her computer bloke with his laptop, and all their associated public servants. Curious. Excited.

Wendy and the ambos were down below.

Everybody else was upside. Carole and Glenda itching to get down and check out the hellhole beneath us.

Someone had even called Greg Farrell and he had showed up in the emergency truck with Norma.

345

Greg wandered over, leaned in and asked "What do you reckon about the barbeque? Yes? No?"

"I reckon we will all be here till dawn" I answered.

"So, yes?"

"Why not?" I said.

Greg fired up the fire brigade's barbeque. Within ten minutes Detective Pete, Berlic and her crew, were all gathered around, grabbing sausages, bread, and sauce. Throwing coins and notes into Norma's ever-hungry cash bucket. Some Jarrajarra normality stamped above the filth below.

I was struggling to wipe the smell, and the sight of the scene, from my memory.

I had another sausage with extra sauce and Greg gave me a double shot black. It was perfect.

Carole and Glenda were waiting for the paramedics to finish up. They were as keen as ever to delve into the blood and gore. I did detect some hesitation about the smell.

"So how bad was it really? Asked Carole.

"The worst thing I have ever smelt in my life," I answered truthfully.

"I'm wearing the mask," said Glenda, "stuff that."

"How long can someone survive without food and water anyway?" Asked Carole.

"He had water," I qualified, "Not exactly your tap water, but wet."

"OK, how long without food?" She asked.

Glenda was on her mobile phone, looking it up on the internet. She was becoming the team geek.

"Two weeks apparently," she answered, reading from her phone screen.

"Geez we were just on the limit when we found him," added Carole. Emphasizing the 'we'.

"We were incredible really," I said.

"We were," they said in harmony.

Finally, the ambos emerged, Folliero strapped into a stretcher. Bottles and tubes attached. I realised, again, there was nowhere the intrepid two, Jack and Jody, would not go to recover a patient. Personally, I didn't care if he lived or died. He was murdering scum, but Wendy and her team would give him the best care he could ever hope to receive. More than he could ever deserve.

Wendy gave me a nod. I took it to mean he was still alive. We watched them pack up their patient and leave.

Carole and Glenda headed down into the pit.

"Coming?" Asked Carole.

"Later," I said. "Much later."

Detective Pete wandered over with Berlic.

"You never cease to amaze me Chris," said Pete.

"Jackpot," said Berlic, smiling. A winner.

"Looks to me, you've got three slam dunk trials ahead of you now. Boofhead, Hughes and now, Folliero," I said, "I'd hate to see Jarrajarra's football coach dragged into number four."

"I reckon three's enough," said Pete, looking at Berlic.

"Three is plenty," she agreed. "Your coach remains a free man."

We all thought in silence for a moment. I didn't have to remind them, it was their very own confidential informant, AJ Davies, who had bought all this evil to my little town.

Some things just don't need to be said out loud. Ever.

"How did you know about Folliero?" Pete asked.

"I guessed. The drop bar came from the council shed. It belonged to the council tractor. I found the tractor near here, over a week ago, all filthy, covered in mud. Ricky Chalmers would never leave it that way, ever. I guessed Kate had used it. After the big confession today, I suspected she'd used it to bury something or someone. I thought if that someone was Folliero then I had urgent reasons to check the property. I did that and I found him in the buried caravan. As you saw him yourself, Pete."

"Where is Kate now?" he asked.

"I have no idea I knocked on the door to ask her permission to look around, but she wasn't home."

I didn't mention the personal note she had left me.

Both Berlic and Pete got that far away look.

"Given what you found," said Pete carefully, "I reckon you had an urgent need to check the safety of an individual inside the property."

"Yes, urgent," I said.

"Looking for a suspected victim of violence," added Berlic.

"Exactly," said Pete. "A potential victim of violence."

They went back to horizon gazing, and soon they were nodding in unison.

"I think we are good," said Berlic.

"I think we're good as gold," said Pete.

"So, all clear on my entry to the property?" I asked.

"Fuck yeah." Said Berlic and we all high fived.

Having found the missing gangster and handed over his second, potential, bitcoin wallet. I had little else to do for the evening except stand around and yawn.

We were into the early morning when Berlic's computer guy came over to our little group and said, "It's another crypto wallet."

"How much?" asked the crown prosecutor.

"Hard to say, but same size at least as the other."

Jessica Berlic QC did a little victory jig. She had the money and the mafioso, it was a huge win for her Royal Commission.

Eventually, I climbed into the cabin of my shiny new truck, with the thermos of coffee Barney had provided. I fell asleep while everyone else managed the mess.

19

SUNDAY, MARCH 25, 2018

Jarrajarra, Nursing Centre.

"I am guessing you know that your sister has gone."

"Yes, we said our goodbyes yesterday after the meeting wrapped up."

It was early morning. After the team packed up at Kate's shed I had gone home for a shower and a run, then came to the Nursing Centre to speak with Ricky Chalmers.

He was sitting up in bed, looking better yet again. His condition improved on every visit.

"You knew about Folliero and the caravan?"

"I do now."

"When did she mention him?"

"After the meeting. She didn't trust me to hold it together during our statements. Kept me out of that loop for my own sake I suppose."

"She told you about the caravan."

"That fucking caravan. Trust me, that thing has history. I don't know why she kept it all these years. Found a purpose in the end I guess."

"She had buried it at the end of a tunnel I think you had built the tunnel, probably."

"Yep. Probably."

"Probably the start of a little man cave for growing stuff."

"Probably."

"But you didn't finish it."

"Nah, I earn more money playing football; and coaching."

"Less risky, too," I added.

"Definitely. Who wants to be in competition with the Mellish boys? I made more money digging their grow caves for them."

We sat in silence. Ricky was too much the straight arrow, to pursue a career in drug growing. It would intervene with his real life. Football.

"Why did Kate insist I come to the meeting yesterday."

"She found out you had been snooping. Figured you would work it out eventually. Maybe she wanted you there to see your reaction. Maybe she just wanted you there because she thought you deserved it. I really don't know."

He thought for a moment then continued.

"Maybe you are the one person in this town she wanted to explain herself to. She was full on my sister, but I think she liked you, as much as she is capable of liking anyone. Particularly a male."

"Me?"

"Yeah you. Work that one out. Gotta say, you didn't have much to beat after the last cop in town."

"She liked you."

"No mate, she loved me, that's way different."

"I saw that."

"What she told you yesterday, about the abuse, that was not even half of it. It was way worse. Not something you can tell really; you just endure it and hope you survive."

"She is certainly a survivor," I said. A gentle prod to keep him talking.

"Oh yeah. A very proactive survivor, you could say."

We shared a laugh.

"Jesus taking on Davies with a drop bar after you beat him up is one thing," I said. "But going to the caravan park and taking on Folliero and Azzie Pisano together, alone. That is crazy brave."

"Not brave, total uncontrollable rage," said Ricky, "Kate can get so angry, fear is just not a factor. Not something you want to see or be around. The Black Mist my mum called it."

"I have not heard that term for years," I said, "my grandmother used to say it about me."

He shrugged, looked at me as though I didn't qualify. "Maybe it's a generational thing. A phrase from the past. I dunno."

"Tell me about the caravan."

"The old man bought it and parked it there behind the shed. Made her sleep out there. Reckoned she wasn't fit to share the house with the rest of us, or some bullshit. His real reason was to get her out there away from mum, for his own sake. She could scream as much as she liked out there."

"Oh."

"Yeah. Oh indeed!" he said looking at me. "She'd run away, Dad and your cop predecessor would find her, bring her home. He took to chaining her up in there. Like leave her there for a week for punishment. Of course, the real punishment was him."

Ricky stopped. Nothing more to add. Nothing further that he wanted to say.

"She killed your dad, didn't she?"

He just nodded.

"It was the first time she used the drop bar," he said. "and it was the last time he raped her, that's for sure."

"You helped her cover it up?"

"I didn't help her. I did that bit myself. All me, that one. Put him in the tractor, tipped it over, on the slope down toward the river. Called the cop, all of that. Death by tractor."

"Death by tractor accessory, as it turned out."

Why did I say that? It slipped out. He laughed, so I didn't apologise.

"How do you tip a tractor?"

He looked at me and shook his head in friendly scorn.

"That is a city boy question if ever I heard one. How don't you tip a tractor would be more accurate. Bit of slope, a bit of leverage, over she goes, easy-peasy."

"OK."

"Dad was pissed, as usual, that helped sell it. I had a bit of luck. The roll bar landed on his head, and squelch went the evidence."

Ricky's sense of humour was as dark as his sister's.

We had a moment of silent thought. I was feeling I had solved the whole crime; I was rather proud of myself.

"Ricky, did you tell any lies in your statement yesterday, anything at all?"

"Not a one."

"Did you know about Folliero during the meeting?"

"Nope."

"Did you know or guess she had buried the caravan with him in it? Before she told you?"

"No, and no. I took off after the fight with Davies because I didn't want to face up to his biker mates. After I came back and went in to see those cops, like you suggested, once that prick Detective Snow got me alone, it was obvious he wanted to make it look like something it wasn't. Not sure what his plan was, not sure where he was going with it.

"Anyway, he started belting into me while I was cuffed to the chair. I got out of that easy enough, and it turned out the fat cunt wasn't as tough as he thought he was. Put him down, then the other detective, Jordan, came into the room, so I dropped him and then got myself out of there, then took off again. You know the rest, mate."

"Alright," I said. "Going forward, if Jordan or Berlic start asking you more questions, just stick to your statement. If you haven't lied, your immunity still applies, and always insist on having Eddie Doolan present."

"I will," he said.

"Both Berlic and Pete told me last night you are still in the clear. I think you will be all right, but after we found Folliero, I think Kate has blown her immunity. That's if they ever find her."

He laughed, "They won't find her, Chris, I promise you that."

We left it there. I went home to have a sleep.

20

MONDAY, SEPTEMBER 17, 2018

Six Months Later

Jarrajarra, Victoria, Australia.

"Morning Killer."

"You know Pete, the only people who call me that are the Crime Service girls. Personally, I don't like it from you, or the lawyers, or any of those public service types."

Detective Pete had called me around 10 A.M. I was in my office, in the station playing Solitaire on my laptop. Not a busy day.

Barney and Joanne were at the front desk planning a fundraiser for something. It was all quiet on the local beat.

"Chris, mate, 'Killer', it's a term of endearment. You're the only one on our side who took out some of theirs. They had it all their own way for decades."

"What was their side? Folliero and his gang? Davies was one of ours, wasn't he?"

"Ouch, mate. Sorry, Chris, it is then, no more 'Killer'. So, how are you Chris, mate?"

"Good, life is quiet again. Just the way I like it."

"You still running ridiculous distance at sparrow's fart? Still punching the bag? Shooting the shit out of the local range?"

"Yes, yes, and yes. Maintaining the strain."

"Good mate. Good. How's our footy coach going?" he asked.

"Played his first game back on Saturday. Did well."

"Great, great."

So that was the introductions done. Detective Pete and I had hardly spoken since the day Kate Chalmers went on the run, and Folliero had turned up not quite dead.

With his absence, I had finally realised what I didn't like about him. He was such a political animal. The case was all he saw. The bigger, the better and always the next one. He was smooth and friendly as far as he needed to be. Probably a sociopath. It just so happened that, in this case, we were on the same side.

As Ricky had predicted, there had been no hint of Kate's whereabouts since the day she left.

The Royal Commission had left town with Folliero and his money. The whole affair had since become a slow procession through the commission and the courts.

"Chris," said Detective Pete, "you will probably, read the news today that our man Folliero is pleading guilty to several charges, a lot, in fact. In particular, he is admitting to organising the murder of Gary Rogers."

"Why the plea?"

"Choice of jail. Minimum term of forty-plus years, whatever, instead of life with no parole. Visitation rights. Retention of enough assets for his wife to survive. Just boilerplate stuff. He is over fifty years old, mate; he is not getting out."

"So, what did he trade for all these benefits?"

"Well, he dobbed a few more of his mates in, so we get a few more prosecutions. Bit more detail about hidden assets. We already have his bitcoin, which is currently tracking at six billion dollars."

"Six billion. Jesus, maybe he should have just stuck to investing."

"Yeah, well, the really interesting bit of info is, he claims he had five million, in cash, with him there in three cases in cabin 143."

"Not one million?"

"No, mate, I think our girl Kate Chalmers told a fib."

She did, but I had guessed that.

"Well, good luck to her," I said. "I hope she finds happiness with all that cash."

Detective Pete just laughed. "Maybe don't say that bit out loud."

"I will take that advice on board. Tell me about Folliero. I hear his right foot was amputated?"

"Yes, and his other foot is just hanging on. Spends his time in a wheelchair. Could probably learn to walk again but, being the horrible little shit he is, he prefers the wheelchair."

"Wow."

"Your girl Kate totally and utterly fucked him over, mate. He is a broken man."

"Well, Kate was a badly damaged woman and some of the men that hurt her paid with their lives. Folliero can count himself lucky."

"Maybe don't say that in public either, not while you are in uniform." He was laughing.

"The reason I called is when you read the papers today, or next week, whenever real news gets down there into the wilderness, you will see that you are going to get a medal."

"Me? Medal?"

"Yes. The Victorian Police Valour Award, for showing exceptional bravery in extremely perilous circumstances."

"What about the Sarge? He was shooting too, remember?"

"Yes, he is getting the Victoria Police Medal for Courage for, let me see, fulfilment of his duties in dangerous and volatile operational circumstances."

"So, let me get this straight. I was in extremely perilous circumstances?"

"Yes."

"While the Sarge was simply in a dangerous and volatile operational circumstance?"

"That's about it exactly."

"He is going to love that. You do remember we were in the same truck."

"Details, mate, mere trivial details."

"OK."

"Right then, I will see you around. Killer."

And he hung up. Thirty seconds later, the mobile rang again. It was the Sarge.

"This is highway robbery," he said. "You were extremely perilous, and I was just merely dangerous. How, on earth, do they decide that?"

And on he went until, eventually, he dropped his fake outrage and congratulated me 'in all seriousness'. He told me I totally deserved all the awards under the sun, and he did nothing and didn't deserve a medal.

The Sarge was back at work, relatively injury free, with no long-term damage and proud as punch at what we had achieved.

Barney and Joanne found the article as well, and we did another round of congratulations.

Joanne thought a party would be good, and we organised a booze-up at the pub for the Cops, the Fireys and the Ambos. In other words, Wendy, Barney, Jody Taggart, all the extended Farrell family, and me.

It was a good night.

What with the celebration, and with all the dead bodies explained in detail, in my mind, the case was now closed.

21

SUNDAY, MARCH 10, 2019

Six Months Later

Six months after the call from Detective Pete, one year to the day after the first of the murders in Jarrajarra, I received an email on my personal email address.

G'day, Chris,

Hope you are well, mate. Still alive here. I saw in the news that Folliero coughed up about the cash I borrowed from his cabin. Just so you know, it was only two million I took. The lying cunt. Still, it was plenty enough for me.

I hear he is not doing so well these days. Got a sore foot, the poor lamb. Pity that. To be honest, I thought the rotten slimy prick was dead. I looked it up on the internet, and the longest you can survive without food and water is a week at best. I should have realised that, with the caravan leaking like a sieve, the thirsty little shit would find something to drink.

After you told me about the offer of a deal, I dragged it on as long as I could before the big confession. I was sure Folliero would have carked it by two weeks, hence my timing. The only time I went down there was to get my evidence.

357

Actually, I may have gone down with a torch and waved the drop bar around to frighten him a couple of times after I got out of your girlfriend's rehab. But the smell was so bad, and he was so fucking piss-weak, it took the fun out of it. Jesus Christ, he cried like a baby whenever I went near him the fucking sook.

He did mention one thing, Folliero. Spilled his guts about Davies. Apparently, he was a police snitch, and they were going to kill him that fucking night.

I assumed that maggot Joey Golino was trying to build up his nerve when Ricky turned up for the first round.

Lucky me. Glad I got him when I still could.

And yeah, I fucking meant it. And I meant to take Folliero and give him the old caravan treatment.

Not boasting, just honest.

Did you like my caravan? That fucking thing had sat out the back of the garage so long no one saw it anymore. Overgrown to buggery. Perfect coffin for my special friend.

Anyway.

I am fucked in the head. I see that. Part of me hopes you can look past that.

I think you worked out the lies I told in my statement. The rest of it, about home and all that stuff, I think you know, is true. I didn't get like this because I wanted to. I am working on the anger. I really am.

Send my love to Wendy. I mean it, no joke. The pair of you really did me a favour. Several favours. I know it. I see it.

You two should get married. You are such a pair of sickeningly honest straight shooters. The world needs more like you. Marry. Breed. I dare you.

Doing well myself, healthy, calm, running a lot, all the good shit. You won't find me. But you're not looking, are ya?

My victims weren't really victims, were they?

Sorry we never got to do that run together. Would have been so much fun. Ricky says you are a plodder, and I would take you easy. If you can't beat Ricky, you won't beat me.

What about our insurance scam, still makes me laugh.

Take care mate.

Kate xx

．　．　．

I read the email several times, memorised the best bits, and then deleted it. Finally, I cleared my junk folder to be sure it was gone.

I didn't want anyone using it to find her.

I was simply glad she was safe and happy, wherever on earth she may be.

ABOUT THE AUTHOR

Geoff crossing the finishing line of the Great Ocean Road Marathon in Apollo Bay.

A colourful childhood amongst the Kensington housing commission flats in Melbourne, Australia. To writing software by the ski-slopes of Colorado, USA. Geoff Davis has lived an eventful life.

Ten grandchildren, an Australia sports medal, multiple wine-producing awards, and over fifty years of marriage to his high school sweetheart have given Davis a unique perspective on life and a wealth of experience to channel into his books. Further informed by a lifetime of ravenous media consumption, with a particular focus on Australian history, conspiracy, and crime. Geoff's original style is equal parts historical fiction, thriller, and small-town black comedy.

THE BLACK MIST is the first book in the Jarrajarra series. Book two, PROVOCATION, is coming soon.

READER'S GROUP

Thank you for reading THE BLACK MIST.

If you'd like to read more of the Jarrajarra series, the first two chapters of book two, PROVOCATION, are currently available for free to members of the Geoff Davis reader's group.

To join the free reader's group, head to:
www.wattlebirdbooks.com/geoffdavis

Warmest regards,
Wattlebird Books

One Last Thing

If you loved Geoff's book and would like to help spread the word to other potential readers, we would be immensely grateful if you could please leave a review on his Amazon page. Your honest feedback will make the world of difference to an emerging independent author.

Thanks again.

Wattlebird Books

wattlebirdbooks.com

Wattlebird Books Publishing Company

Copyright © Geoff Davis, 2023

Published by Wattlebird Books Publishing Company

Book design by Dune Assembly

ISBN: 978-0-6457513-0-7 (ebook)

ISBN: 978-0-6457513-1-4 (paperback)

Version: 230403_1727

Printed in Great Britain
by Amazon

26368489R00208